image COMICS PRESENTS



# INVINCIBLE™
## GROWING PAINS

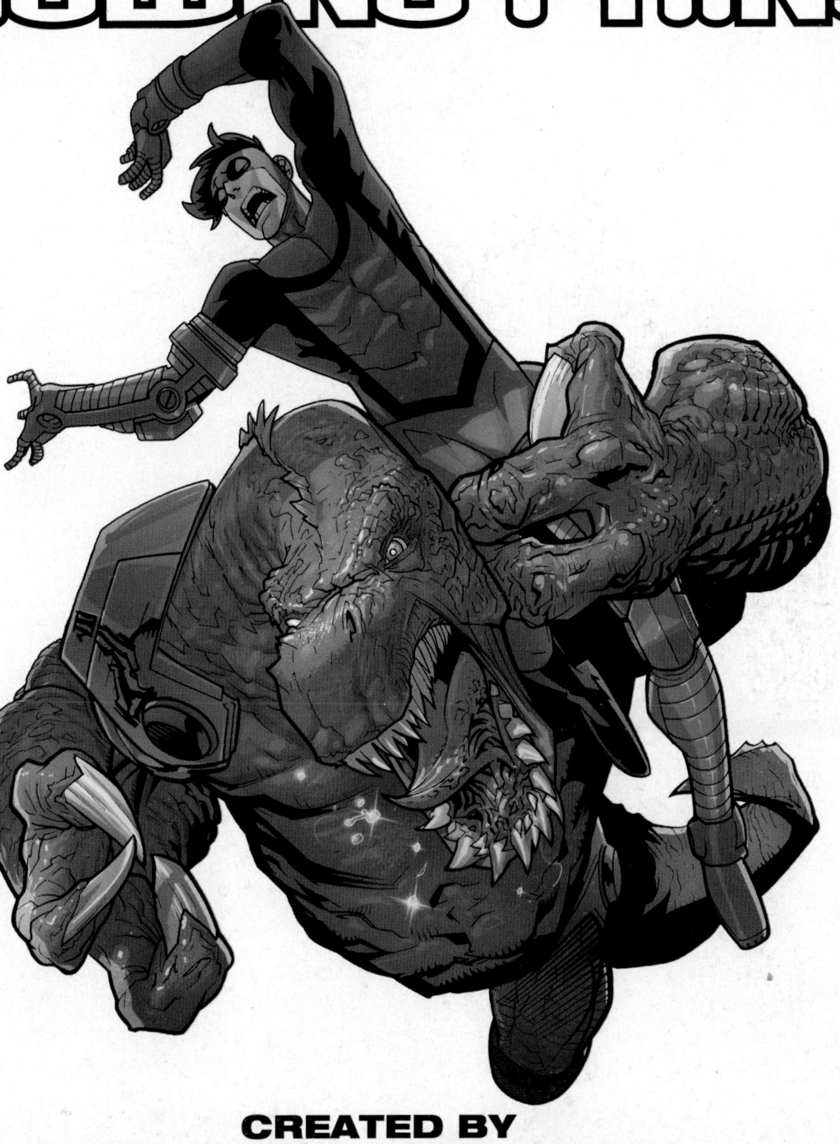

CREATED BY
**ROBERT KIRKMAN**
**& CORY WALKER**

image®

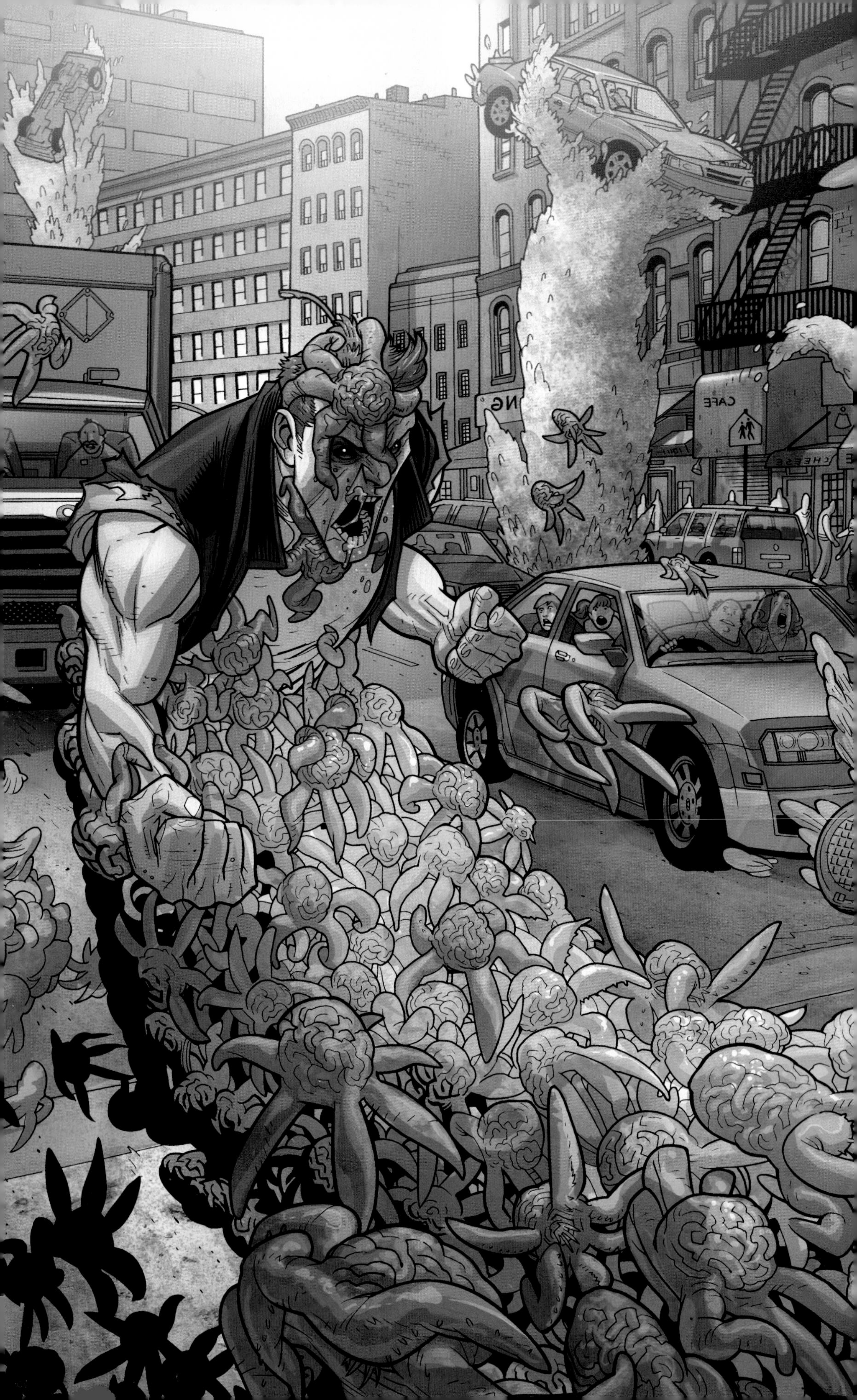
CAFE

### writer
# ROBERT KIRKMAN

### penciler
# CORY WALKER
#### (chapters 1-2, 6 backup story)
# RYAN OTTLEY
#### (chapters 3-5, 6 main story)

### inker
# CORY WALKER
#### (chapters 1-2, 6 backup story)
# CLIFF RATHBURN
#### (chapters 3-5, 6 main story)

### colorist
# DAVE MCCAIG
#### (chapters 1-2)
# FCO PLASCENCIA
#### (chapters 3-6)

### letterer
# RUS WOOTON

### editor
# SINA GRACE
#### original series editor
## AUBREY SITTERSON

### cover
# RYAN OTTLEY
# & FCO PLASCENCIA

ISBN: 978-1-60706-251-6
INVINCIBLE, VOL. 13: GROWING PAINS
First Printing

SKYBOUND ENTERTAINMENT
www.skyboundent.com

Robert Kirkman - CEO
J.J. Didde - President
Sina Grace - Editorial Director
Chad Manion - Assistant to Mr. Grace

IMAGE COMICS, INC.
www.imagecomics.com

Robert Kirkman - Chief Operating Officer
Erik Larsen - Chief Financial Officer
Todd McFarlane - President
Marc Silvestri - CEO
Jim Valentino - Vice-President

Eric Stephenson - Publisher
Todd Martinez - Sales & Licensing Coordinator
Betsy Gomez - PR & Marketing Coordinator
Branwyn Bigglestone - Accounts Manager
Sarah deLaine - Administrative Assistant
Tyler Shainline - Traffic Manager
Drew Gill - Art Director
Jonathan Chan - Production Artist
Monica Howard - Production Artist
Vincent Kukua - Production Artist
Kevin Yuen - Production Artist

Published by Image Comics, Inc. Office of publication: 2134 Allston Way, 2nd Floor, Berkeley, California 94704. Image and its logos are ® and © 2010 Image Comics Inc. All rights reserved. Originally published in single magazine form as INVINCIBLE #66-70 and INVINCIBLE RETURNS #1. INVINCIBLE and all character likenesses are ™ and © 2010, Robert Kirkman and Cory Walker. All rights reserved. All names, characters, events and locales in this publication are entirely fictional. Any resemblance to actual persons (living or dead), events or places, without satiric intent, is coincidental. No part of this publication may be reproduced or transmitted, in any form or by any means (except for short excerpts for review purposes) without the express written permission of the copyright holder. PRINTED IN U.S.A. For information regarding the CPSIA on this printed material call: 203-595-3636 and provide reference # EAST –67095

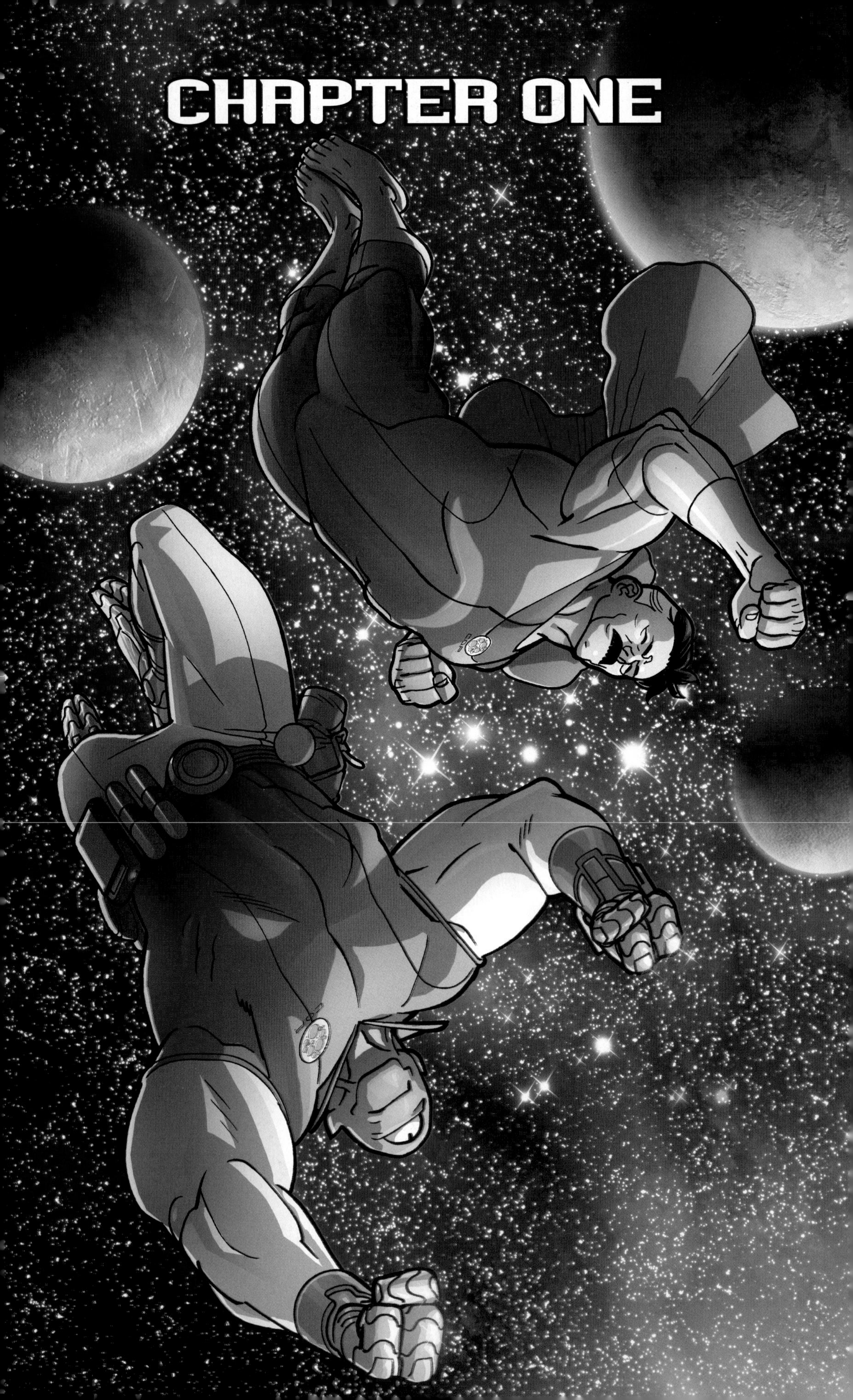
CHAPTER ONE

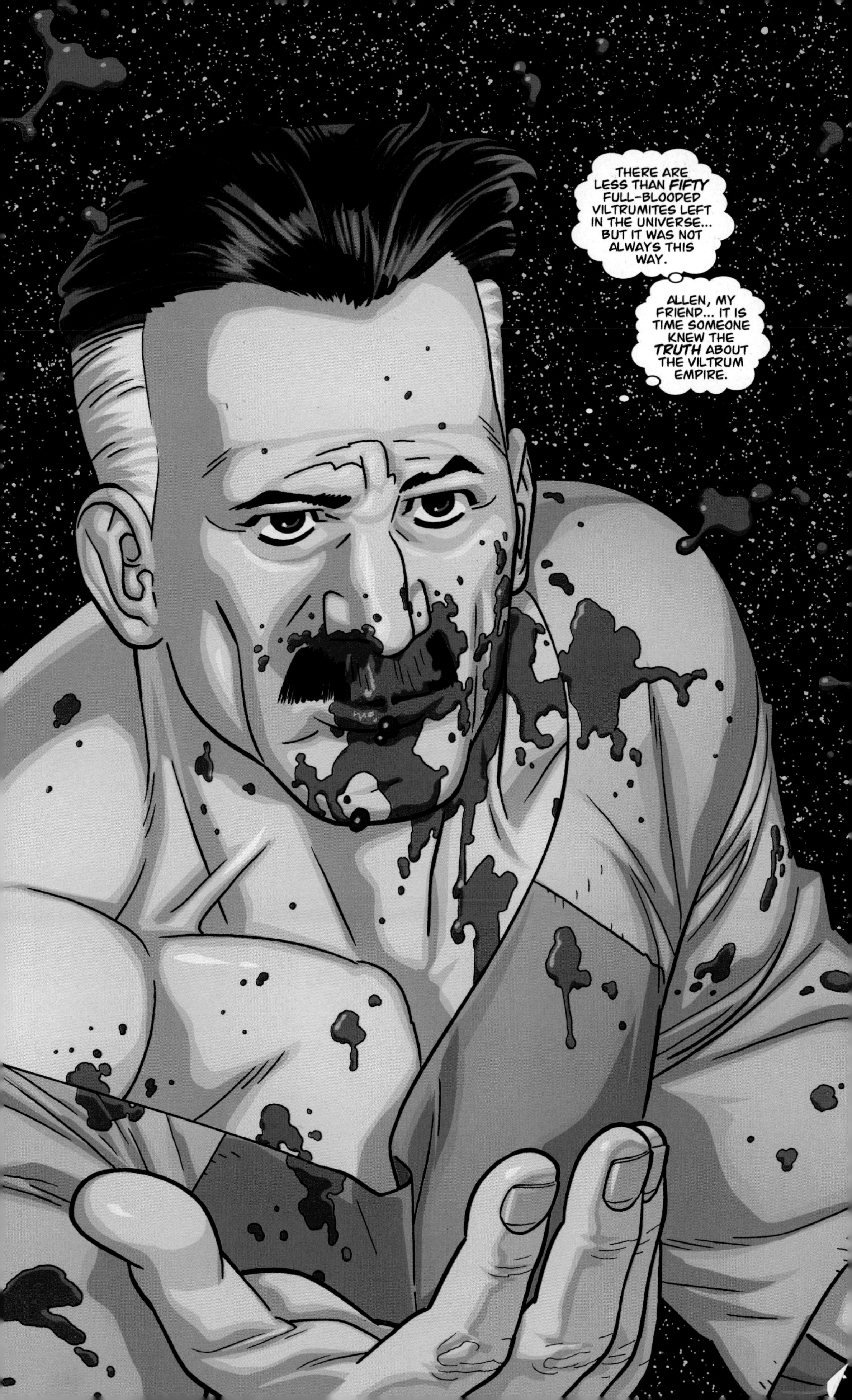
THERE ARE LESS THAN FIFTY FULL-BLOODED VILTRUMITES LEFT IN THE UNIVERSE... BUT IT WAS NOT ALWAYS THIS WAY.
ALLEN, MY FRIEND... IT IS TIME SOMEONE KNEW THE TRUTH ABOUT THE VILTRUM EMPIRE.

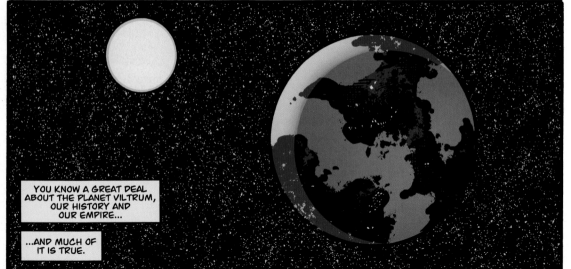

YOU KNOW A GREAT DEAL ABOUT THE PLANET VILTRUM, OUR HISTORY AND OUR EMPIRE...

...AND MUCH OF IT IS TRUE.

WE WERE A VIOLENT RACE WHO VALUED STRENGTH ABOVE ALL ELSE.

TO RID OURSELVES OF ANY WEAKNESS WE SLAUGHTERED EACH OTHER UNTIL WE WERE BRED INTO THE VILTRUMITES YOU KNOW TODAY.

EVENTUALLY, OUR PEOPLE UNITED, AND WE TURNED OUR ATTENTION OUTWARD, ESTABLISHING THE VILTRUM EMPIRE.

AN EMPIRE THAT CONTINUED TO EXPAND AT AN ASTOUNDING RATE FOR NEARLY ONE-THOUSAND YEARS.

UNTIL OUR ENEMIES MADE A WEAPON CAPABLE OF HURTING US.

THEY MADE A VIRUS.

UNIQUE TO OUR GENETIC CODE, THE VIRUS WAS *DEVASTATING.* IT SWEPT THROUGH MY PEOPLE AT AN ALARMING RATE.

IT APPEARED THERE WAS NO WAY OF STOPPING IT. OUR ENTIRE EMPIRE WAS IN JEOPARDY.

ATTEMPTS WERE MADE TO QUARANTINE THOSE WHO BECAME INFECTED... BUT IT WAS TOO LATE.

ALMOST THE ENTIRE POPULATION WAS INFECTED WITH WHAT WOULD BECOME KNOWN AS *THE SCOURGE VIRUS.*

THOSE WHO *SURVIVED* THE VIRUS DISCOVERED ITS DEADLY AFTER EFFECTS.

THERE WAS A SHORT PERIOD OF TIME AFTER THE VIRUS HAD LEFT THEIR SYSTEM, WHERE THEIR STRENGTH AND INVULNERABILITY HAD BEEN GREATLY DIMINISHED.

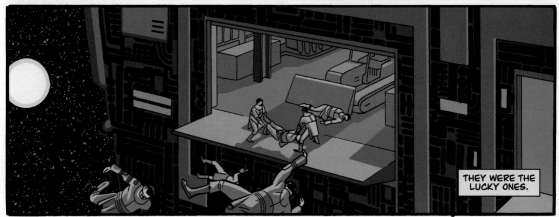

THEY WERE THE LUCKY ONES.

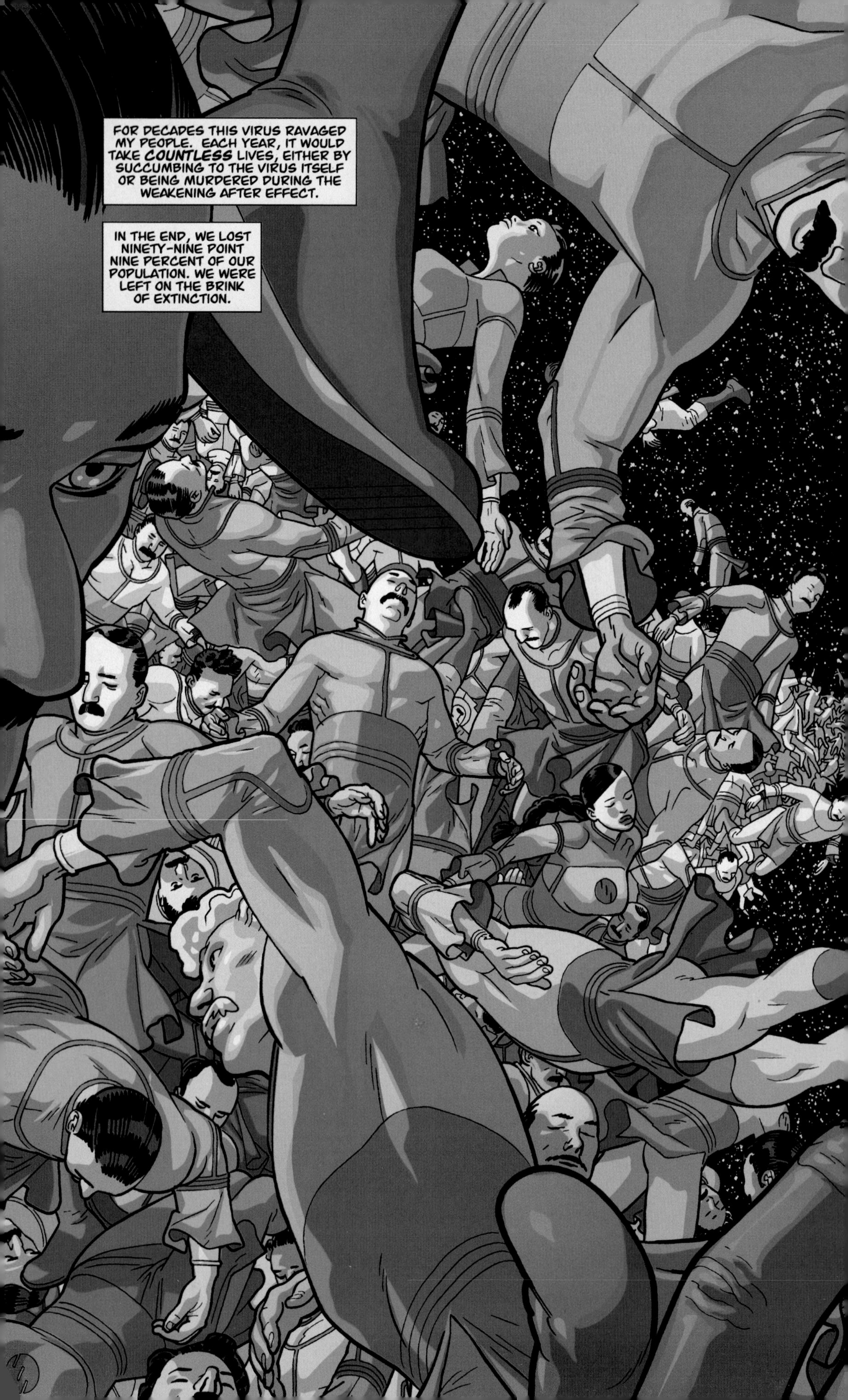
FOR DECADES THIS VIRUS RAVAGED MY PEOPLE. EACH YEAR, IT WOULD TAKE COUNTLESS LIVES, EITHER BY SUCCUMBING TO THE VIRUS ITSELF OR BEING MURDERED DURING THE WEAKENING AFTER EFFECT.
IN THE END, WE LOST NINETY-NINE POINT NINE PERCENT OF OUR POPULATION. WE WERE LEFT ON THE BRINK OF EXTINCTION.

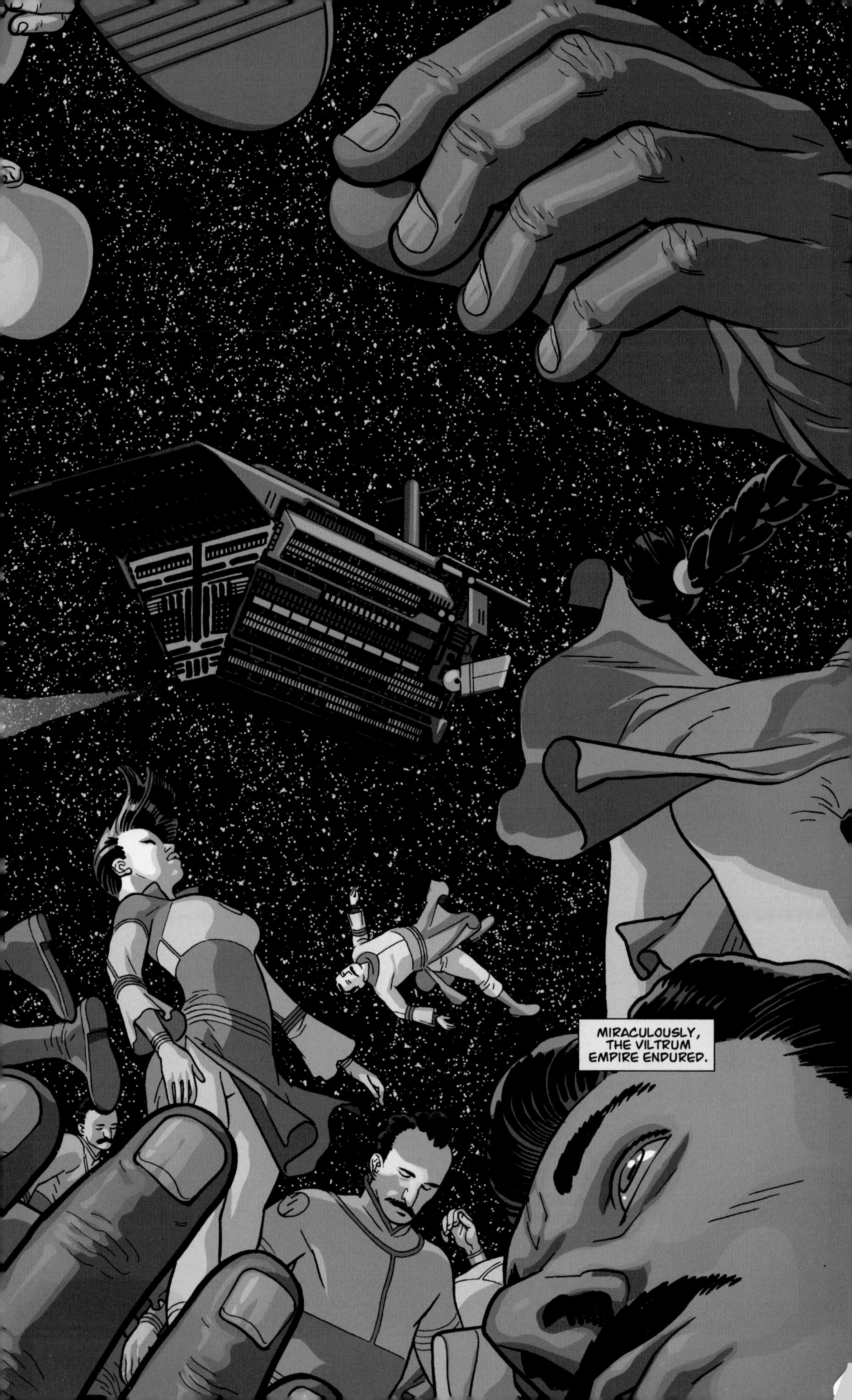
MIRACULOUSLY, THE VILTRUM EMPIRE ENDURED.

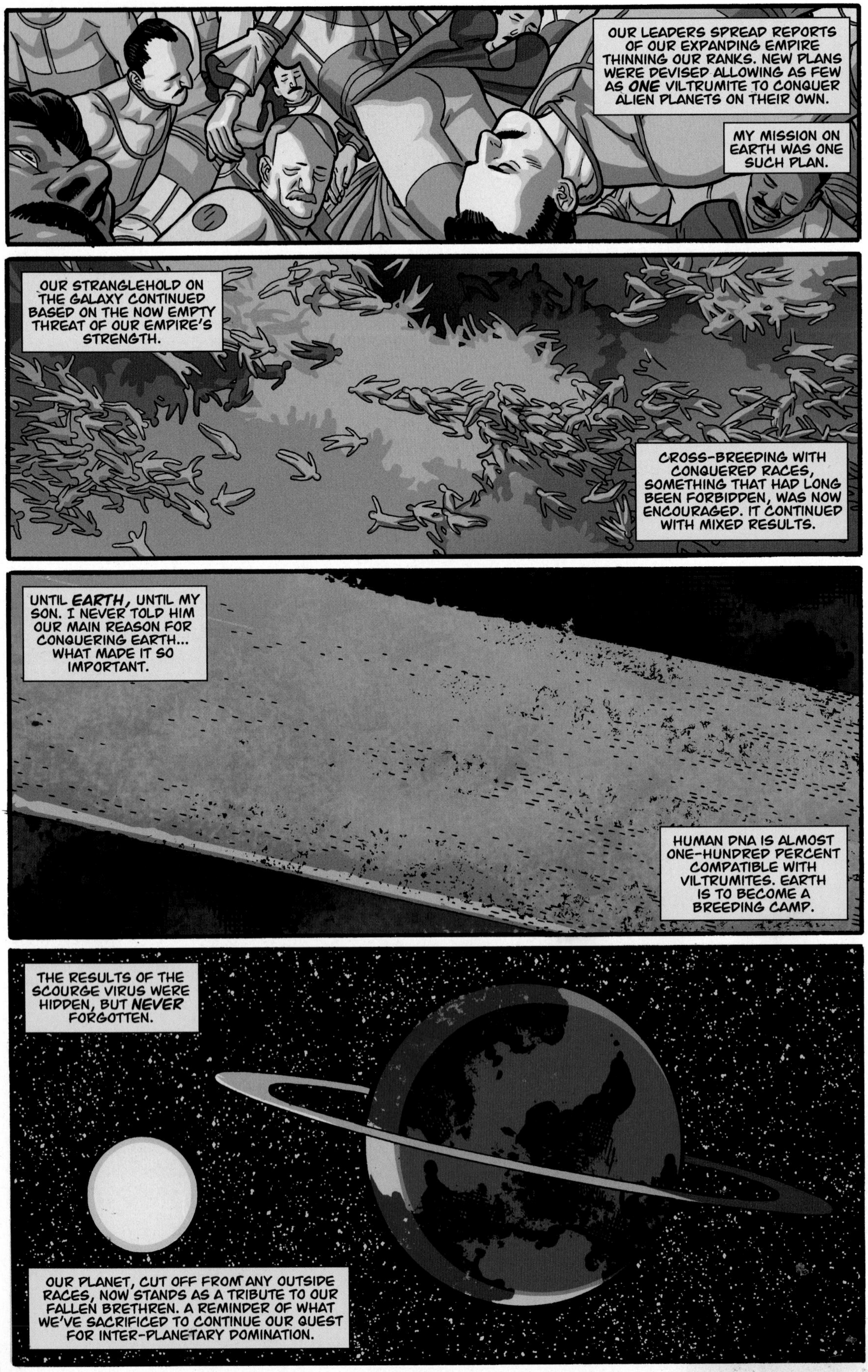
OUR LEADERS SPREAD REPORTS OF OUR EXPANDING EMPIRE THINNING OUR RANKS. NEW PLANS WERE DEVISED ALLOWING AS FEW AS ONE VILTRUMITE TO CONQUER ALIEN PLANETS ON THEIR OWN.
MY MISSION ON EARTH WAS ONE SUCH PLAN.
OUR STRANGLEHOLD ON THE GALAXY CONTINUED BASED ON THE NOW EMPTY THREAT OF OUR EMPIRE'S STRENGTH.
CROSS-BREEDING WITH CONQUERED RACES, SOMETHING THAT HAD LONG BEEN FORBIDDEN, WAS NOW ENCOURAGED. IT CONTINUED WITH MIXED RESULTS.
UNTIL EARTH, UNTIL MY SON. I NEVER TOLD HIM OUR MAIN REASON FOR CONQUERING EARTH... WHAT MADE IT SO IMPORTANT.
HUMAN DNA IS ALMOST ONE-HUNDRED PERCENT COMPATIBLE WITH VILTRUMITES. EARTH IS TO BECOME A BREEDING CAMP.
THE RESULTS OF THE SCOURGE VIRUS WERE HIDDEN, BUT NEVER FORGOTTEN.
OUR PLANET, CUT OFF FROM ANY OUTSIDE RACES, NOW STANDS AS A TRIBUTE TO OUR FALLEN BRETHREN. A REMINDER OF WHAT WE'VE SACRIFICED TO CONTINUE OUR QUEST FOR INTER-PLANETARY DOMINATION.

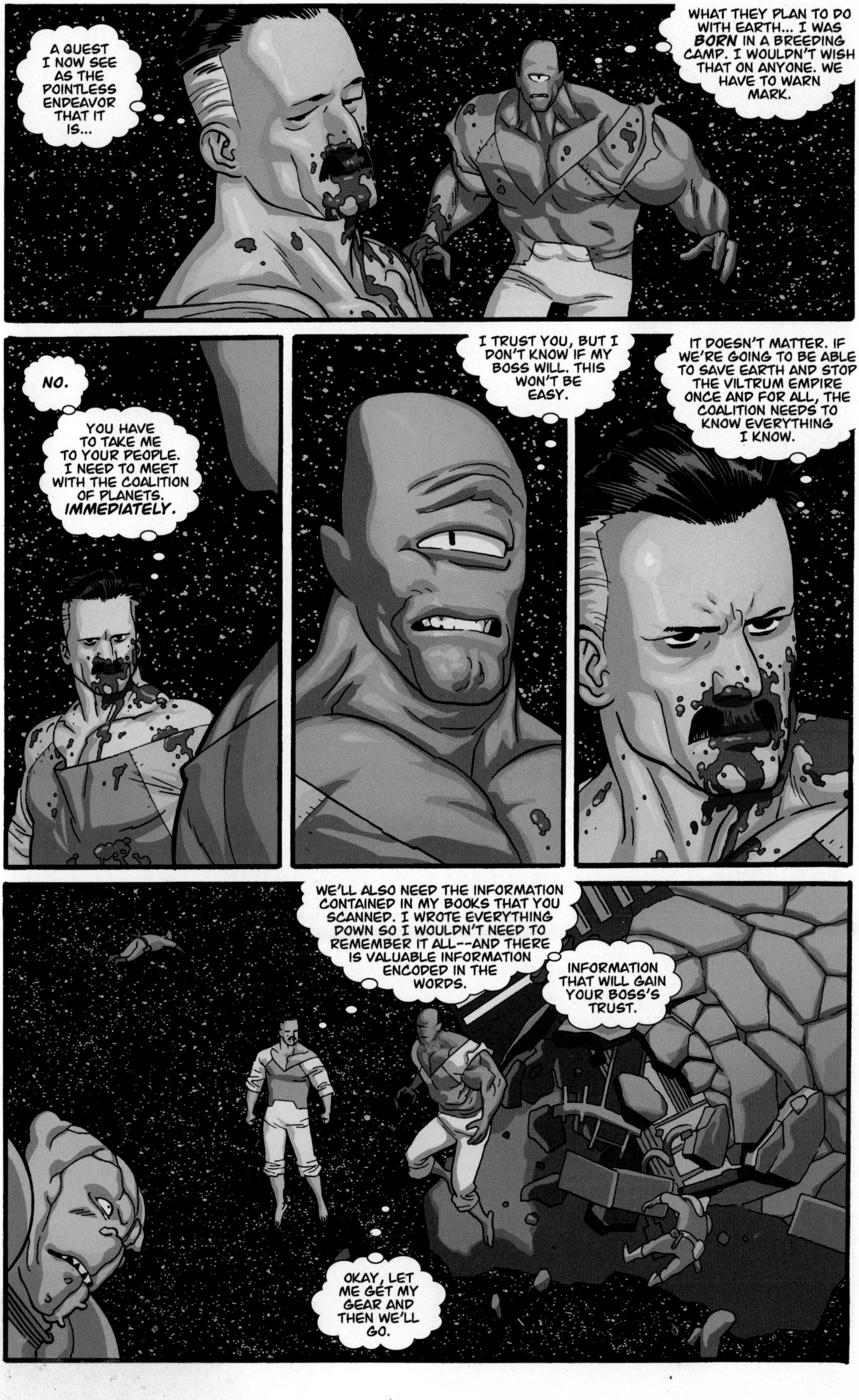
A QUEST I NOW SEE AS THE POINTLESS ENDEAVOR THAT IT IS...
WHAT THEY PLAN TO DO WITH EARTH... I WAS BORN IN A BREEDING CAMP. I WOULDN'T WISH THAT ON ANYONE. WE HAVE TO WARN MARK.
NO.
YOU HAVE TO TAKE ME TO YOUR PEOPLE. I NEED TO MEET WITH THE COALITION OF PLANETS. IMMEDIATELY.
I TRUST YOU, BUT I DON'T KNOW IF MY BOSS WILL. THIS WON'T BE EASY.
IT DOESN'T MATTER. IF WE'RE GOING TO BE ABLE TO SAVE EARTH AND STOP THE VILTRUM EMPIRE ONCE AND FOR ALL, THE COALITION NEEDS TO KNOW EVERYTHING I KNOW.
WE'LL ALSO NEED THE INFORMATION CONTAINED IN MY BOOKS THAT YOU SCANNED. I WROTE EVERYTHING DOWN SO I WOULDN'T NEED TO REMEMBER IT ALL--AND THERE IS VALUABLE INFORMATION ENCODED IN THE WORDS.
INFORMATION THAT WILL GAIN YOUR BOSS'S TRUST.
OKAY, LET ME GET MY GEAR AND THEN WE'LL GO.

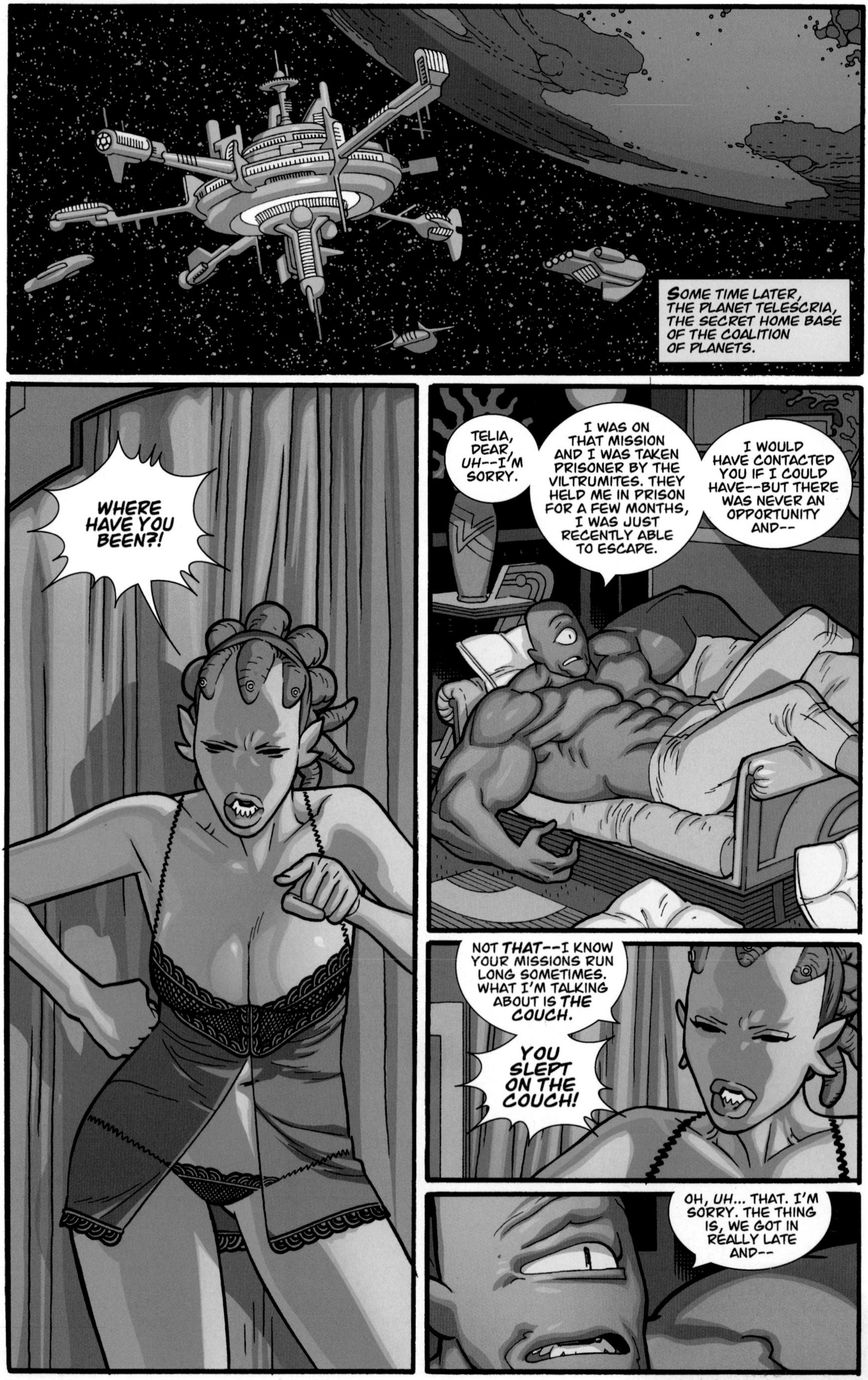
SOME TIME LATER, THE PLANET TELESCRIA, THE SECRET HOME BASE OF THE COALITION OF PLANETS.
WHERE HAVE YOU BEEN?!
TELIA, DEAR, UH--I'M SORRY.
I WAS ON THAT MISSION AND I WAS TAKEN PRISONER BY THE VILTRUMITES. THEY HELD ME IN PRISON FOR A FEW MONTHS, I WAS JUST RECENTLY ABLE TO ESCAPE.
I WOULD HAVE CONTACTED YOU IF I COULD HAVE--BUT THERE WAS NEVER AN OPPORTUNITY AND--
NOT THAT--I KNOW YOUR MISSIONS RUN LONG SOMETIMES. WHAT I'M TALKING ABOUT IS THE COUCH.
YOU SLEPT ON THE COUCH!
OH, UH... THAT. I'M SORRY. THE THING IS, WE GOT IN REALLY LATE AND--

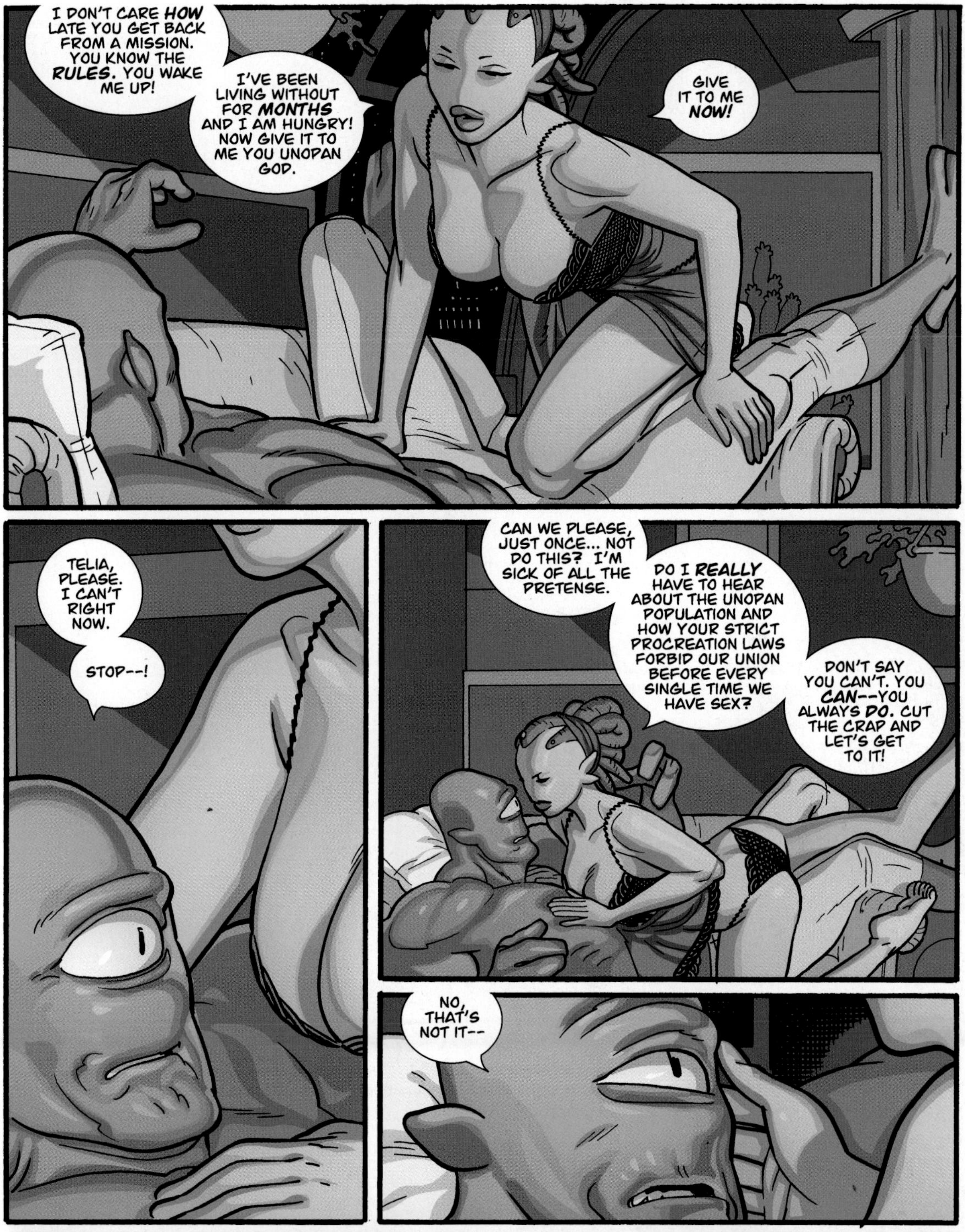
I DON'T CARE HOW LATE YOU GET BACK FROM A MISSION. YOU KNOW THE RULES. YOU WAKE ME UP!
I'VE BEEN LIVING WITHOUT FOR MONTHS AND I AM HUNGRY! NOW GIVE IT TO ME YOU UNOPAN GOD.
GIVE IT TO ME NOW!
TELIA, PLEASE. I CAN'T RIGHT NOW.
STOP--!
CAN WE PLEASE, JUST ONCE... NOT DO THIS? I'M SICK OF ALL THE PRETENSE.
DO I REALLY HAVE TO HEAR ABOUT THE UNOPAN POPULATION AND HOW YOUR STRICT PROCREATION LAWS FORBID OUR UNION BEFORE EVERY SINGLE TIME WE HAVE SEX?
DON'T SAY YOU CAN'T. YOU CAN--YOU ALWAYS DO. CUT THE CRAP AND LET'S GET TO IT!
NO, THAT'S NOT IT--
WAIT A MINUTE... DID YOU SAY "WE" GOT IN REALLY LATE?

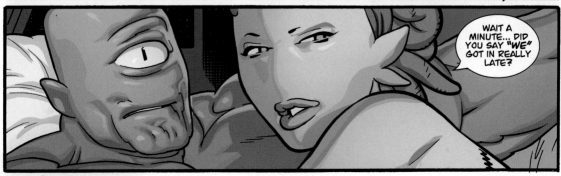

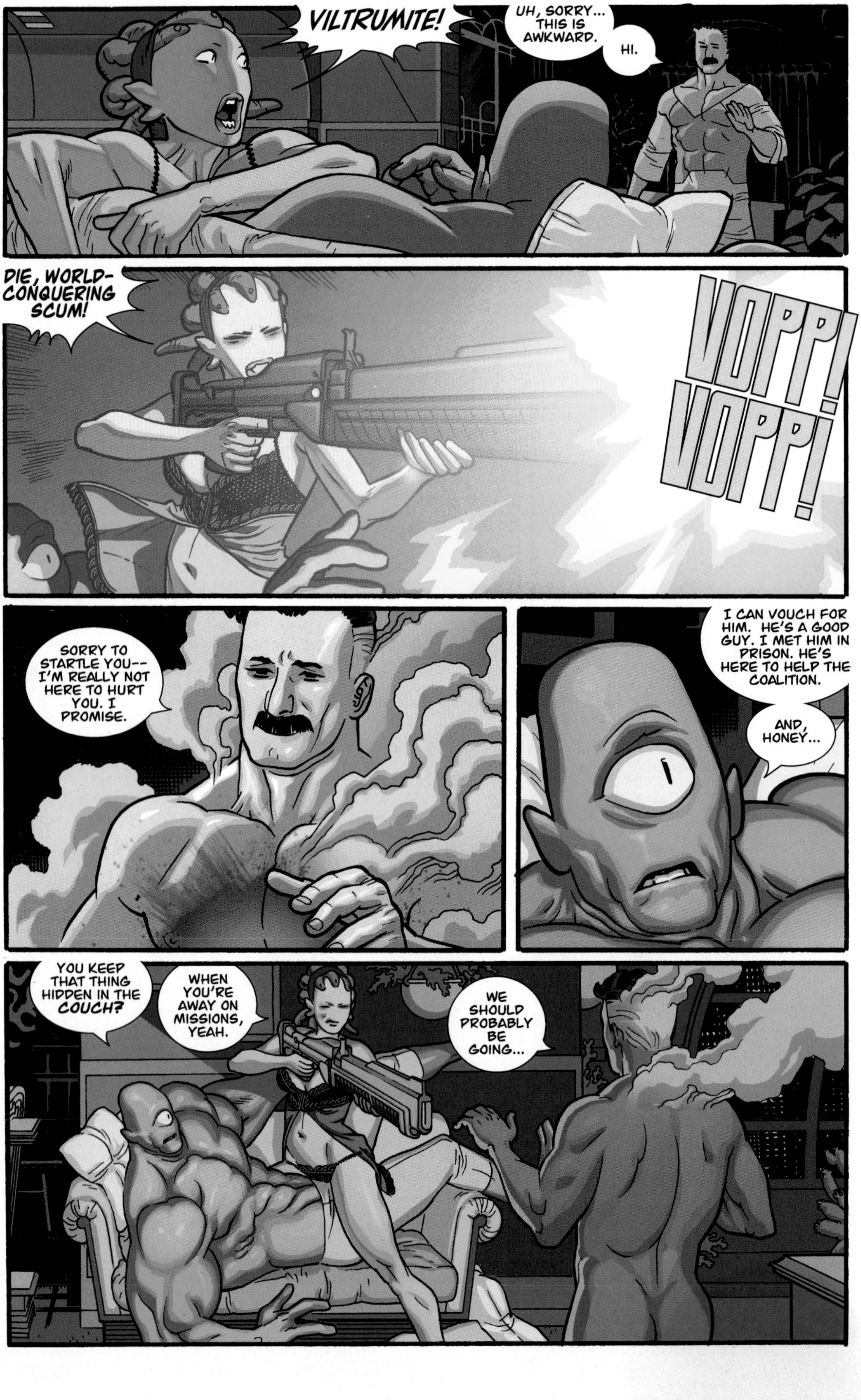
VILTRUMITE!
UH, SORRY... THIS IS AWKWARD.
HI.
DIE, WORLD-CONQUERING SCUM!
VOPP! VOPP!
SORRY TO STARTLE YOU-- I'M REALLY NOT HERE TO HURT YOU. I PROMISE.
I CAN VOUCH FOR HIM. HE'S A GOOD GUY. I MET HIM IN PRISON. HE'S HERE TO HELP THE COALITION.
AND, HONEY...
YOU KEEP THAT THING HIDDEN IN THE COUCH?
WHEN YOU'RE AWAY ON MISSIONS, YEAH.
WE SHOULD PROBABLY BE GOING...

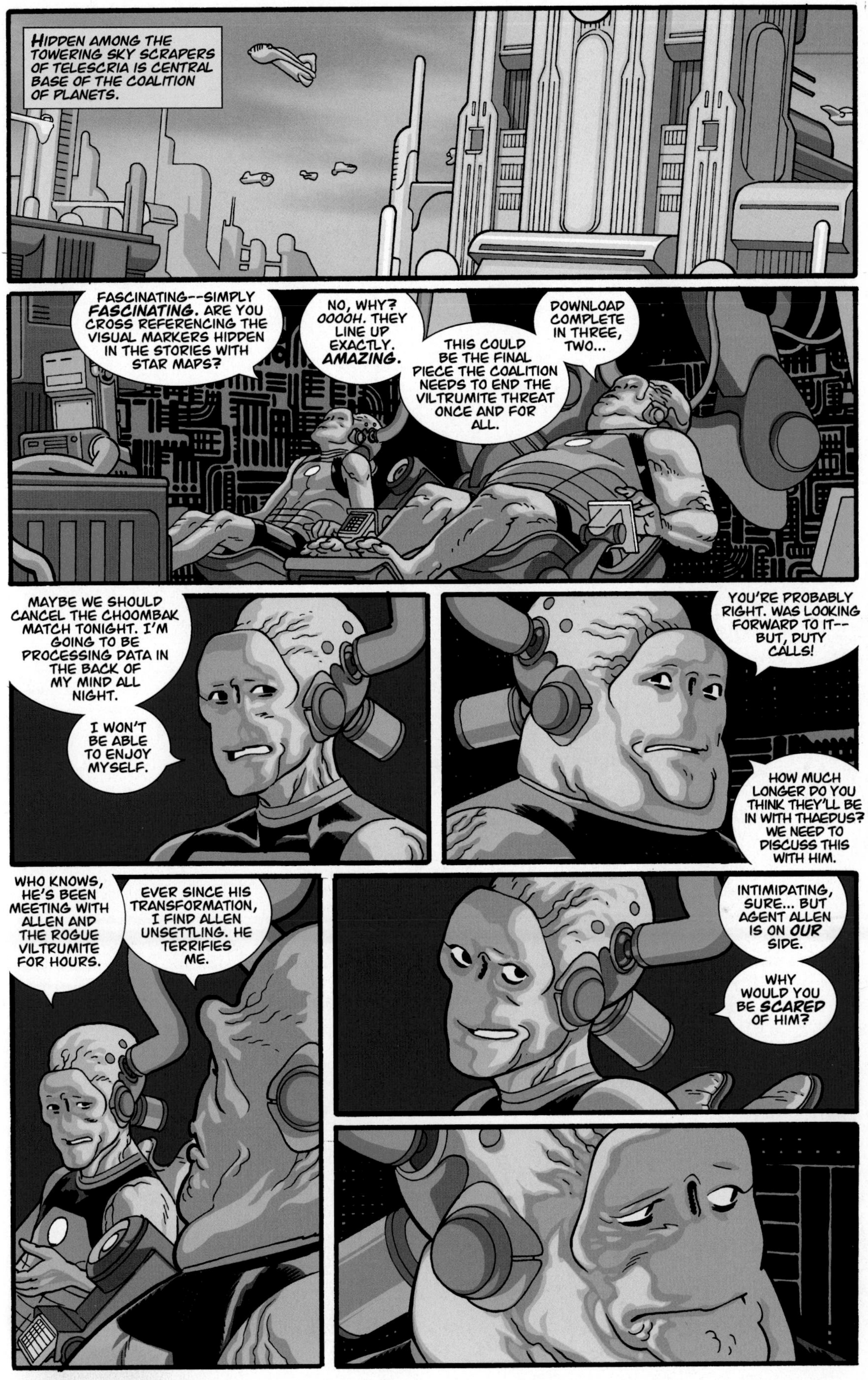
HIDDEN AMONG THE TOWERING SKY SCRAPERS OF TELESCRIA IS CENTRAL BASE OF THE COALITION OF PLANETS.
FASCINATING--SIMPLY FASCINATING. ARE YOU CROSS REFERENCING THE VISUAL MARKERS HIDDEN IN THE STORIES WITH STAR MAPS?
NO, WHY? OOOOH. THEY LINE UP EXACTLY. AMAZING.
THIS COULD BE THE FINAL PIECE THE COALITION NEEDS TO END THE VILTRUMITE THREAT ONCE AND FOR ALL.
DOWNLOAD COMPLETE IN THREE, TWO...
MAYBE WE SHOULD CANCEL THE CHOOMBAK MATCH TONIGHT. I'M GOING TO BE PROCESSING DATA IN THE BACK OF MY MIND ALL NIGHT.
I WON'T BE ABLE TO ENJOY MYSELF.
YOU'RE PROBABLY RIGHT. WAS LOOKING FORWARD TO IT--BUT, DUTY CALLS!
HOW MUCH LONGER DO YOU THINK THEY'LL BE IN WITH THAEDUS? WE NEED TO DISCUSS THIS WITH HIM.
WHO KNOWS, HE'S BEEN MEETING WITH ALLEN AND THE ROGUE VILTRUMITE FOR HOURS.
EVER SINCE HIS TRANSFORMATION, I FIND ALLEN UNSETTLING. HE TERRIFIES ME.
INTIMIDATING, SURE... BUT AGENT ALLEN IS ON OUR SIDE.
WHY WOULD YOU BE SCARED OF HIM?

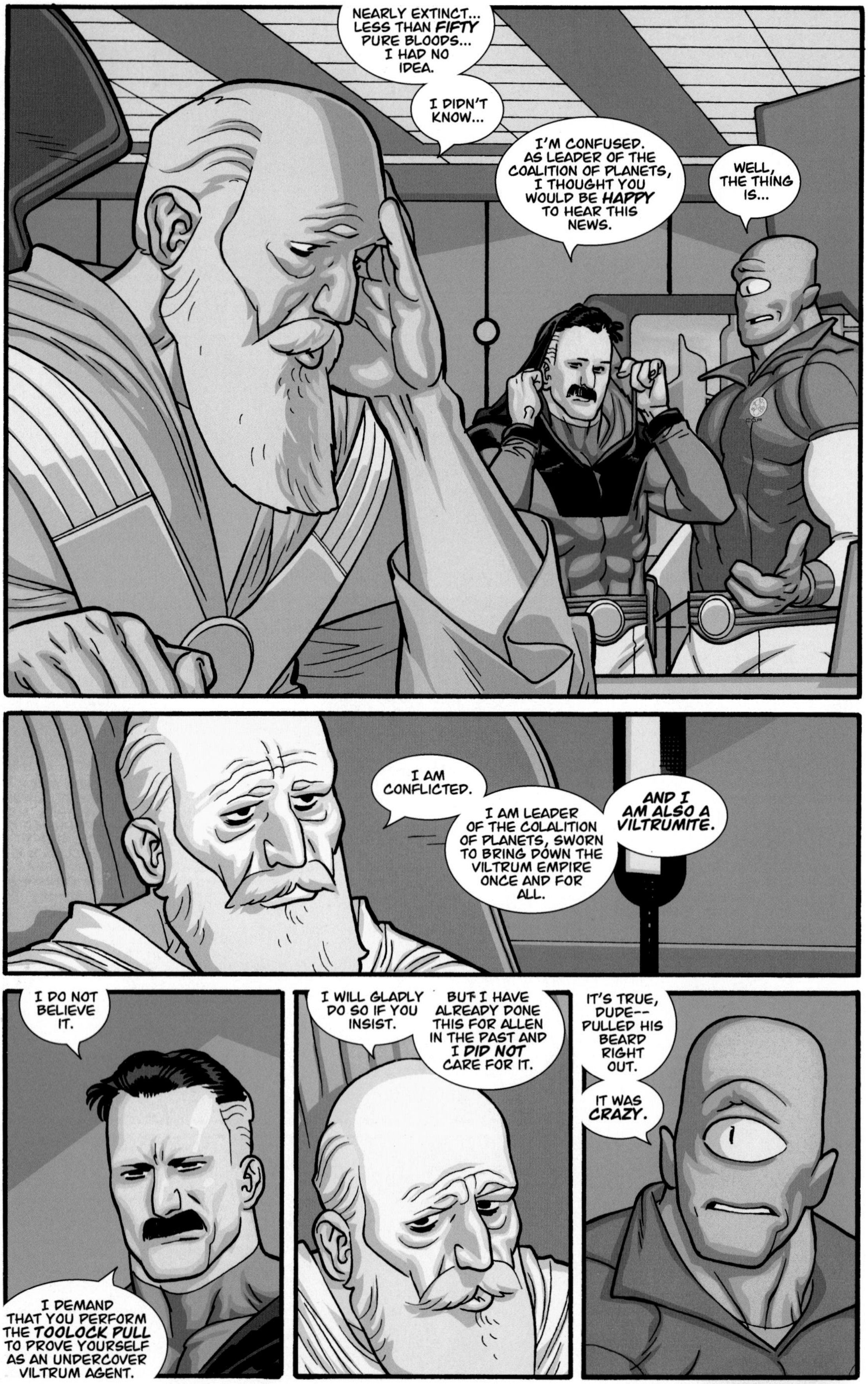
NEARLY EXTINCT... LESS THAN FIFTY PURE BLOODS... I HAD NO IDEA.
I DIDN'T KNOW...
I'M CONFUSED. AS LEADER OF THE COALITION OF PLANETS, I THOUGHT YOU WOULD BE HAPPY TO HEAR THIS NEWS.
WELL, THE THING IS...
I AM CONFLICTED.
I AM LEADER OF THE COLALITION OF PLANETS, SWORN TO BRING DOWN THE VILTRUM EMPIRE ONCE AND FOR ALL.
AND I AM ALSO A VILTRUMITE.
I DO NOT BELIEVE IT.
I DEMAND THAT YOU PERFORM THE TOOLOCK PULL TO PROVE YOURSELF AS AN UNDERCOVER VILTRUM AGENT.
I WILL GLADLY DO SO IF YOU INSIST.
BUT I HAVE ALREADY DONE THIS FOR ALLEN IN THE PAST AND I DID NOT CARE FOR IT.
IT'S TRUE, DUDE-- PULLED HIS BEARD RIGHT OUT.
IT WAS CRAZY.

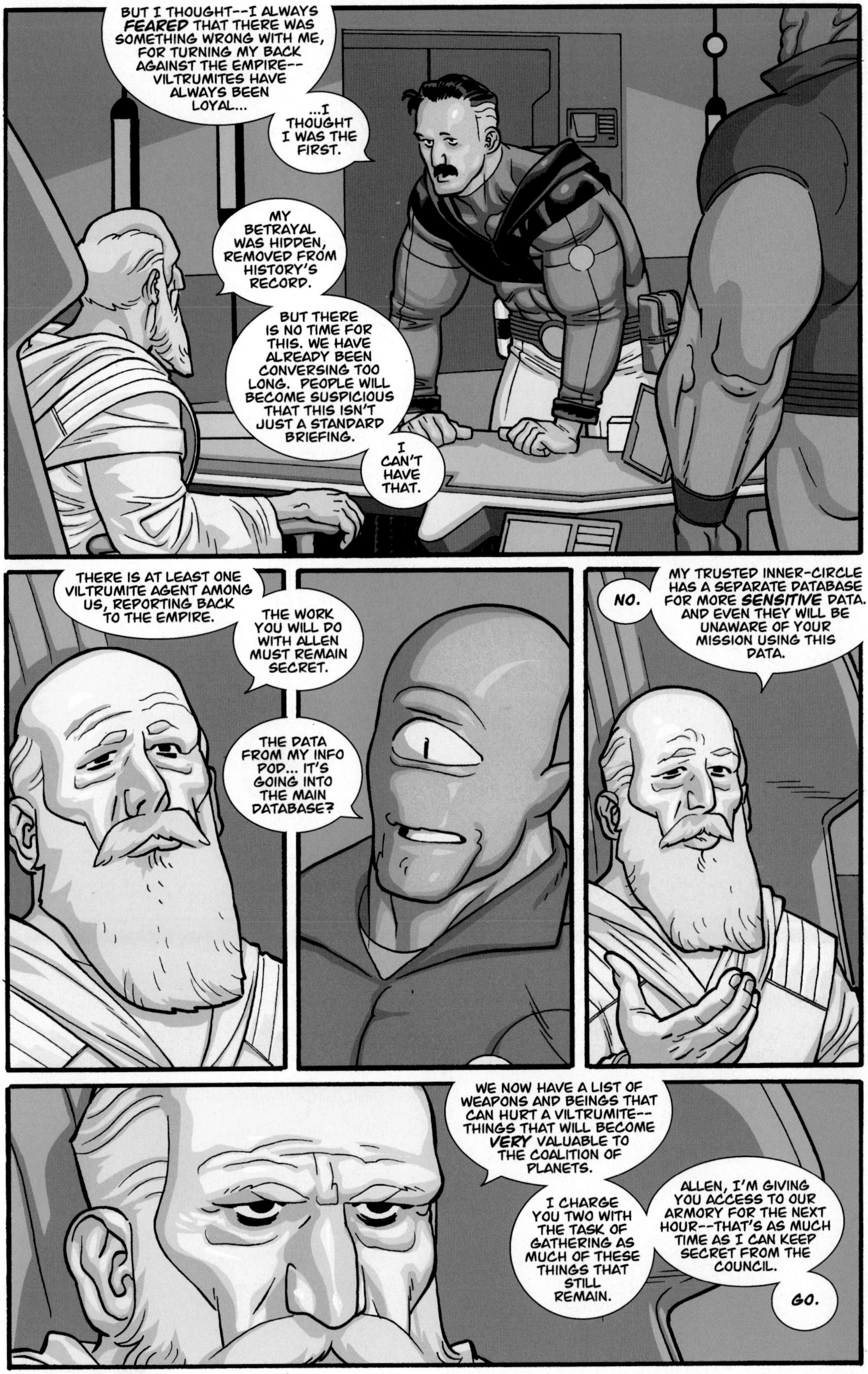

BUT I THOUGHT--I ALWAYS FEARED THAT THERE WAS SOMETHING WRONG WITH ME, FOR TURNING MY BACK AGAINST THE EMPIRE--VILTRUMITES HAVE ALWAYS BEEN LOYAL...
...I THOUGHT I WAS THE FIRST.
MY BETRAYAL WAS HIDDEN, REMOVED FROM HISTORY'S RECORD.
BUT THERE IS NO TIME FOR THIS. WE HAVE ALREADY BEEN CONVERSING TOO LONG. PEOPLE WILL BECOME SUSPICIOUS THAT THIS ISN'T JUST A STANDARD BRIEFING.
I CAN'T HAVE THAT.
THERE IS AT LEAST ONE VILTRUMITE AGENT AMONG US, REPORTING BACK TO THE EMPIRE.
THE WORK YOU WILL DO WITH ALLEN MUST REMAIN SECRET.
THE DATA FROM MY INFO POD... IT'S GOING INTO THE MAIN DATABASE?
NO.
MY TRUSTED INNER-CIRCLE HAS A SEPARATE DATABASE FOR MORE SENSITIVE DATA. AND EVEN THEY WILL BE UNAWARE OF YOUR MISSION USING THIS DATA.
WE NOW HAVE A LIST OF WEAPONS AND BEINGS THAT CAN HURT A VILTRUMITE--THINGS THAT WILL BECOME VERY VALUABLE TO THE COALITION OF PLANETS.
I CHARGE YOU TWO WITH THE TASK OF GATHERING AS MUCH OF THESE THINGS THAT STILL REMAIN.
ALLEN, I'M GIVING YOU ACCESS TO OUR ARMORY FOR THE NEXT HOUR--THAT'S AS MUCH TIME AS I CAN KEEP SECRET FROM THE COUNCIL.
GO.

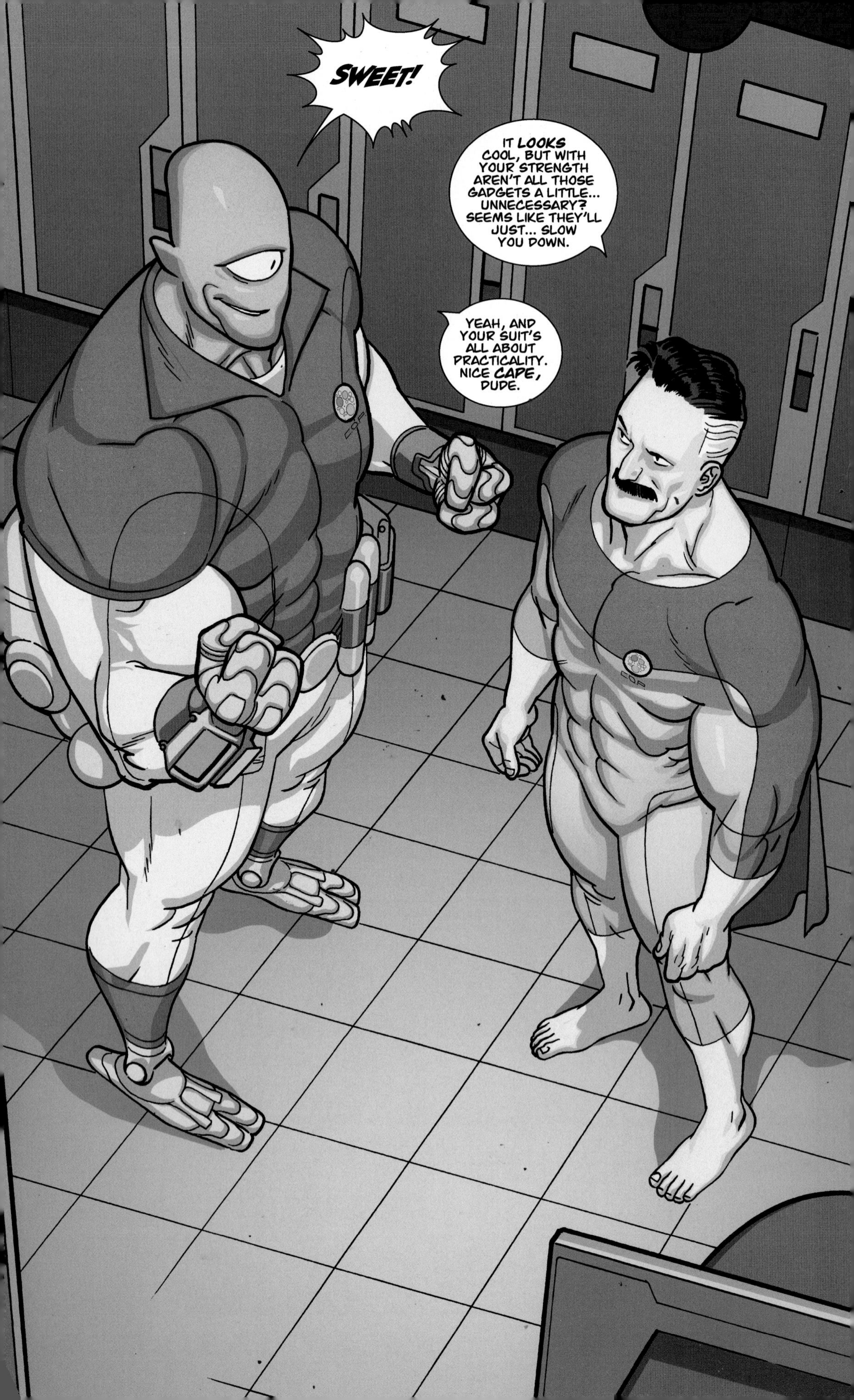
SWEET!
IT LOOKS COOL, BUT WITH YOUR STRENGTH AREN'T ALL THOSE GADGETS A LITTLE... UNNECESSARY? SEEMS LIKE THEY'LL JUST... SLOW YOU DOWN.
YEAH, AND YOUR SUIT'S ALL ABOUT PRACTICALITY. NICE CAPE, DUDE.

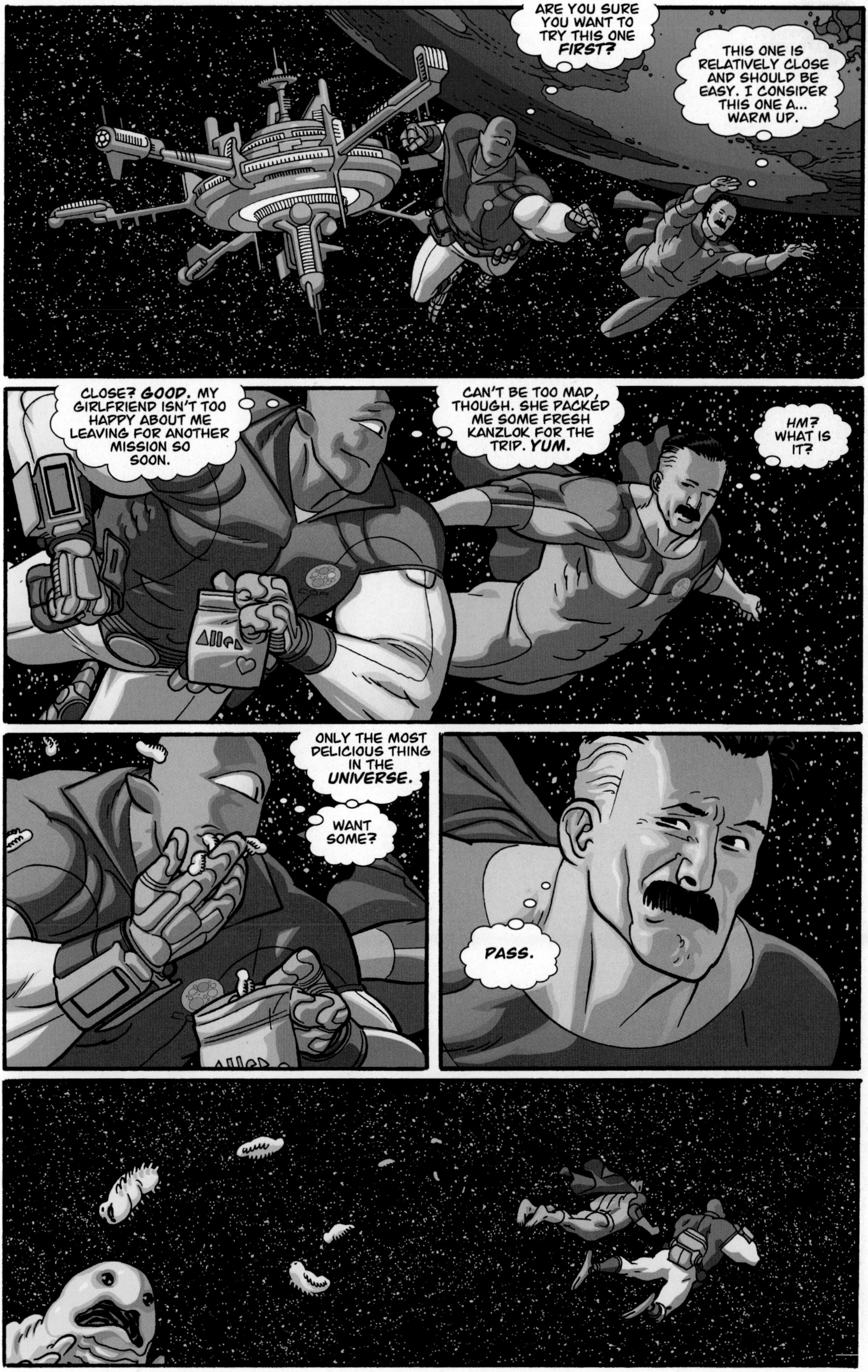
ARE YOU SURE YOU WANT TO TRY THIS ONE FIRST?
THIS ONE IS RELATIVELY CLOSE AND SHOULD BE EASY. I CONSIDER THIS ONE A... WARM UP.
CLOSE? GOOD. MY GIRLFRIEND ISN'T TOO HAPPY ABOUT ME LEAVING FOR ANOTHER MISSION SO SOON.
CAN'T BE TOO MAD, THOUGH. SHE PACKED ME SOME FRESH KANZLOK FOR THE TRIP. YUM.
HM? WHAT IS IT?
ONLY THE MOST DELICIOUS THING IN THE UNIVERSE.
WANT SOME?
PASS.

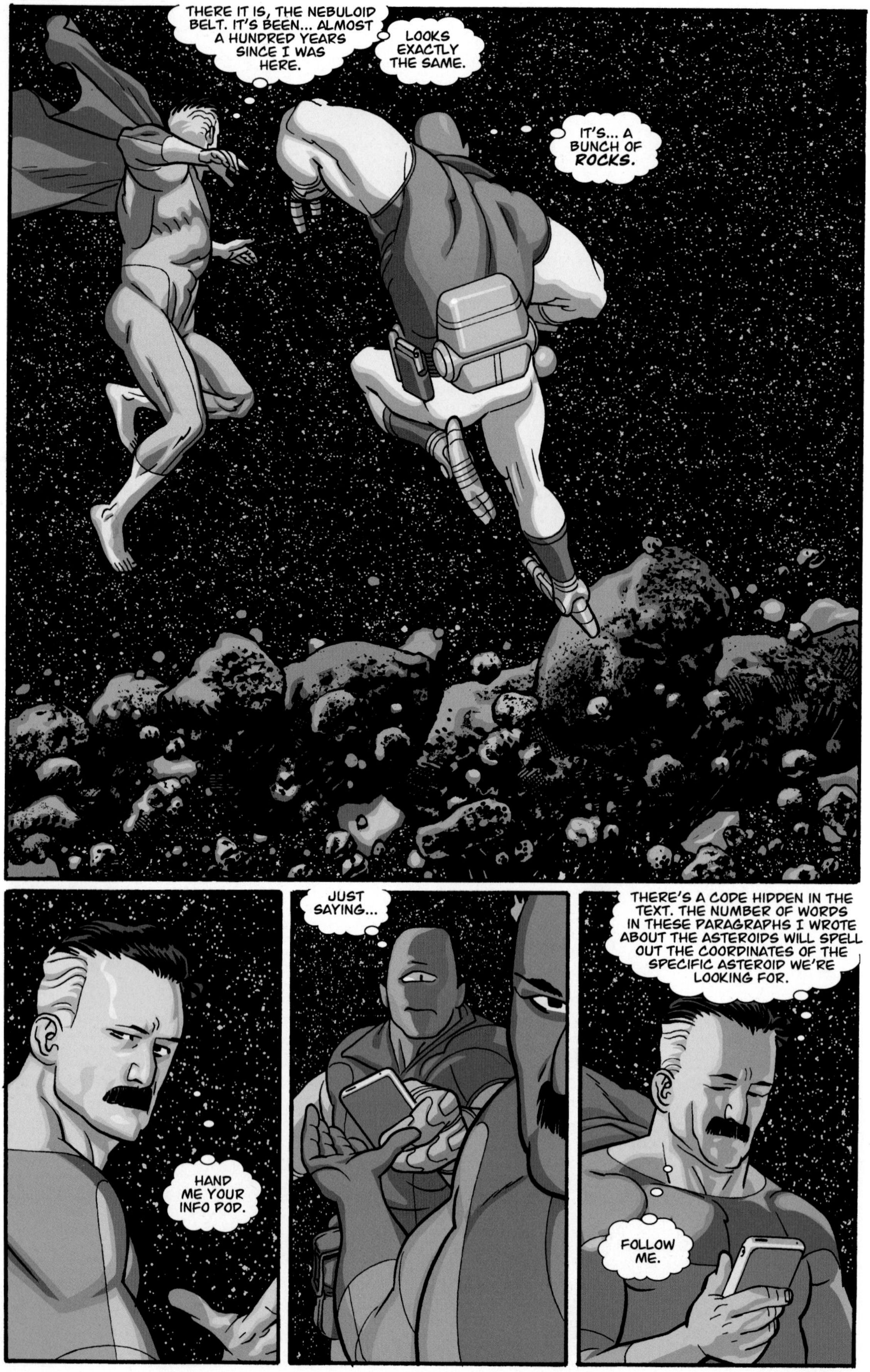
THERE IT IS, THE NEBULOID BELT. IT'S BEEN... ALMOST A HUNDRED YEARS SINCE I WAS HERE.
LOOKS EXACTLY THE SAME.
IT'S... A BUNCH OF ROCKS.
HAND ME YOUR INFO POD.
JUST SAYING...
THERE'S A CODE HIDDEN IN THE TEXT. THE NUMBER OF WORDS IN THESE PARAGRAPHS I WROTE ABOUT THE ASTEROIDS WILL SPELL OUT THE COORDINATES OF THE SPECIFIC ASTEROID WE'RE LOOKING FOR.
FOLLOW ME.

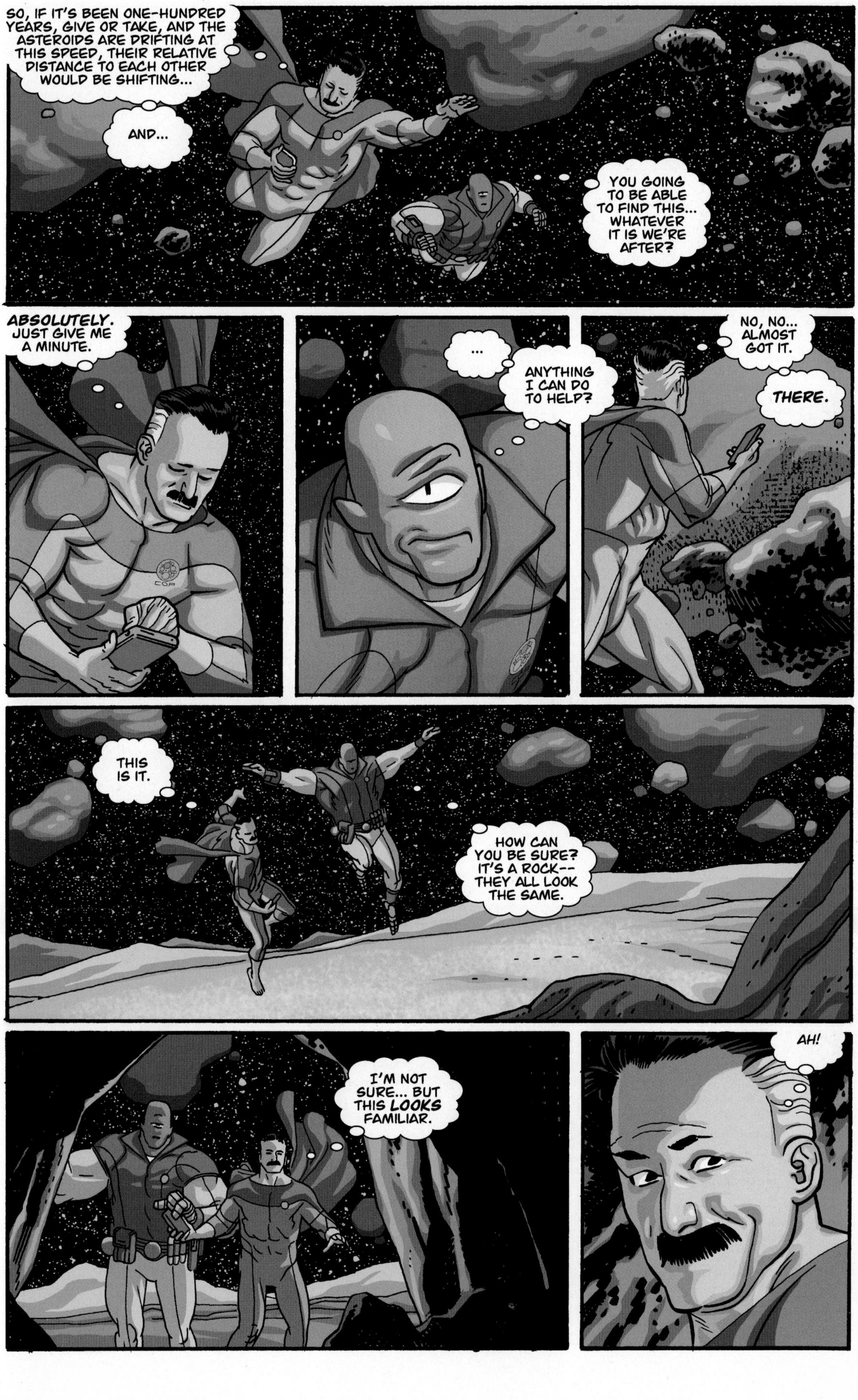
SO, IF IT'S BEEN ONE-HUNDRED YEARS, GIVE OR TAKE, AND THE ASTEROIDS ARE DRIFTING AT THIS SPEED, THEIR RELATIVE DISTANCE TO EACH OTHER WOULD BE SHIFTING...
AND...
YOU GOING TO BE ABLE TO FIND THIS... WHATEVER IT IS WE'RE AFTER?
ABSOLUTELY. JUST GIVE ME A MINUTE.
...
ANYTHING I CAN DO TO HELP?
NO, NO... ALMOST GOT IT.
THERE.
THIS IS IT.
HOW CAN YOU BE SURE? IT'S A ROCK-- THEY ALL LOOK THE SAME.
I'M NOT SURE... BUT THIS LOOKS FAMILIAR.
AH!

THERE IT IS.

WAIT, *WHAT?*

I DON'T UNDERSTAND. THE GUN HAS JUST BEEN LYING HERE FOR ALMOST *ONE-HUNDRED YEARS?* THAT MAKES NO SENSE.

WHY DIDN'T YOU JUST TAKE IT BACK TO THE VILTRUM EMPIRE? WHY'D YOU LEAVE IT HERE?

THIS GUN BELONGS TO THE *SPACE RACER.* YOU REALLY KNOW NOTHING ABOUT HIM?

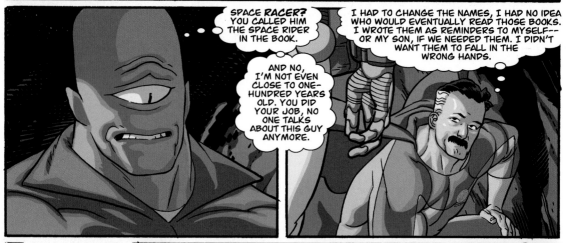

SPACE *RACER?* YOU CALLED HIM THE SPACE RIDER IN THE BOOK.

AND NO, I'M NOT EVEN CLOSE TO ONE-HUNDRED YEARS OLD. YOU DID YOUR JOB, NO ONE TALKS ABOUT THIS GUY ANYMORE.

I HAD TO CHANGE THE NAMES, I HAD NO IDEA WHO WOULD EVENTUALLY READ THOSE BOOKS. I WROTE THEM AS REMINDERS TO MYSELF-- OR MY SON, IF WE NEEDED THEM. I DIDN'T WANT THEM TO FALL IN THE WRONG HANDS.

THE SPACE RACER'S GUN--THE ONE THAT FIRES INDESTRUCTIBLE BLASTS THAT WILL SHOOT THROUGH ANYTHING--CAN ONLY BE FIRED BY *HIM.*

HE'S GOT SOME KIND OF BOND WITH THE GUN--IF ANYONE TRIES TO TAKE IT OR USE IT... IF I HAD TOUCHED IT WHILE HE WAS STILL ALIVE IT WOULD HAVE FLOWN INTO THE CENTER OF THE PILE OF RUBBLE I BURIED HIM UNDER AND GIVEN HIM THE MEANS TO ESCAPE.

MY ONLY OPTION WAS TO LEAVE IT EXACTLY WHERE HE DROPPED IT.

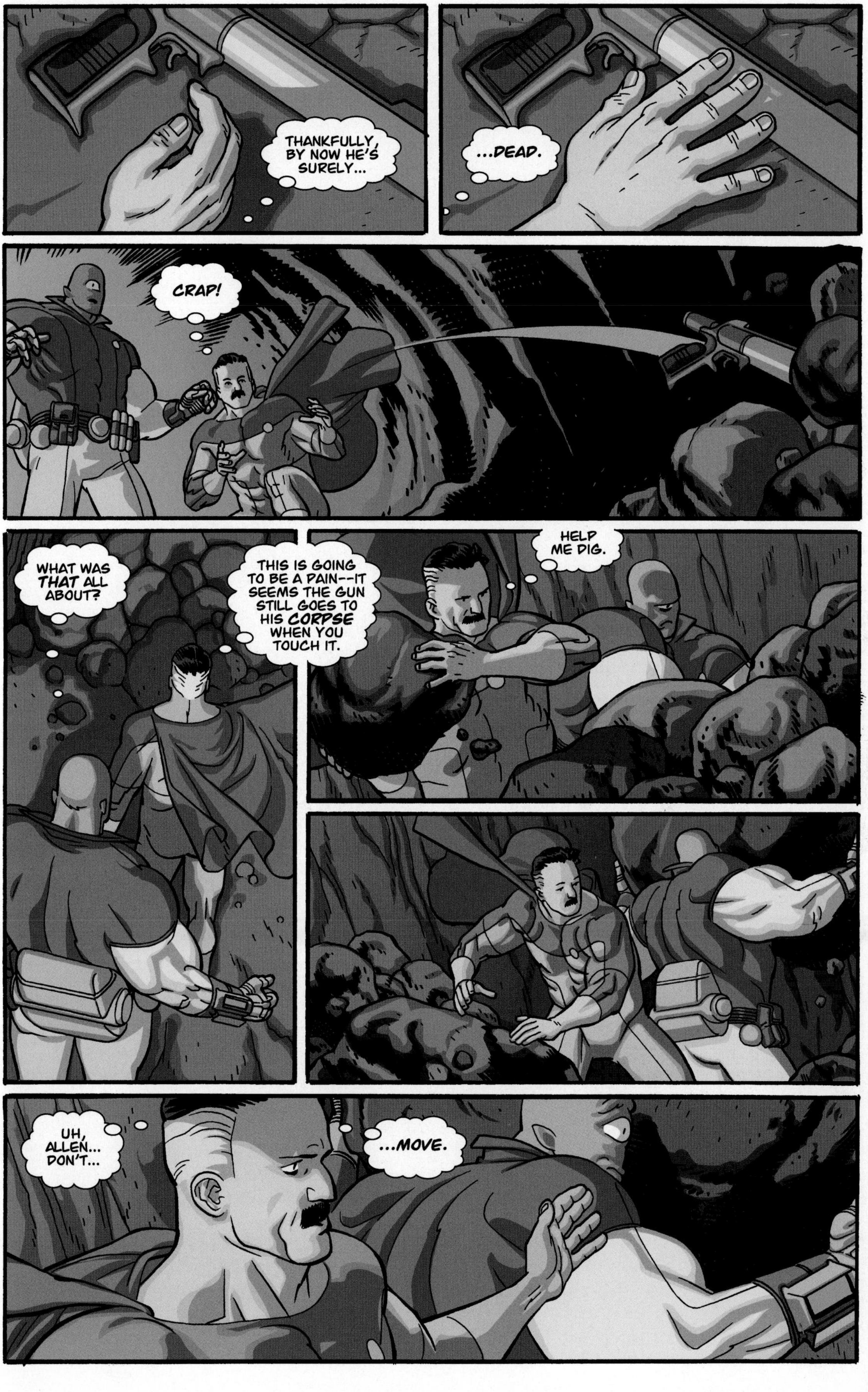
THANKFULLY, BY NOW HE'S SURELY...
...DEAD.
CRAP!
WHAT WAS THAT ALL ABOUT?
THIS IS GOING TO BE A PAIN--IT SEEMS THE GUN STILL GOES TO HIS CORPSE WHEN YOU TOUCH IT.
HELP ME DIG.
UH, ALLEN... DON'T...
...MOVE.

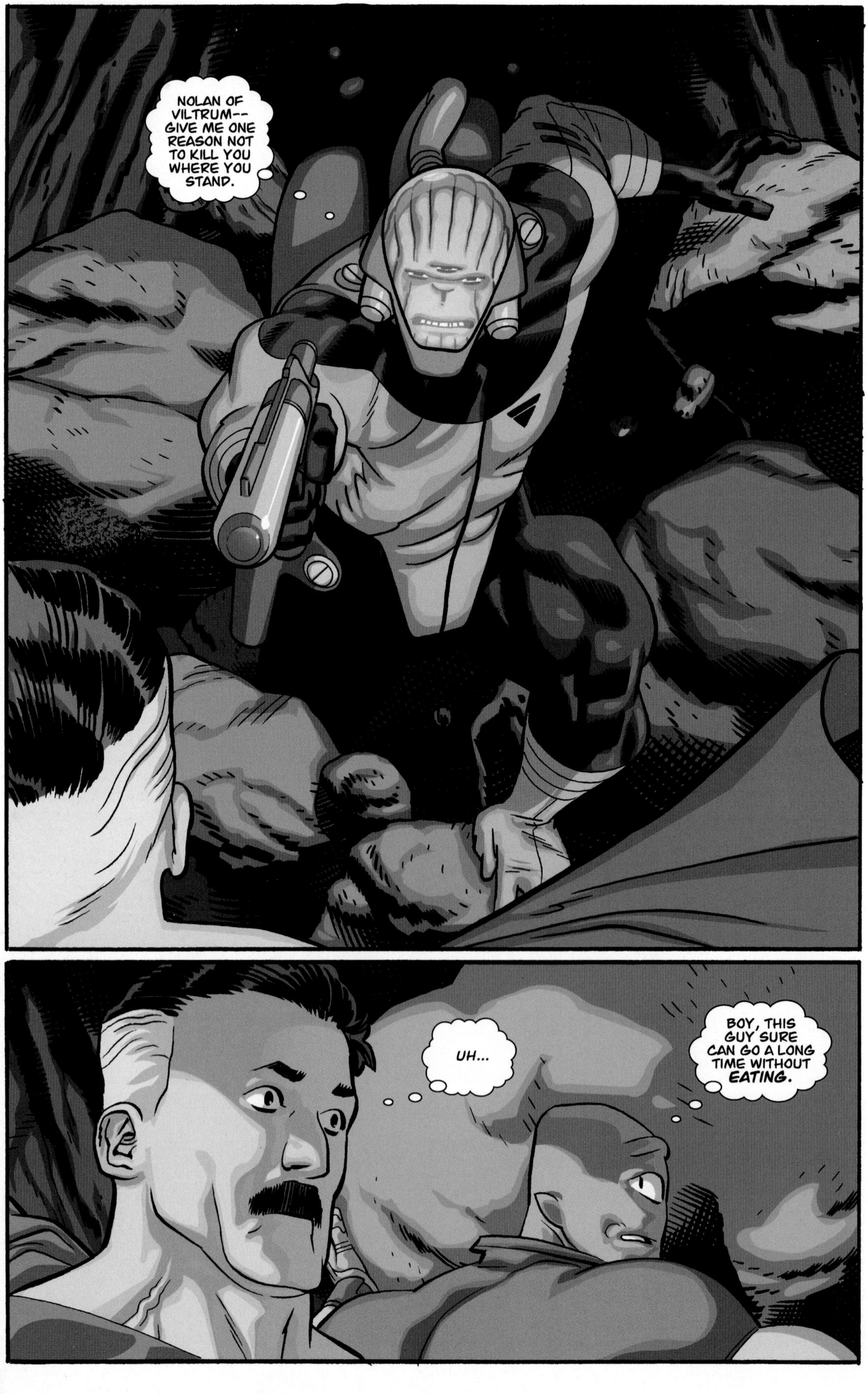
NOLAN OF VILTRUM-- GIVE ME ONE REASON NOT TO KILL YOU WHERE YOU STAND.
UH...
BOY, THIS GUY SURE CAN GO A LONG TIME WITHOUT EATING.

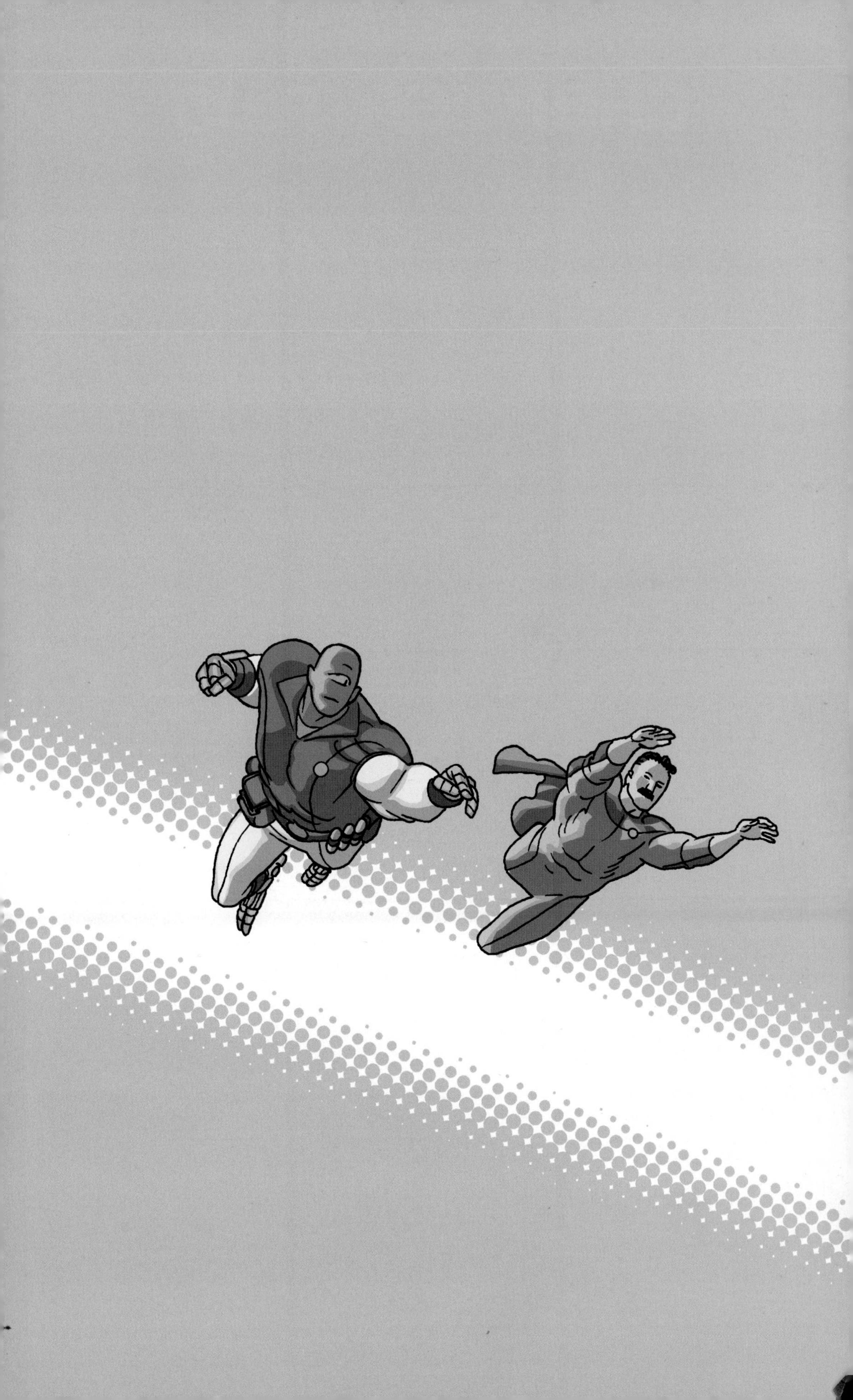

# CHAPTER TWO

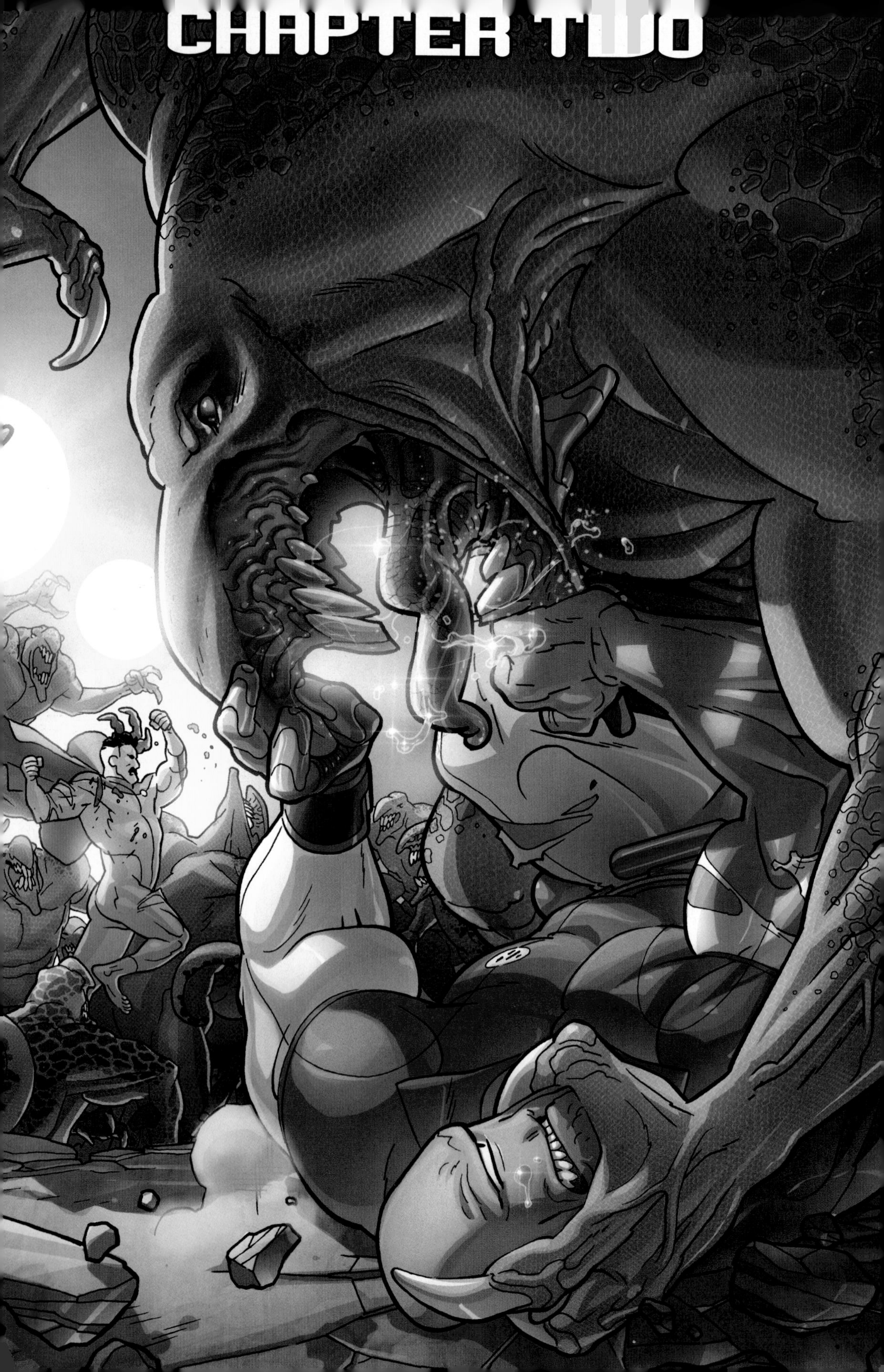

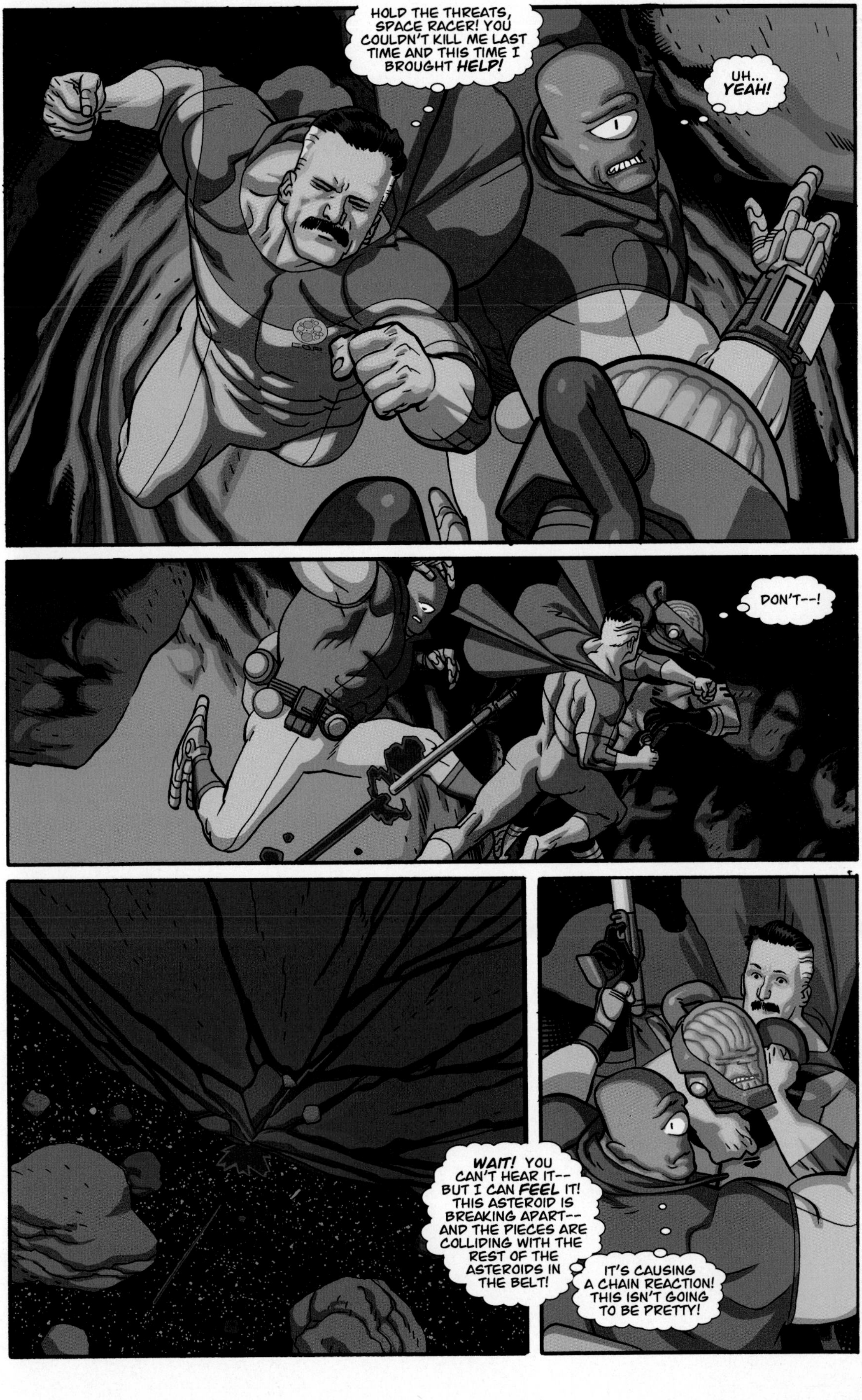
HOLD THE THREATS, SPACE RACER! YOU COULDN'T KILL ME LAST TIME AND THIS TIME I BROUGHT **HELP!**
UH... **YEAH!**
DON'T--!
***WAIT!*** YOU CAN'T HEAR IT-- BUT I CAN ***FEEL*** IT! THIS ASTEROID IS BREAKING APART-- AND THE PIECES ARE COLLIDING WITH THE REST OF THE ASTEROIDS IN THE BELT!
IT'S CAUSING A CHAIN REACTION! THIS ISN'T GOING TO BE PRETTY!

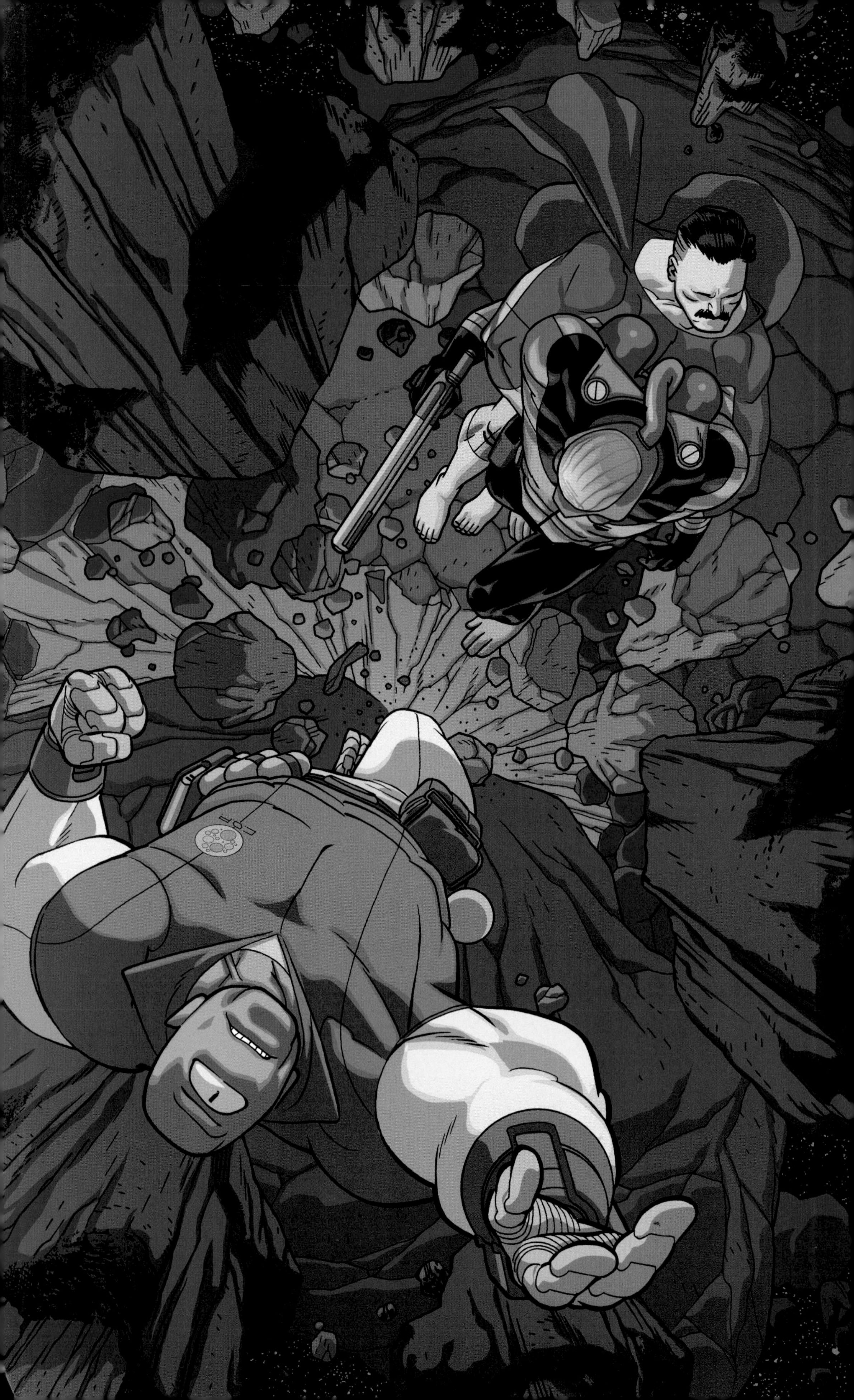

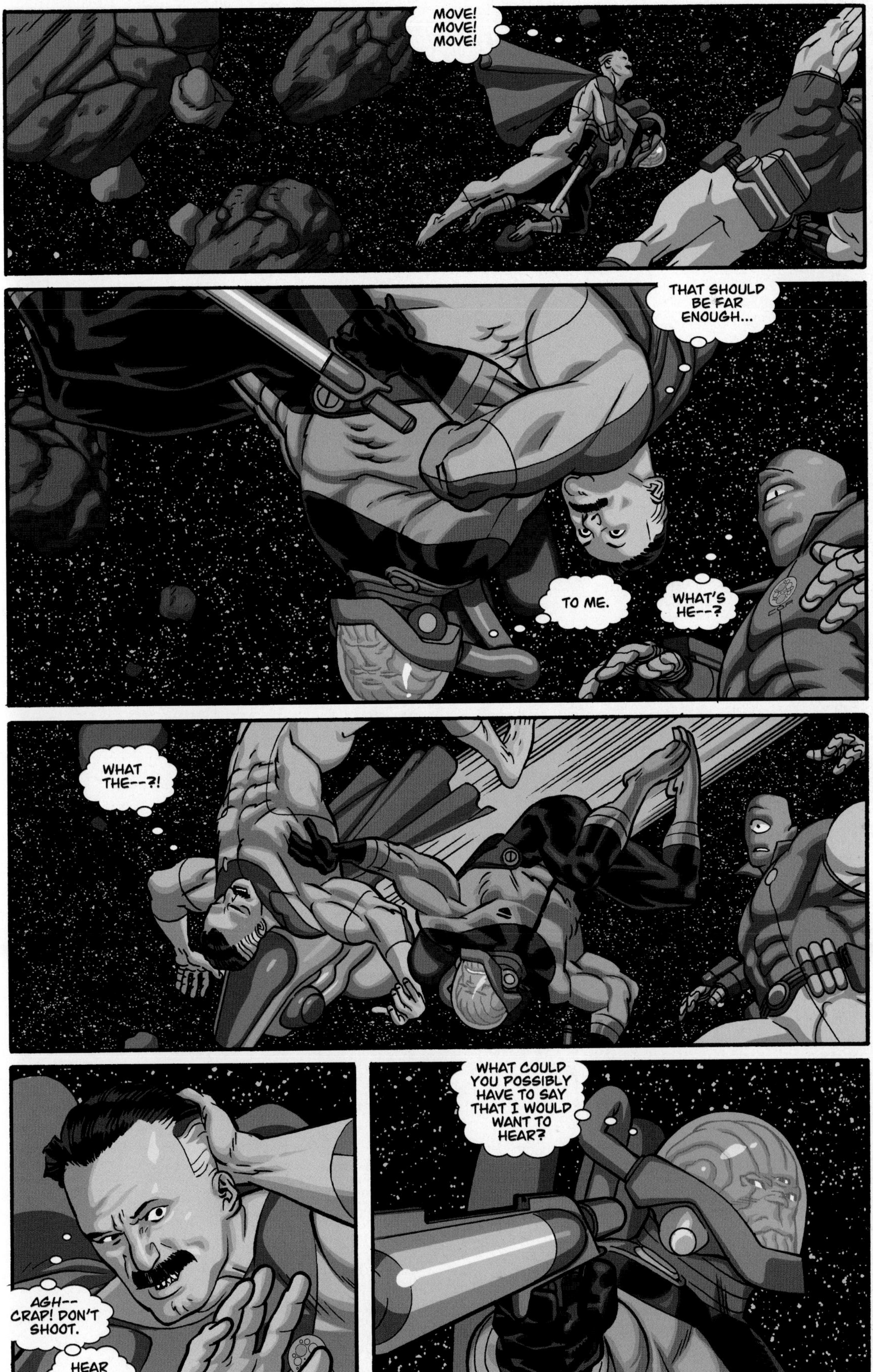
MOVE! MOVE! MOVE!
THAT SHOULD BE FAR ENOUGH...
TO ME.
WHAT'S HE--?
WHAT THE--?!
AGH-- CRAP! DON'T SHOOT.
HEAR ME OUT.
WHAT COULD YOU POSSIBLY HAVE TO SAY THAT I WOULD WANT TO HEAR?

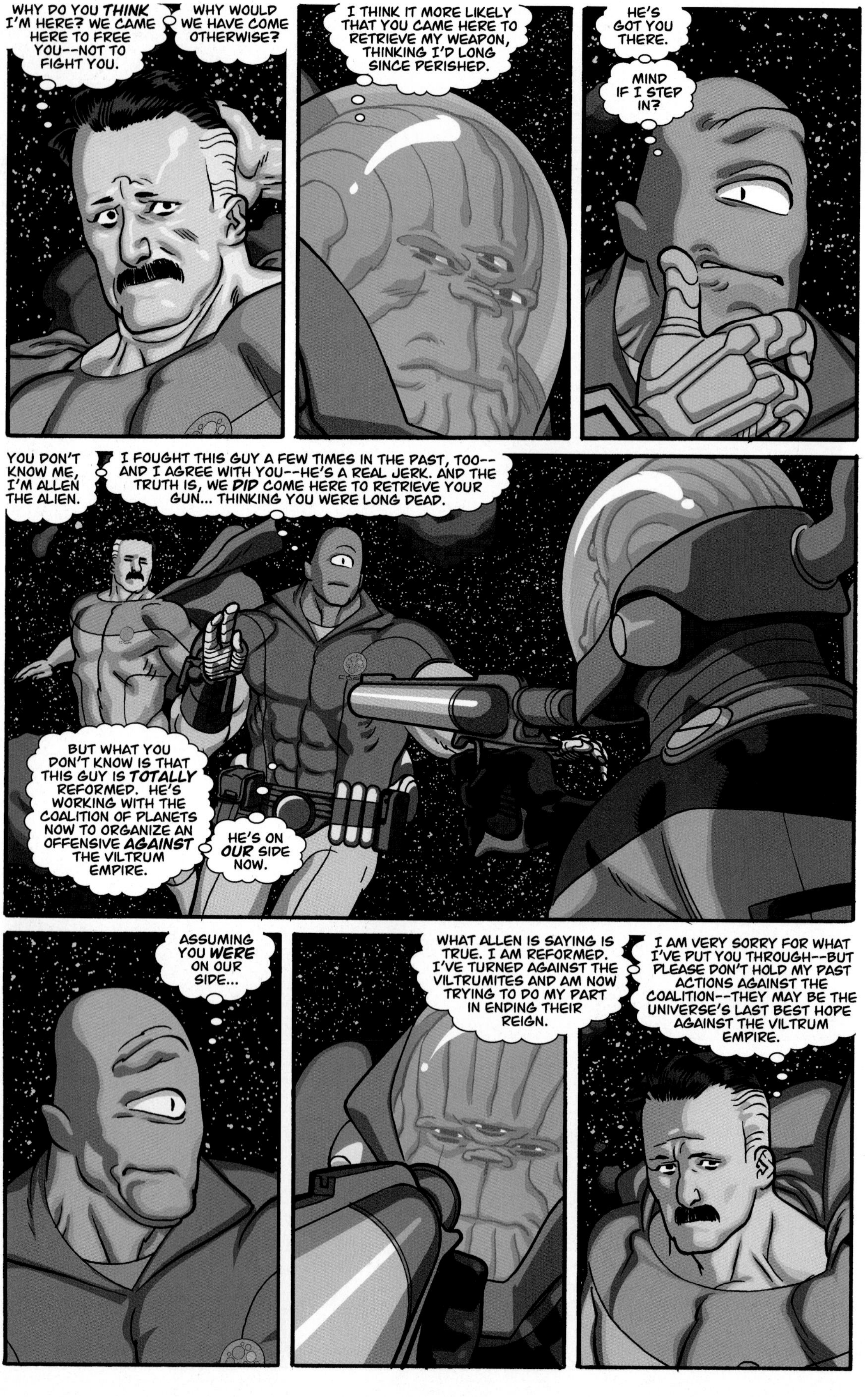
WHY DO YOU THINK I'M HERE? WE CAME HERE TO FREE YOU--NOT TO FIGHT YOU.
WHY WOULD WE HAVE COME OTHERWISE?
I THINK IT MORE LIKELY THAT YOU CAME HERE TO RETRIEVE MY WEAPON, THINKING I'D LONG SINCE PERISHED.
HE'S GOT YOU THERE.
MIND IF I STEP IN?
YOU DON'T KNOW ME, I'M ALLEN THE ALIEN.
I FOUGHT THIS GUY A FEW TIMES IN THE PAST, TOO-- AND I AGREE WITH YOU--HE'S A REAL JERK. AND THE TRUTH IS, WE DID COME HERE TO RETRIEVE YOUR GUN... THINKING YOU WERE LONG DEAD.
BUT WHAT YOU DON'T KNOW IS THAT THIS GUY IS TOTALLY REFORMED. HE'S WORKING WITH THE COALITION OF PLANETS NOW TO ORGANIZE AN OFFENSIVE AGAINST THE VILTRUM EMPIRE.
HE'S ON OUR SIDE NOW.
ASSUMING YOU WERE ON OUR SIDE...
WHAT ALLEN IS SAYING IS TRUE. I AM REFORMED. I'VE TURNED AGAINST THE VILTRUMITES AND AM NOW TRYING TO DO MY PART IN ENDING THEIR REIGN.
I AM VERY SORRY FOR WHAT I'VE PUT YOU THROUGH--BUT PLEASE DON'T HOLD MY PAST ACTIONS AGAINST THE COALITION--THEY MAY BE THE UNIVERSE'S LAST BEST HOPE AGAINST THE VILTRUM EMPIRE.

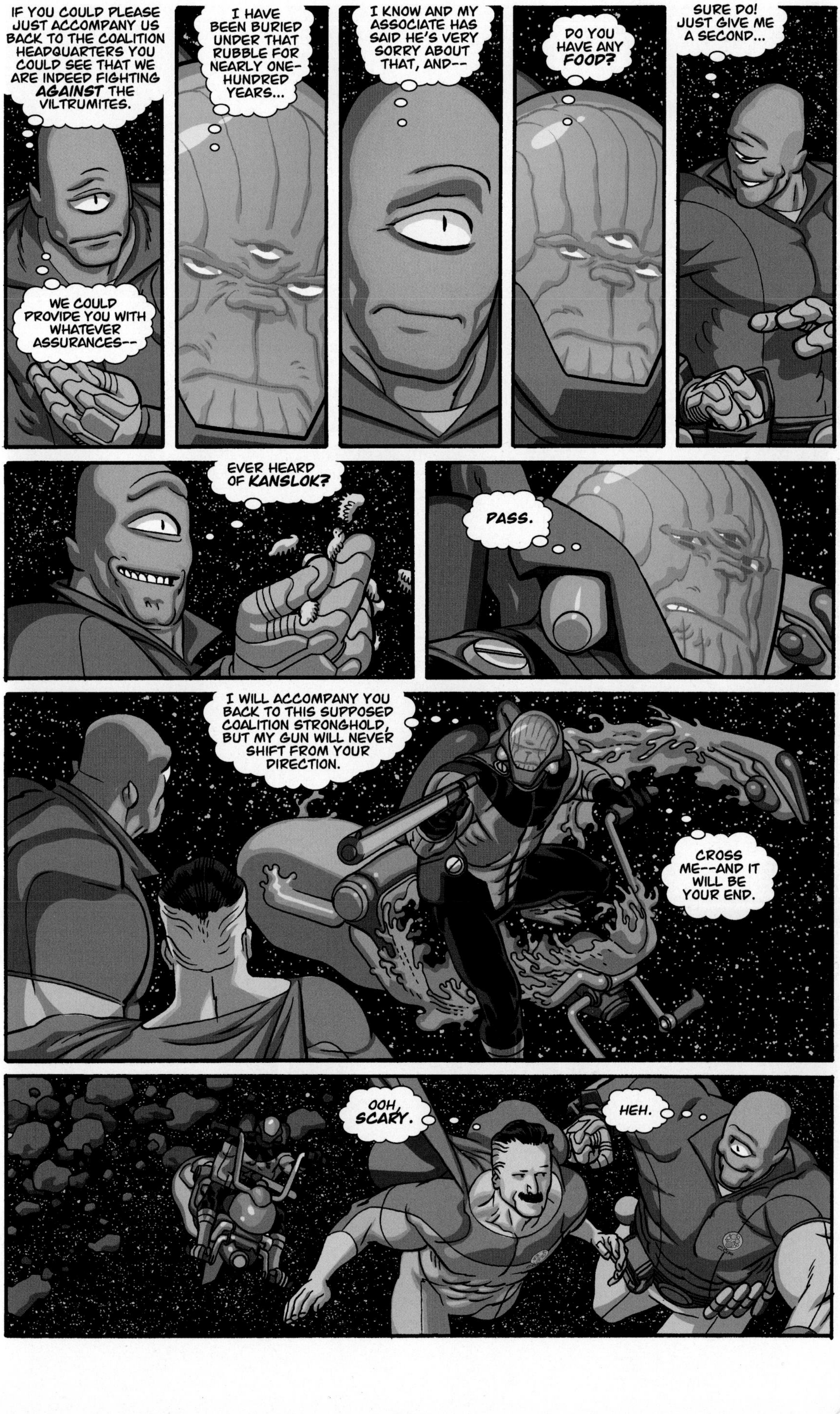
IF YOU COULD PLEASE JUST ACCOMPANY US BACK TO THE COALITION HEADQUARTERS YOU COULD SEE THAT WE ARE INDEED FIGHTING AGAINST THE VILTRUMITES.
WE COULD PROVIDE YOU WITH WHATEVER ASSURANCES--
I HAVE BEEN BURIED UNDER THAT RUBBLE FOR NEARLY ONE-HUNDRED YEARS...
I KNOW AND MY ASSOCIATE HAS SAID HE'S VERY SORRY ABOUT THAT, AND--
DO YOU HAVE ANY FOOD?
SURE DO! JUST GIVE ME A SECOND...
EVER HEARD OF KANSLOK?
PASS.
I WILL ACCOMPANY YOU BACK TO THIS SUPPOSED COALITION STRONGHOLD, BUT MY GUN WILL NEVER SHIFT FROM YOUR DIRECTION.
CROSS ME--AND IT WILL BE YOUR END.
OOH, SCARY.
HEH.

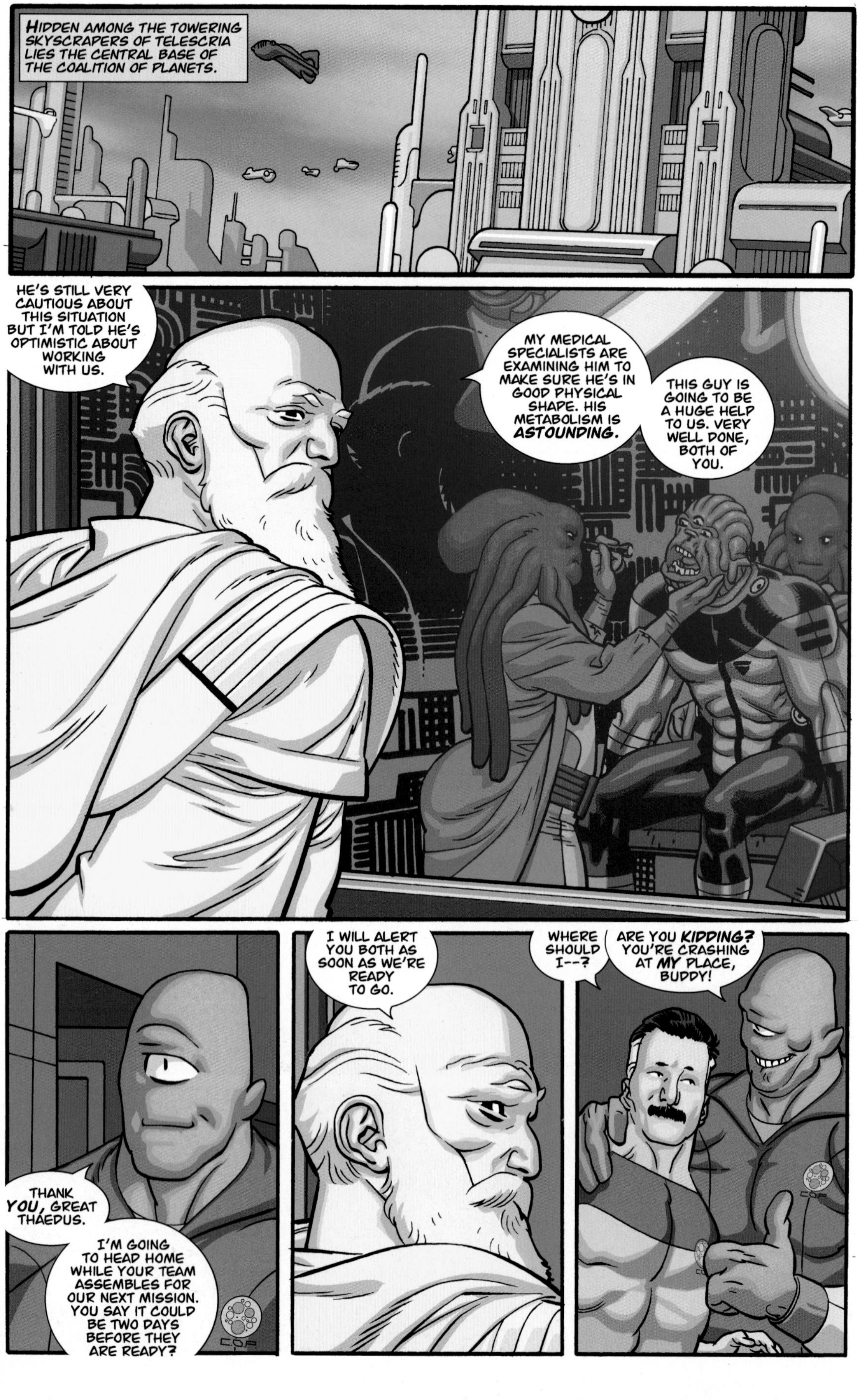
HIDDEN AMONG THE TOWERING SKYSCRAPERS OF TELESCRIA LIES THE CENTRAL BASE OF THE COALITION OF PLANETS.
HE'S STILL VERY CAUTIOUS ABOUT THIS SITUATION BUT I'M TOLD HE'S OPTIMISTIC ABOUT WORKING WITH US.
MY MEDICAL SPECIALISTS ARE EXAMINING HIM TO MAKE SURE HE'S IN GOOD PHYSICAL SHAPE. HIS METABOLISM IS ASTOUNDING.
THIS GUY IS GOING TO BE A HUGE HELP TO US. VERY WELL DONE, BOTH OF YOU.
THANK YOU, GREAT THAEDUS.
I'M GOING TO HEAD HOME WHILE YOUR TEAM ASSEMBLES FOR OUR NEXT MISSION. YOU SAY IT COULD BE TWO DAYS BEFORE THEY ARE READY?
I WILL ALERT YOU BOTH AS SOON AS WE'RE READY TO GO.
WHERE SHOULD I--?
ARE YOU KIDDING? YOU'RE CRASHING AT MY PLACE, BUDDY!

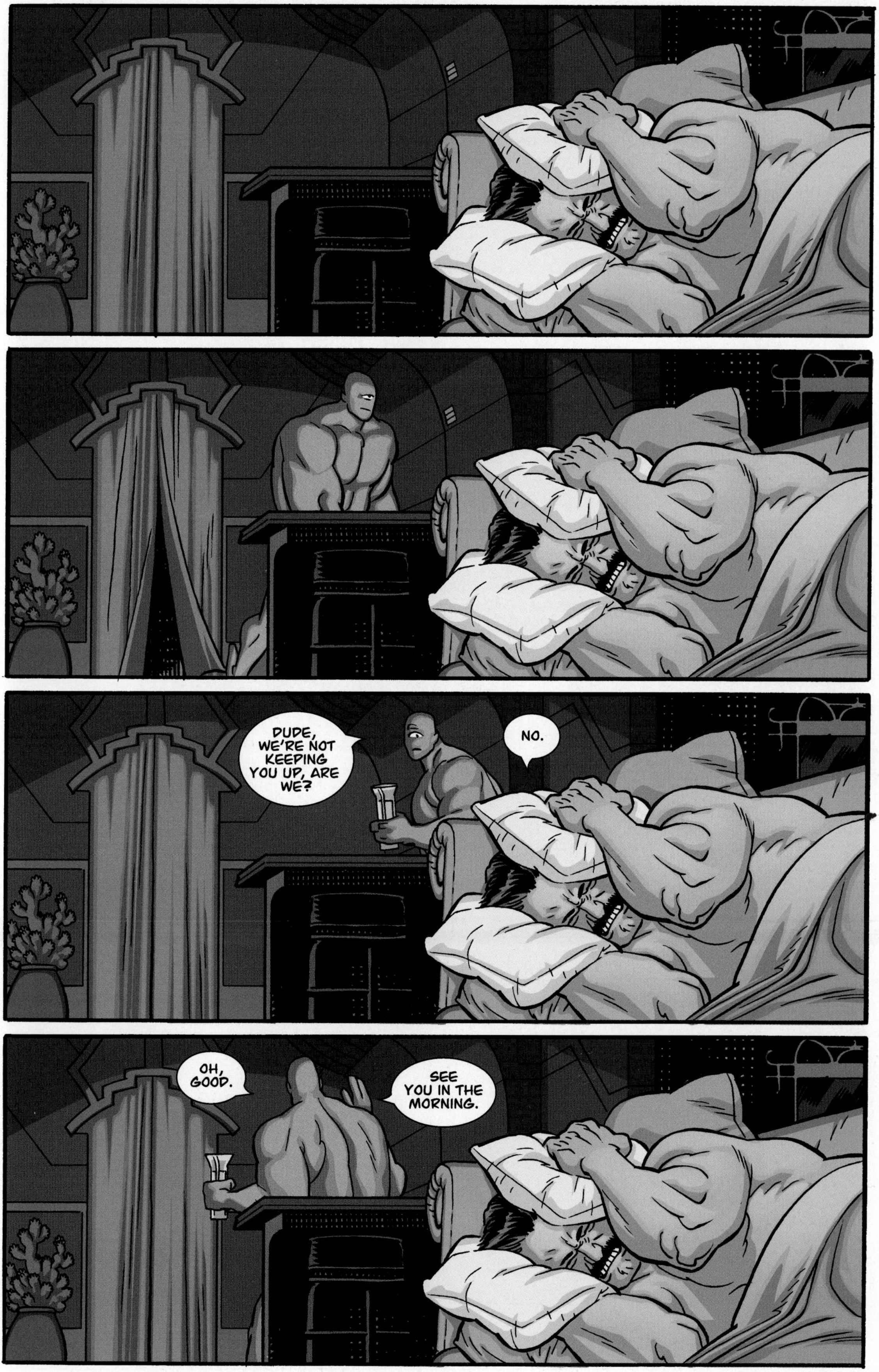
DUDE, WE'RE NOT KEEPING YOU UP, ARE WE?
NO.
OH, GOOD.
SEE YOU IN THE MORNING.

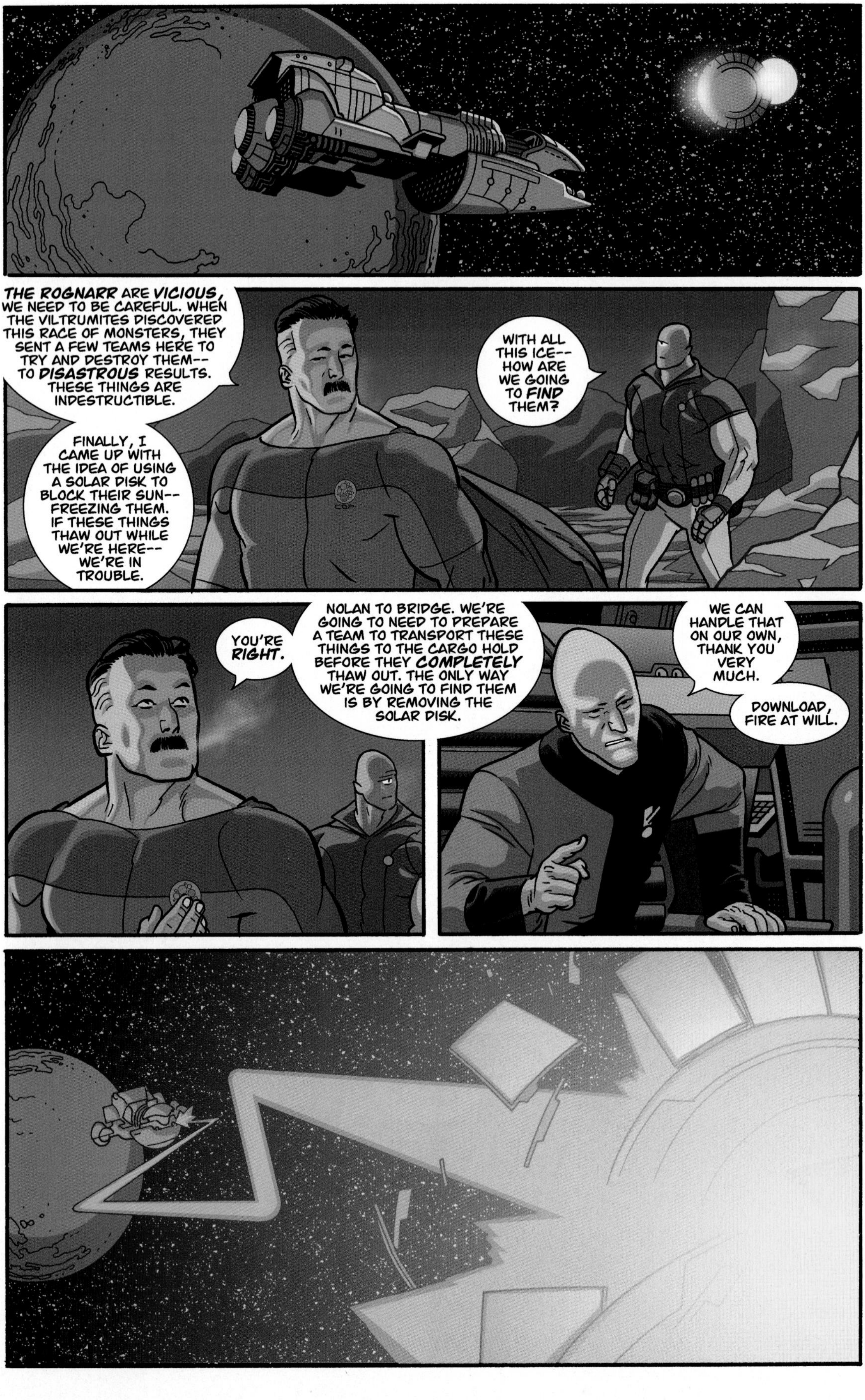
THE ROGNARR ARE VICIOUS, WE NEED TO BE CAREFUL. WHEN THE VILTRUMITES DISCOVERED THIS RACE OF MONSTERS, THEY SENT A FEW TEAMS HERE TO TRY AND DESTROY THEM-- TO DISASTROUS RESULTS. THESE THINGS ARE INDESTRUCTIBLE.
FINALLY, I CAME UP WITH THE IDEA OF USING A SOLAR DISK TO BLOCK THEIR SUN-- FREEZING THEM. IF THESE THINGS THAW OUT WHILE WE'RE HERE-- WE'RE IN TROUBLE.
WITH ALL THIS ICE-- HOW ARE WE GOING TO FIND THEM?
YOU'RE RIGHT.
NOLAN TO BRIDGE. WE'RE GOING TO NEED TO PREPARE A TEAM TO TRANSPORT THESE THINGS TO THE CARGO HOLD BEFORE THEY COMPLETELY THAW OUT. THE ONLY WAY WE'RE GOING TO FIND THEM IS BY REMOVING THE SOLAR DISK.
WE CAN HANDLE THAT ON OUR OWN, THANK YOU VERY MUCH.
DOWNLOAD, FIRE AT WILL.

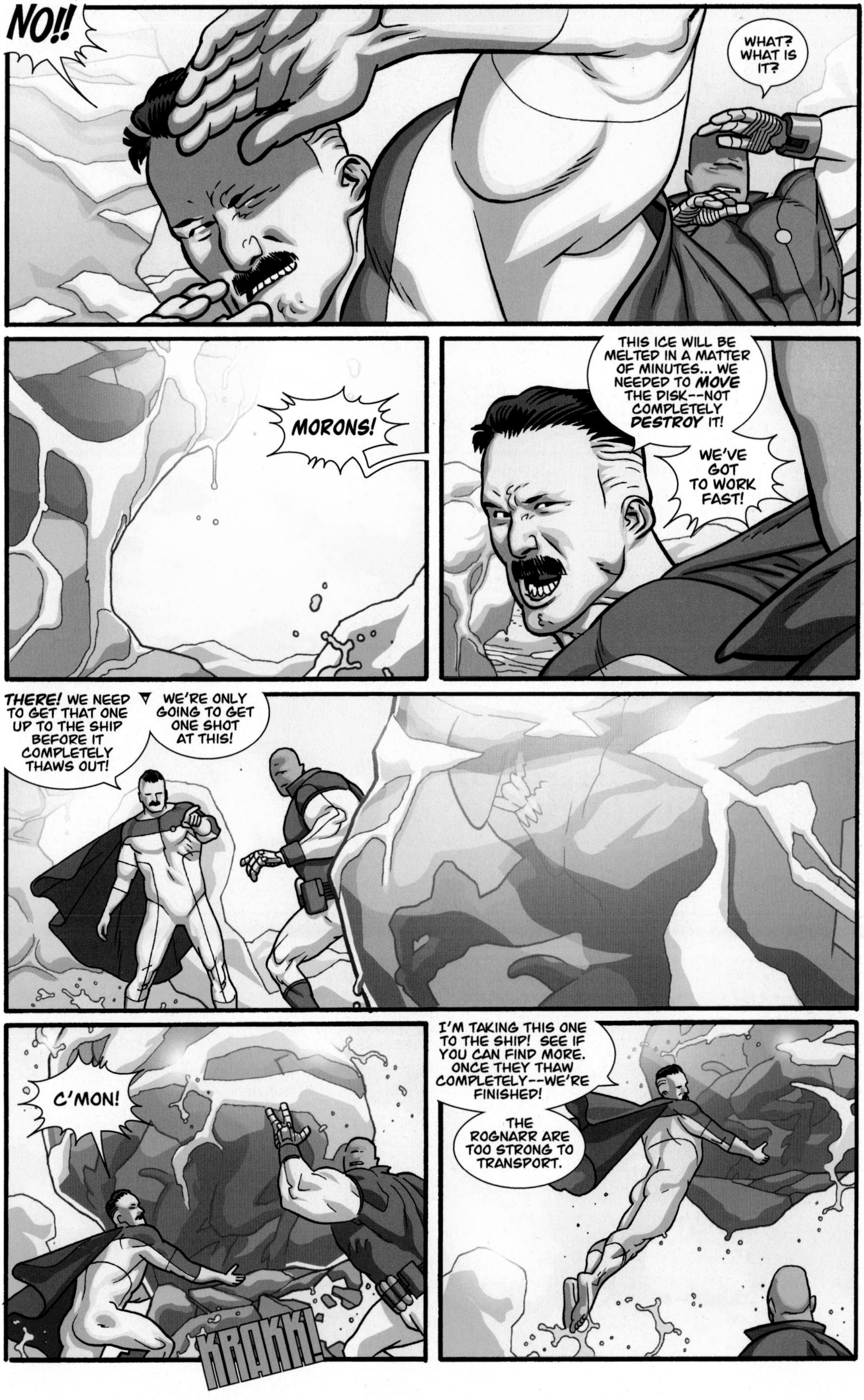
NO!!
WHAT? WHAT IS IT?
MORONS!
THIS ICE WILL BE MELTED IN A MATTER OF MINUTES... WE NEEDED TO MOVE THE DISK--NOT COMPLETELY DESTROY IT!
WE'VE GOT TO WORK FAST!
THERE! WE NEED TO GET THAT ONE UP TO THE SHIP BEFORE IT COMPLETELY THAWS OUT!
WE'RE ONLY GOING TO GET ONE SHOT AT THIS!
C'MON!
KRAKK!
I'M TAKING THIS ONE TO THE SHIP! SEE IF YOU CAN FIND MORE. ONCE THEY THAW COMPLETELY--WE'RE FINISHED!
THE ROGNARR ARE TOO STRONG TO TRANSPORT.

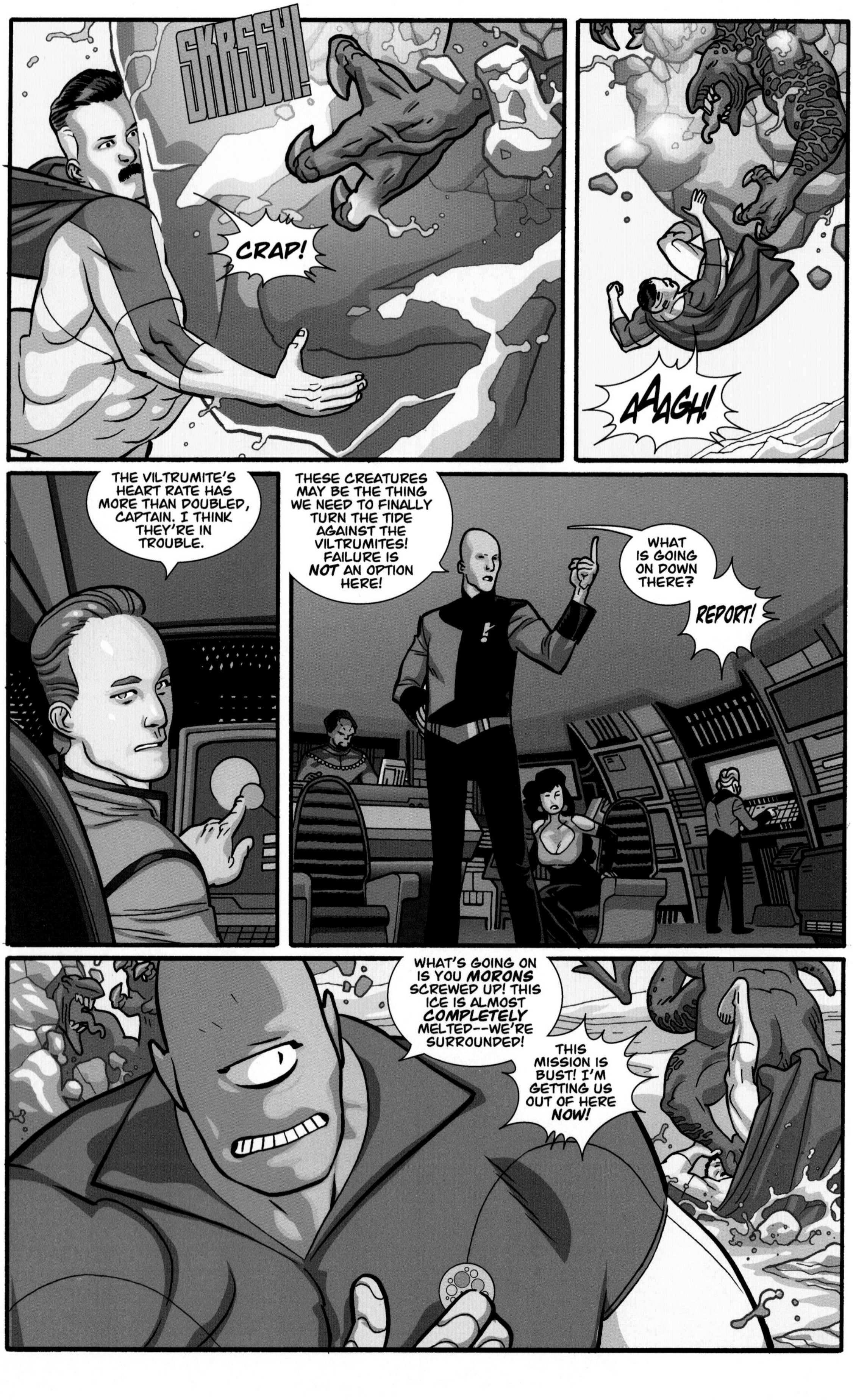
SKRSSH!
CRAP!
AAAGH!
THE VILTRUMITE'S HEART RATE HAS MORE THAN DOUBLED, CAPTAIN. I THINK THEY'RE IN TROUBLE.
THESE CREATURES MAY BE THE THING WE NEED TO FINALLY TURN THE TIDE AGAINST THE VILTRUMITES! FAILURE IS NOT AN OPTION HERE!
WHAT IS GOING ON DOWN THERE?
REPORT!
WHAT'S GOING ON IS YOU MORONS SCREWED UP! THIS ICE IS ALMOST COMPLETELY MELTED--WE'RE SURROUNDED!
THIS MISSION IS BUST! I'M GETTING US OUT OF HERE NOW!

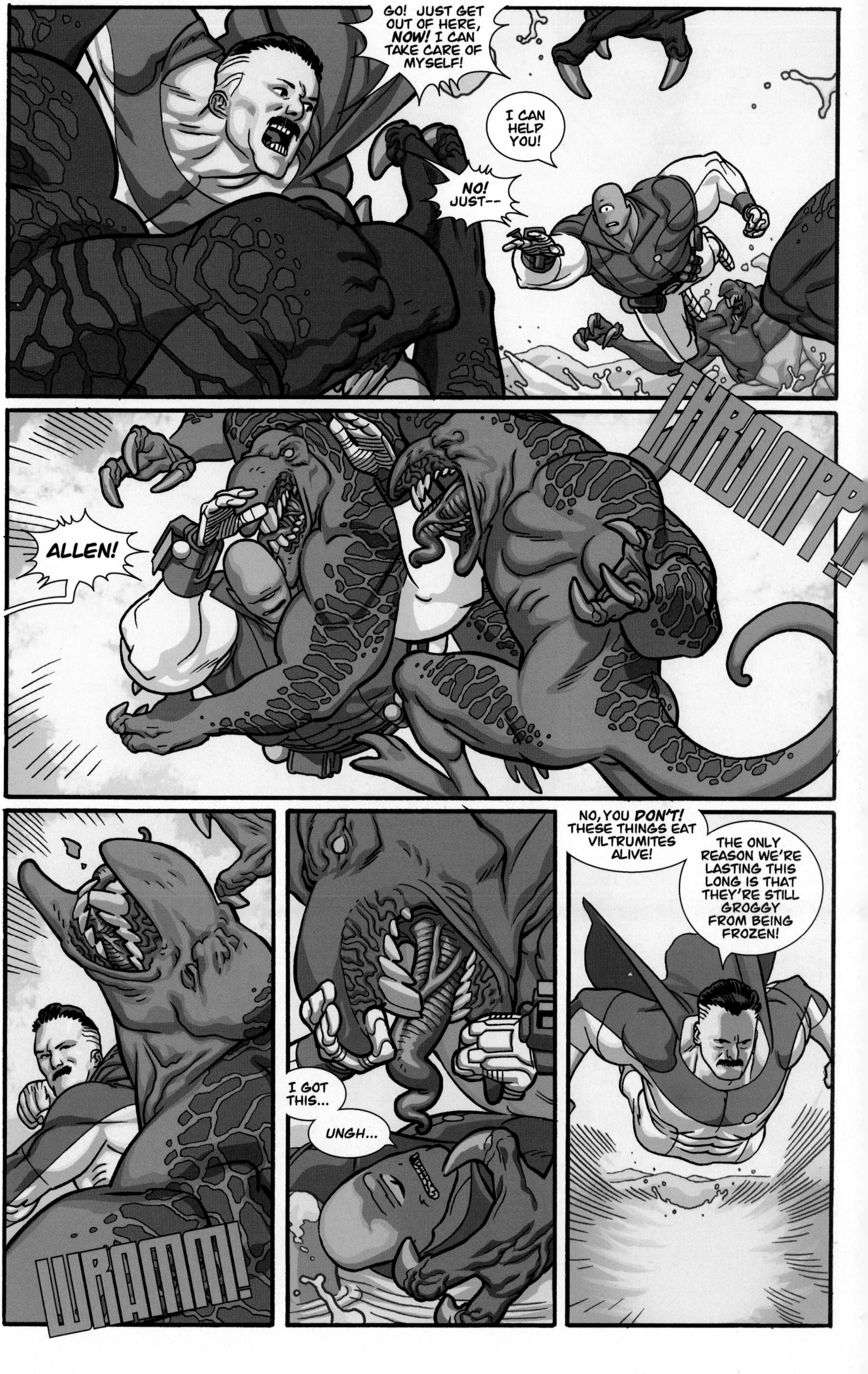
GO! JUST GET OUT OF HERE, NOW! I CAN TAKE CARE OF MYSELF!
I CAN HELP YOU!
NO! JUST--
THROMPP!!
ALLEN!
WRAMM!
I GOT THIS...
UNGH...
NO, YOU DON'T! THESE THINGS EAT VILTRUMITES ALIVE!
THE ONLY REASON WE'RE LASTING THIS LONG IS THAT THEY'RE STILL GROGGY FROM BEING FROZEN!

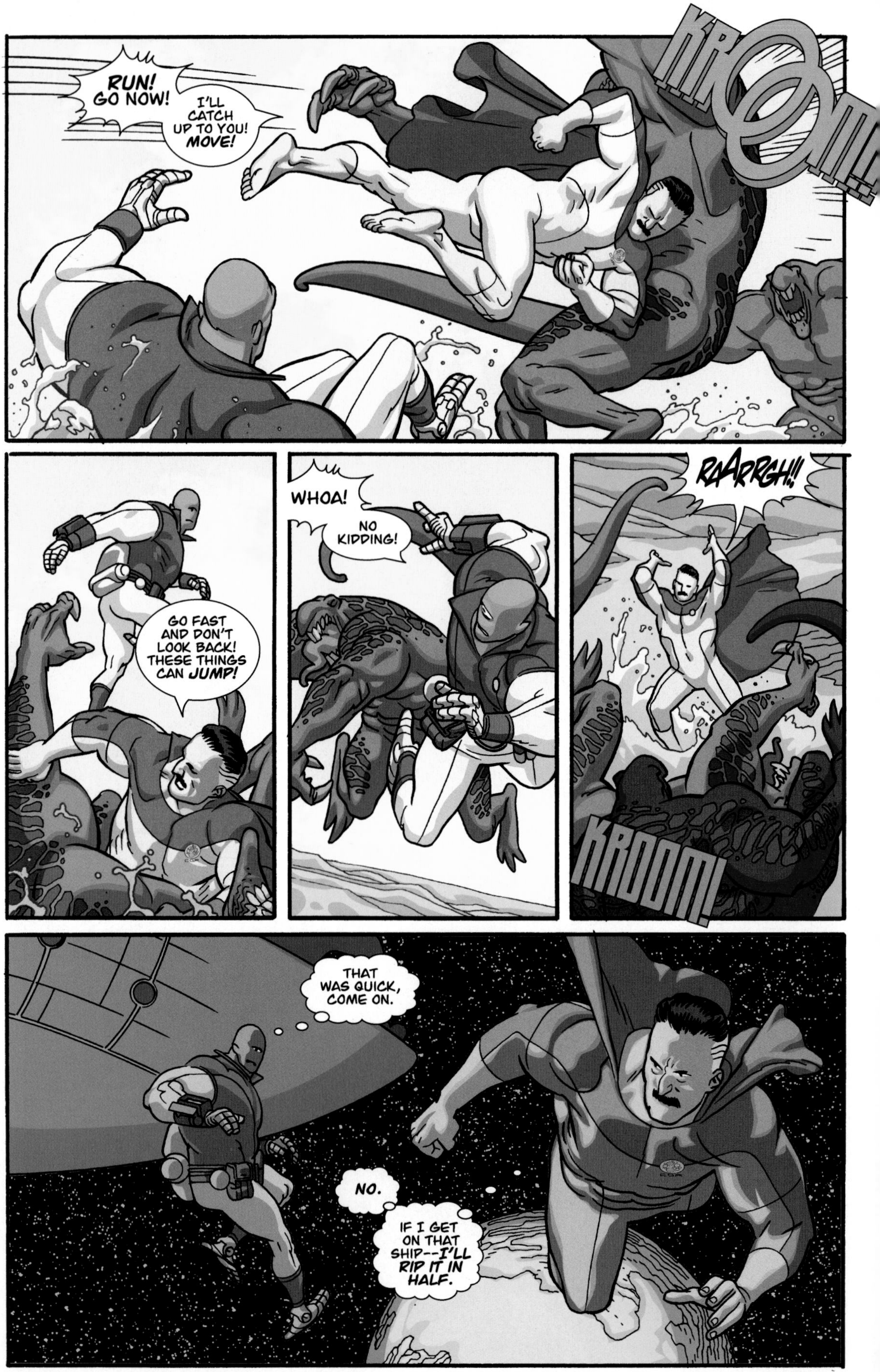
KROOM!
RUN! GO NOW!
I'LL CATCH UP TO YOU! MOVE!
GO FAST AND DON'T LOOK BACK! THESE THINGS CAN JUMP!
WHOA!
NO KIDDING!
RAARRGH!!
KROOM!
THAT WAS QUICK, COME ON.
NO.
IF I GET ON THAT SHIP--I'LL RIP IT IN HALF.

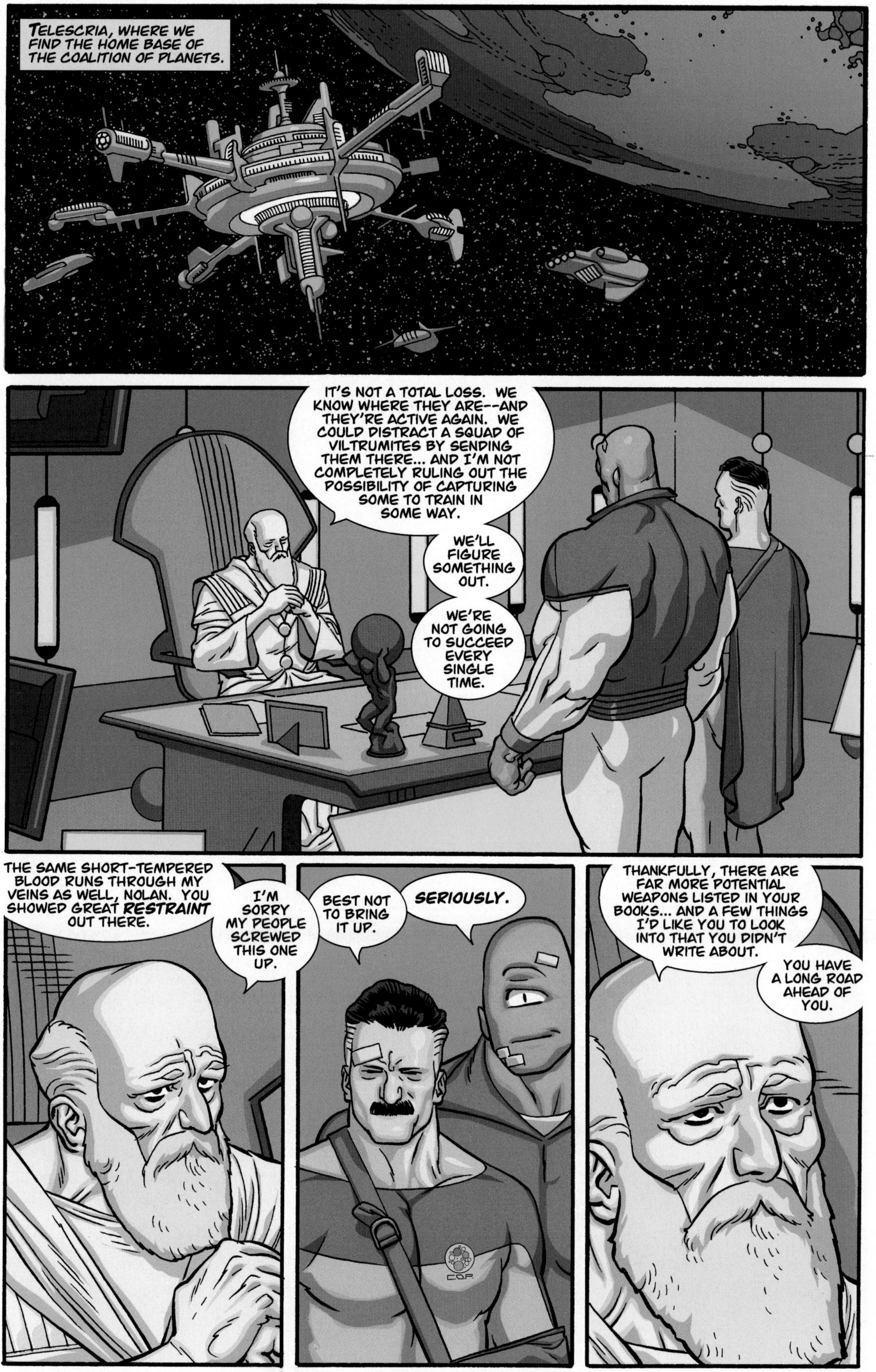
TELESCRIA, WHERE WE FIND THE HOME BASE OF THE COALITION OF PLANETS.
IT'S NOT A TOTAL LOSS. WE KNOW WHERE THEY ARE--AND THEY'RE ACTIVE AGAIN. WE COULD DISTRACT A SQUAD OF VILTRUMITES BY SENDING THEM THERE... AND I'M NOT COMPLETELY RULING OUT THE POSSIBILITY OF CAPTURING SOME TO TRAIN IN SOME WAY.
WE'LL FIGURE SOMETHING OUT.
WE'RE NOT GOING TO SUCCEED EVERY SINGLE TIME.
THE SAME SHORT-TEMPERED BLOOD RUNS THROUGH MY VEINS AS WELL, NOLAN. YOU SHOWED GREAT RESTRAINT OUT THERE.
I'M SORRY MY PEOPLE SCREWED THIS ONE UP.
BEST NOT TO BRING IT UP.
SERIOUSLY.
C.O.P.
THANKFULLY, THERE ARE FAR MORE POTENTIAL WEAPONS LISTED IN YOUR BOOKS... AND A FEW THINGS I'D LIKE YOU TO LOOK INTO THAT YOU DIDN'T WRITE ABOUT.
YOU HAVE A LONG ROAD AHEAD OF YOU.

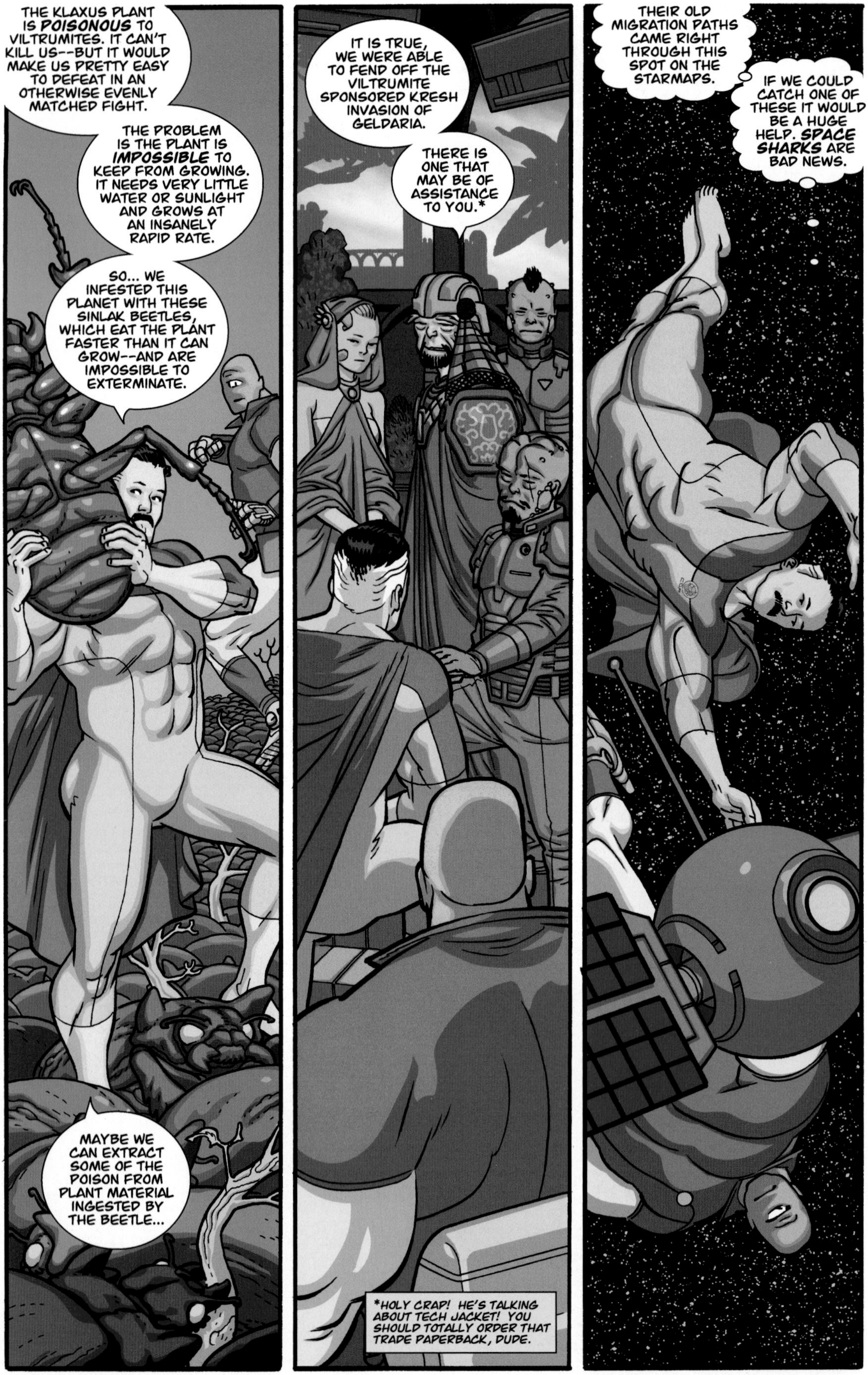
THE KLAXUS PLANT IS POISONOUS TO VILTRUMITES. IT CAN'T KILL US--BUT IT WOULD MAKE US PRETTY EASY TO DEFEAT IN AN OTHERWISE EVENLY MATCHED FIGHT.
THE PROBLEM IS THE PLANT IS IMPOSSIBLE TO KEEP FROM GROWING. IT NEEDS VERY LITTLE WATER OR SUNLIGHT AND GROWS AT AN INSANELY RAPID RATE.
SO... WE INFESTED THIS PLANET WITH THESE SINLAK BEETLES, WHICH EAT THE PLANT FASTER THAN IT CAN GROW--AND ARE IMPOSSIBLE TO EXTERMINATE.
MAYBE WE CAN EXTRACT SOME OF THE POISON FROM PLANT MATERIAL INGESTED BY THE BEETLE...
IT IS TRUE, WE WERE ABLE TO FEND OFF THE VILTRUMITE SPONSORED KRESH INVASION OF GELDARIA.
THERE IS ONE THAT MAY BE OF ASSISTANCE TO YOU.*
*HOLY CRAP! HE'S TALKING ABOUT TECH JACKET! YOU SHOULD TOTALLY ORDER THAT TRADE PAPERBACK, DUDE.
THEIR OLD MIGRATION PATHS CAME RIGHT THROUGH THIS SPOT ON THE STARMAPS.
IF WE COULD CATCH ONE OF THESE IT WOULD BE A HUGE HELP. SPACE SHARKS ARE BAD NEWS.

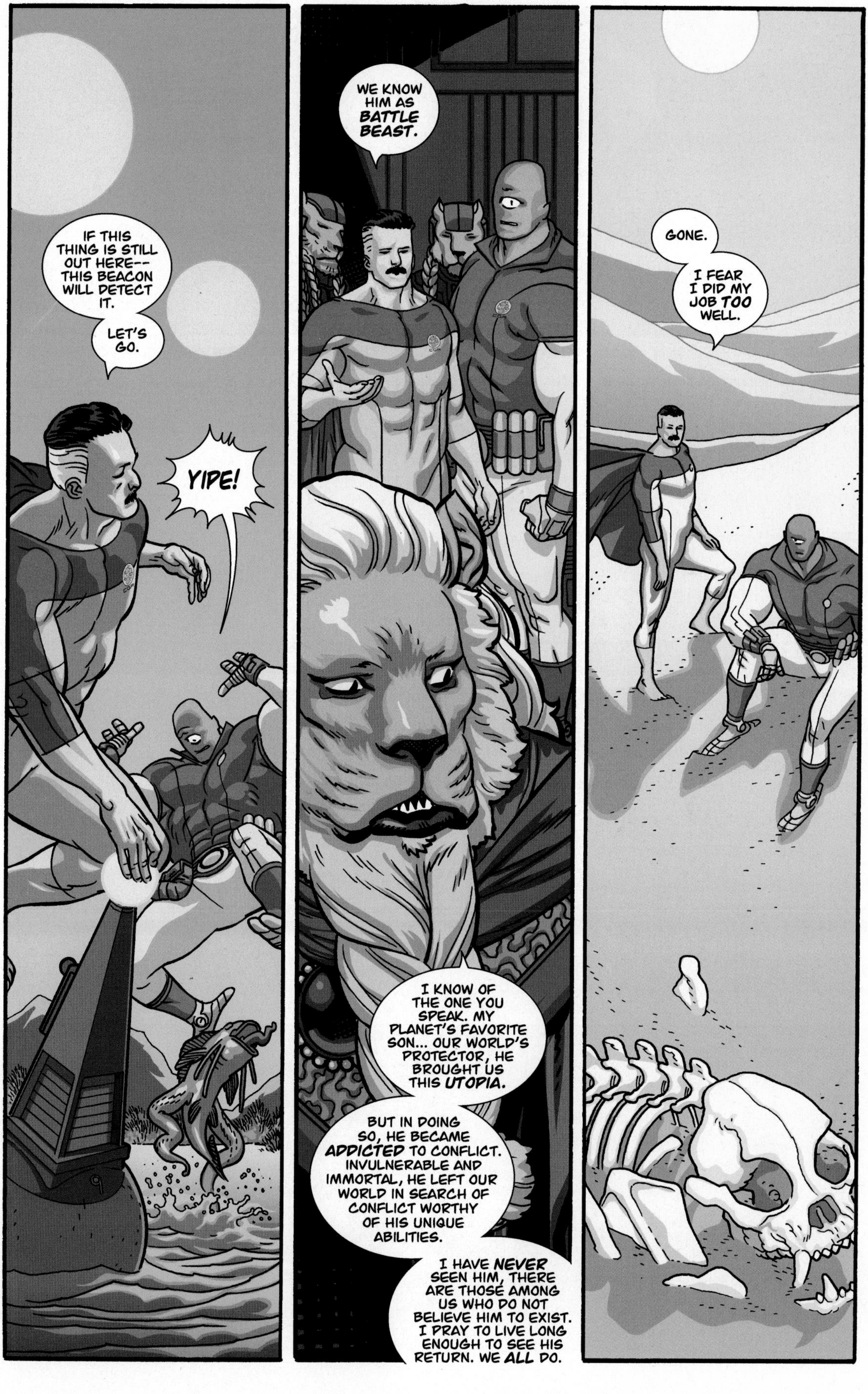
IF THIS THING IS STILL OUT HERE-- THIS BEACON WILL DETECT IT.
LET'S GO.
YIPE!
WE KNOW HIM AS BATTLE BEAST.
I KNOW OF THE ONE YOU SPEAK. MY PLANET'S FAVORITE SON... OUR WORLD'S PROTECTOR, HE BROUGHT US THIS UTOPIA.
BUT IN DOING SO, HE BECAME ADDICTED TO CONFLICT. INVULNERABLE AND IMMORTAL, HE LEFT OUR WORLD IN SEARCH OF CONFLICT WORTHY OF HIS UNIQUE ABILITIES.
I HAVE NEVER SEEN HIM, THERE ARE THOSE AMONG US WHO DO NOT BELIEVE HIM TO EXIST. I PRAY TO LIVE LONG ENOUGH TO SEE HIS RETURN. WE ALL DO.
GONE.
I FEAR I DID MY JOB TOO WELL.

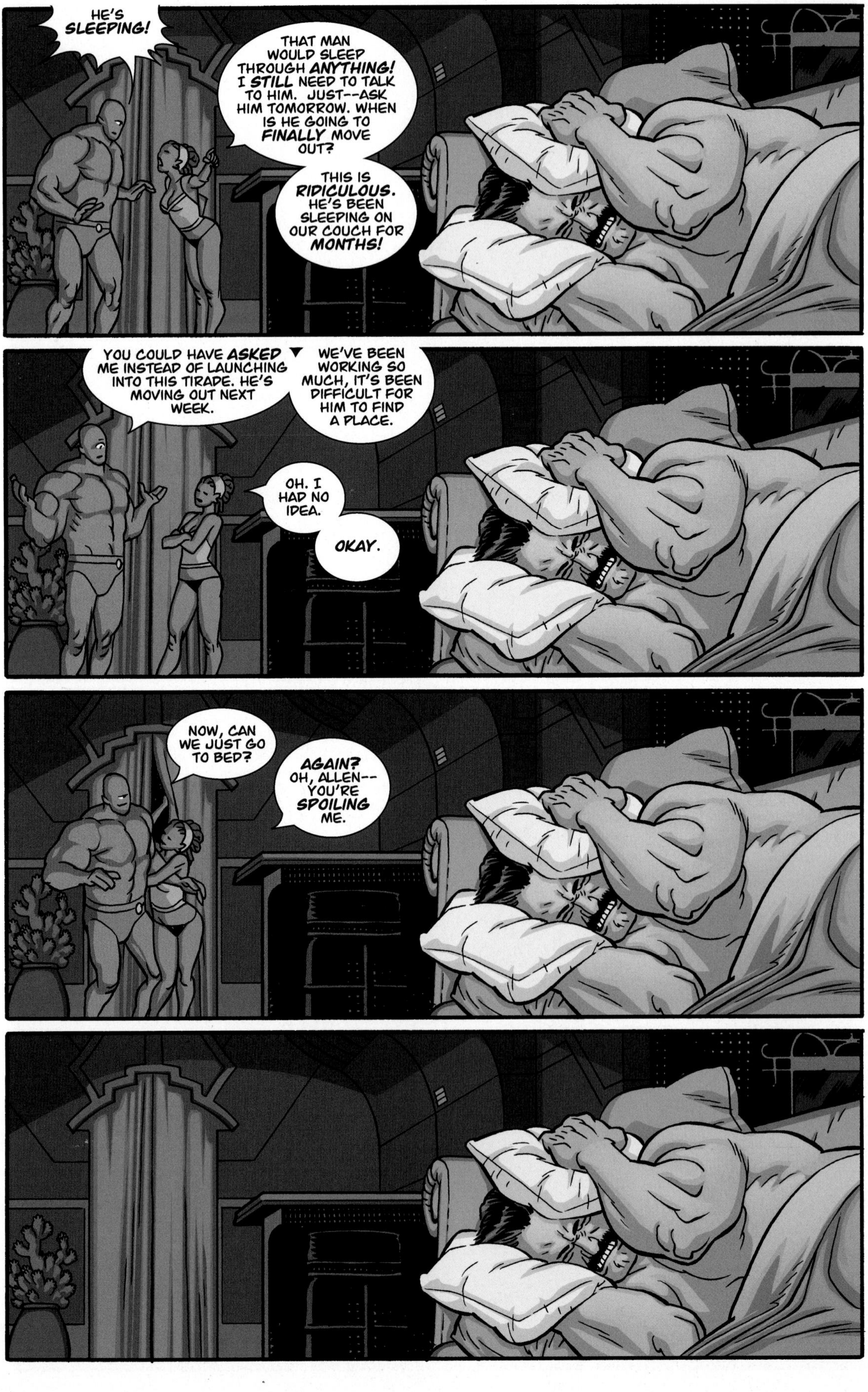
HE'S SLEEPING!
THAT MAN WOULD SLEEP THROUGH ANYTHING! I STILL NEED TO TALK TO HIM. JUST--ASK HIM TOMORROW. WHEN IS HE GOING TO FINALLY MOVE OUT?
THIS IS RIDICULOUS. HE'S BEEN SLEEPING ON OUR COUCH FOR MONTHS!
YOU COULD HAVE ASKED ME INSTEAD OF LAUNCHING INTO THIS TIRADE. HE'S MOVING OUT NEXT WEEK.
WE'VE BEEN WORKING SO MUCH, IT'S BEEN DIFFICULT FOR HIM TO FIND A PLACE.
OH. I HAD NO IDEA.
OKAY.
NOW, CAN WE JUST GO TO BED?
AGAIN? OH, ALLEN--YOU'RE SPOILING ME.

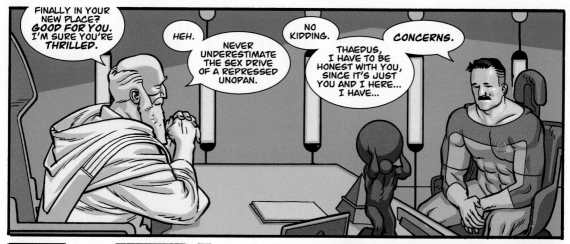

FINALLY IN YOUR NEW PLACE? GOOD FOR YOU. I'M SURE YOU'RE *THRILLED.*

HEH.

NEVER UNDERESTIMATE THE SEX DRIVE OF A REPRESSED UNOPAN.

NO KIDDING.

CONCERNS.

THAEDUS, I HAVE TO BE HONEST WITH YOU, SINCE IT'S JUST YOU AND I HERE... I HAVE...

I SHARE THEM.

COME WITH ME.

WE HAVE SPACE RACER WORKING WITH US. WE WERE ABLE TO EXTRACT A DILUTED SAMPLE OF THE KLAXUS POISON FROM THE SINTAK BEETLE.

THERE ARE OTHER POTENTIAL ITEMS OF INTEREST-- BUT I FEAR IT WON'T BE ENOUGH.

IT *WILL* BE.

COME.

THE TIME TO STRIKE IS *NOW.* YOU NEED TO GO TO EARTH.

GET YOUR SON AND THAT BOY WITH THE GELDARIAN WEAPON-- AND WHOEVER ELSE YOU THINK CAN HELP US.

WE WILL DO OUR BEST TO ARRANGE AS MANY THREATS TO THE VILTRUMITES AS WE CAN WHILE YOU ARE AWAY.

NOW...

...THERE IS SOMETHING I MUST REVEAL TO YOU.

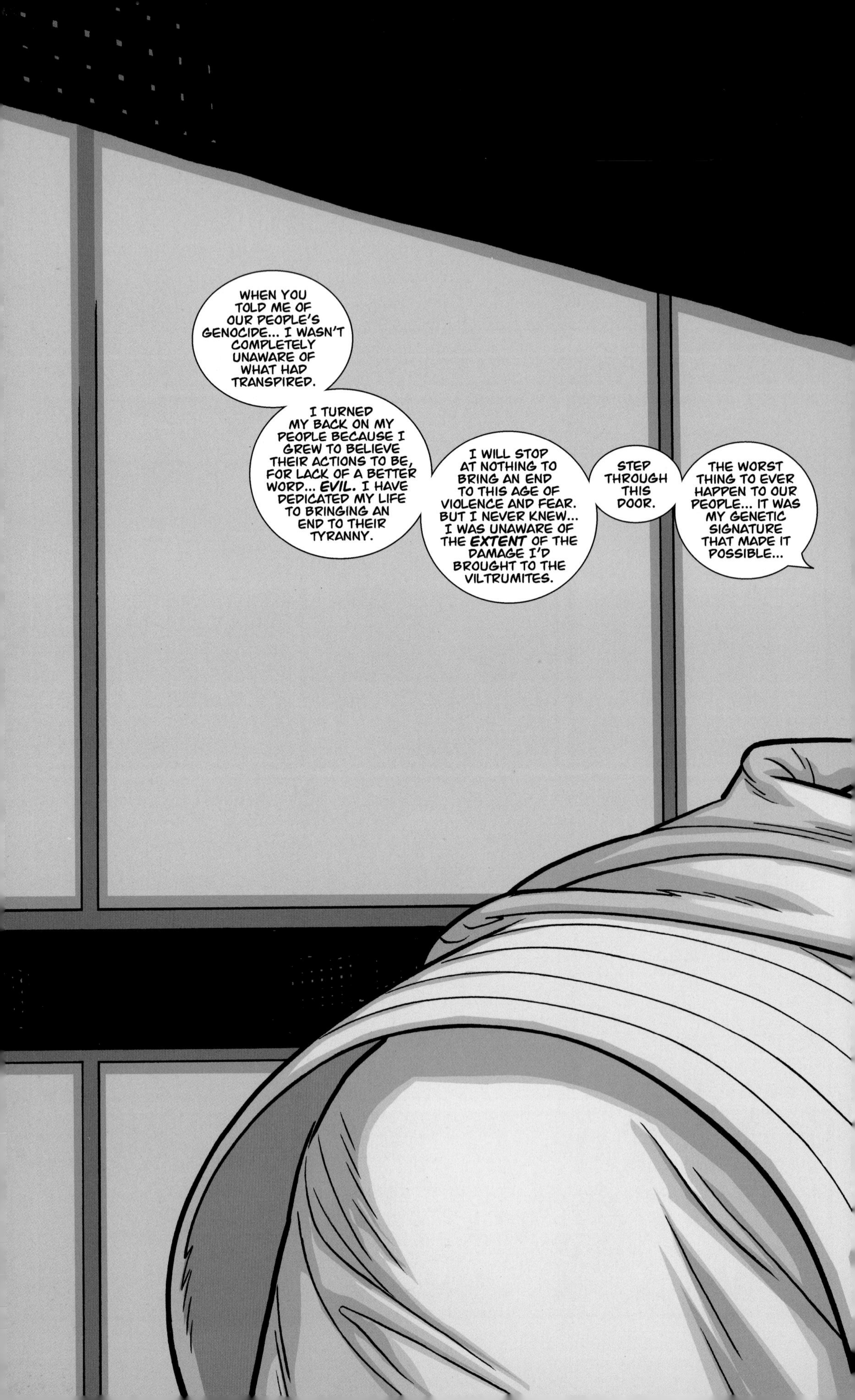
WHEN YOU TOLD ME OF OUR PEOPLE'S GENOCIDE... I WASN'T COMPLETELY UNAWARE OF WHAT HAD TRANSPIRED.
I TURNED MY BACK ON MY PEOPLE BECAUSE I GREW TO BELIEVE THEIR ACTIONS TO BE, FOR LACK OF A BETTER WORD... EVIL. I HAVE DEDICATED MY LIFE TO BRINGING AN END TO THEIR TYRANNY.
I WILL STOP AT NOTHING TO BRING AN END TO THIS AGE OF VIOLENCE AND FEAR. BUT I NEVER KNEW... I WAS UNAWARE OF THE EXTENT OF THE DAMAGE I'D BROUGHT TO THE VILTRUMITES.
STEP THROUGH THIS DOOR.
THE WORST THING TO EVER HAPPEN TO OUR PEOPLE... IT WAS MY GENETIC SIGNATURE THAT MADE IT POSSIBLE...

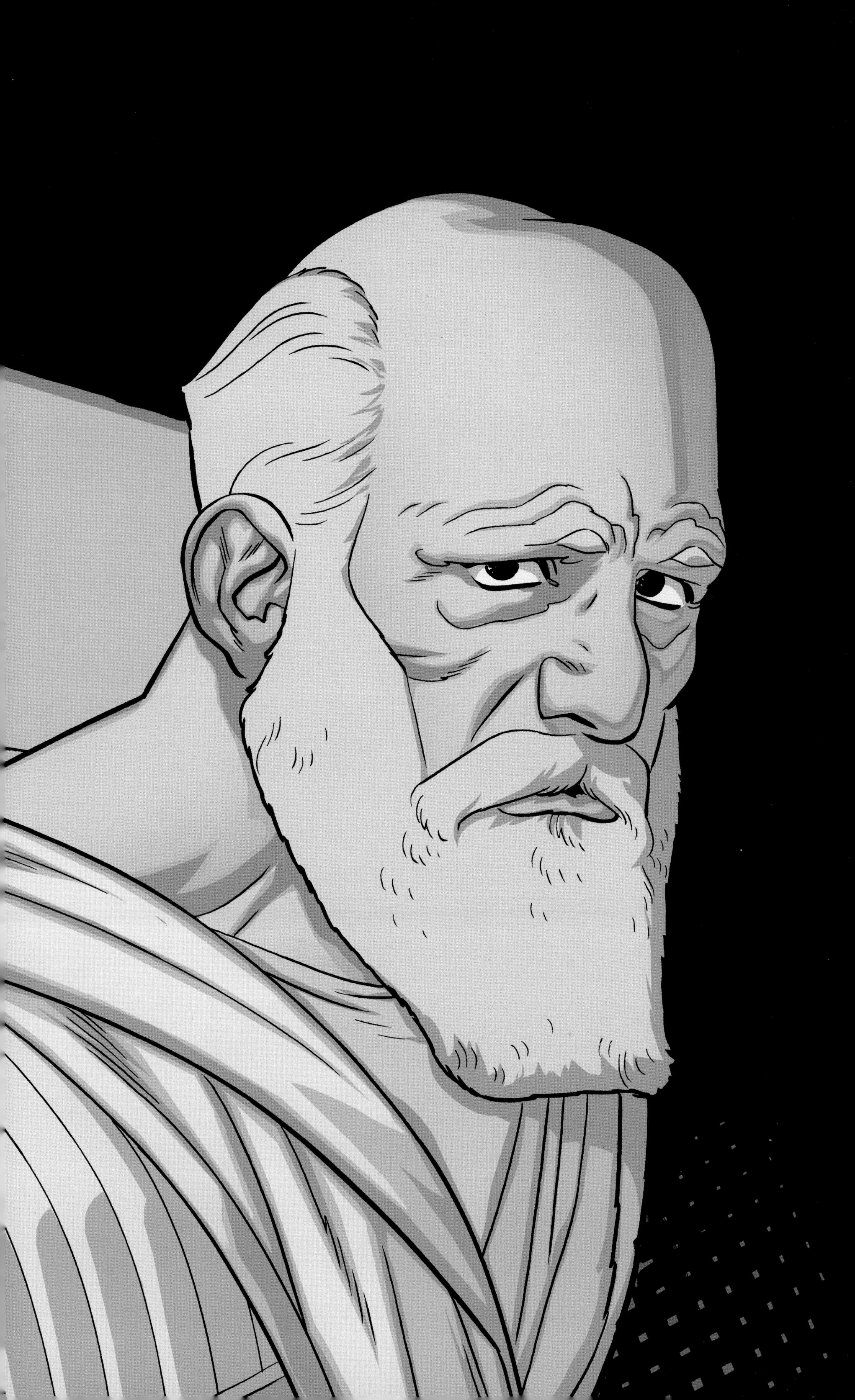

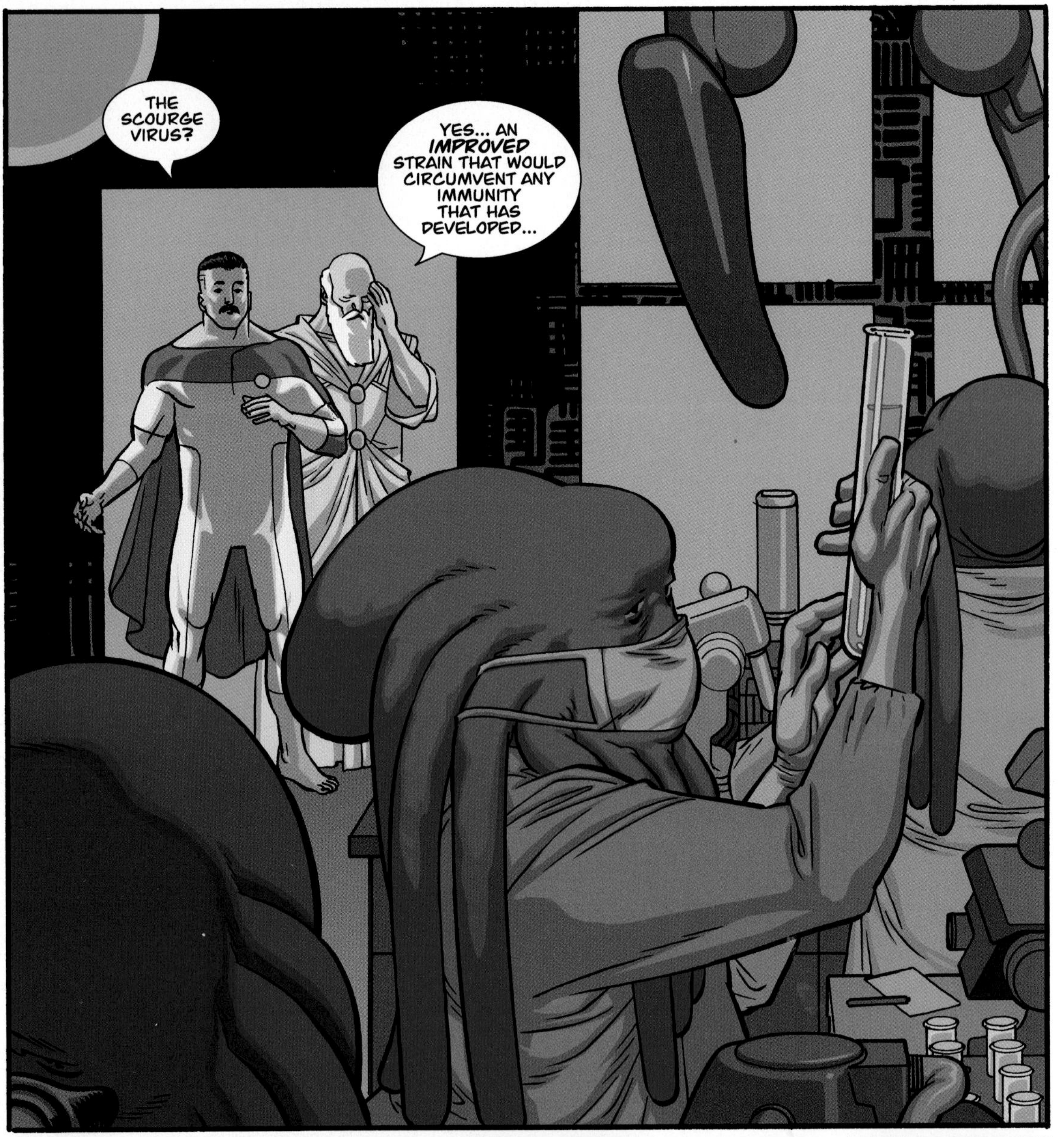
THE SCOURGE VIRUS?
YES... AN IMPROVED STRAIN THAT WOULD CIRCUMVENT ANY IMMUNITY THAT HAS DEVELOPED...

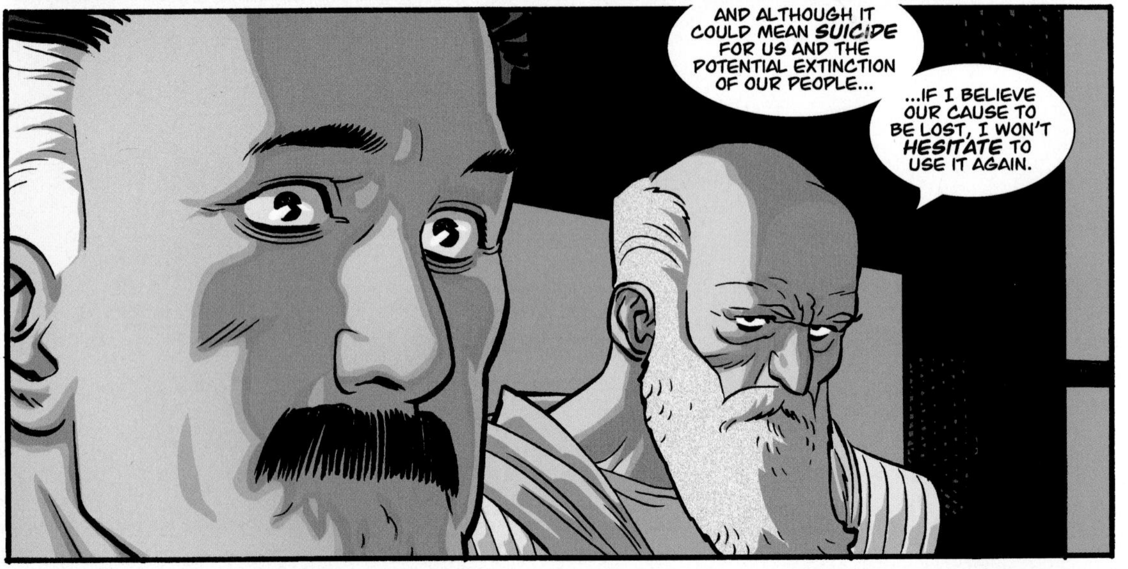
AND ALTHOUGH IT COULD MEAN SUICIDE FOR US AND THE POTENTIAL EXTINCTION OF OUR PEOPLE...
...IF I BELIEVE OUR CAUSE TO BE LOST, I WON'T HESITATE TO USE IT AGAIN.

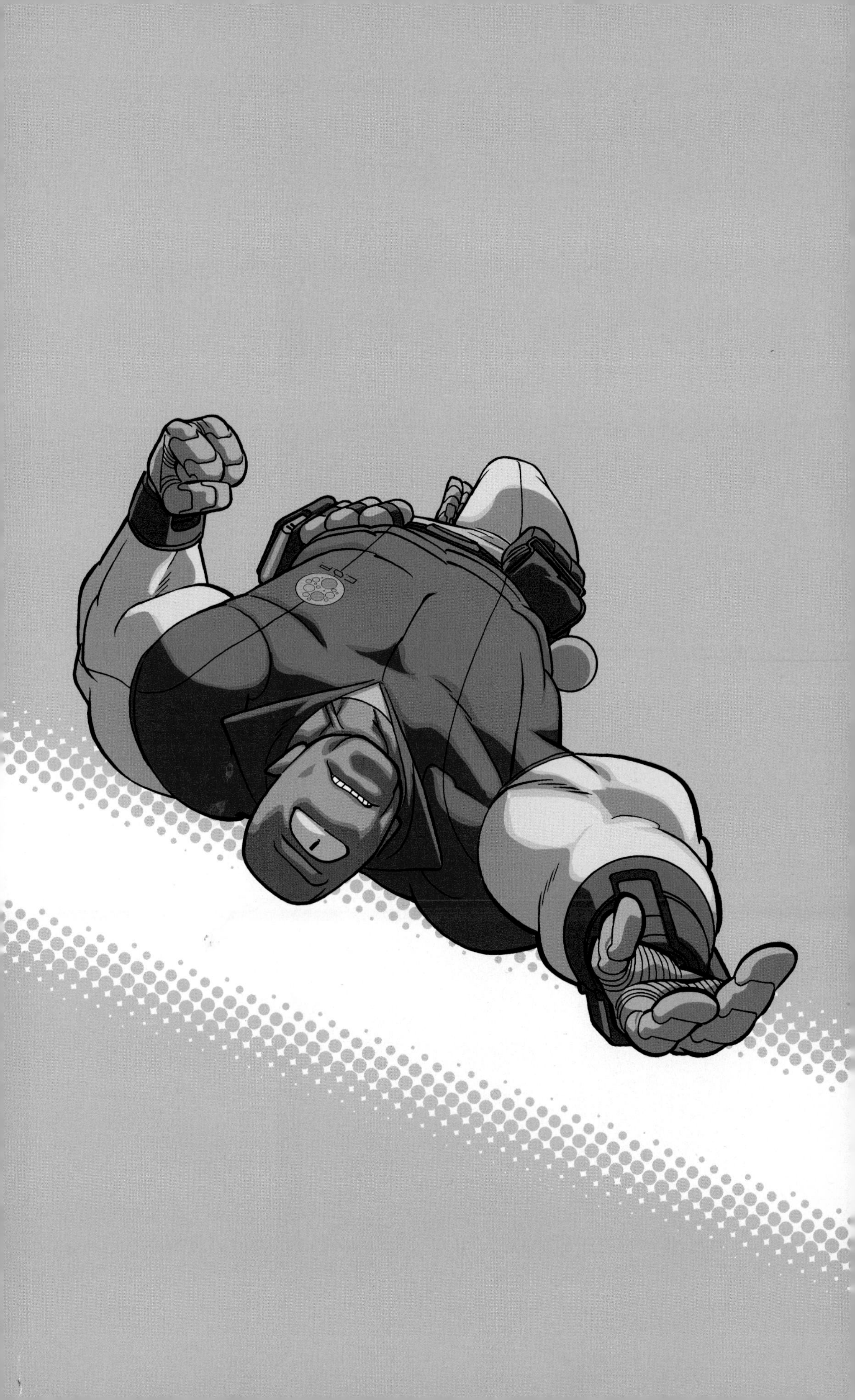

# CHAPTER THREE

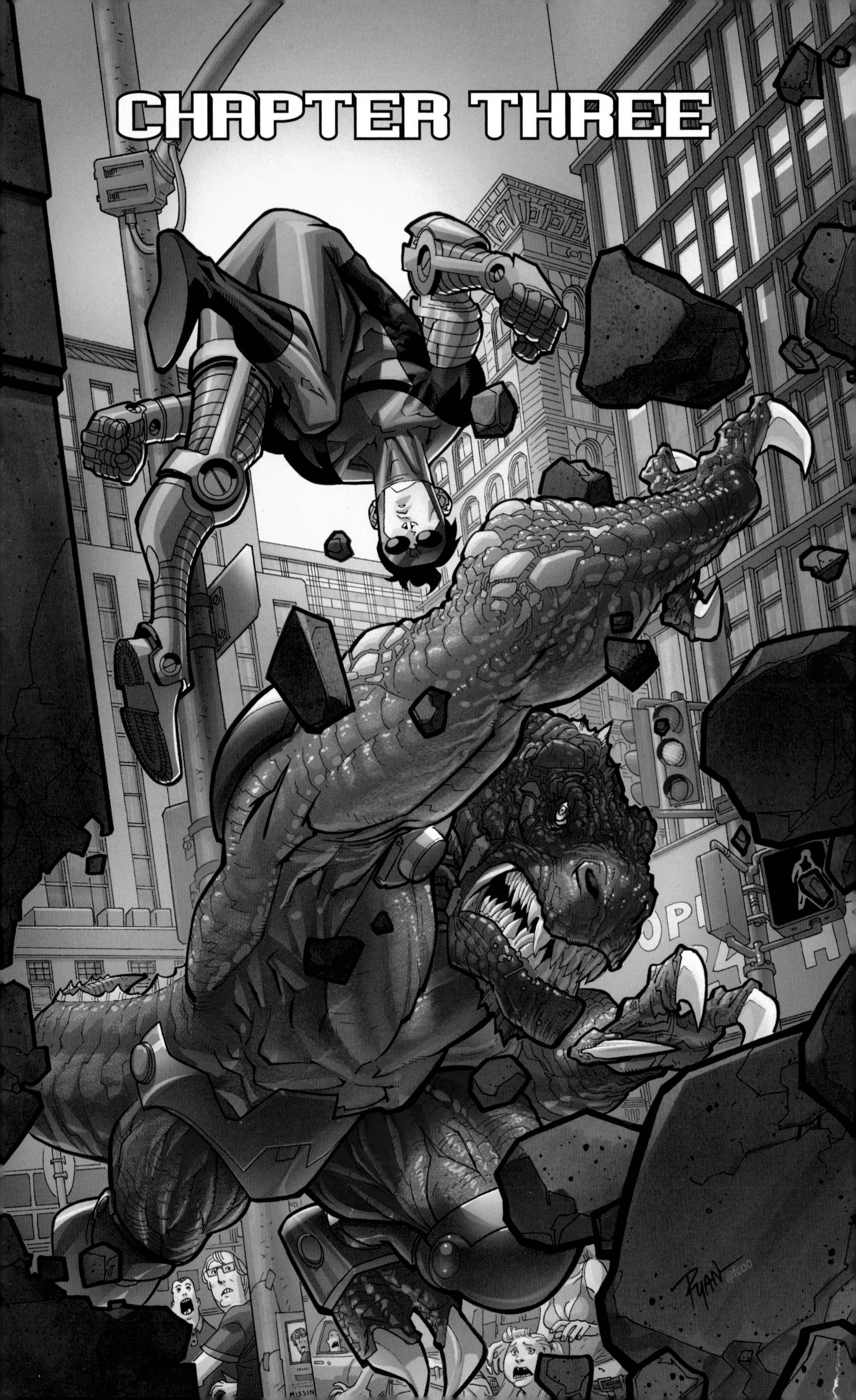

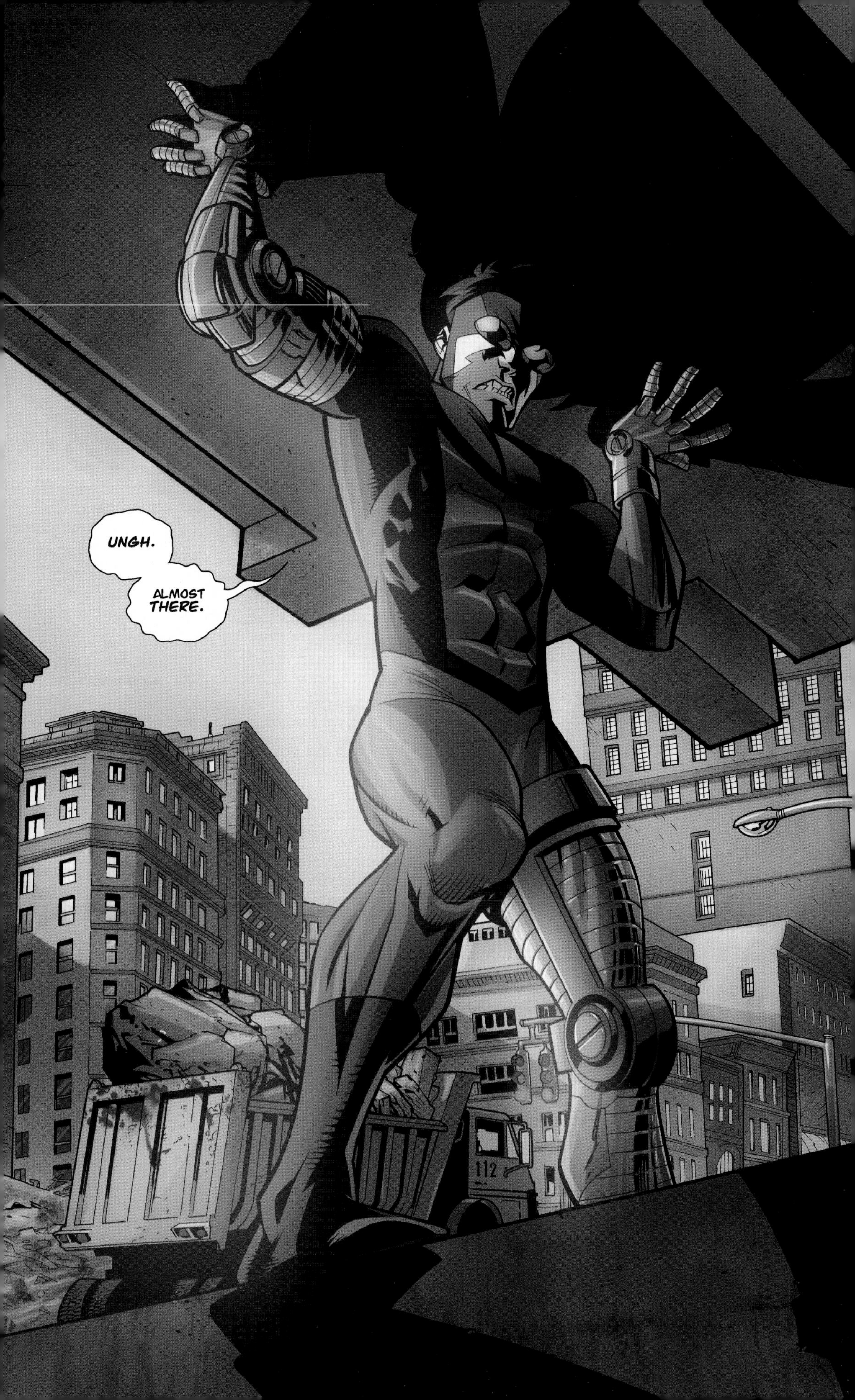
UNGH.
ALMOST THERE.

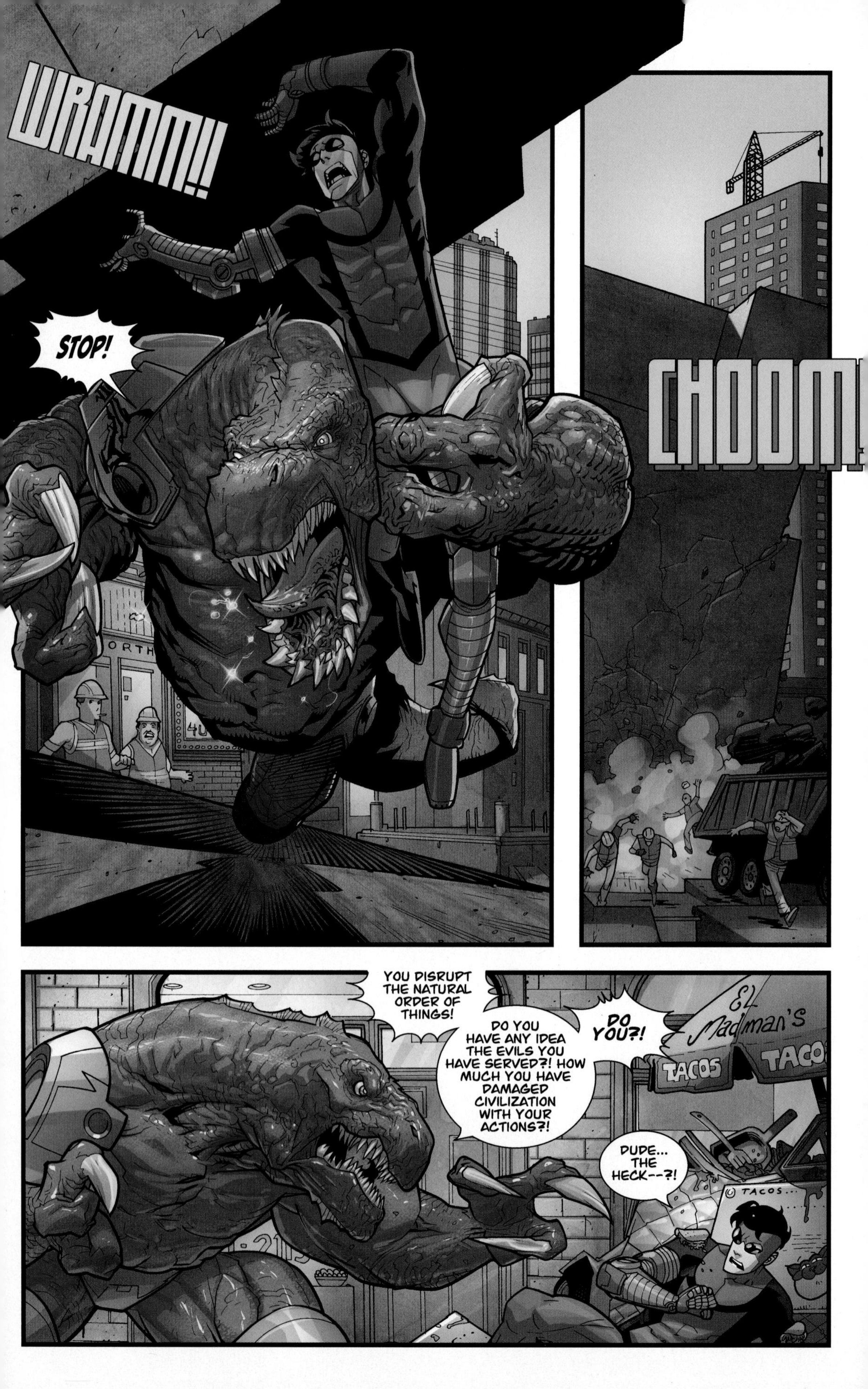
WRAMM!!
STOP!
CHOOM
YOU DISRUPT THE NATURAL ORDER OF THINGS!
DO YOU HAVE ANY IDEA THE EVILS YOU HAVE SERVED?! HOW MUCH YOU HAVE DAMAGED CIVILIZATION WITH YOUR ACTIONS?!
DO YOU?!
El Madman's
TACOS
DUDE... THE HECK--?!
TACOS...

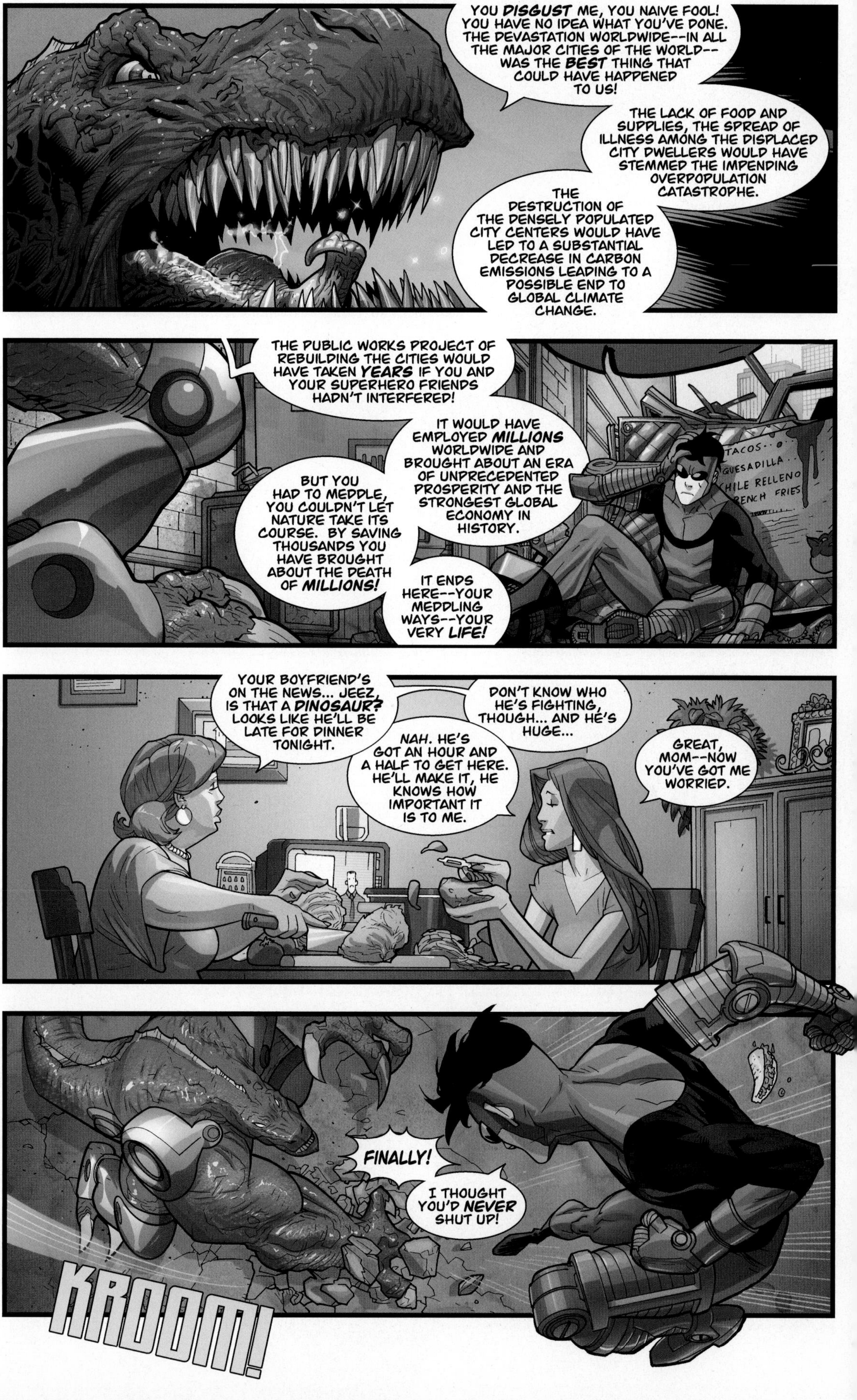
YOU DISGUST ME, YOU NAIVE FOOL! YOU HAVE NO IDEA WHAT YOU'VE DONE. THE DEVASTATION WORLDWIDE--IN ALL THE MAJOR CITIES OF THE WORLD--WAS THE BEST THING THAT COULD HAVE HAPPENED TO US!
THE LACK OF FOOD AND SUPPLIES, THE SPREAD OF ILLNESS AMONG THE DISPLACED CITY DWELLERS WOULD HAVE STEMMED THE IMPENDING OVERPOPULATION CATASTROPHE.
THE DESTRUCTION OF THE DENSELY POPULATED CITY CENTERS WOULD HAVE LED TO A SUBSTANTIAL DECREASE IN CARBON EMISSIONS LEADING TO A POSSIBLE END TO GLOBAL CLIMATE CHANGE.
THE PUBLIC WORKS PROJECT OF REBUILDING THE CITIES WOULD HAVE TAKEN YEARS IF YOU AND YOUR SUPERHERO FRIENDS HADN'T INTERFERED!
IT WOULD HAVE EMPLOYED MILLIONS WORLDWIDE AND BROUGHT ABOUT AN ERA OF UNPRECEDENTED PROSPERITY AND THE STRONGEST GLOBAL ECONOMY IN HISTORY.
BUT YOU HAD TO MEDDLE, YOU COULDN'T LET NATURE TAKE ITS COURSE. BY SAVING THOUSANDS YOU HAVE BROUGHT ABOUT THE DEATH OF MILLIONS!
IT ENDS HERE--YOUR MEDDLING WAYS--YOUR VERY LIFE!
TACOS
QUESADILLA
CHILE RELLENO
FRENCH FRIES
YOUR BOYFRIEND'S ON THE NEWS... JEEZ, IS THAT A DINOSAUR? LOOKS LIKE HE'LL BE LATE FOR DINNER TONIGHT.
NAH. HE'S GOT AN HOUR AND A HALF TO GET HERE. HE'LL MAKE IT, HE KNOWS HOW IMPORTANT IT IS TO ME.
DON'T KNOW WHO HE'S FIGHTING, THOUGH... AND HE'S HUGE...
GREAT, MOM--NOW YOU'VE GOT ME WORRIED.
FINALLY!
I THOUGHT YOU'D NEVER SHUT UP!
KROOM!

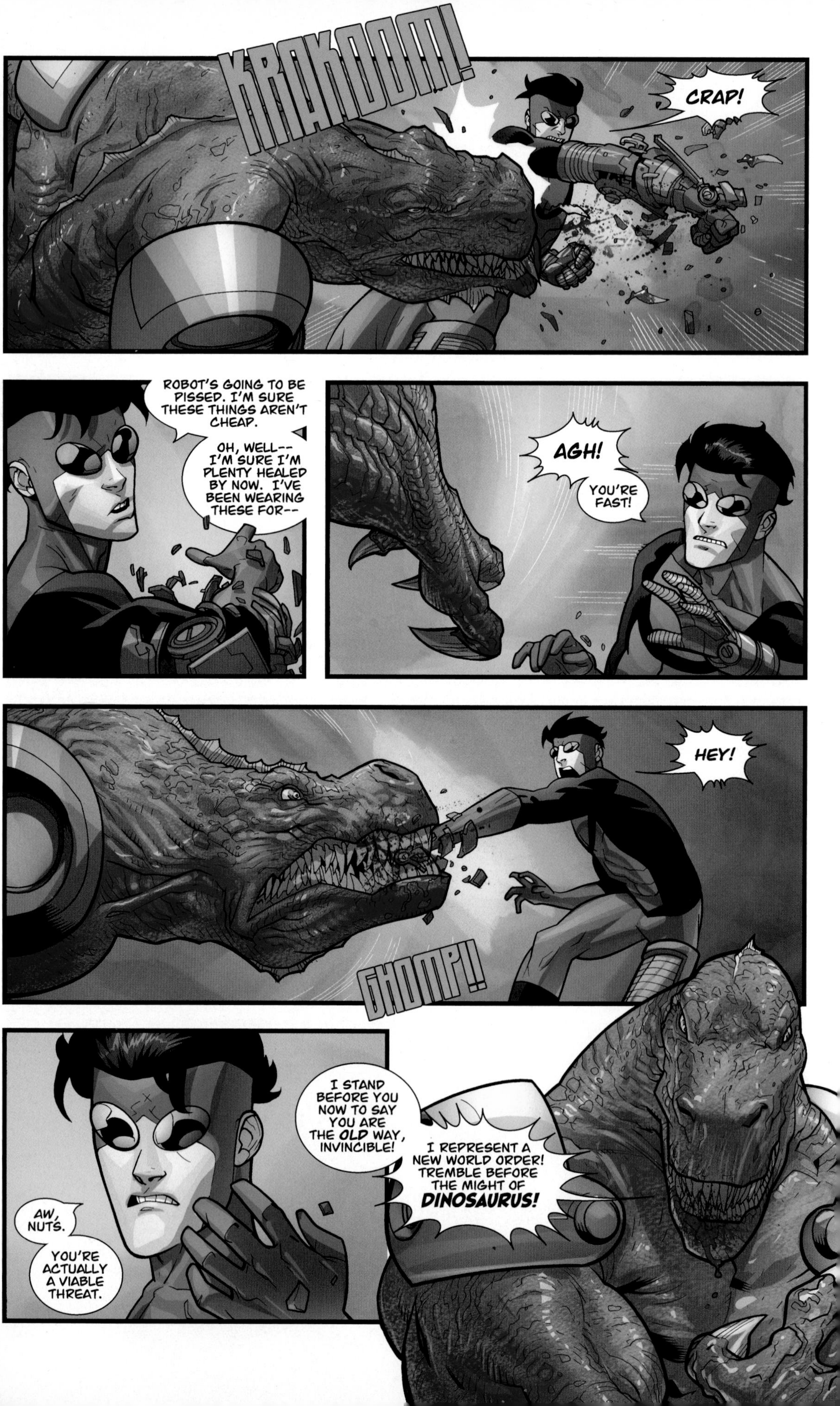
KRAKOOM!
CRAP!
ROBOT'S GOING TO BE PISSED. I'M SURE THESE THINGS AREN'T CHEAP.
OH, WELL-- I'M SURE I'M PLENTY HEALED BY NOW. I'VE BEEN WEARING THESE FOR--
AGH!
YOU'RE FAST!
HEY!
GHOMP!!
I STAND BEFORE YOU NOW TO SAY YOU ARE THE OLD WAY, INVINCIBLE!
I REPRESENT A NEW WORLD ORDER! TREMBLE BEFORE THE MIGHT OF DINOSAURUS!
AW, NUTS.
YOU'RE ACTUALLY A VIABLE THREAT.

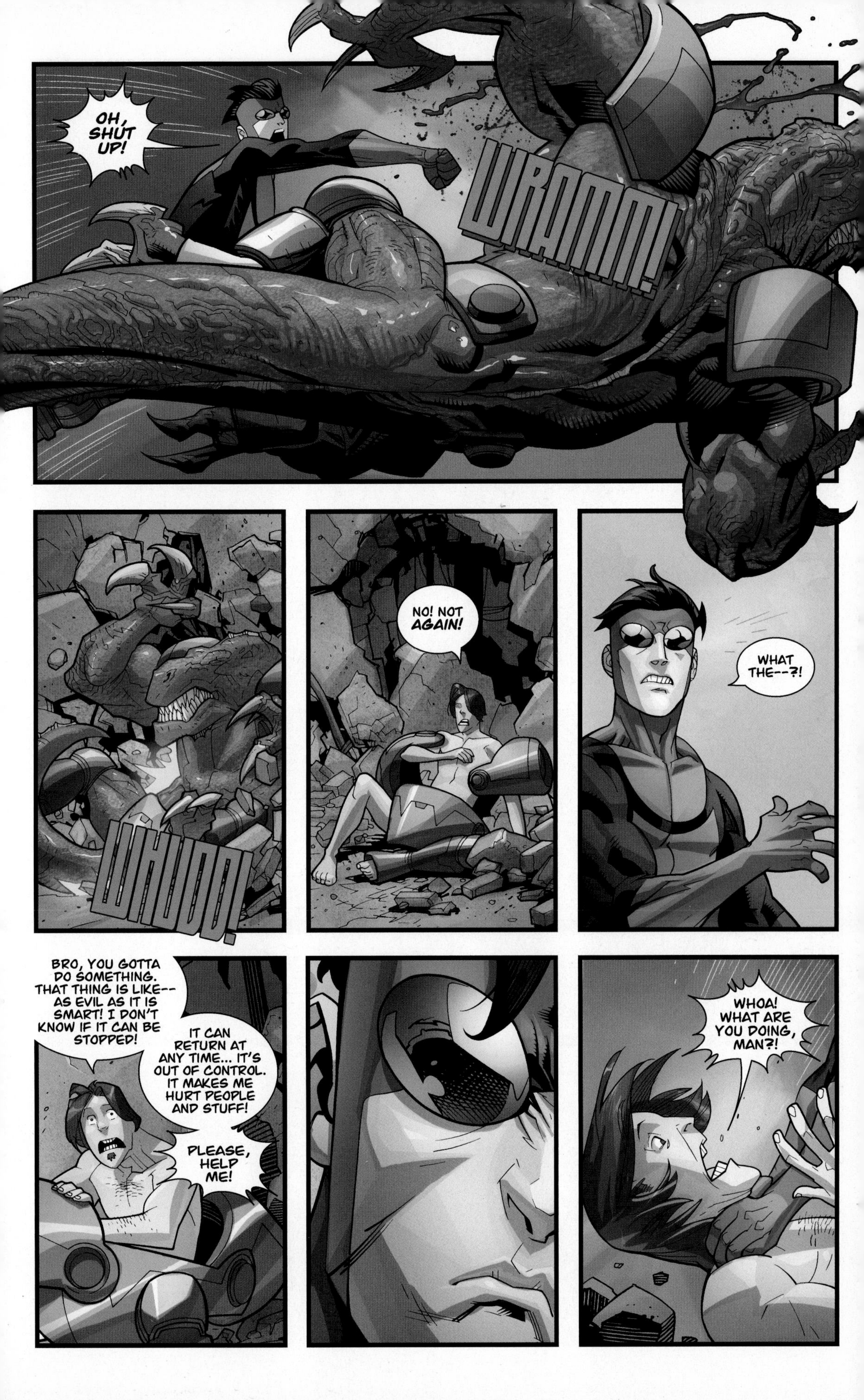
OH, SHUT UP!
WRAMM!
WHUDD!
NO! NOT AGAIN!
WHAT THE--?!
BRO, YOU GOTTA DO SOMETHING. THAT THING IS LIKE-- AS EVIL AS IT IS SMART! I DON'T KNOW IF IT CAN BE STOPPED!
IT CAN RETURN AT ANY TIME... IT'S OUT OF CONTROL. IT MAKES ME HURT PEOPLE AND STUFF!
PLEASE, HELP ME!
WHOA! WHAT ARE YOU DOING, MAN?!

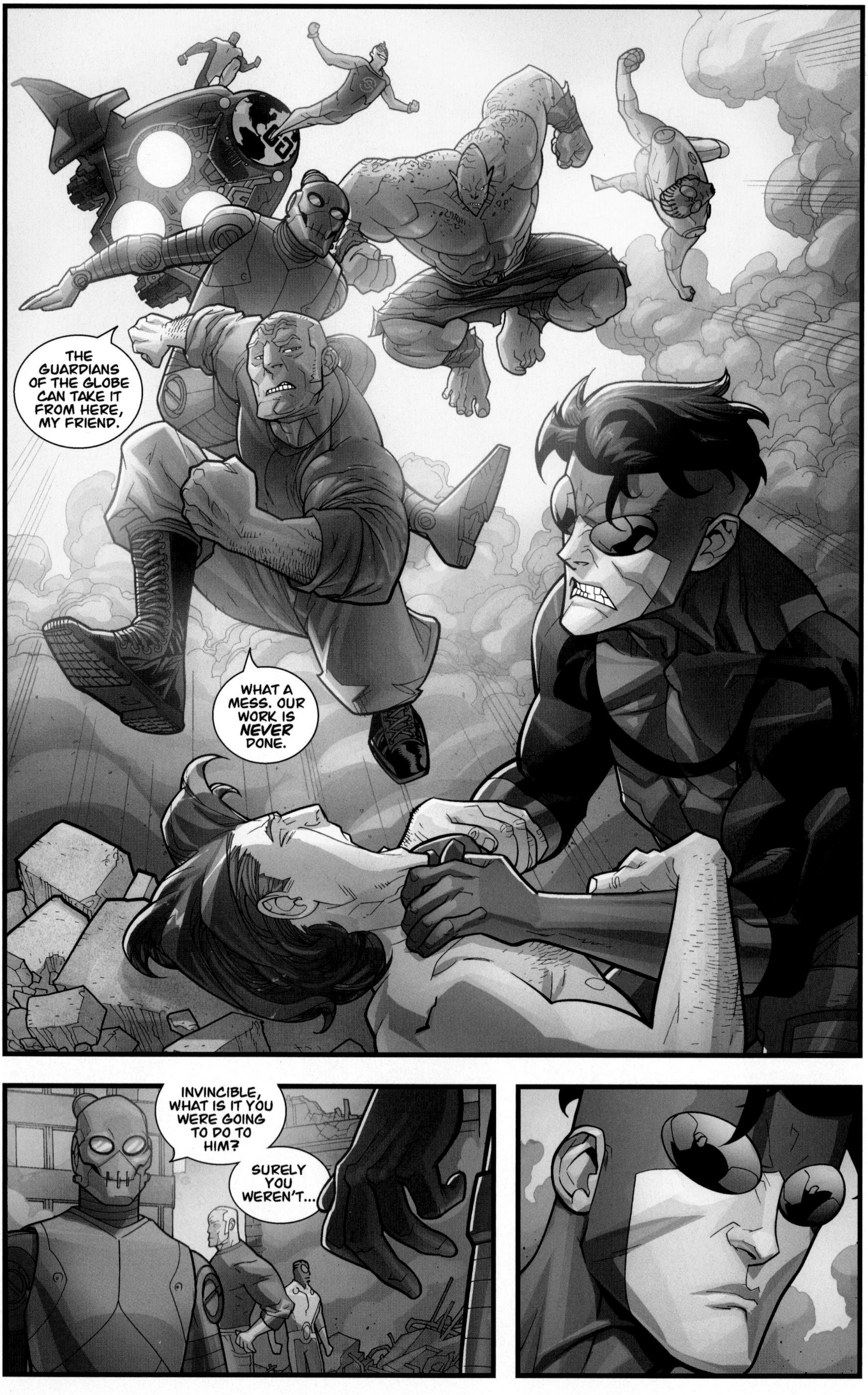
THE GUARDIANS OF THE GLOBE CAN TAKE IT FROM HERE, MY FRIEND.
WHAT A MESS. OUR WORK IS *NEVER* DONE.
INVINCIBLE, WHAT IS IT YOU WERE GOING TO DO TO HIM?
SURELY YOU WEREN'T...

I DIDN'T KNOW WHAT TO SAY.

"YEAH. I WAS GOING TO KILL HIM." WAS THE FIRST THING THAT POPPED INTO MY HEAD... AND HEARING IT PUT SO PLAINLY LIKE THAT...

IT JUST FELT SO... WRONG.

WERE YOU GOING TO KILL HIM? COULD YOU?

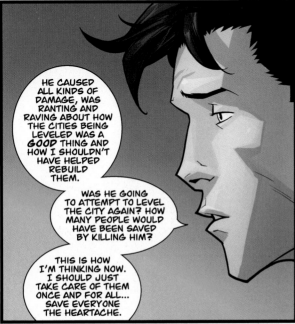

HE CAUSED ALL KINDS OF DAMAGE, WAS RANTING AND RAVING ABOUT HOW THE CITIES BEING LEVELED WAS A GOOD THING AND HOW I SHOULDN'T HAVE HELPED REBUILD THEM.

WAS HE GOING TO ATTEMPT TO LEVEL THE CITY AGAIN? HOW MANY PEOPLE WOULD HAVE BEEN SAVED BY KILLING HIM?

THIS IS HOW I'M THINKING NOW. I SHOULD JUST TAKE CARE OF THEM ONCE AND FOR ALL... SAVE EVERYONE THE HEARTACHE.

BUT COULD YOU?

I DON'T KNOW. CONQUEST... ANGSTROM... I HAD A PERSONAL STAKE IN THAT. I SNAPPED.

THIS GUY WAS JUST SOME IDIOT FRAT BOY. I FELT SORRY FOR HIM... BUT... I THINK I WAS GOING TO.

I DON'T KNOW.

THAT'S GOOD... I THINK THAT'S A GOOD THING... YOU NOT KNOWING.

LET'S GO EAT. MY PARENTS PROBABLY THINK WE'RE AVOIDING THEM.

THANKS FOR DOING THIS. THEY'RE EXCITED.

NO PROBLEM, EVE.

HOW BAD COULD IT BE?

...

WHAT DID I SAY?

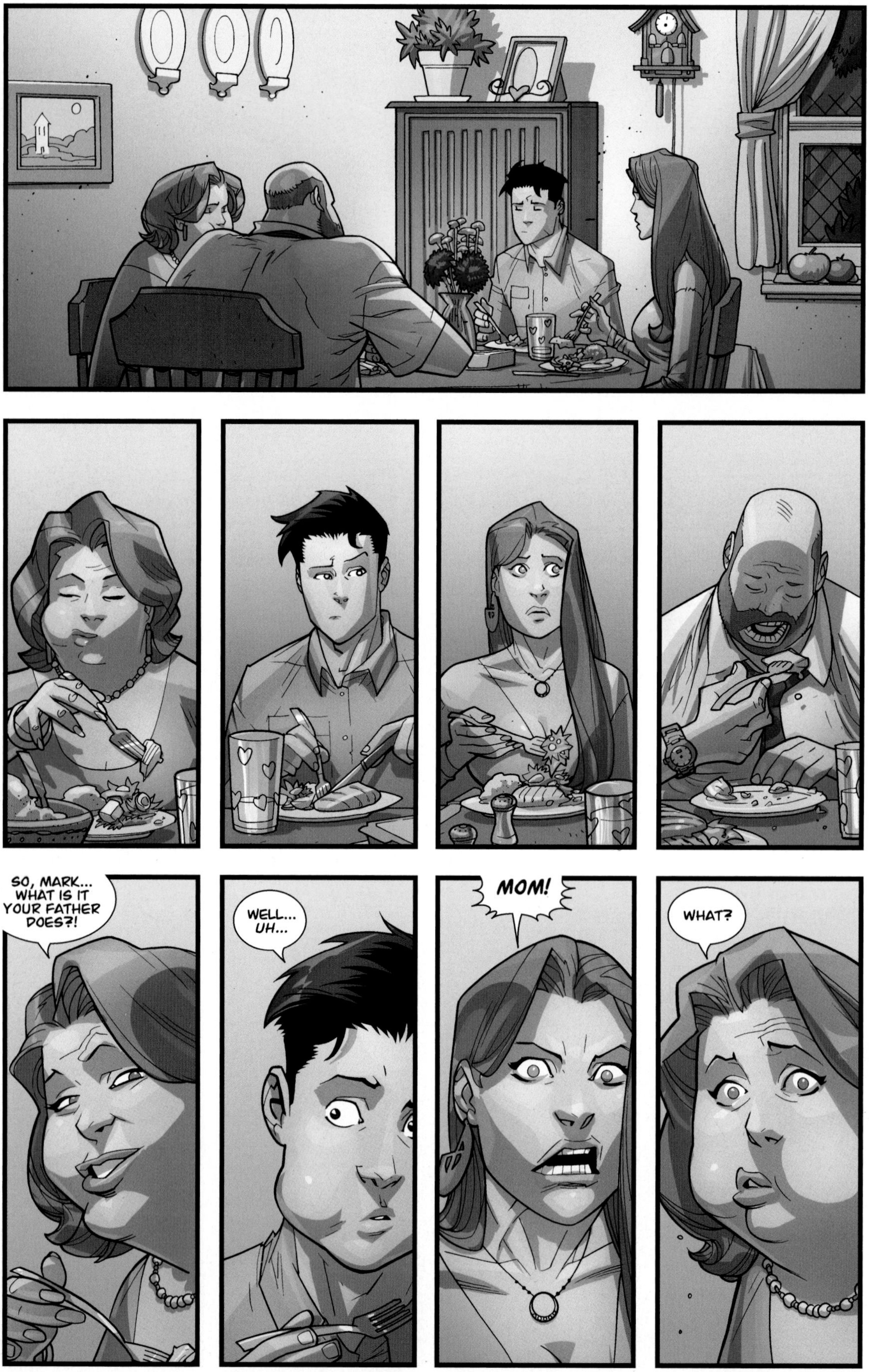
SO, MARK... WHAT IS IT YOUR FATHER DOES?!
WELL... UH...
MOM!
WHAT?

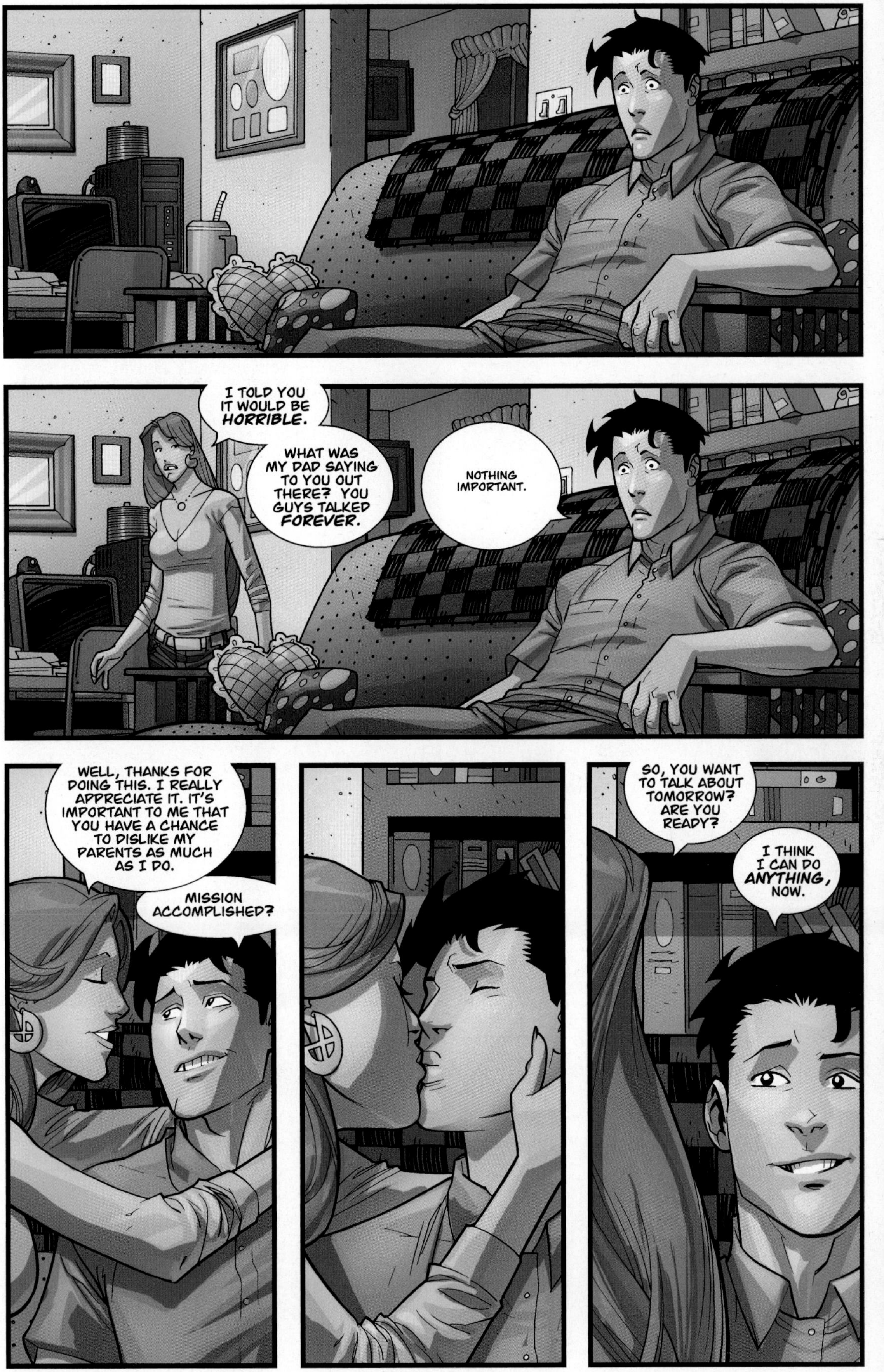
I TOLD YOU IT WOULD BE HORRIBLE.
WHAT WAS MY DAD SAYING TO YOU OUT THERE? YOU GUYS TALKED FOREVER.
NOTHING IMPORTANT.
WELL, THANKS FOR DOING THIS. I REALLY APPRECIATE IT. IT'S IMPORTANT TO ME THAT YOU HAVE A CHANCE TO DISLIKE MY PARENTS AS MUCH AS I DO.
MISSION ACCOMPLISHED?
SO, YOU WANT TO TALK ABOUT TOMORROW? ARE YOU READY?
I THINK I CAN DO ANYTHING, NOW.

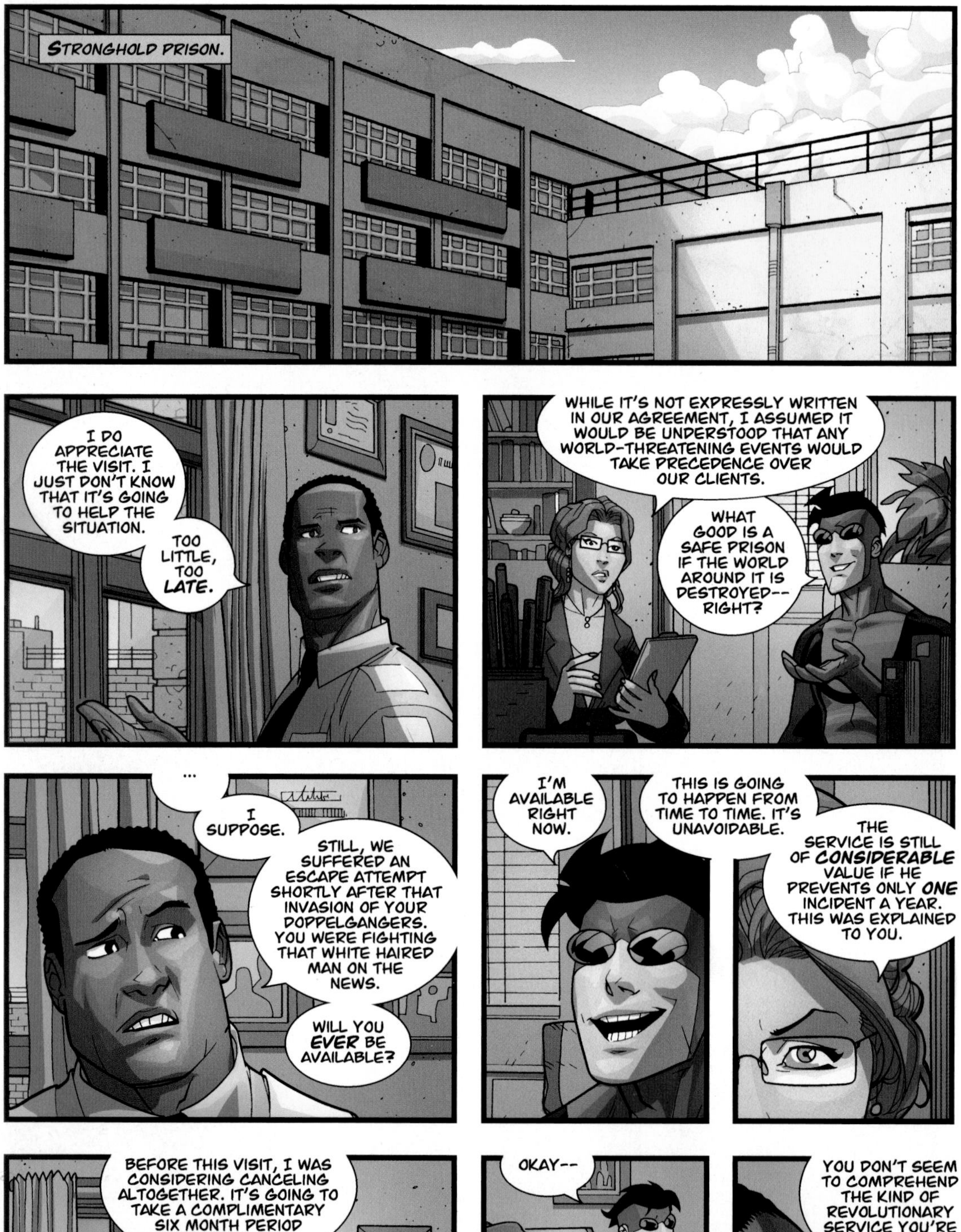
STRONGHOLD PRISON.
I DO APPRECIATE THE VISIT. I JUST DON'T KNOW THAT IT'S GOING TO HELP THE SITUATION.
TOO LITTLE, TOO LATE.
WHILE IT'S NOT EXPRESSLY WRITTEN IN OUR AGREEMENT, I ASSUMED IT WOULD BE UNDERSTOOD THAT ANY WORLD-THREATENING EVENTS WOULD TAKE PRECEDENCE OVER OUR CLIENTS.
WHAT GOOD IS A SAFE PRISON IF THE WORLD AROUND IT IS DESTROYED-- RIGHT?
...
I SUPPOSE.
STILL, WE SUFFERED AN ESCAPE ATTEMPT SHORTLY AFTER THAT INVASION OF YOUR DOPPELGANGERS. YOU WERE FIGHTING THAT WHITE HAIRED MAN ON THE NEWS.
WILL YOU EVER BE AVAILABLE?
I'M AVAILABLE RIGHT NOW.
THIS IS GOING TO HAPPEN FROM TIME TO TIME. IT'S UNAVOIDABLE.
THE SERVICE IS STILL OF CONSIDERABLE VALUE IF HE PREVENTS ONLY ONE INCIDENT A YEAR. THIS WAS EXPLAINED TO YOU.
BEFORE THIS VISIT, I WAS CONSIDERING CANCELING ALTOGETHER. IT'S GOING TO TAKE A COMPLIMENTARY SIX MONTH PERIOD TO KEEP ME.
BOTTOM LINE.
OKAY--
THREE MONTHS, TAKE IT OR LEAVE IT. WE'LL SEE HOW OFTEN MY CLIENT OFFERS ASSISTANCE WHEN YOU'RE NOT IN THE ROTATION.
YOU DON'T SEEM TO COMPREHEND THE KIND OF REVOLUTIONARY SERVICE YOU'RE A PART OF.
SIGH
FINE.

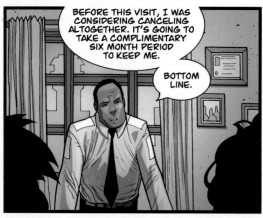

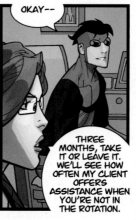

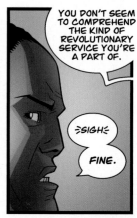

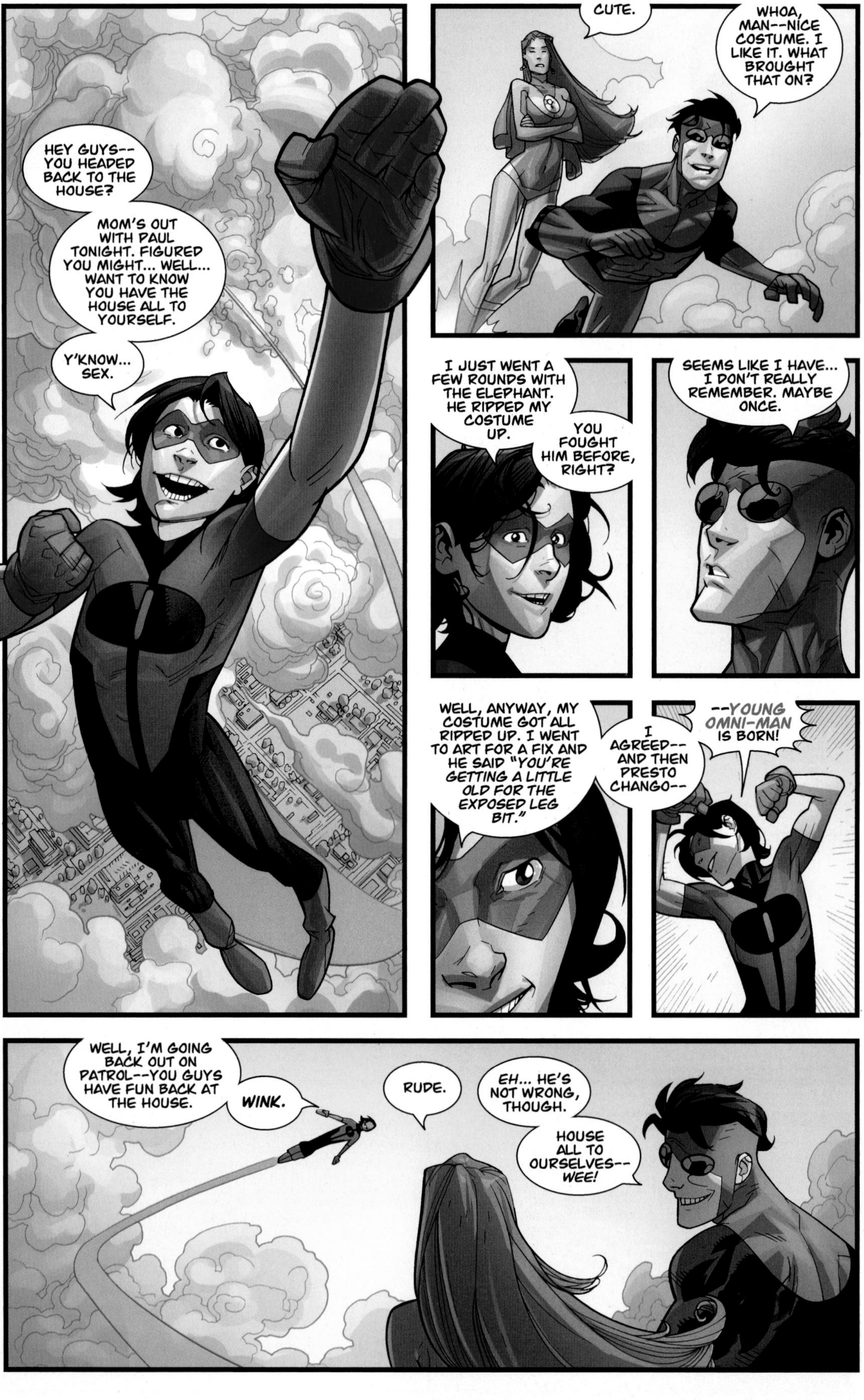

HEY GUYS--
YOU HEADED BACK TO THE HOUSE?
MOM'S OUT WITH PAUL TONIGHT. FIGURED YOU MIGHT... WELL... WANT TO KNOW YOU HAVE THE HOUSE ALL TO YOURSELF.
Y'KNOW... SEX.
CUTE.
WHOA, MAN--NICE COSTUME. I LIKE IT. WHAT BROUGHT THAT ON?
I JUST WENT A FEW ROUNDS WITH THE ELEPHANT. HE RIPPED MY COSTUME UP.
YOU FOUGHT HIM BEFORE, RIGHT?
SEEMS LIKE I HAVE... I DON'T REALLY REMEMBER. MAYBE ONCE.
WELL, ANYWAY, MY COSTUME GOT ALL RIPPED UP. I WENT TO ART FOR A FIX AND HE SAID "YOU'RE GETTING A LITTLE OLD FOR THE EXPOSED LEG BIT."
I AGREED--AND THEN PRESTO CHANGO--
--YOUNG OMNI-MAN IS BORN!
WELL, I'M GOING BACK OUT ON PATROL--YOU GUYS HAVE FUN BACK AT THE HOUSE.
WINK.
RUDE.
EH... HE'S NOT WRONG, THOUGH.
HOUSE ALL TO OURSELVES--WEE!

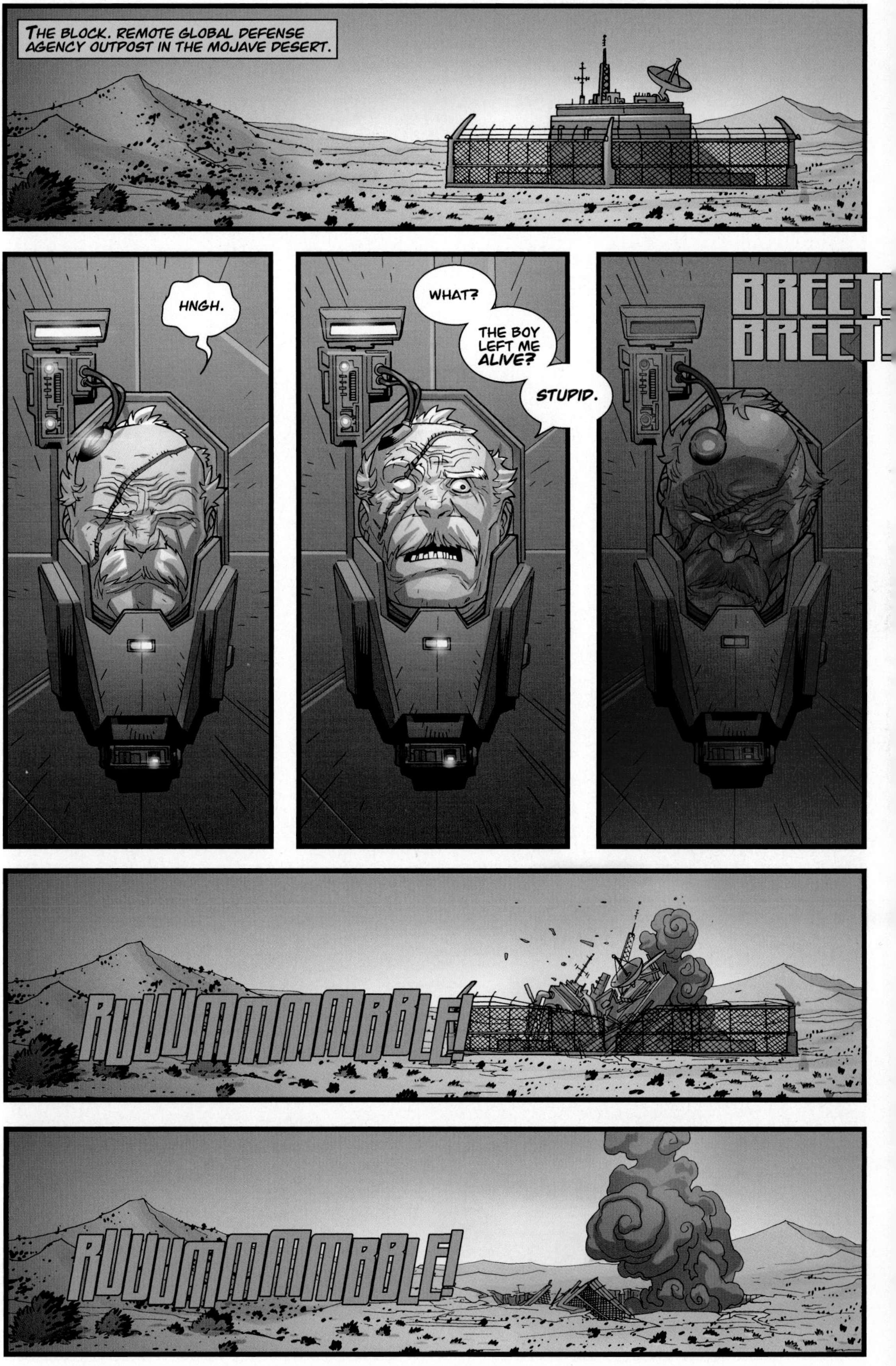
THE BLOCK. REMOTE GLOBAL DEFENSE AGENCY OUTPOST IN THE MOJAVE DESERT.
HNGH.
WHAT?
THE BOY LEFT ME ALIVE?
STUPID.
BREET!
BREET!
RUUUMMMMMBBLE!
RUUUMMMMMBBLE!

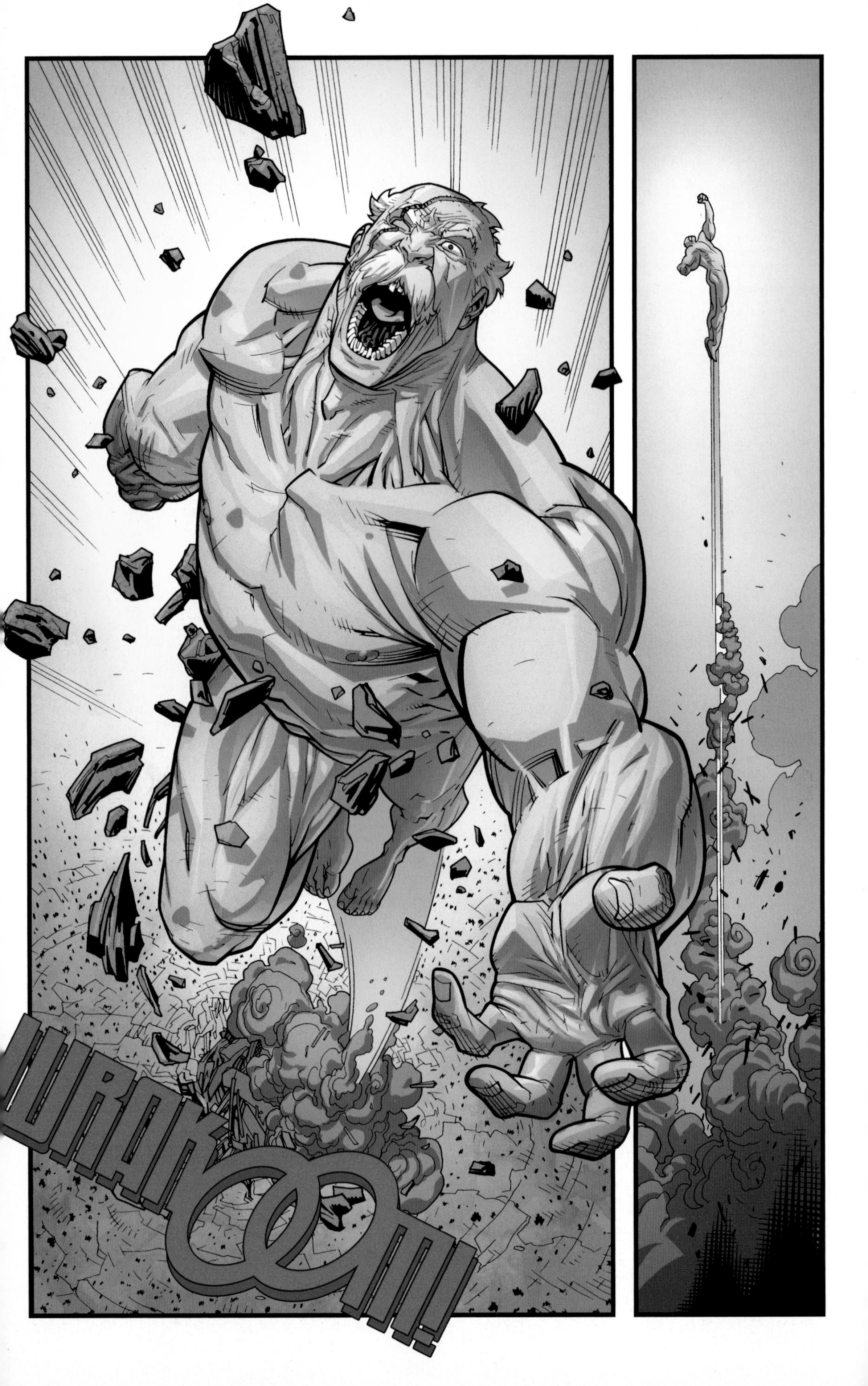
WRAKOOM!!

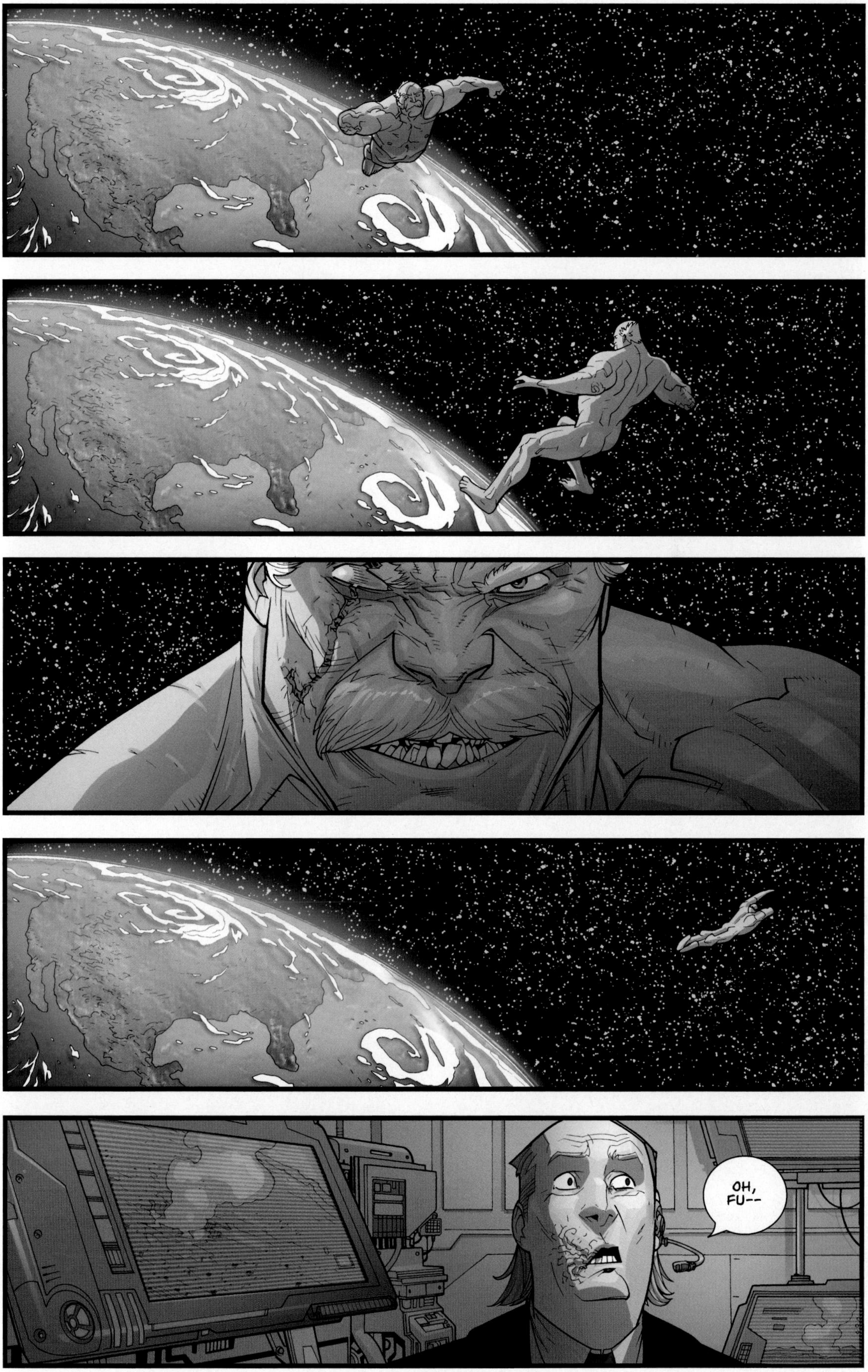
OH, FU--

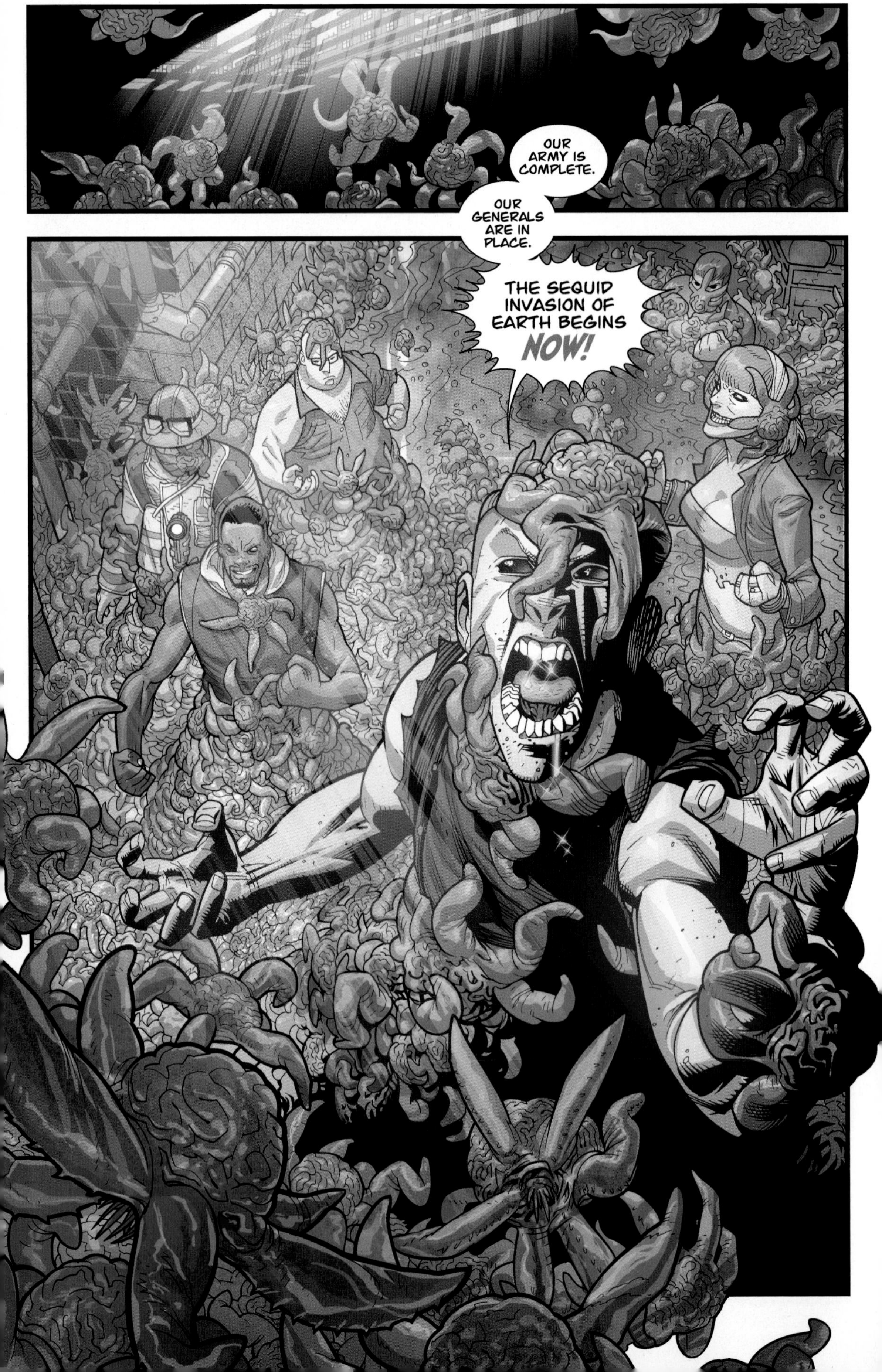
OUR ARMY IS COMPLETE.
OUR GENERALS ARE IN PLACE.
THE SEQUID INVASION OF EARTH BEGINS NOW!

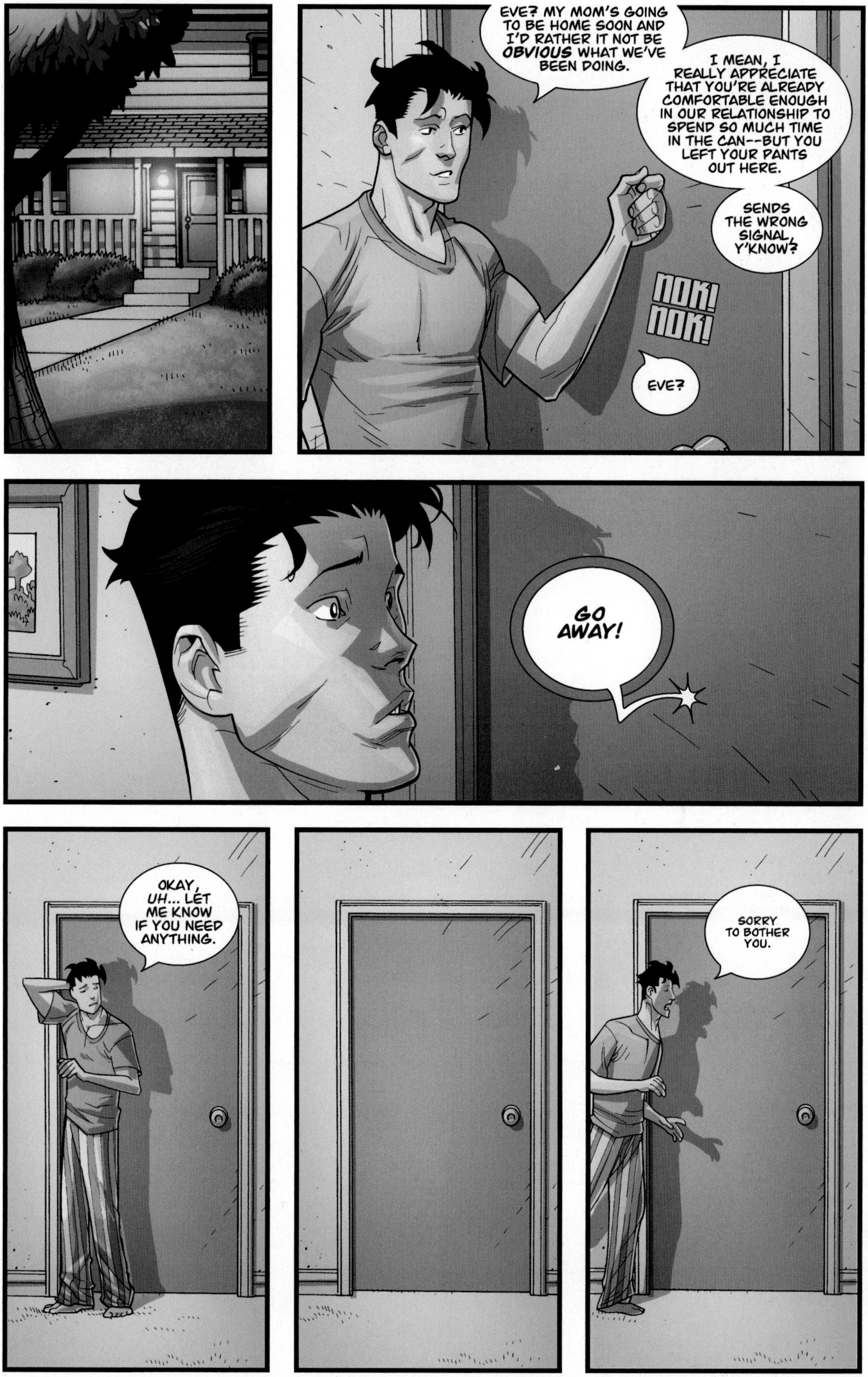
EVE? MY MOM'S GOING TO BE HOME SOON AND I'D RATHER IT NOT BE OBVIOUS WHAT WE'VE BEEN DOING.
I MEAN, I REALLY APPRECIATE THAT YOU'RE ALREADY COMFORTABLE ENOUGH IN OUR RELATIONSHIP TO SPEND SO MUCH TIME IN THE CAN--BUT YOU LEFT YOUR PANTS OUT HERE.
SENDS THE WRONG SIGNAL, Y'KNOW?
NOK! NOK!
EVE?
GO AWAY!
OKAY, UH... LET ME KNOW IF YOU NEED ANYTHING.
SORRY TO BOTHER YOU.

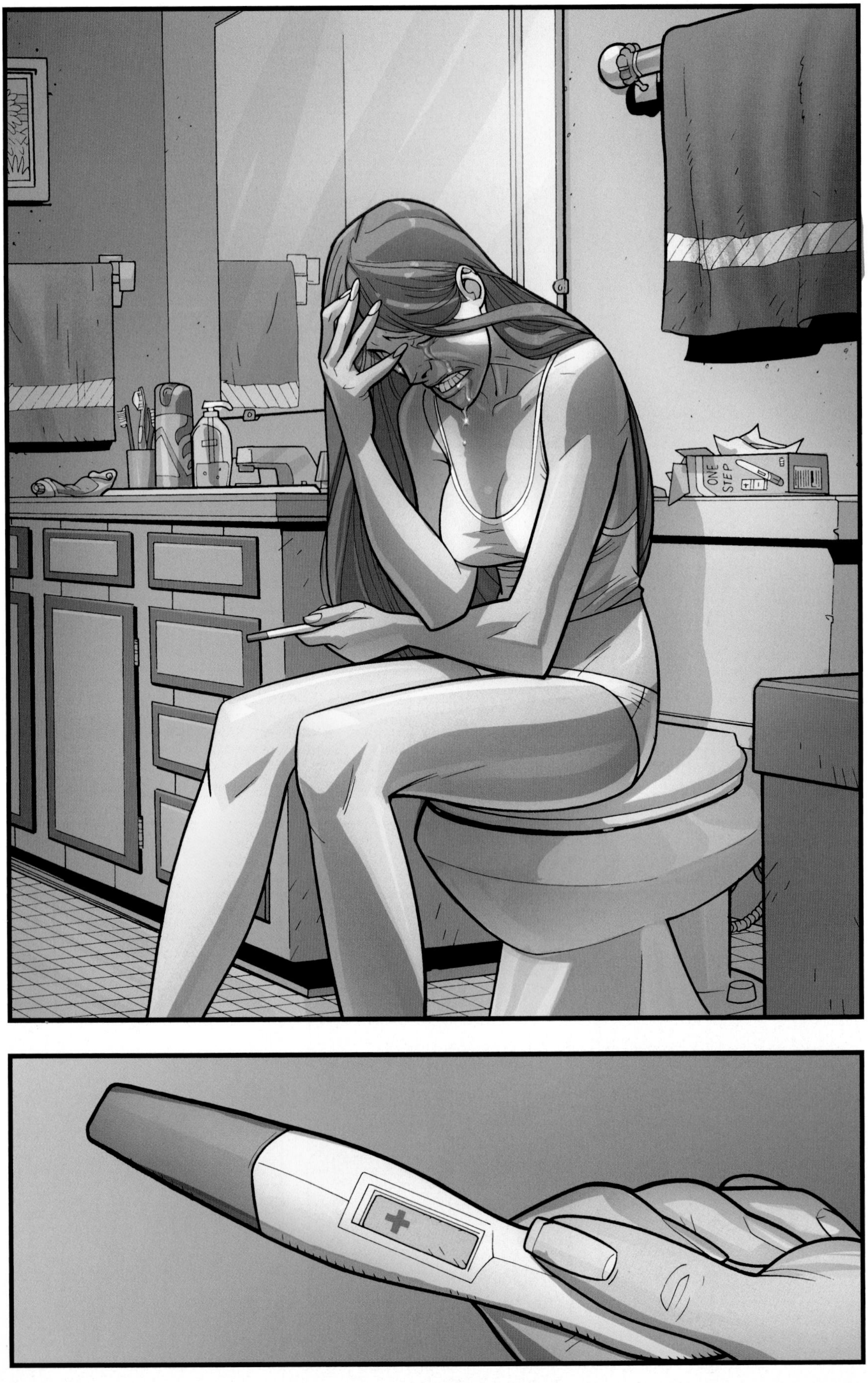
ONE STEP

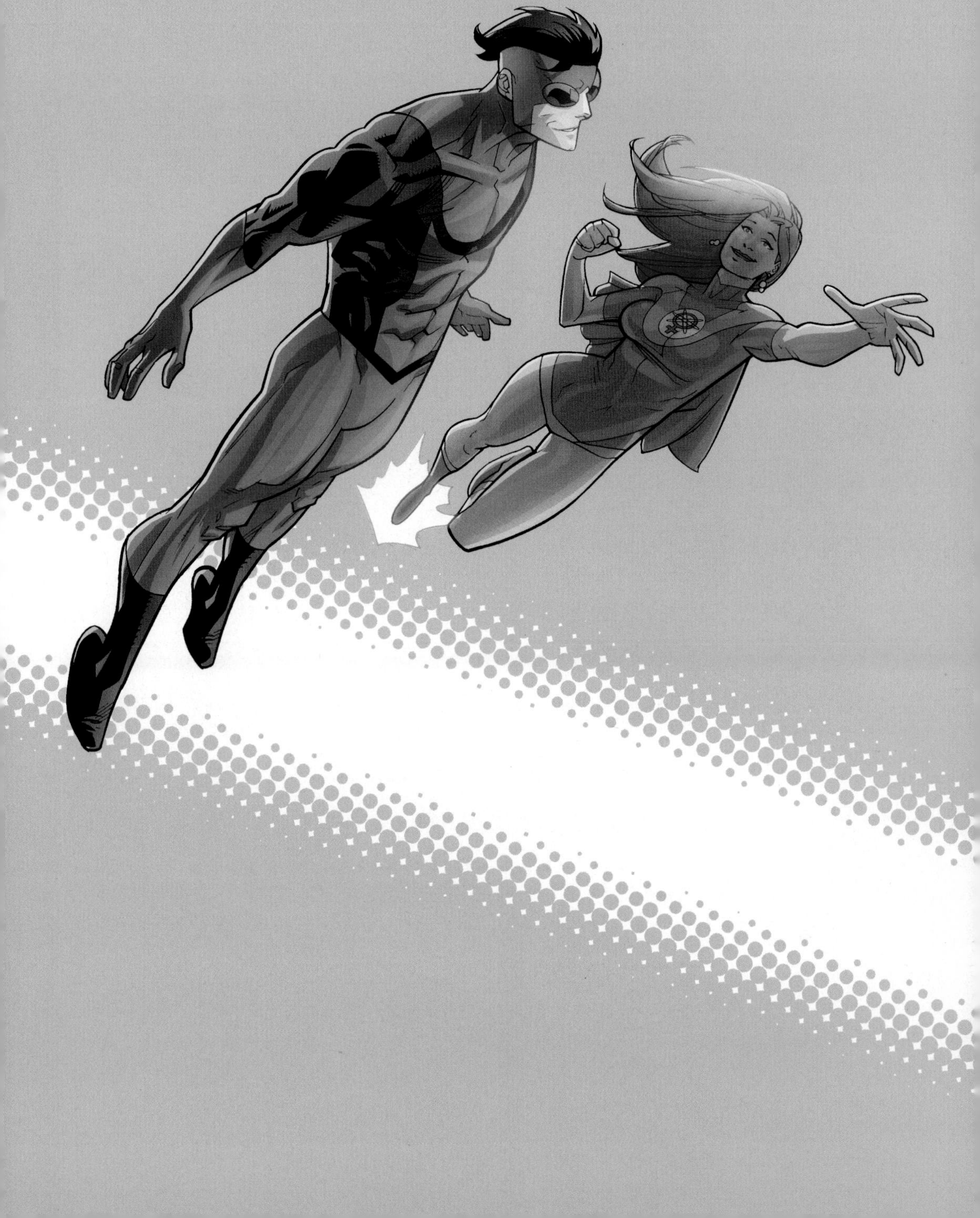

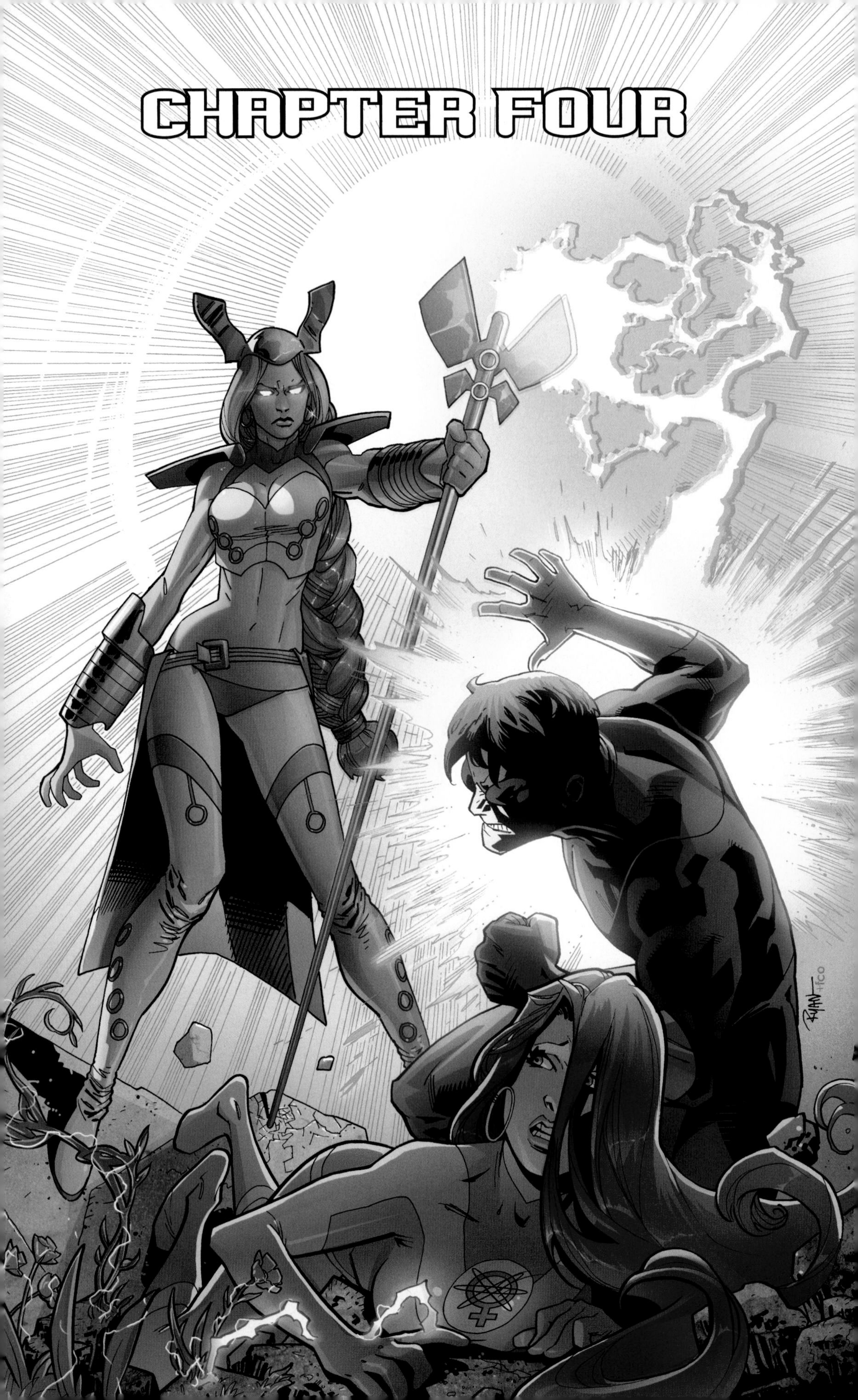
CHAPTER FOUR

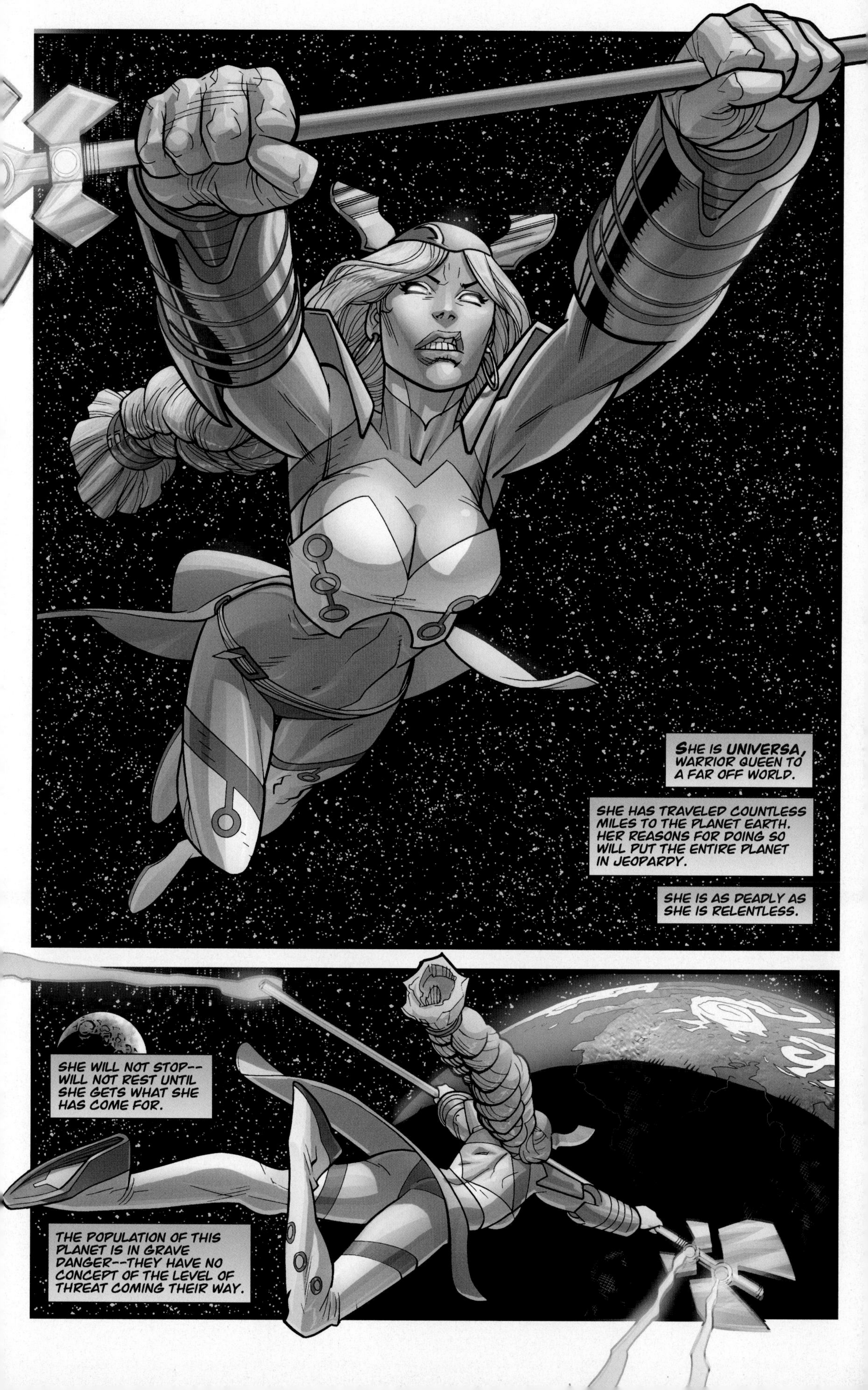
SHE IS UNIVERSA, WARRIOR QUEEN TO A FAR OFF WORLD.
SHE HAS TRAVELED COUNTLESS MILES TO THE PLANET EARTH. HER REASONS FOR DOING SO WILL PUT THE ENTIRE PLANET IN JEOPARDY.
SHE IS AS DEADLY AS SHE IS RELENTLESS.
SHE WILL NOT STOP-- WILL NOT REST UNTIL SHE GETS WHAT SHE HAS COME FOR.
THE POPULATION OF THIS PLANET IS IN GRAVE DANGER--THEY HAVE NO CONCEPT OF THE LEVEL OF THREAT COMING THEIR WAY.

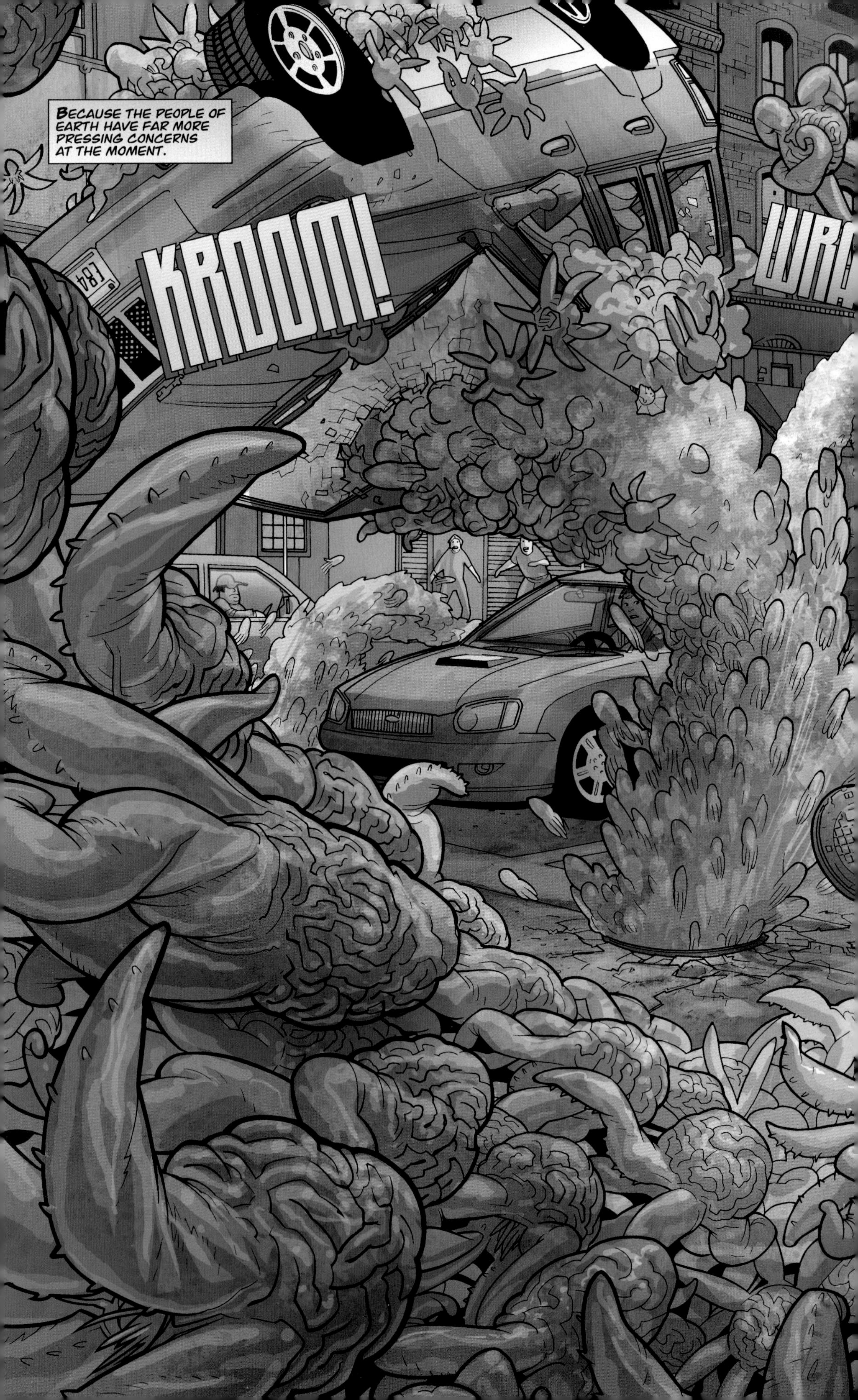
BECAUSE THE PEOPLE OF EARTH HAVE FAR MORE PRESSING CONCERNS AT THE MOMENT.
KROOM!

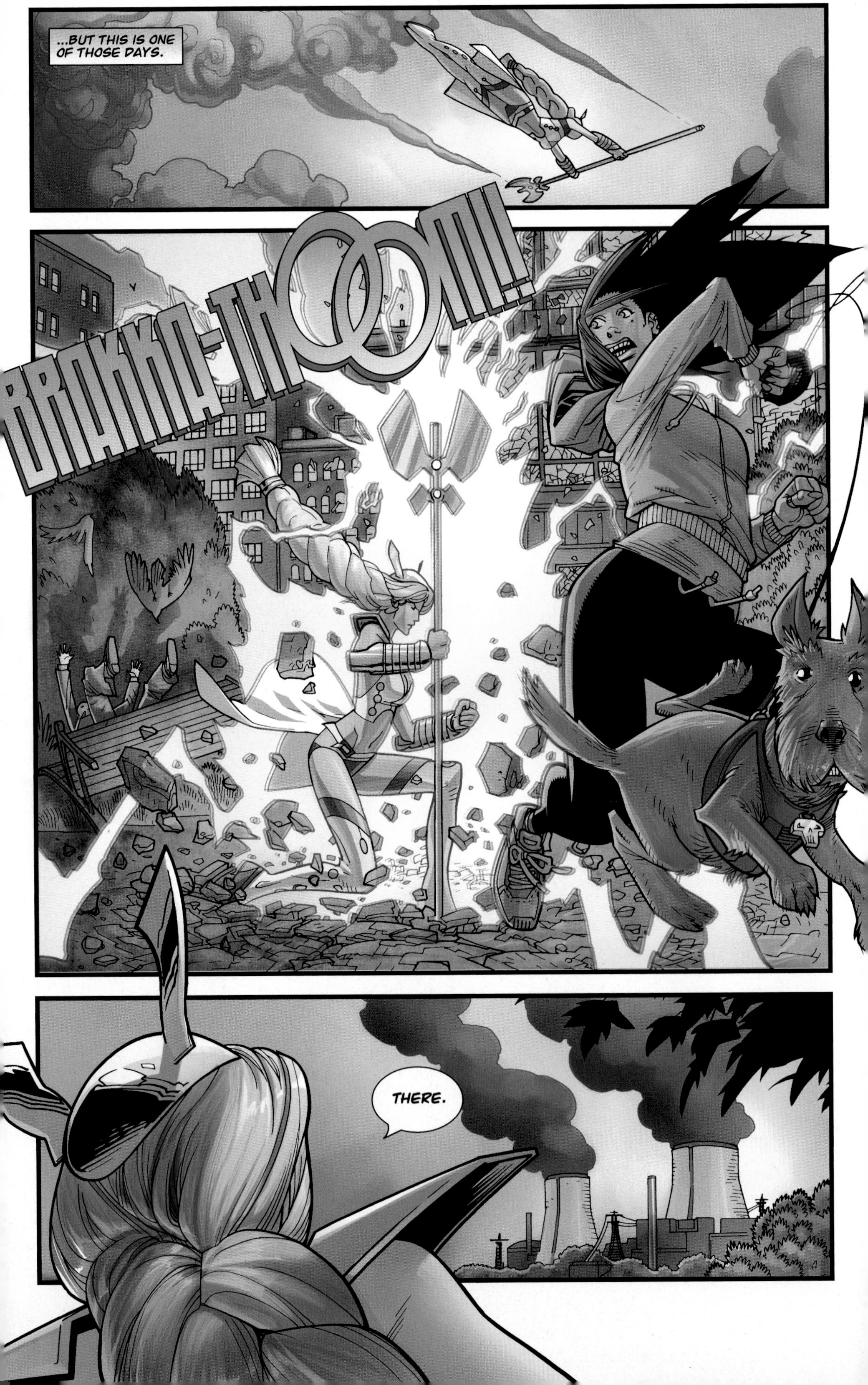
...BUT THIS IS ONE OF THOSE DAYS.
BRAKKA-THOOM!!
THERE.

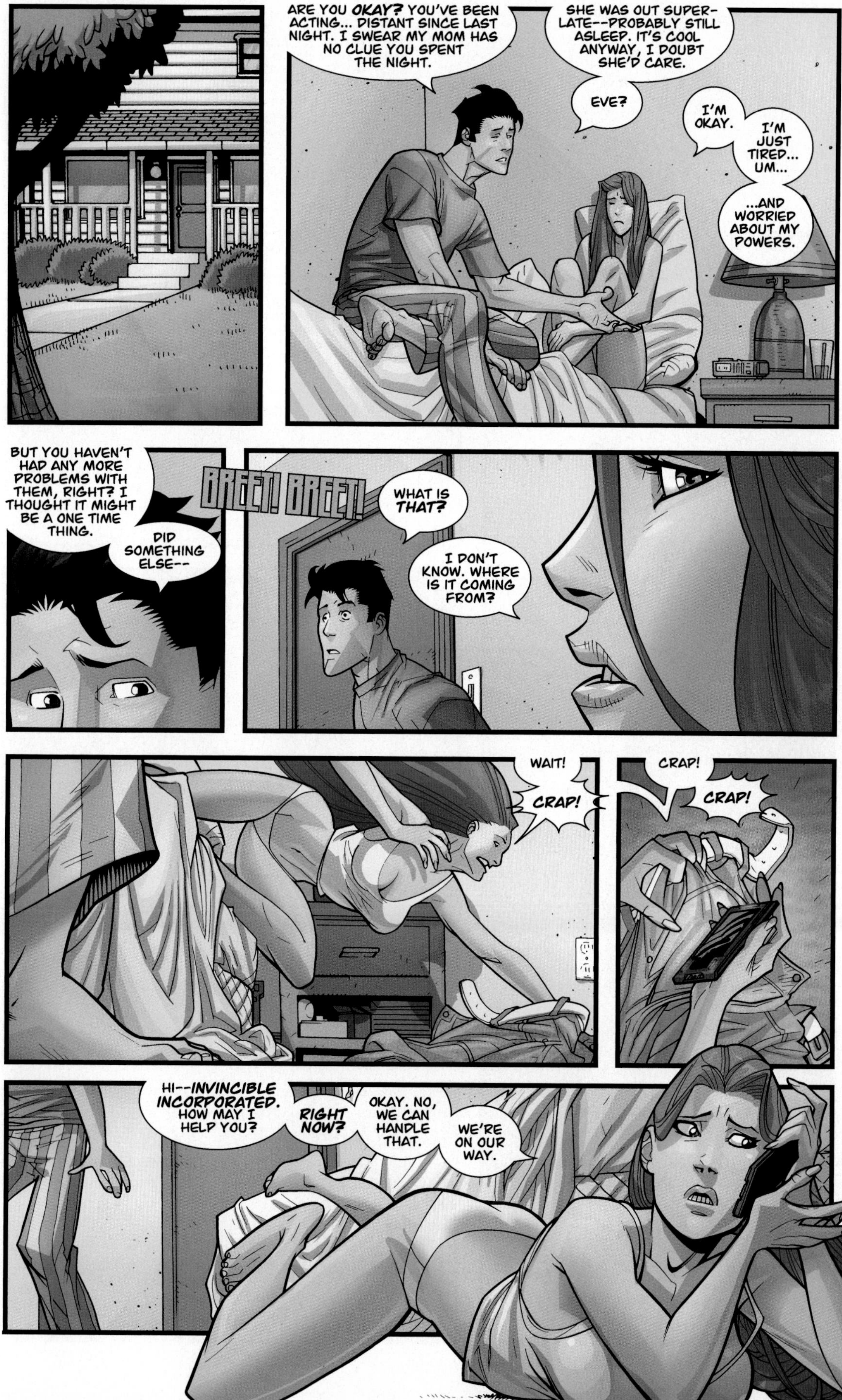
ARE YOU OKAY? YOU'VE BEEN ACTING... DISTANT SINCE LAST NIGHT. I SWEAR MY MOM HAS NO CLUE YOU SPENT THE NIGHT.
SHE WAS OUT SUPER-LATE--PROBABLY STILL ASLEEP. IT'S COOL ANYWAY, I DOUBT SHE'D CARE.
EVE?
I'M OKAY.
I'M JUST TIRED... UM...
...AND WORRIED ABOUT MY POWERS.
BUT YOU HAVEN'T HAD ANY MORE PROBLEMS WITH THEM, RIGHT? I THOUGHT IT MIGHT BE A ONE TIME THING.
DID SOMETHING ELSE--
BREET! BREET!
WHAT IS THAT?
I DON'T KNOW. WHERE IS IT COMING FROM?
WAIT!
CRAP!
CRAP!
CRAP!
HI--INVINCIBLE INCORPORATED. HOW MAY I HELP YOU?
RIGHT NOW?
OKAY. NO, WE CAN HANDLE THAT.
WE'RE ON OUR WAY.

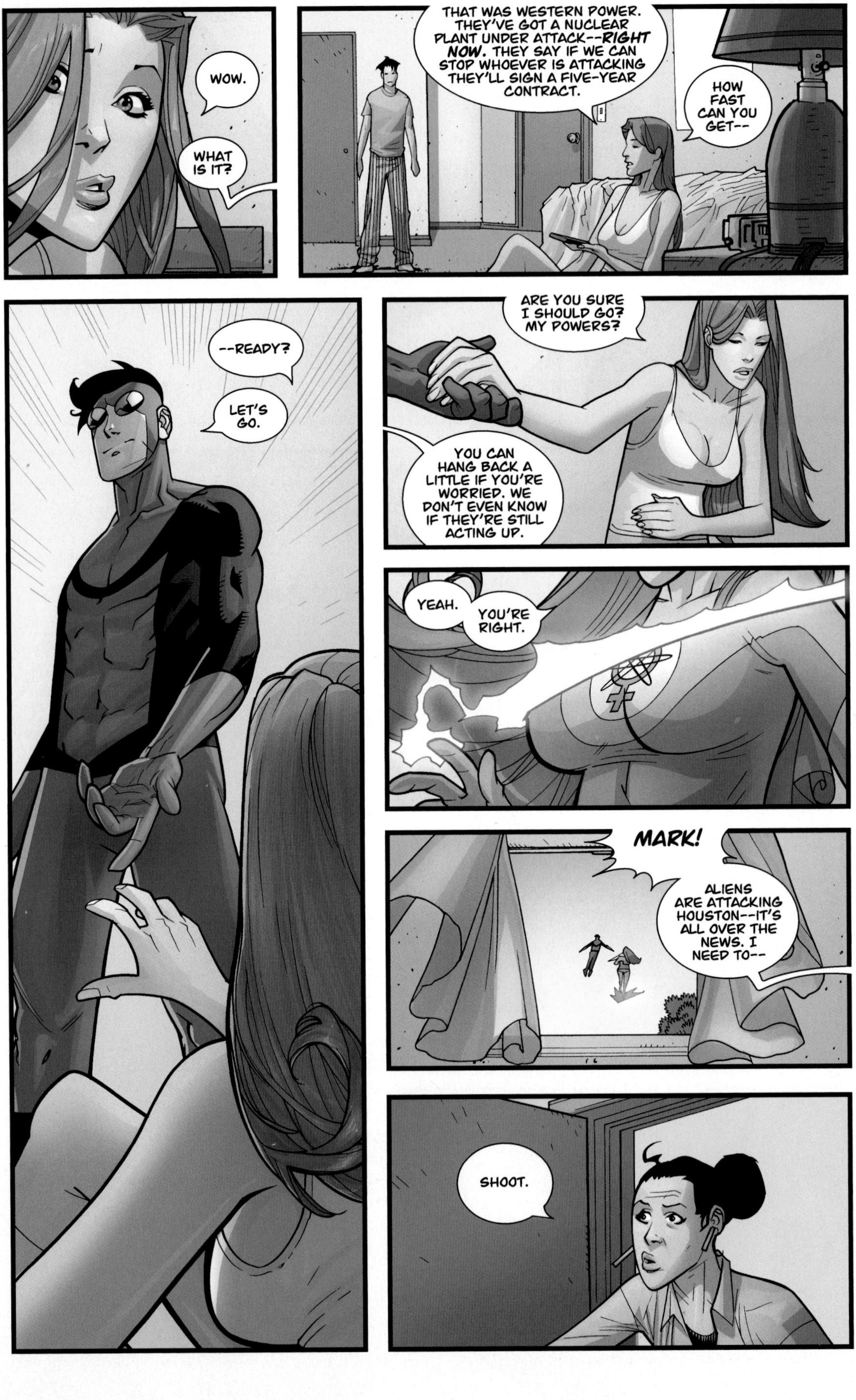
WOW.
WHAT IS IT?
THAT WAS WESTERN POWER. THEY'VE GOT A NUCLEAR PLANT UNDER ATTACK--RIGHT NOW. THEY SAY IF WE CAN STOP WHOEVER IS ATTACKING THEY'LL SIGN A FIVE-YEAR CONTRACT.
HOW FAST CAN YOU GET--
--READY?
LET'S GO.
ARE YOU SURE I SHOULD GO? MY POWERS?
YOU CAN HANG BACK A LITTLE IF YOU'RE WORRIED. WE DON'T EVEN KNOW IF THEY'RE STILL ACTING UP.
YEAH.
YOU'RE RIGHT.
MARK!
ALIENS ARE ATTACKING HOUSTON--IT'S ALL OVER THE NEWS. I NEED TO--
SHOOT.

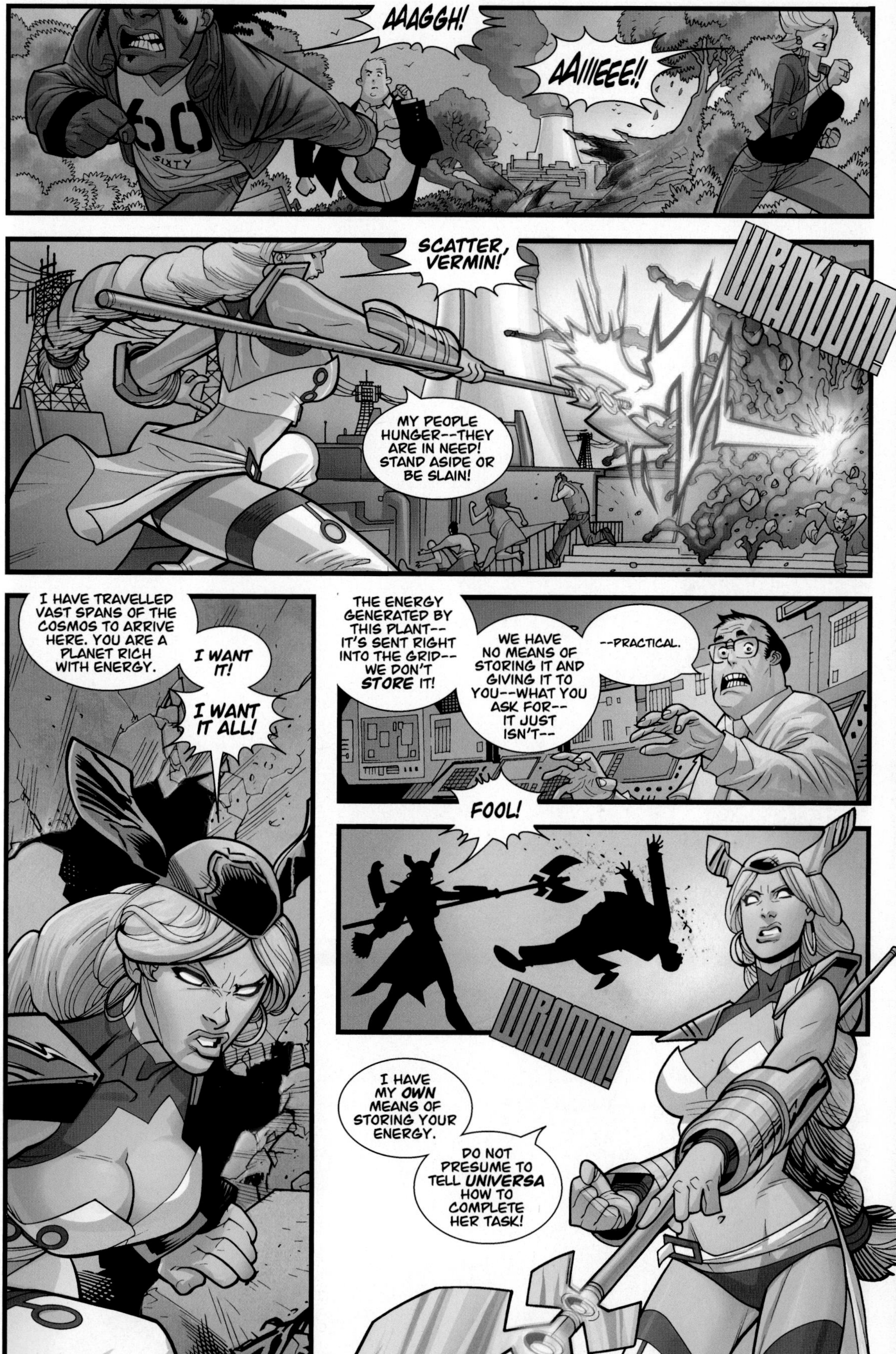
AAAGGH!
AAIIIEEE!!
SCATTER, VERMIN!
WRKOOM!
MY PEOPLE HUNGER--THEY ARE IN NEED! STAND ASIDE OR BE SLAIN!
I HAVE TRAVELLED VAST SPANS OF THE COSMOS TO ARRIVE HERE. YOU ARE A PLANET RICH WITH ENERGY.
I WANT IT!
I WANT IT ALL!
THE ENERGY GENERATED BY THIS PLANT-- IT'S SENT RIGHT INTO THE GRID-- WE DON'T STORE IT!
WE HAVE NO MEANS OF STORING IT AND GIVING IT TO YOU--WHAT YOU ASK FOR-- IT JUST ISN'T--
--PRACTICAL.
FOOL!
WRMM!
I HAVE MY OWN MEANS OF STORING YOUR ENERGY.
DO NOT PRESUME TO TELL UNIVERSA HOW TO COMPLETE HER TASK!

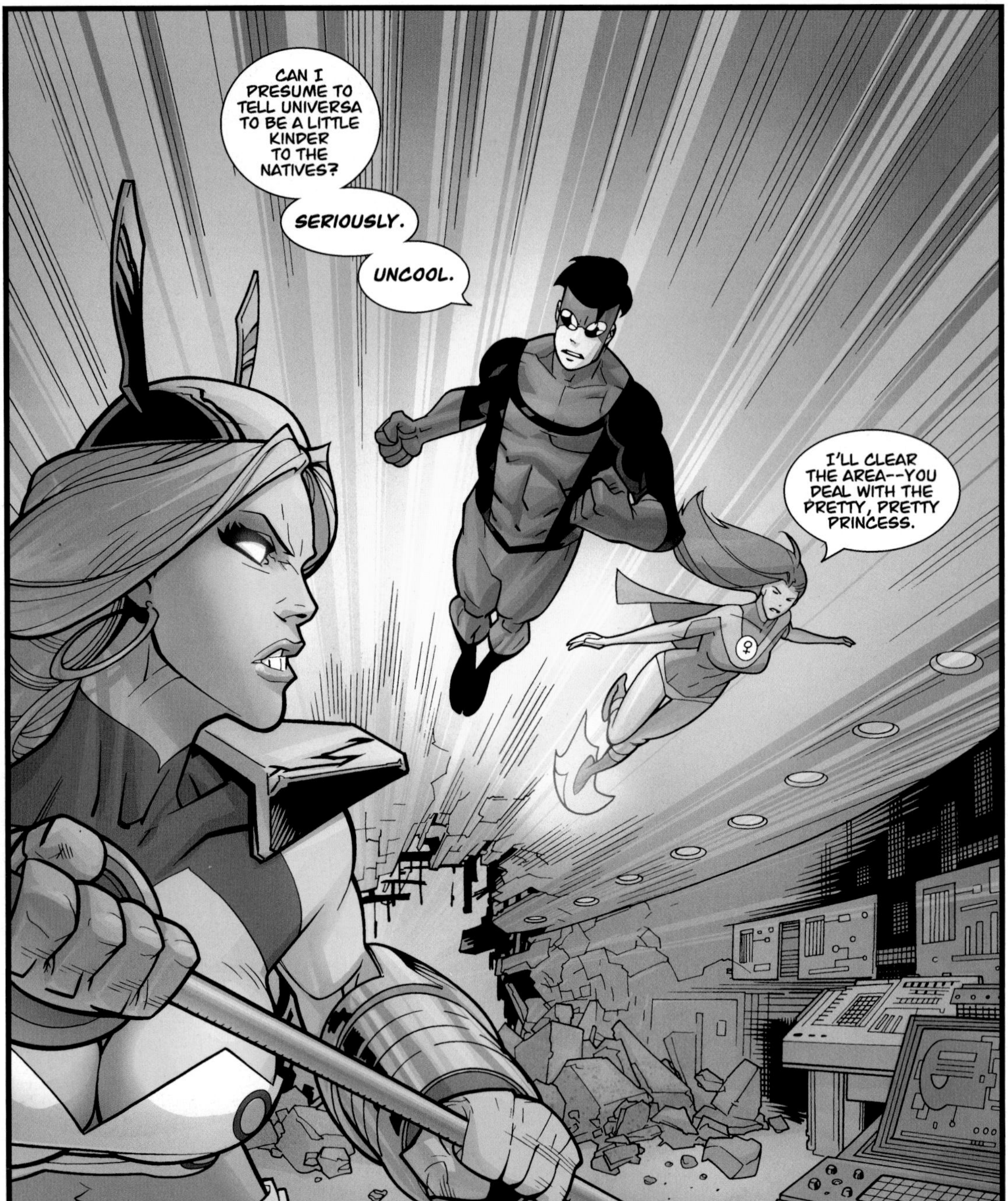
CAN I PRESUME TO TELL UNIVERSA TO BE A LITTLE KINDER TO THE NATIVES?
SERIOUSLY.
UNCOOL.
I'LL CLEAR THE AREA--YOU DEAL WITH THE PRETTY, PRETTY PRINCESS.

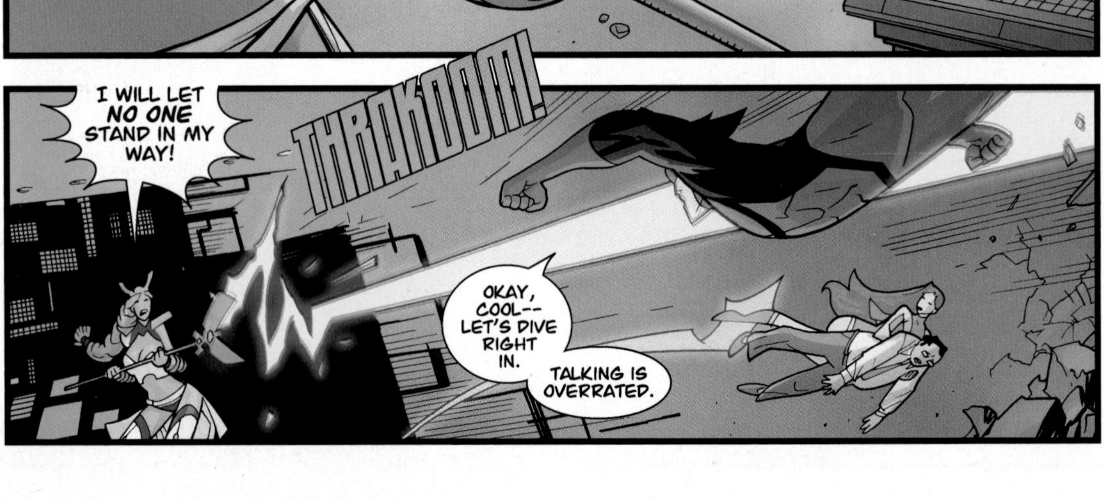
I WILL LET NO ONE STAND IN MY WAY!
THRAKOOM!
OKAY, COOL-- LET'S DIVE RIGHT IN.
TALKING IS OVERRATED.

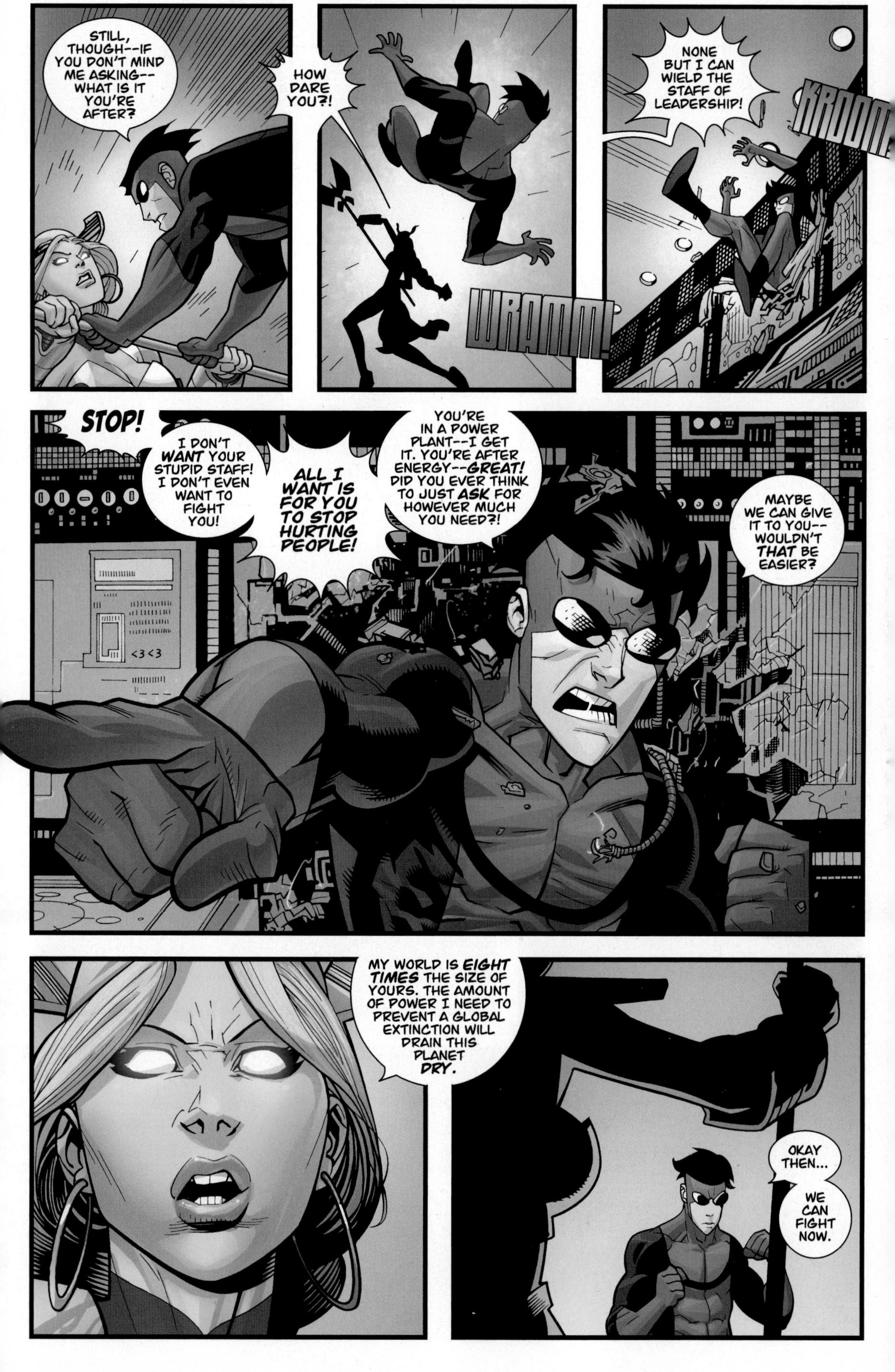
STILL, THOUGH--IF YOU DON'T MIND ME ASKING--WHAT IS IT YOU'RE AFTER?
HOW DARE YOU?!
WRAMM!
NONE BUT I CAN WIELD THE STAFF OF LEADERSHIP!
KROOM
STOP!
I DON'T WANT YOUR STUPID STAFF! I DON'T EVEN WANT TO FIGHT YOU!
ALL I WANT IS FOR YOU TO STOP HURTING PEOPLE!
YOU'RE IN A POWER PLANT--I GET IT. YOU'RE AFTER ENERGY--GREAT! DID YOU EVER THINK TO JUST ASK FOR HOWEVER MUCH YOU NEED?!
MAYBE WE CAN GIVE IT TO YOU--WOULDN'T THAT BE EASIER?
<3 <3
MY WORLD IS EIGHT TIMES THE SIZE OF YOURS. THE AMOUNT OF POWER I NEED TO PREVENT A GLOBAL EXTINCTION WILL DRAIN THIS PLANET DRY.
OKAY THEN...
WE CAN FIGHT NOW.

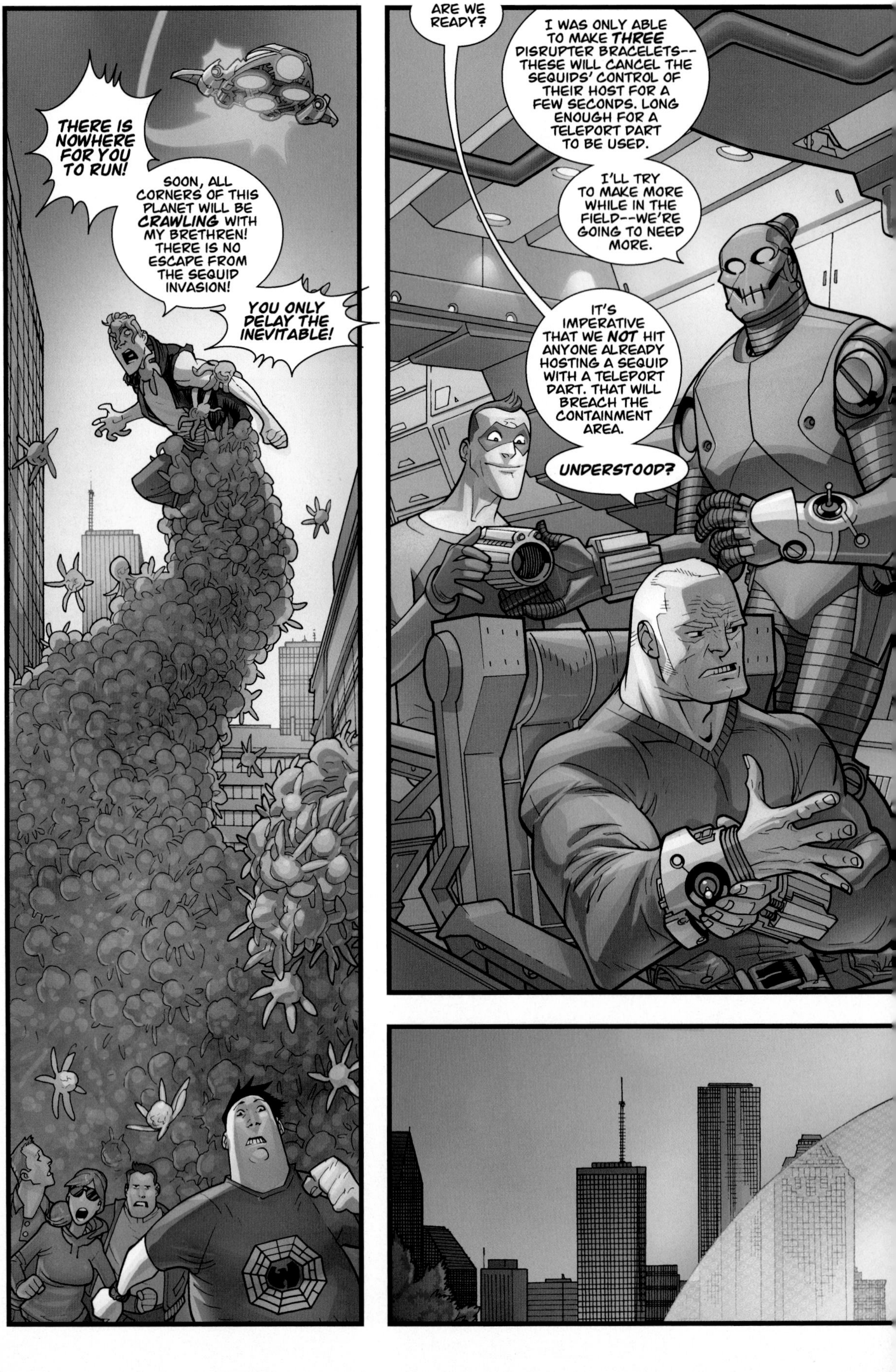
THERE IS NOWHERE FOR YOU TO RUN!
SOON, ALL CORNERS OF THIS PLANET WILL BE CRAWLING WITH MY BRETHREN! THERE IS NO ESCAPE FROM THE SEQUID INVASION!
YOU ONLY DELAY THE INEVITABLE!
ARE WE READY?
I WAS ONLY ABLE TO MAKE THREE DISRUPTER BRACELETS-- THESE WILL CANCEL THE SEQUIDS' CONTROL OF THEIR HOST FOR A FEW SECONDS. LONG ENOUGH FOR A TELEPORT DART TO BE USED.
I'LL TRY TO MAKE MORE WHILE IN THE FIELD--WE'RE GOING TO NEED MORE.
IT'S IMPERATIVE THAT WE NOT HIT ANYONE ALREADY HOSTING A SEQUID WITH A TELEPORT DART. THAT WILL BREACH THE CONTAINMENT AREA.
UNDERSTOOD?

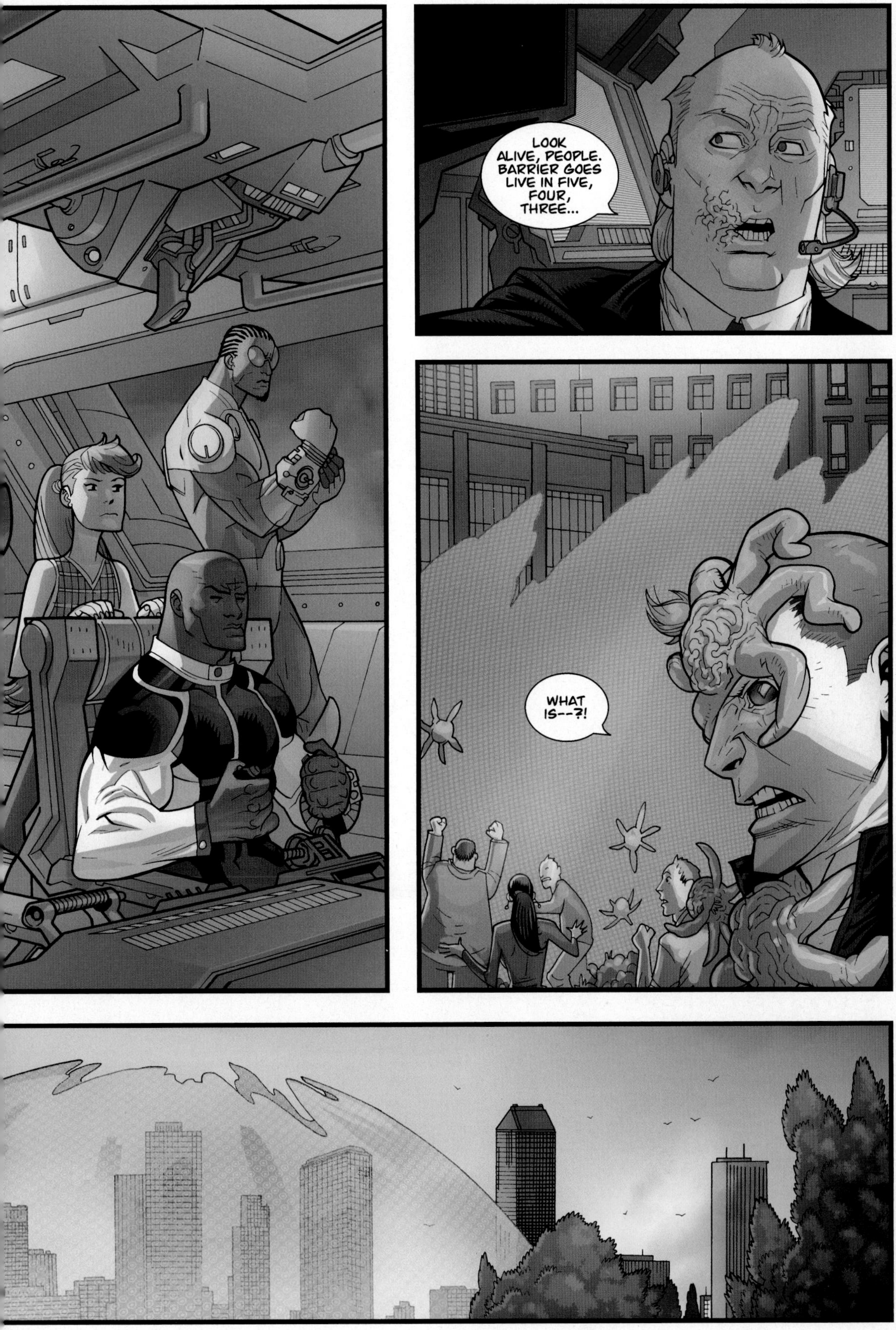
LOOK ALIVE, PEOPLE. BARRIER GOES LIVE IN FIVE, FOUR, THREE...
WHAT IS--?!

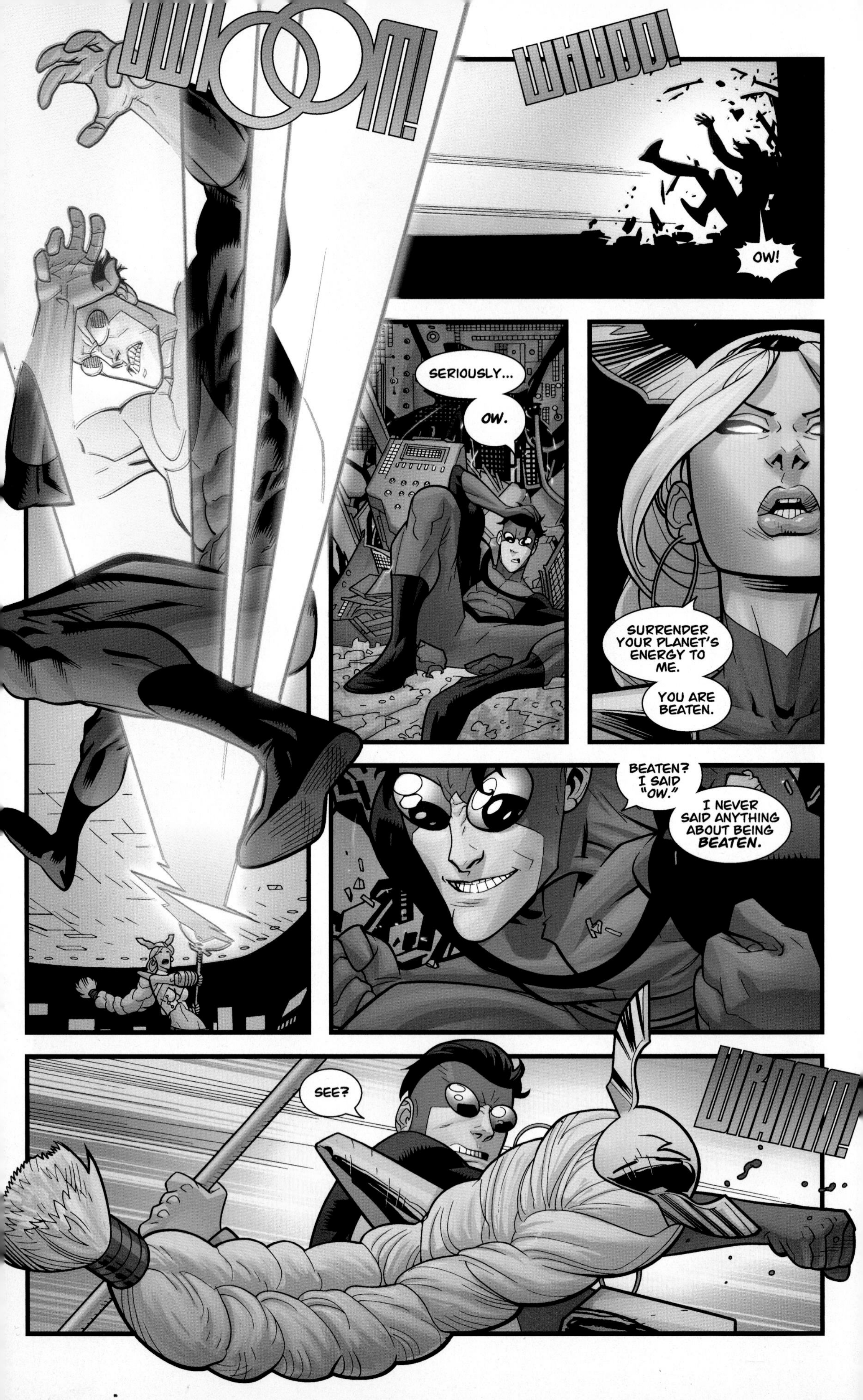
DWOOOM!
WHUDD!
OW!
SERIOUSLY...
OW.
SURRENDER YOUR PLANET'S ENERGY TO ME.
YOU ARE BEATEN.
BEATEN? I SAID "OW."
I NEVER SAID ANYTHING ABOUT BEING BEATEN.
SEE?
WRAMM!

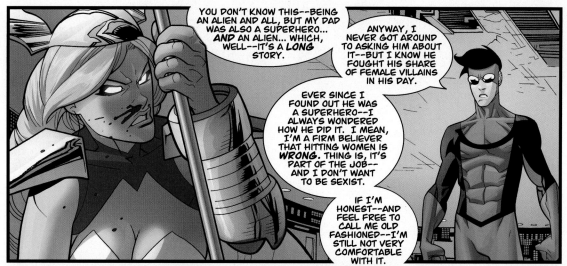

YOU DON'T KNOW THIS--BEING AN ALIEN AND ALL, BUT MY DAD WAS ALSO A SUPERHERO... *AND* AN ALIEN... WHICH, WELL--IT'S A *LONG* STORY.

ANYWAY, I NEVER GOT AROUND TO ASKING HIM ABOUT IT--BUT I KNOW HE FOUGHT HIS SHARE OF FEMALE VILLAINS IN HIS DAY.

EVER SINCE I FOUND OUT HE WAS A SUPERHERO--I ALWAYS WONDERED HOW HE DID IT. I MEAN, I'M A FIRM BELIEVER THAT HITTING WOMEN IS *WRONG.* THING IS, IT'S PART OF THE JOB-- AND I DON'T WANT TO BE SEXIST.

IF I'M HONEST--AND FEEL FREE TO CALL ME OLD FASHIONED--I'M STILL NOT VERY COMFORTABLE WITH IT.

VTOOM!

SILENCE!

OW, AGAIN!

GETTING MORE COMFORTABLE WITH IT...

...AND WHAT THE HELL *IS* THAT THING?

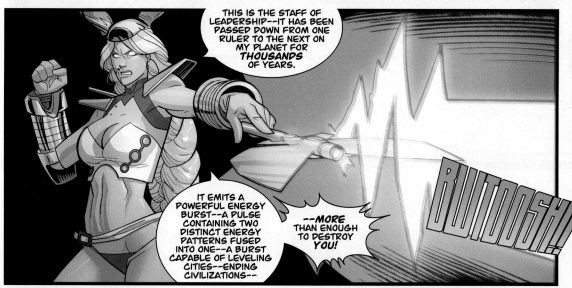

THIS IS THE STAFF OF LEADERSHIP--IT HAS BEEN PASSED DOWN FROM ONE RULER TO THE NEXT ON MY PLANET FOR *THOUSANDS* OF YEARS.

IT EMITS A POWERFUL ENERGY BURST--A PULSE CONTAINING TWO DISTINCT ENERGY PATTERNS FUSED INTO ONE--A BURST CAPABLE OF LEVELING CITIES--ENDING CIVILIZATIONS--

--MORE THAN ENOUGH TO DESTROY *YOU!*

BWIDOSH!

NNNGGH!

--CAN'T!

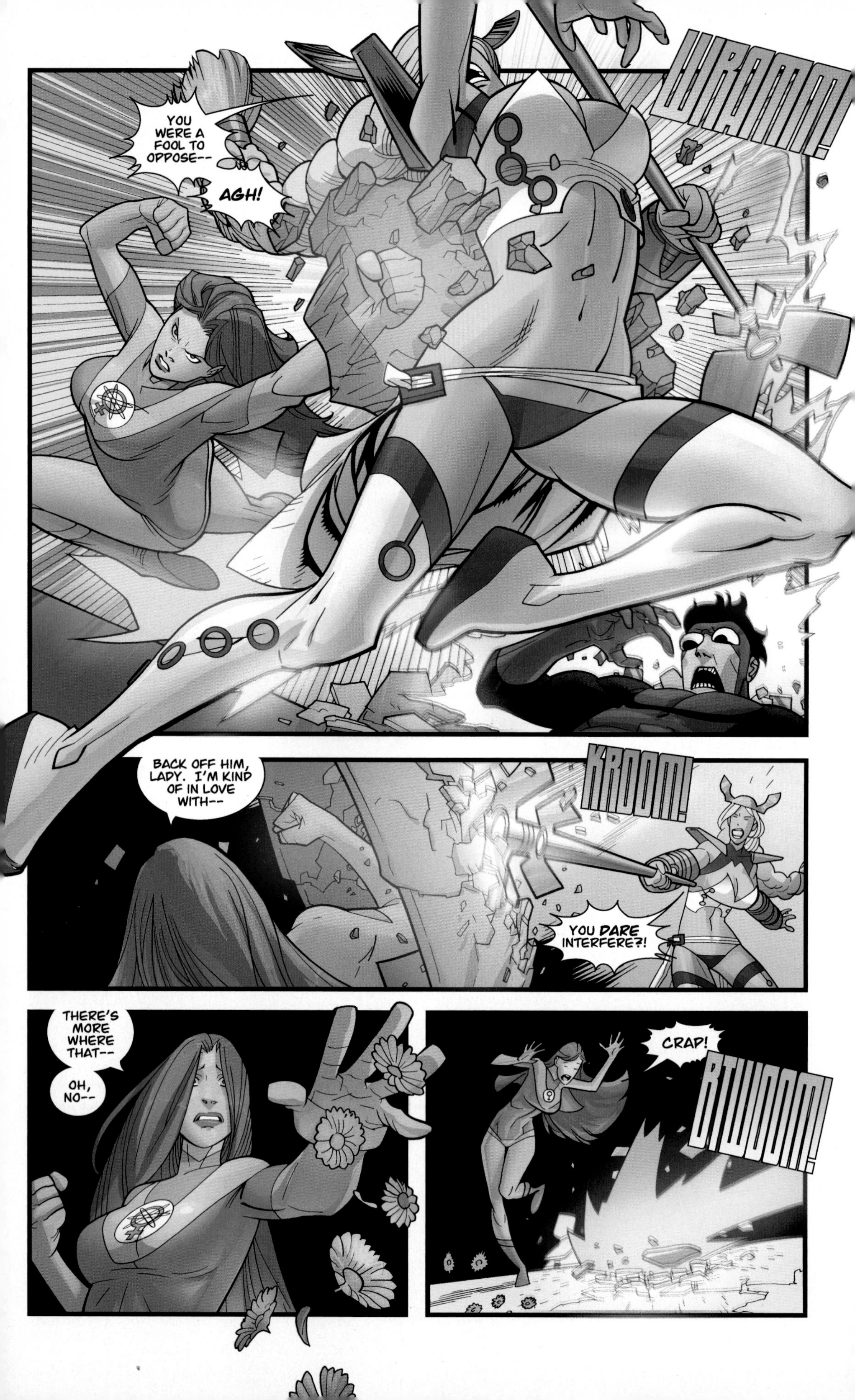
WROOM!
YOU WERE A FOOL TO OPPOSE--
AGH!
BACK OFF HIM, LADY. I'M KIND OF IN LOVE WITH--
KROOM!
YOU DARE INTERFERE?!
THERE'S MORE WHERE THAT--
OH, NO--
CRAP!
BTWOOM!

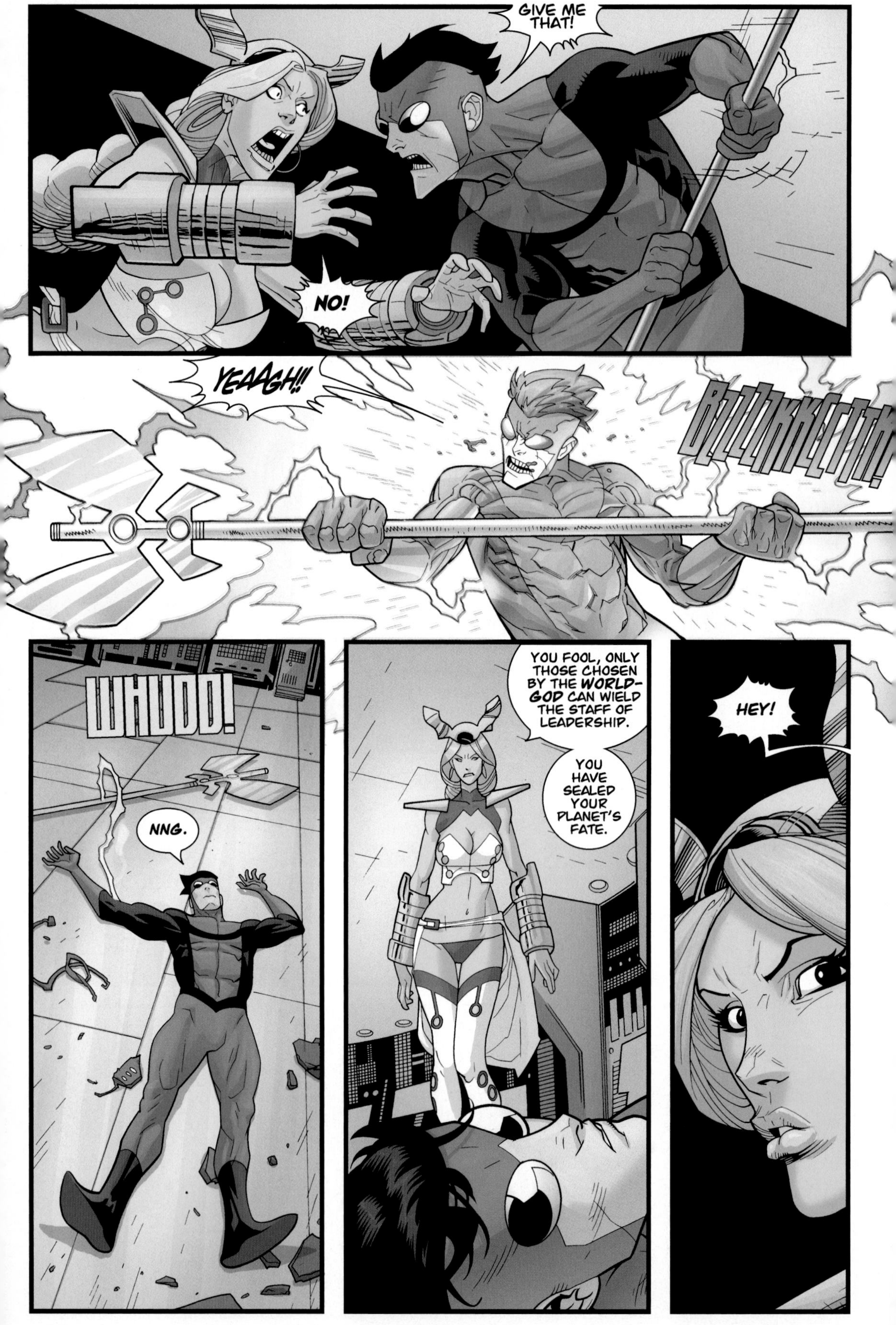
GIVE ME THAT!
NO!
YEAAAGH!!
BZZZKKKCTTH!
WHUDD!
NNG.
YOU FOOL, ONLY THOSE CHOSEN BY THE WORLD-GOD CAN WIELD THE STAFF OF LEADERSHIP.
YOU HAVE SEALED YOUR PLANET'S FATE.
HEY!

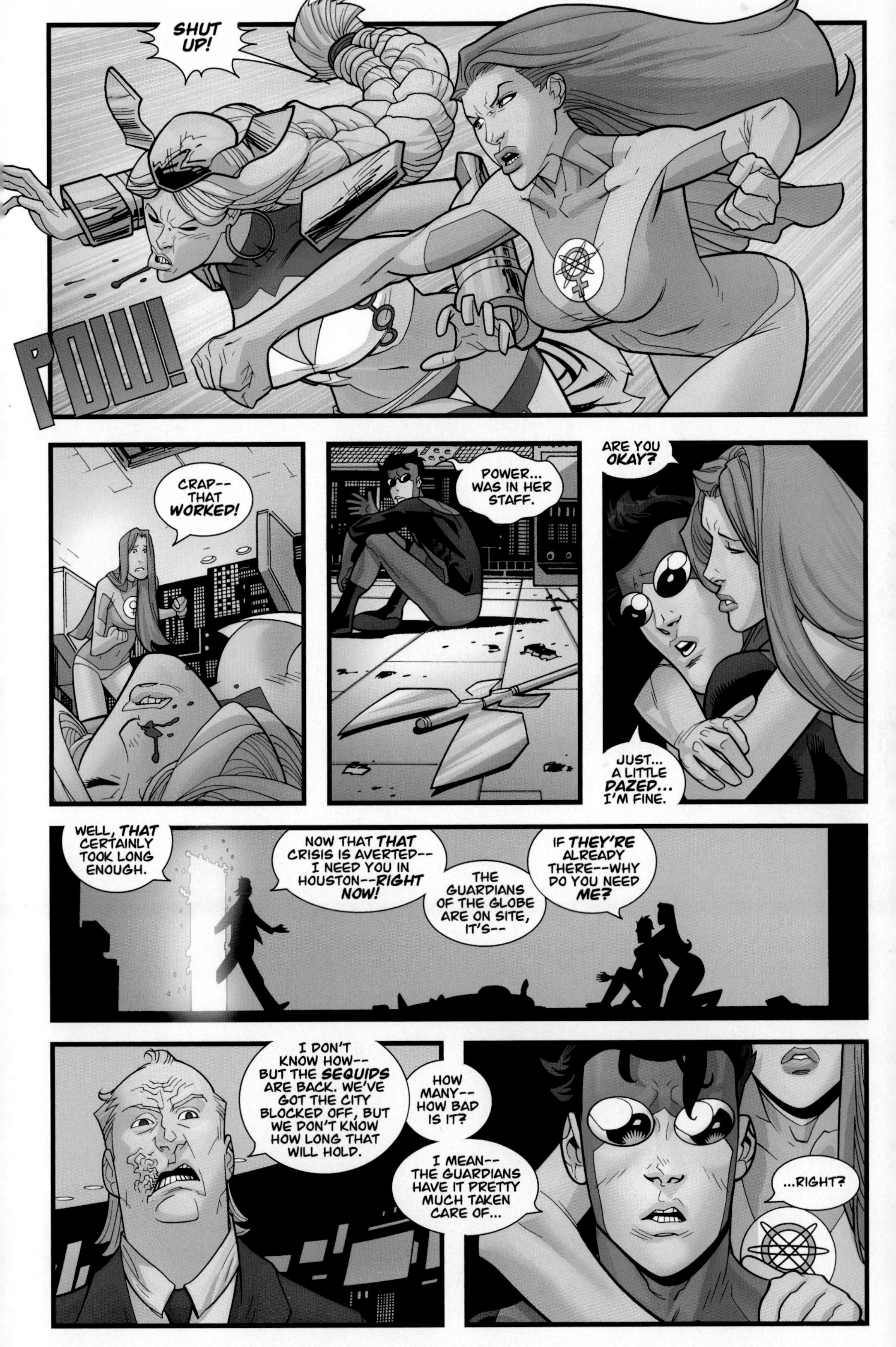
SHUT UP!
POW!
CRAP-- THAT WORKED!
POWER... WAS IN HER STAFF.
ARE YOU OKAY?
JUST... A LITTLE DAZED... I'M FINE.
WELL, THAT CERTAINLY TOOK LONG ENOUGH.
NOW THAT THAT CRISIS IS AVERTED-- I NEED YOU IN HOUSTON--RIGHT NOW!
THE GUARDIANS OF THE GLOBE ARE ON SITE, IT'S--
IF THEY'RE ALREADY THERE--WHY DO YOU NEED ME?
I DON'T KNOW HOW-- BUT THE SEQUIDS ARE BACK. WE'VE GOT THE CITY BLOCKED OFF, BUT WE DON'T KNOW HOW LONG THAT WILL HOLD.
HOW MANY-- HOW BAD IS IT?
I MEAN-- THE GUARDIANS HAVE IT PRETTY MUCH TAKEN CARE OF...
...RIGHT?

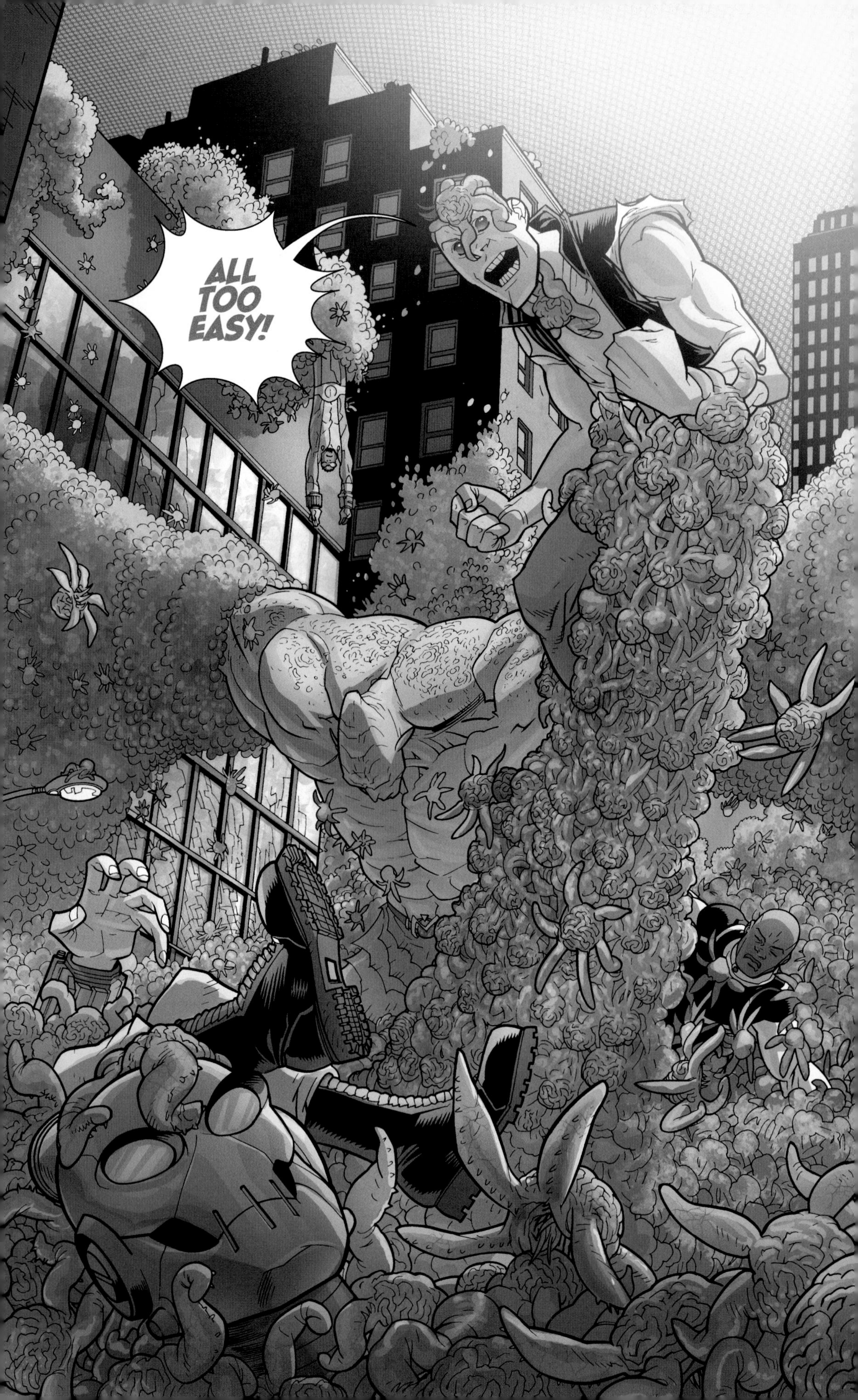
ALL TOO EASY!

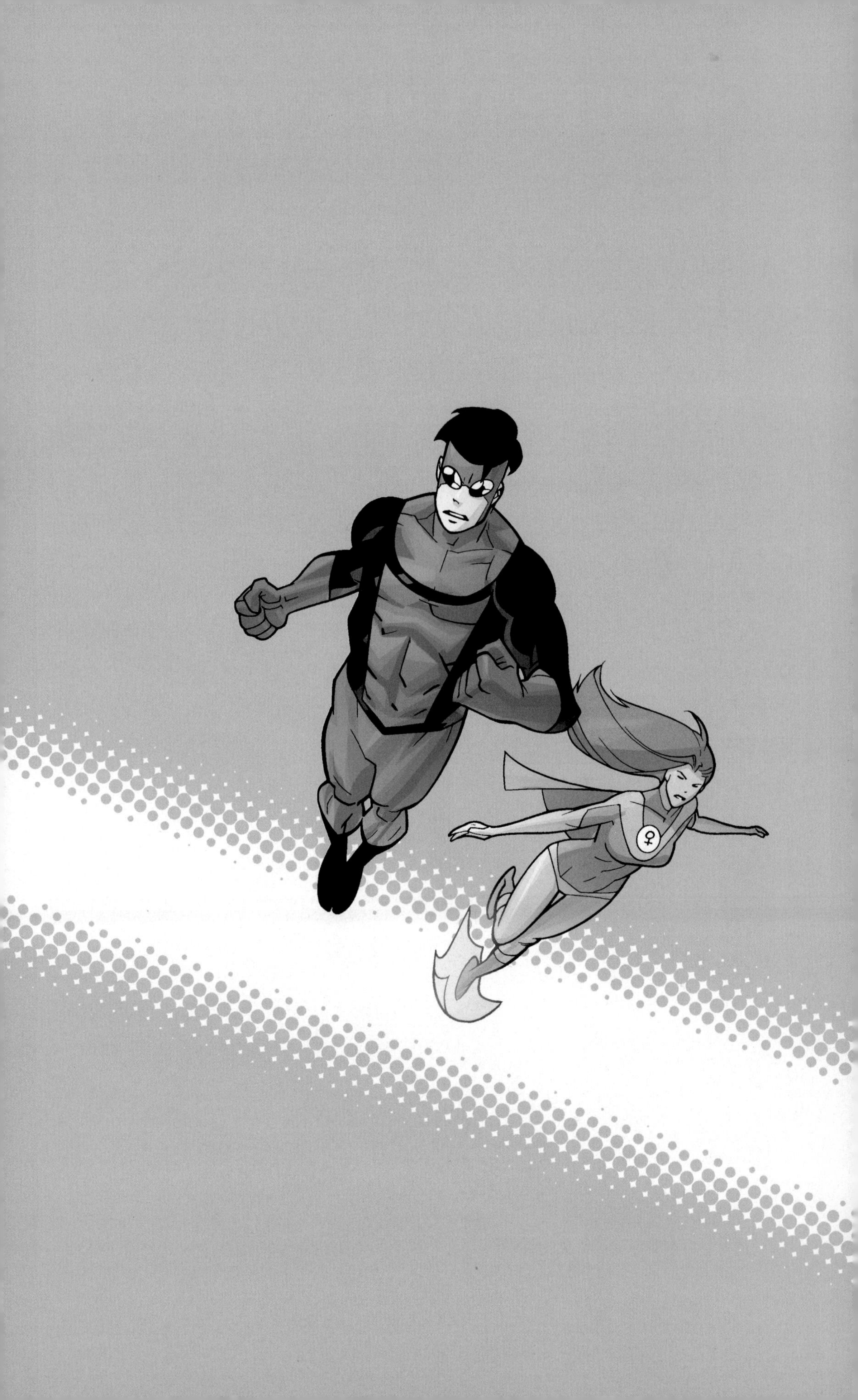

# CHAPTER FIVE

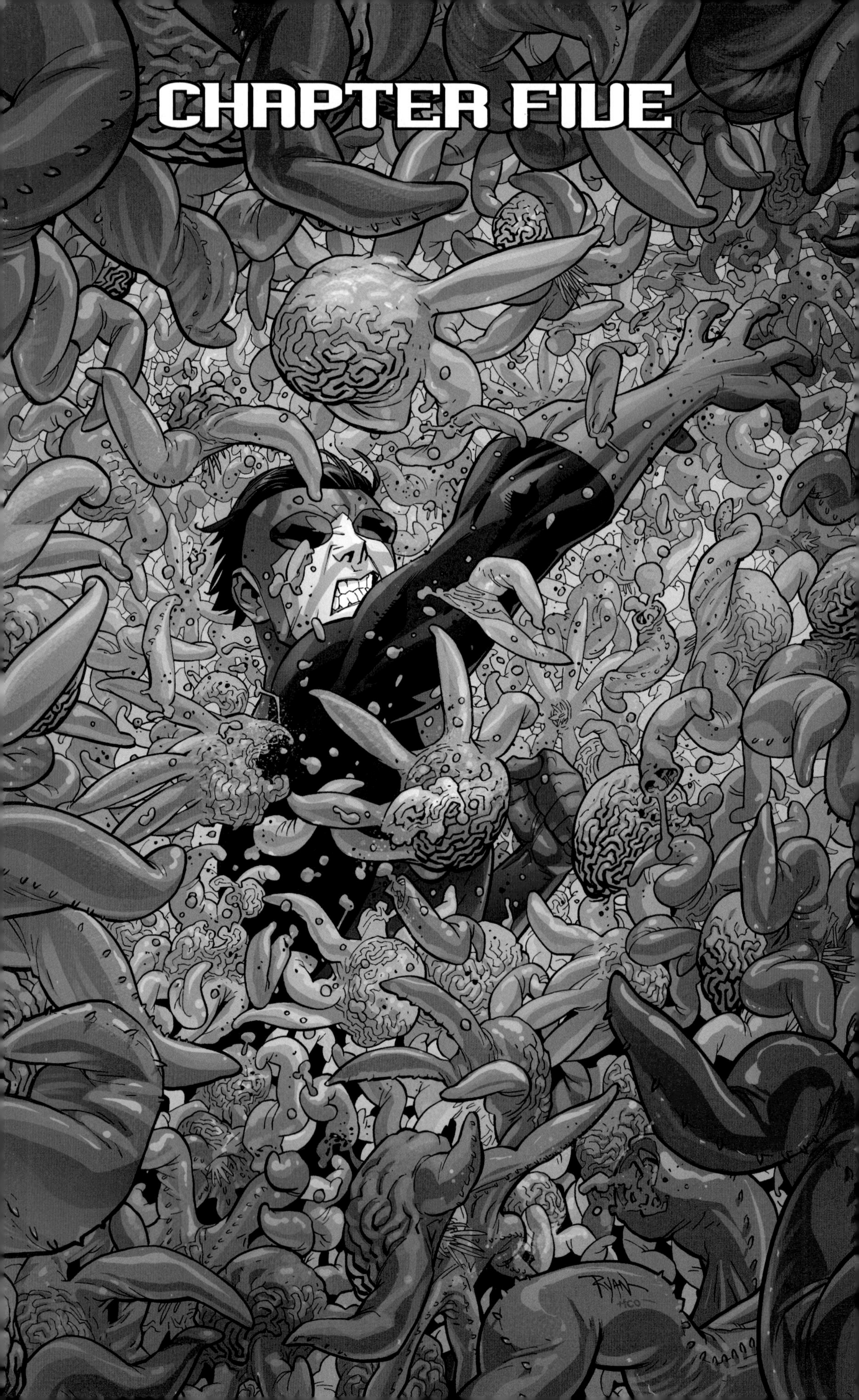

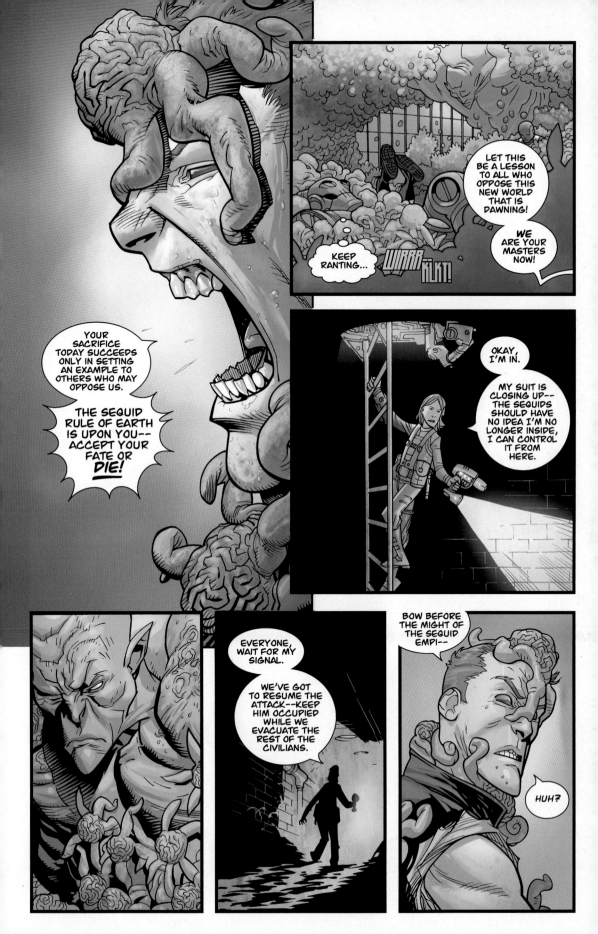

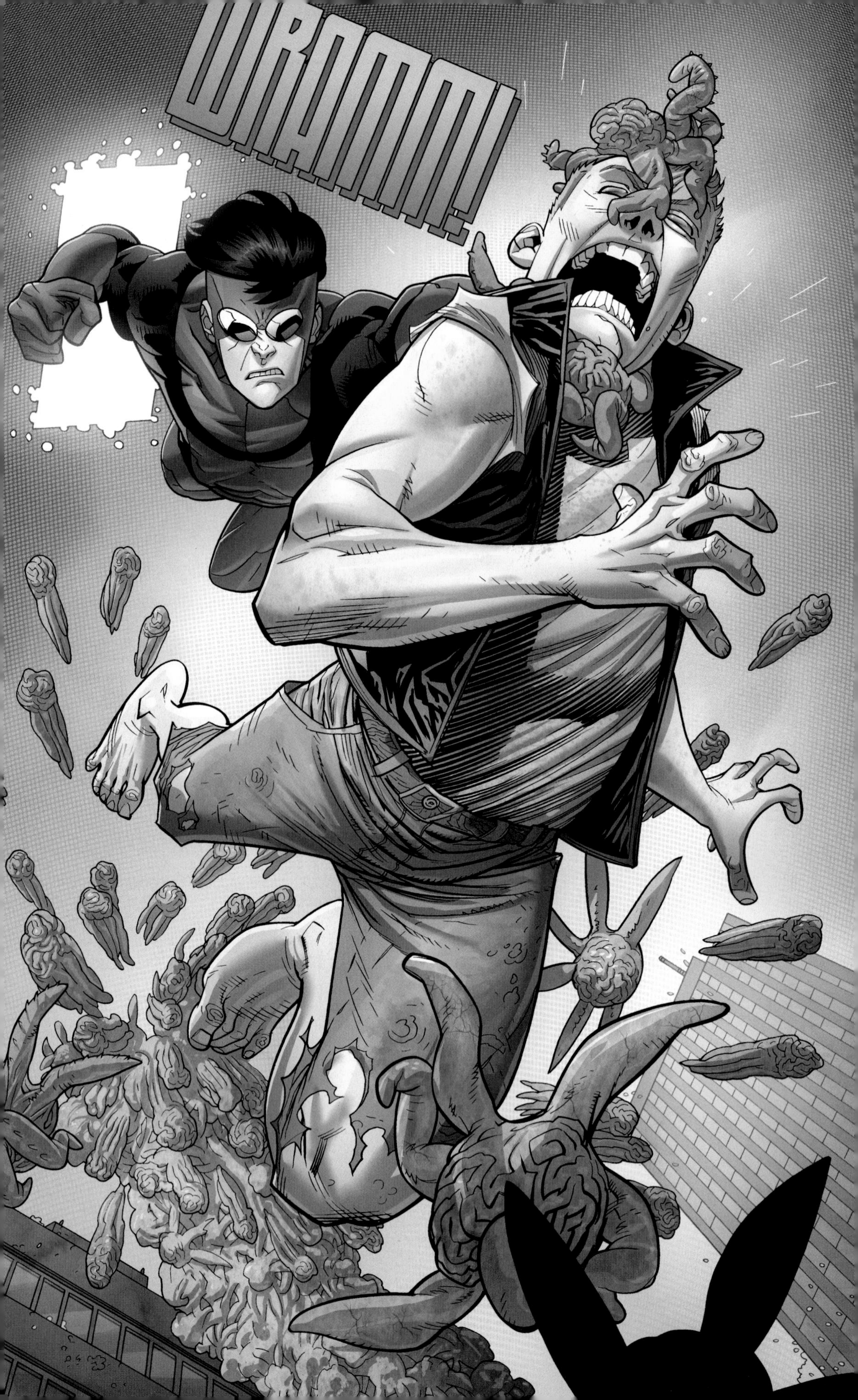
WRAMM!!

HOW?!
HOW IN THE HECK ARE YOU BACK?!
CHOOM!
DID YOU REALLY THINK THAT WOULD HURT US?! IS THAT THE EXTENT OF YOUR PLAN?
A TACKLE?!
PATHETIC.
I WAS JUST TRYING TO GET YOUR ATTENTION.
THAT PLAN WORKED.
TO CONTINUE-- HOW ARE YOU HERE?! YOU WERE LEFT WITH THE MARTIANS, YOU HAD NO HOST-- THEY TOOK YOU BACK TO MARS.
RIGHT? I MEAN, OBVIOUSLY NOT... BUT WHAT HAPPENED? DID THE MARTIANS SEND YOU HERE? WAS IT AN ATTACK?
THIS ONE, THE BODY YOU SEE BEFORE YOU-- OUR ORIGINAL HOST. WE NEVER LEFT IT. YOU BROUGHT US HERE.

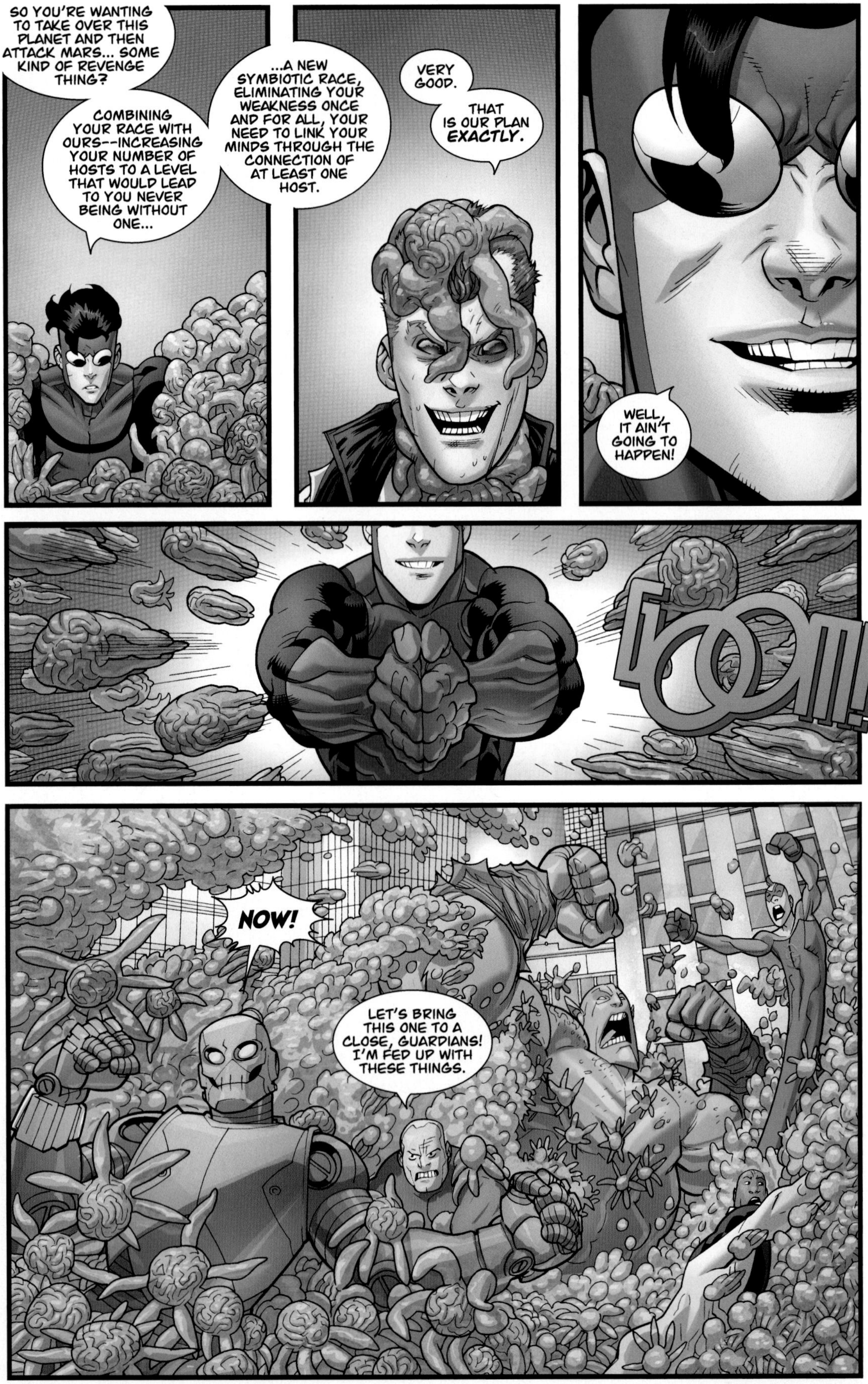
SO YOU'RE WANTING TO TAKE OVER THIS PLANET AND THEN ATTACK MARS... SOME KIND OF REVENGE THING?
COMBINING YOUR RACE WITH OURS--INCREASING YOUR NUMBER OF HOSTS TO A LEVEL THAT WOULD LEAD TO YOU NEVER BEING WITHOUT ONE...
...A NEW SYMBIOTIC RACE, ELIMINATING YOUR WEAKNESS ONCE AND FOR ALL, YOUR NEED TO LINK YOUR MINDS THROUGH THE CONNECTION OF AT LEAST ONE HOST.
VERY GOOD.
THAT IS OUR PLAN EXACTLY.
WELL, IT AIN'T GOING TO HAPPEN!
BOOM!
NOW!
LET'S BRING THIS ONE TO A CLOSE, GUARDIANS! I'M FED UP WITH THESE THINGS.

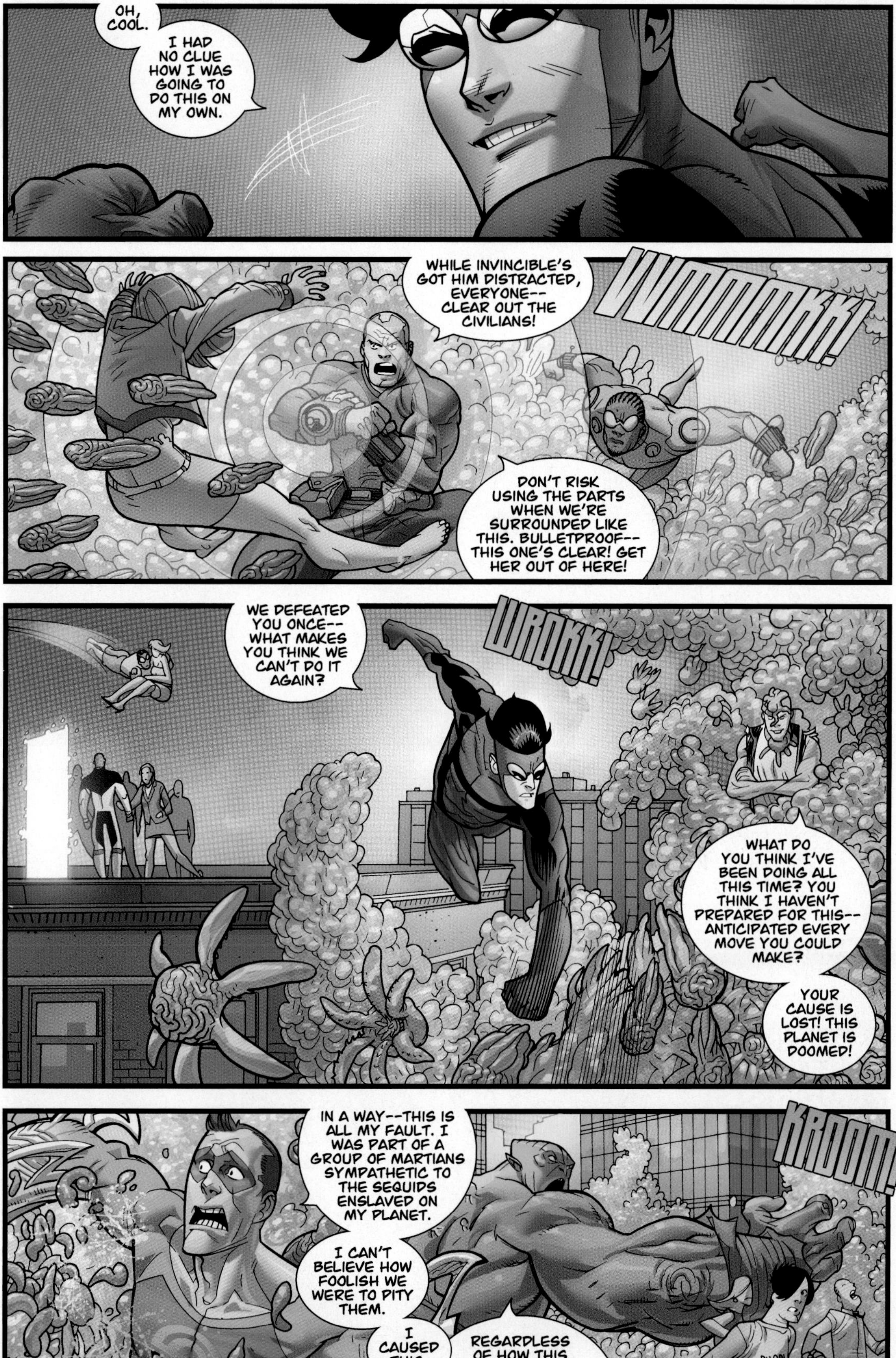

OH, COOL.
I HAD NO CLUE HOW I WAS GOING TO DO THIS ON MY OWN.
WHILE INVINCIBLE'S GOT HIM DISTRACTED, EVERYONE-- CLEAR OUT THE CIVILIANS!
VVMMMMKK!
DON'T RISK USING THE DARTS WHEN WE'RE SURROUNDED LIKE THIS. BULLETPROOF-- THIS ONE'S CLEAR! GET HER OUT OF HERE!
WE DEFEATED YOU ONCE-- WHAT MAKES YOU THINK WE CAN'T DO IT AGAIN?
WROKK!
WHAT DO YOU THINK I'VE BEEN DOING ALL THIS TIME? YOU THINK I HAVEN'T PREPARED FOR THIS-- ANTICIPATED EVERY MOVE YOU COULD MAKE?
YOUR CAUSE IS LOST! THIS PLANET IS DOOMED!
IN A WAY--THIS IS ALL MY FAULT. I WAS PART OF A GROUP OF MARTIANS SYMPATHETIC TO THE SEQUIDS ENSLAVED ON MY PLANET.
KROOM!
I CAN'T BELIEVE HOW FOOLISH WE WERE TO PITY THEM.
I CAUSED THIS.
REGARDLESS OF HOW THIS SHAKES DOWN-- YOU'RE PROBABLY GOING TO WANT TO START KEEPING THAT TO YOURSELF.

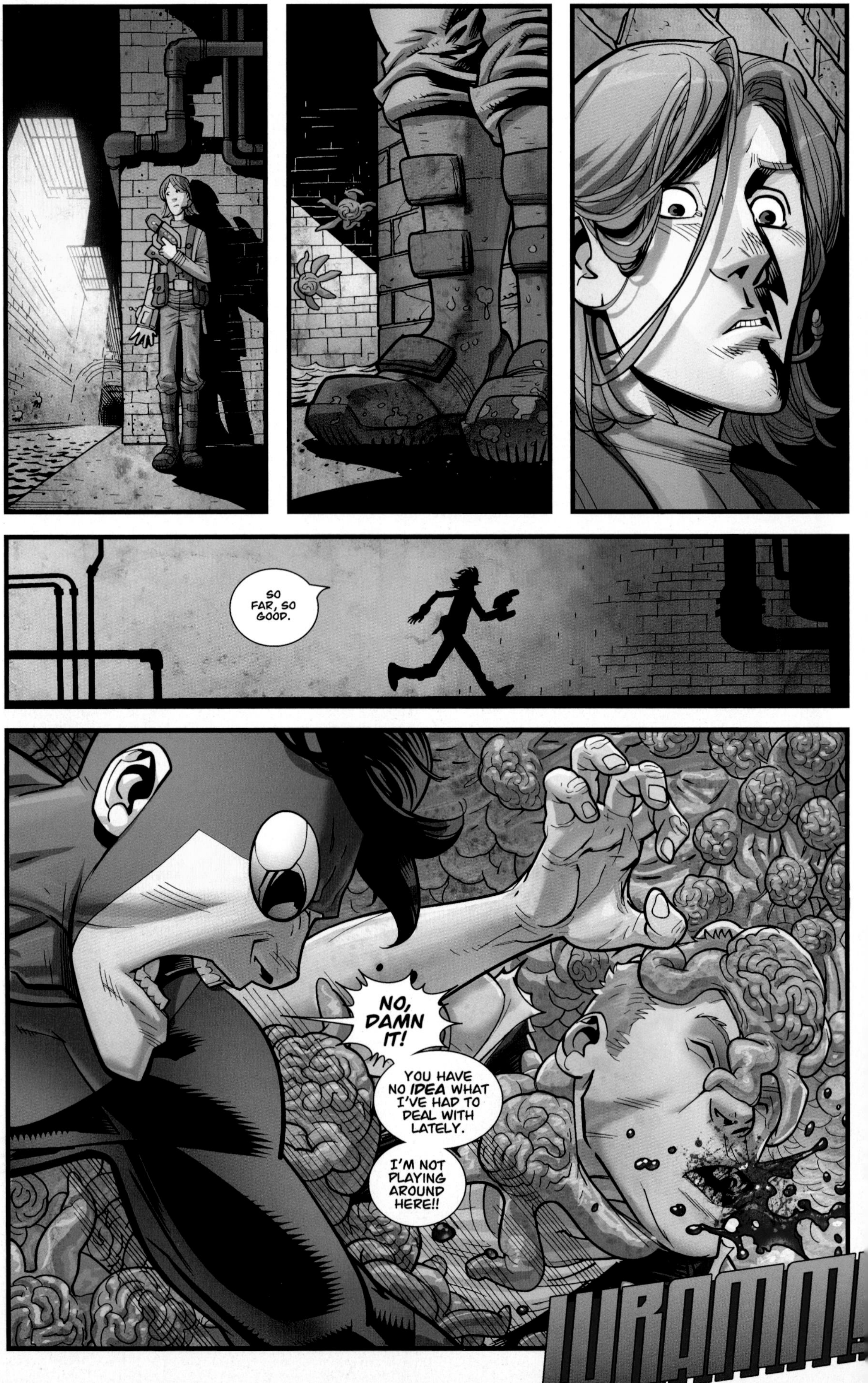
SO FAR, SO GOOD.
NO, DAMN IT!
YOU HAVE NO IDEA WHAT I'VE HAD TO DEAL WITH LATELY.
I'M NOT PLAYING AROUND HERE!!
WRAMM!

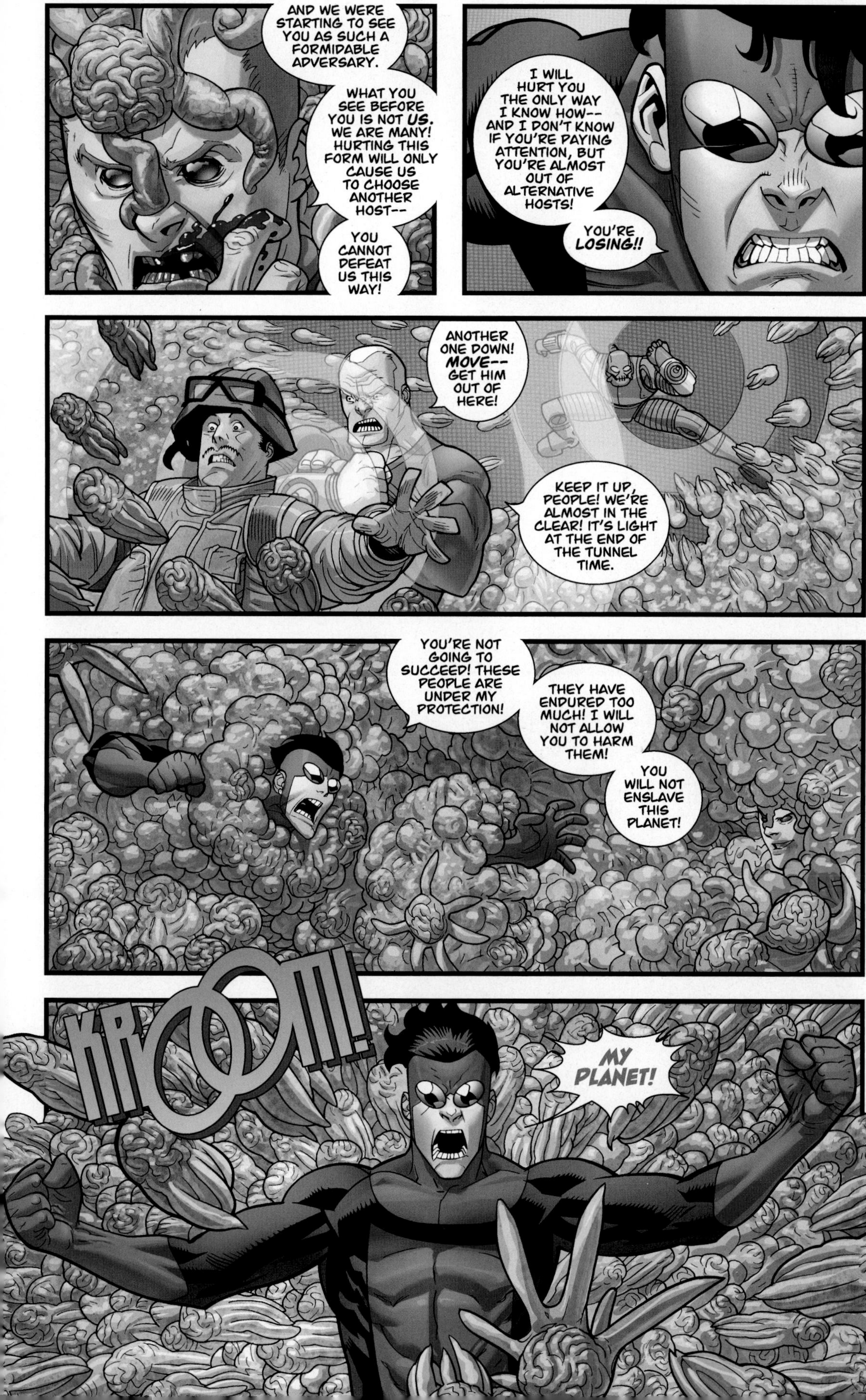
AND WE WERE STARTING TO SEE YOU AS SUCH A FORMIDABLE ADVERSARY.
WHAT YOU SEE BEFORE YOU IS NOT US. WE ARE MANY! HURTING THIS FORM WILL ONLY CAUSE US TO CHOOSE ANOTHER HOST--
YOU CANNOT DEFEAT US THIS WAY!
I WILL HURT YOU THE ONLY WAY I KNOW HOW-- AND I DON'T KNOW IF YOU'RE PAYING ATTENTION, BUT YOU'RE ALMOST OUT OF ALTERNATIVE HOSTS!
YOU'RE LOSING!!
ANOTHER ONE DOWN! MOVE-- GET HIM OUT OF HERE!
KEEP IT UP, PEOPLE! WE'RE ALMOST IN THE CLEAR! IT'S LIGHT AT THE END OF THE TUNNEL TIME.
YOU'RE NOT GOING TO SUCCEED! THESE PEOPLE ARE UNDER MY PROTECTION!
THEY HAVE ENDURED TOO MUCH! I WILL NOT ALLOW YOU TO HARM THEM!
YOU WILL NOT ENSLAVE THIS PLANET!
KROOM!
MY PLANET!

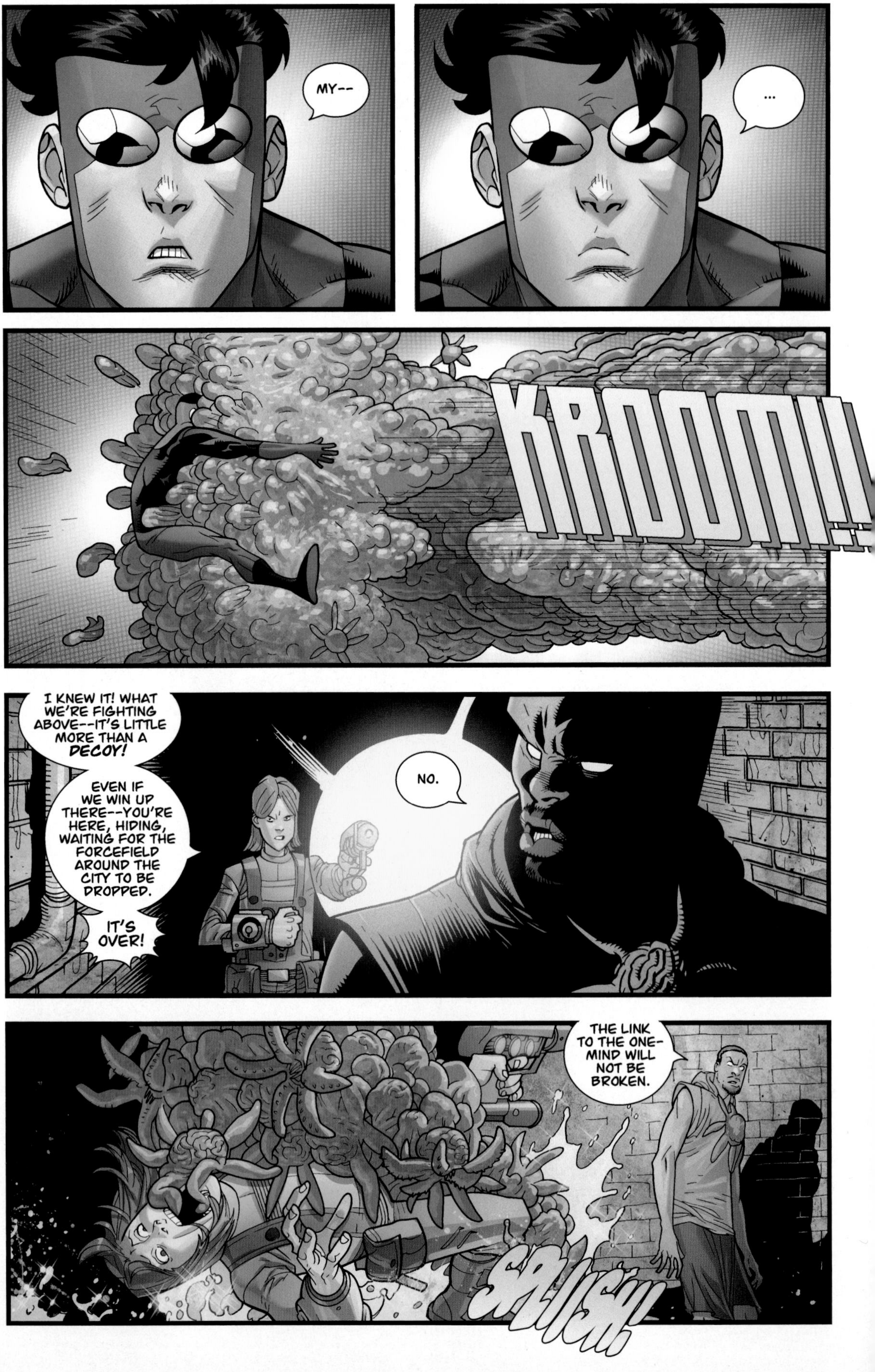
MY--
...
KROOM!!!
I KNEW IT! WHAT WE'RE FIGHTING ABOVE--IT'S LITTLE MORE THAN A DECOY!
EVEN IF WE WIN UP THERE--YOU'RE HERE, HIDING, WAITING FOR THE FORCEFIELD AROUND THE CITY TO BE DROPPED.
IT'S OVER!
NO.
THE LINK TO THE ONE-MIND WILL NOT BE BROKEN.
SPLISH!

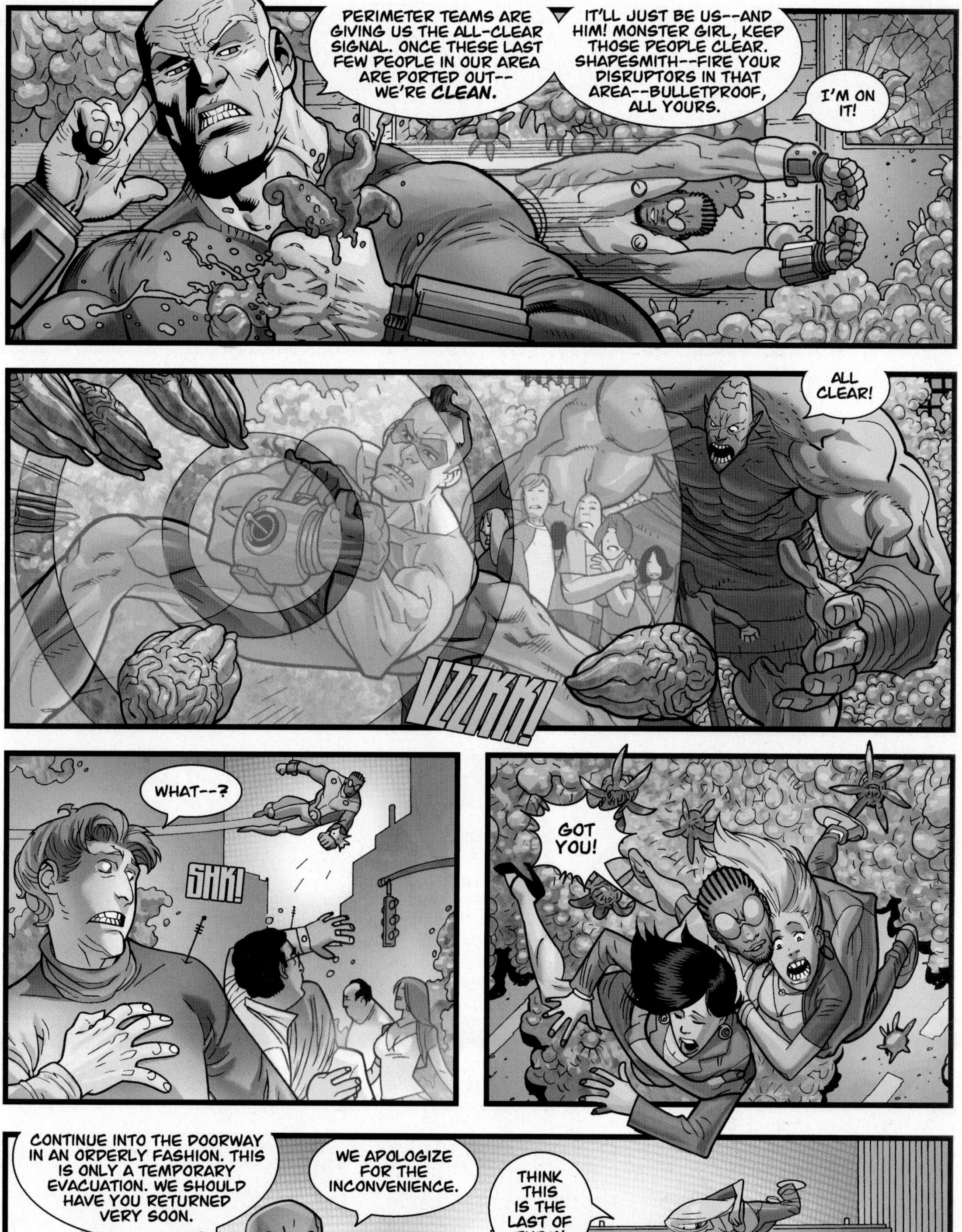

PERIMETER TEAMS ARE GIVING US THE ALL-CLEAR SIGNAL. ONCE THESE LAST FEW PEOPLE IN OUR AREA ARE PORTED OUT-- WE'RE CLEAN.
IT'LL JUST BE US--AND HIM! MONSTER GIRL, KEEP THOSE PEOPLE CLEAR. SHAPESMITH--FIRE YOUR DISRUPTORS IN THAT AREA--BULLETPROOF, ALL YOURS.
I'M ON IT!
ALL CLEAR!
VZZKK!
WHAT--?
SHK!
GOT YOU!
CONTINUE INTO THE DOORWAY IN AN ORDERLY FASHION. THIS IS ONLY A TEMPORARY EVACUATION. WE SHOULD HAVE YOU RETURNED VERY SOON.
WE APOLOGIZE FOR THE INCONVENIENCE.
THINK THIS IS THE LAST OF THEM!

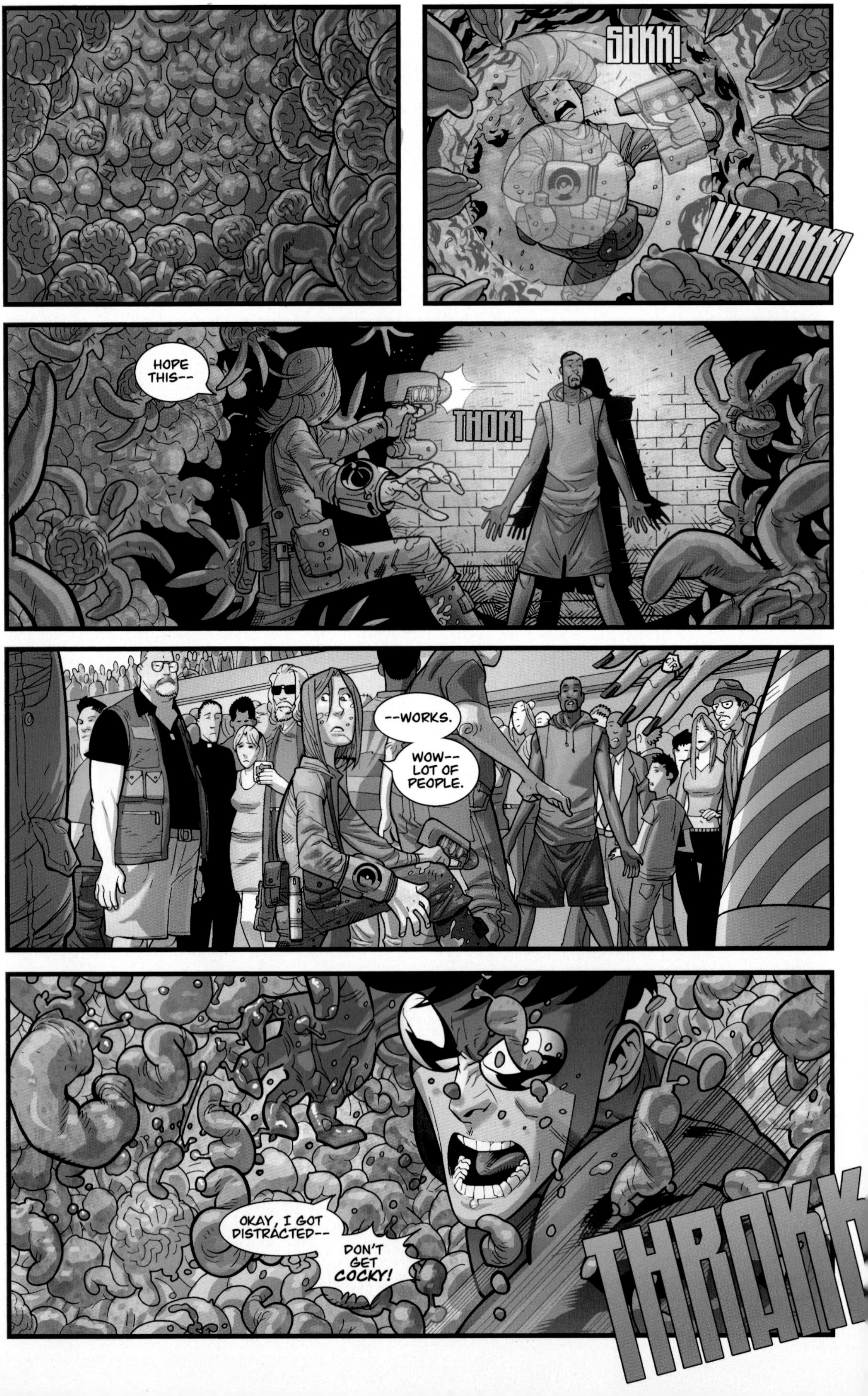
SHKK!
VZZZKKK!
HOPE THIS--
THOK!
--WORKS.
WOW-- LOT OF PEOPLE.
OKAY, I GOT DISTRACTED--
DON'T GET COCKY!
THRAKK

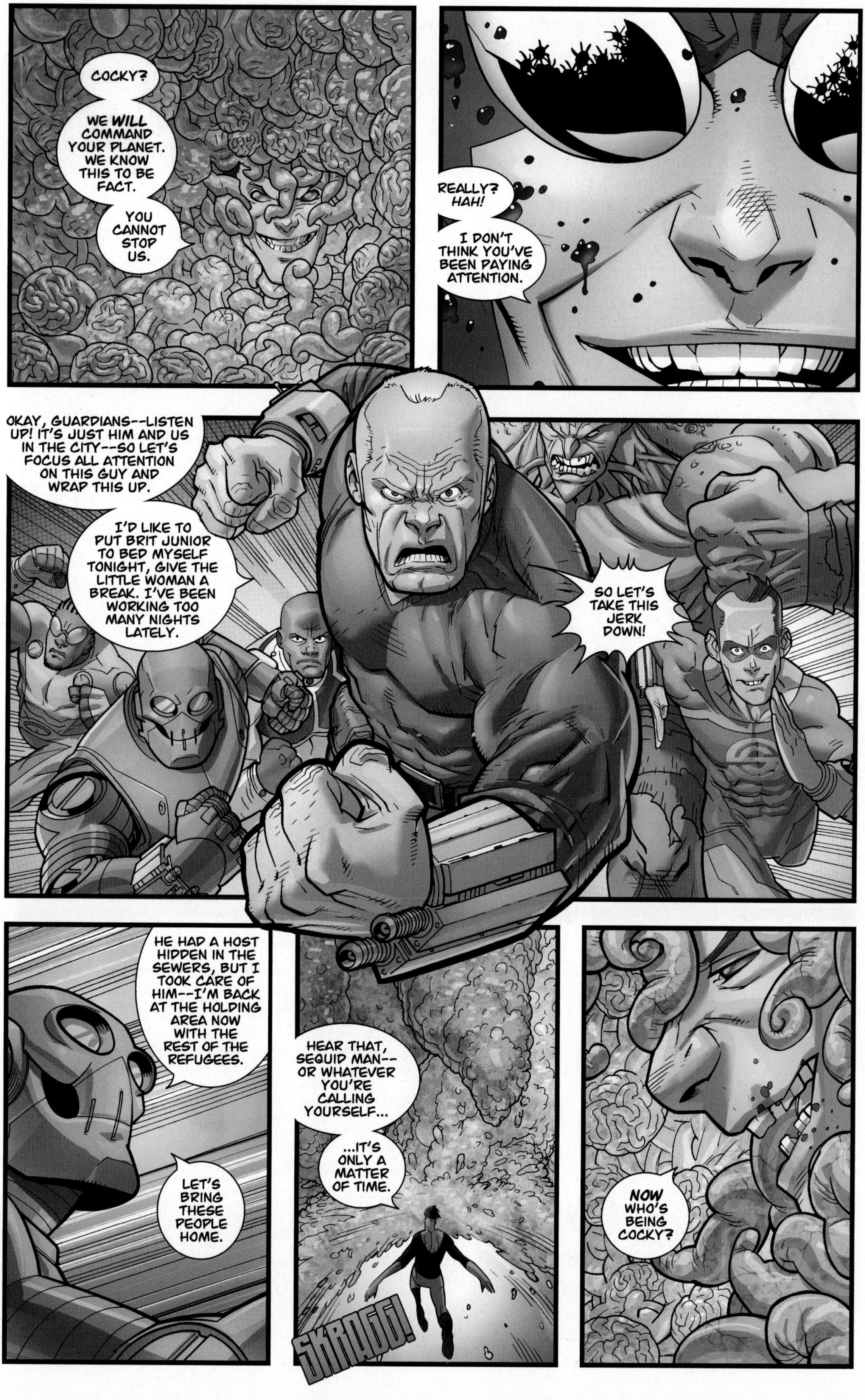
COCKY?
WE WILL COMMAND YOUR PLANET. WE KNOW THIS TO BE FACT.
YOU CANNOT STOP US.
REALLY? HAH!
I DON'T THINK YOU'VE BEEN PAYING ATTENTION.
OKAY, GUARDIANS--LISTEN UP! IT'S JUST HIM AND US IN THE CITY--SO LET'S FOCUS ALL ATTENTION ON THIS GUY AND WRAP THIS UP.
I'D LIKE TO PUT BRIT JUNIOR TO BED MYSELF TONIGHT, GIVE THE LITTLE WOMAN A BREAK. I'VE BEEN WORKING TOO MANY NIGHTS LATELY.
SO LET'S TAKE THIS JERK DOWN!
HE HAD A HOST HIDDEN IN THE SEWERS, BUT I TOOK CARE OF HIM--I'M BACK AT THE HOLDING AREA NOW WITH THE REST OF THE REFUGEES.
LET'S BRING THESE PEOPLE HOME.
HEAR THAT, SEQUID MAN--OR WHATEVER YOU'RE CALLING YOURSELF...
...IT'S ONLY A MATTER OF TIME.
SKRAGG!
NOW WHO'S BEING COCKY?

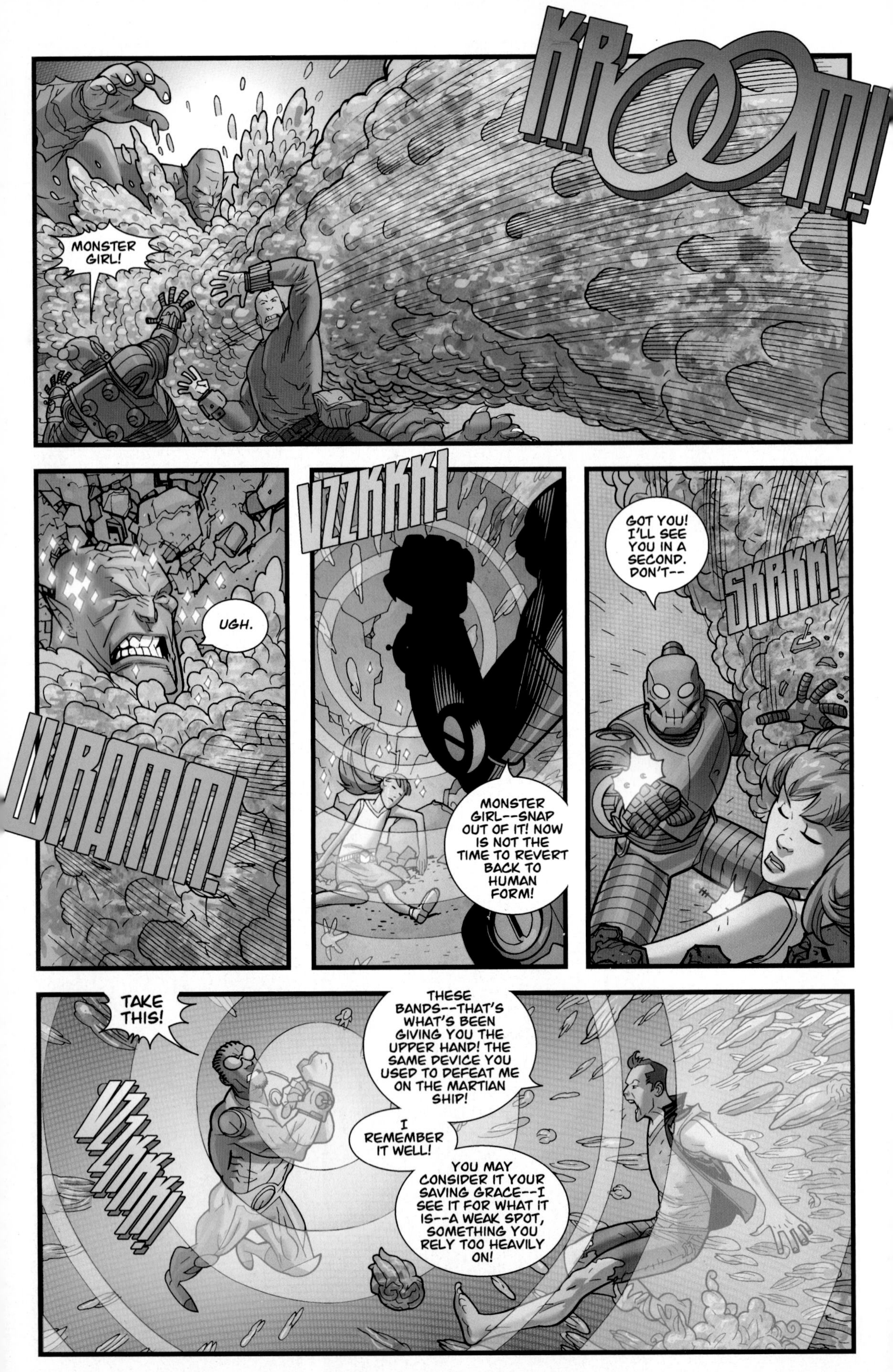
KROOM!!
MONSTER GIRL!
UGH.
WROMM!
VZZKKK!
MONSTER GIRL--SNAP OUT OF IT! NOW IS NOT THE TIME TO REVERT BACK TO HUMAN FORM!
GOT YOU! I'LL SEE YOU IN A SECOND. DON'T--
SKRKK!
TAKE THIS!
VZNKK!
THESE BANDS--THAT'S WHAT'S BEEN GIVING YOU THE UPPER HAND! THE SAME DEVICE YOU USED TO DEFEAT ME ON THE MARTIAN SHIP!
I REMEMBER IT WELL!
YOU MAY CONSIDER IT YOUR SAVING GRACE--I SEE IT FOR WHAT IT IS--A WEAK SPOT, SOMETHING YOU RELY TOO HEAVILY ON!

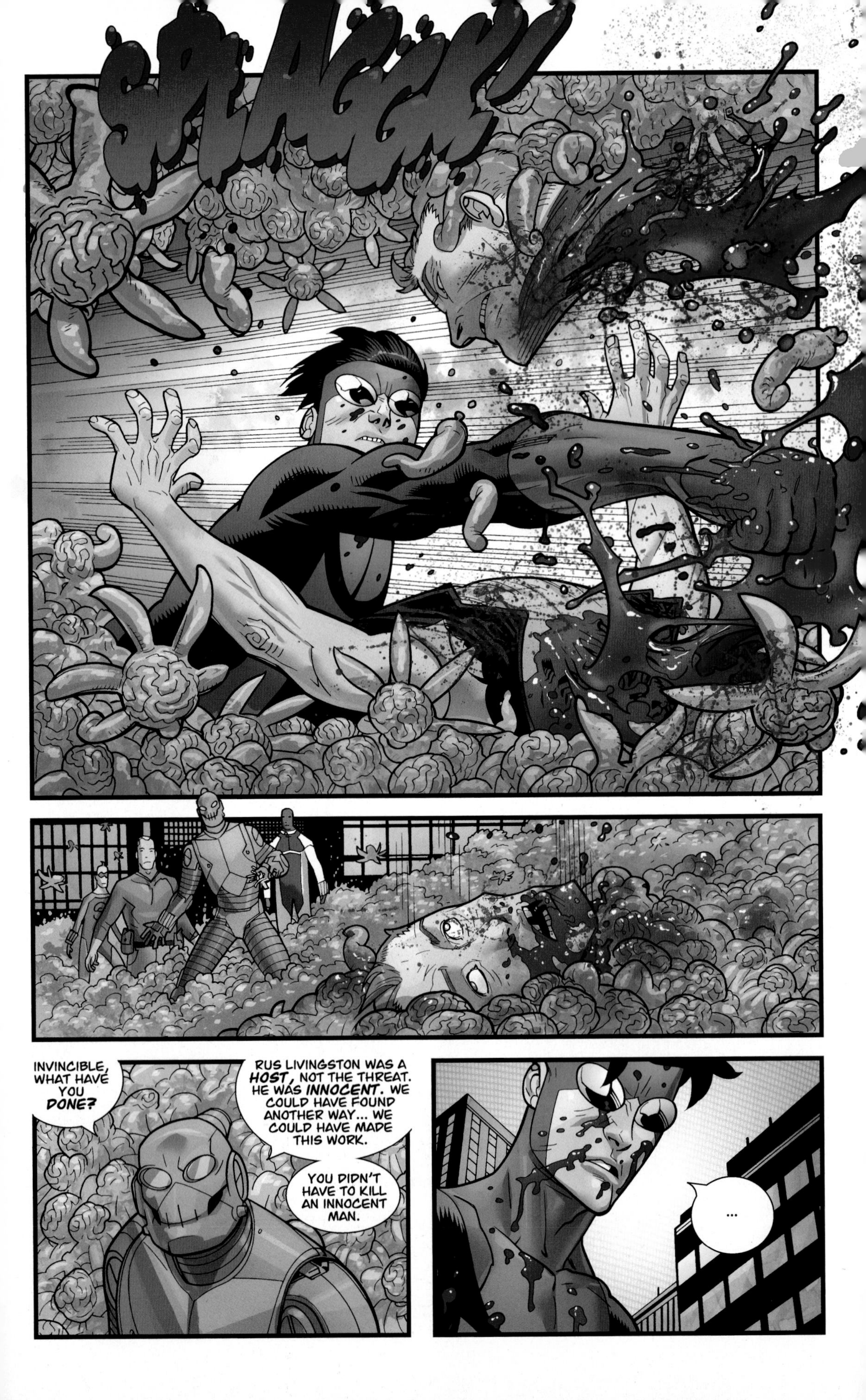
INVINCIBLE, WHAT HAVE YOU DONE?
RUS LIVINGSTON WAS A HOST, NOT THE THREAT. HE WAS INNOCENT. WE COULD HAVE FOUND ANOTHER WAY... WE COULD HAVE MADE THIS WORK.
YOU DIDN'T HAVE TO KILL AN INNOCENT MAN.
...

UNITED STATES **PENTAGON**
Parking in Rear

DID HE JUST *KILL* HIM?

I CAN'T BELIEVE--

*I CAN.* BOY'S HAD A LOT TO DEAL WITH RECENTLY. IT WOULD APPEAR THAT HE'S BEEN PUSHED OVER THE EDGE.

THAT IS DEFINITELY A MAJOR CONCERN.

BUT I DON'T HAVE TIME TO DEAL WITH THAT RIGHT NOW. WE'VE GOT A GOOD PORTION OF A MAJOR AMERICAN CITY OVERRUN WITH MINDLESS ALIEN LIFE-FORMS WHO UNDER NO CIRCUMSTANCES CAN BE ALLOWED TO COME INTO CONTACT WITH A HUMAN.

THAT FORCE FIELD HAS HELD UP NICELY SO FAR--BUT WE'VE DONE LITTLE FIELD TESTING, WE HAVE NO IDEA HOW LONG IT CAN HOLD.

IDEAS?

WAY AHEAD OF YOU, ACTUALLY.

ONCE THE GUARDIANS OF THE GLOBE ARE REMOVED FROM THE AREA, WE'RE GOING TO PIPE IN AN AIRBORNE PATHOGEN. THIS PATHOGEN WHEN CONTAINED WITHIN THE FORCE FIELD WILL CONCENTRATE, INFECTING ALL THE SEQUIDS CONTAINED WITHIN.

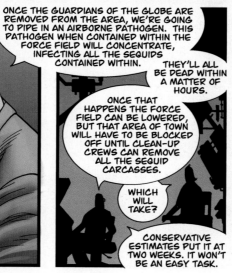

THEY'LL ALL BE DEAD WITHIN A MATTER OF HOURS.

ONCE THAT HAPPENS THE FORCE FIELD CAN BE LOWERED, BUT THAT AREA OF TOWN WILL HAVE TO BE BLOCKED OFF UNTIL CLEAN-UP CREWS CAN REMOVE ALL THE SEQUID CARCASSES.

WHICH WILL TAKE?

CONSERVATIVE ESTIMATES PUT IT AT TWO WEEKS. IT WON'T BE AN EASY TASK.

INVINCIBLE IS TRYING TO LEAVE THE PROTECTED AREA, SIR.

LET HIM GO. I KNOW WHERE TO FIND HIM.

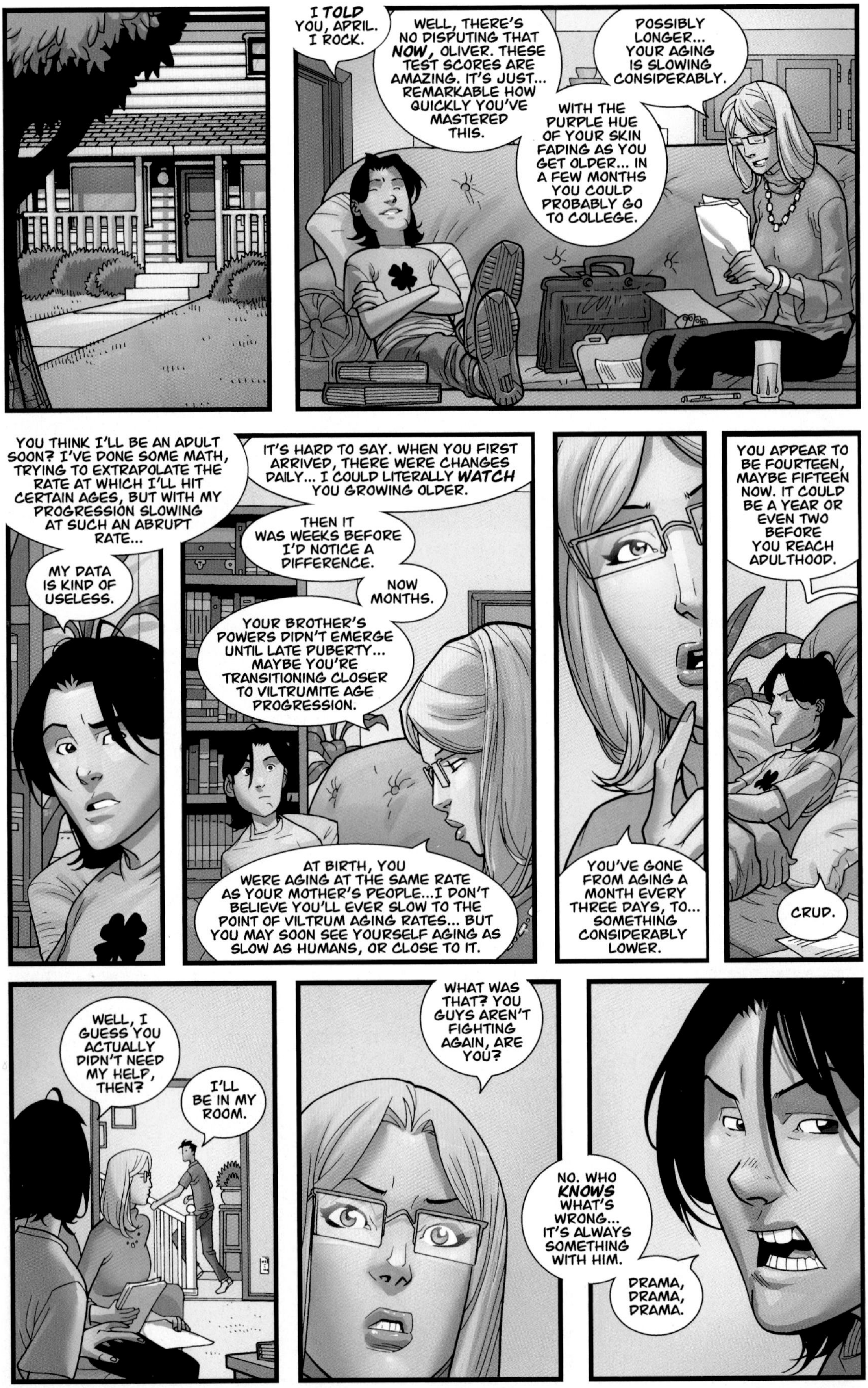
I TOLD YOU, APRIL. I ROCK.
WELL, THERE'S NO DISPUTING THAT NOW, OLIVER. THESE TEST SCORES ARE AMAZING. IT'S JUST... REMARKABLE HOW QUICKLY YOU'VE MASTERED THIS.
POSSIBLY LONGER... YOUR AGING IS SLOWING CONSIDERABLY.
WITH THE PURPLE HUE OF YOUR SKIN FADING AS YOU GET OLDER... IN A FEW MONTHS YOU COULD PROBABLY GO TO COLLEGE.
YOU THINK I'LL BE AN ADULT SOON? I'VE DONE SOME MATH, TRYING TO EXTRAPOLATE THE RATE AT WHICH I'LL HIT CERTAIN AGES, BUT WITH MY PROGRESSION SLOWING AT SUCH AN ABRUPT RATE...
MY DATA IS KIND OF USELESS.
IT'S HARD TO SAY. WHEN YOU FIRST ARRIVED, THERE WERE CHANGES DAILY... I COULD LITERALLY WATCH YOU GROWING OLDER.
THEN IT WAS WEEKS BEFORE I'D NOTICE A DIFFERENCE.
NOW MONTHS.
YOUR BROTHER'S POWERS DIDN'T EMERGE UNTIL LATE PUBERTY... MAYBE YOU'RE TRANSITIONING CLOSER TO VILTRUMITE AGE PROGRESSION.
AT BIRTH, YOU WERE AGING AT THE SAME RATE AS YOUR MOTHER'S PEOPLE...I DON'T BELIEVE YOU'LL EVER SLOW TO THE POINT OF VILTRUM AGING RATES... BUT YOU MAY SOON SEE YOURSELF AGING AS SLOW AS HUMANS, OR CLOSE TO IT.
YOU'VE GONE FROM AGING A MONTH EVERY THREE DAYS, TO... SOMETHING CONSIDERABLY LOWER.
YOU APPEAR TO BE FOURTEEN, MAYBE FIFTEEN NOW. IT COULD BE A YEAR OR EVEN TWO BEFORE YOU REACH ADULTHOOD.
CRUD.
WELL, I GUESS YOU ACTUALLY DIDN'T NEED MY HELP, THEN?
I'LL BE IN MY ROOM.
WHAT WAS THAT? YOU GUYS AREN'T FIGHTING AGAIN, ARE YOU?
NO. WHO KNOWS WHAT'S WRONG... IT'S ALWAYS SOMETHING WITH HIM.
DRAMA, DRAMA, DRAMA.

I'VE KNOWN INVINCIBLE FOR A LONG TIME. I FEAR HE'S GONE TOO FAR THIS TIME. HE **MURDERED** THAT MAN.

I WATCHED HIM.

I--I COULDN'T BELIEVE IT.

IT'S IN CECIL'S HANDS NOW. HE'LL KNOW WHAT TO DO. SHADY AS THAT MAN IS, HE KNOWS WHAT HE'S DOING.

KNOWS HOW TO PUSH OUR BUTTONS.

I HOPE THE TELEPORTATION WASN'T TOO JARRING FOR YOU. I WAS SO WORRIED ABOUT YOU.

IT--

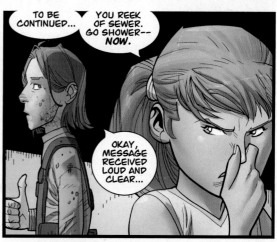

TO BE CONTINUED...

YOU REEK OF SEWER. GO SHOWER-- **NOW.**

OKAY, MESSAGE RECEIVED LOUD AND CLEAR...

QUICK SHOWER...

ANYTHING FOR MY--

≥KOFF!≤

≥HUURK!≤

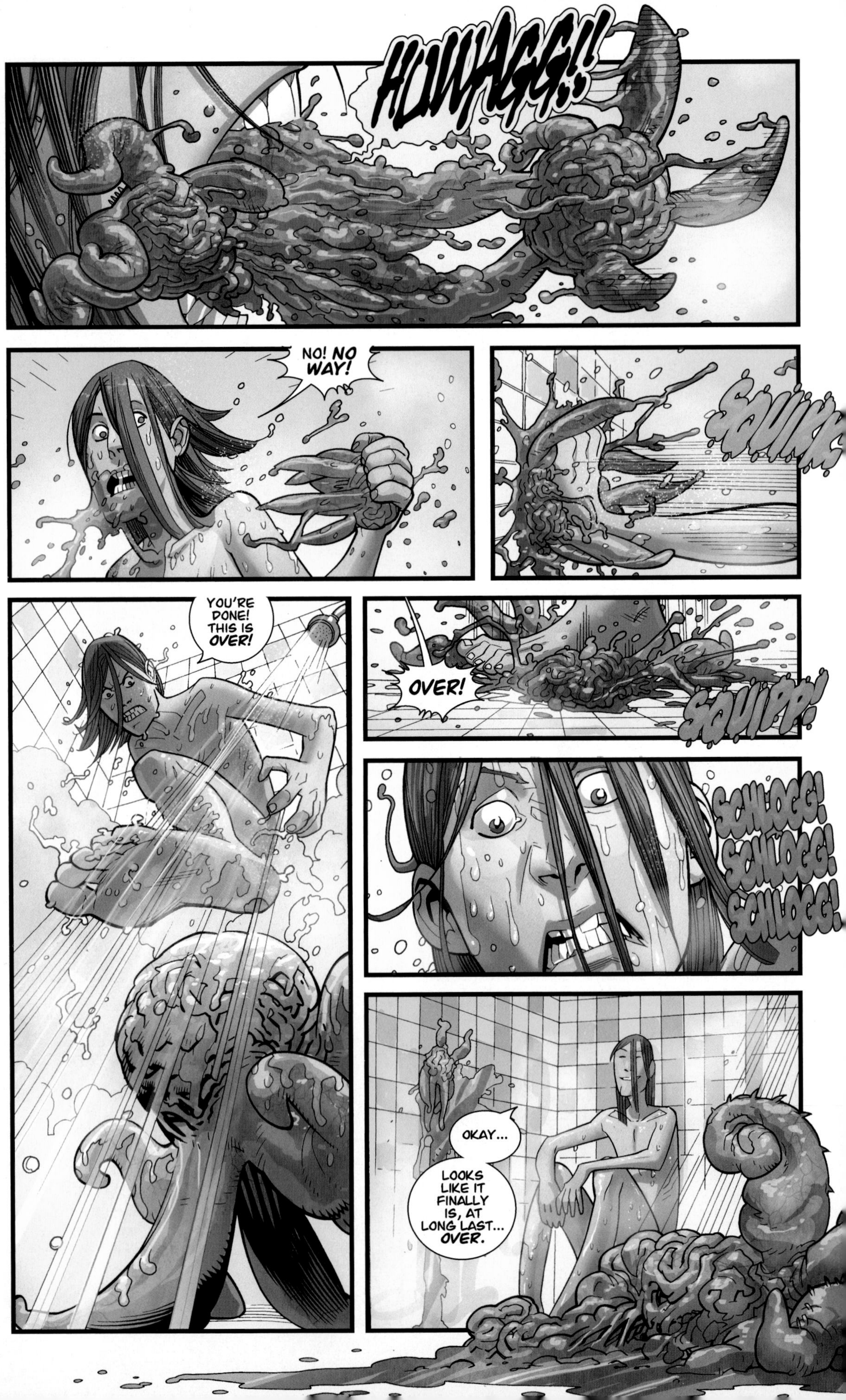
HUWAGG!!
NO! NO WAY!
SQUIKK!
YOU'RE DONE! THIS IS OVER!
OVER!
SQUIPP!
SCHLOGG! SCHLOGG! SCHLOGG!
OKAY...
LOOKS LIKE IT FINALLY IS, AT LONG LAST... OVER.

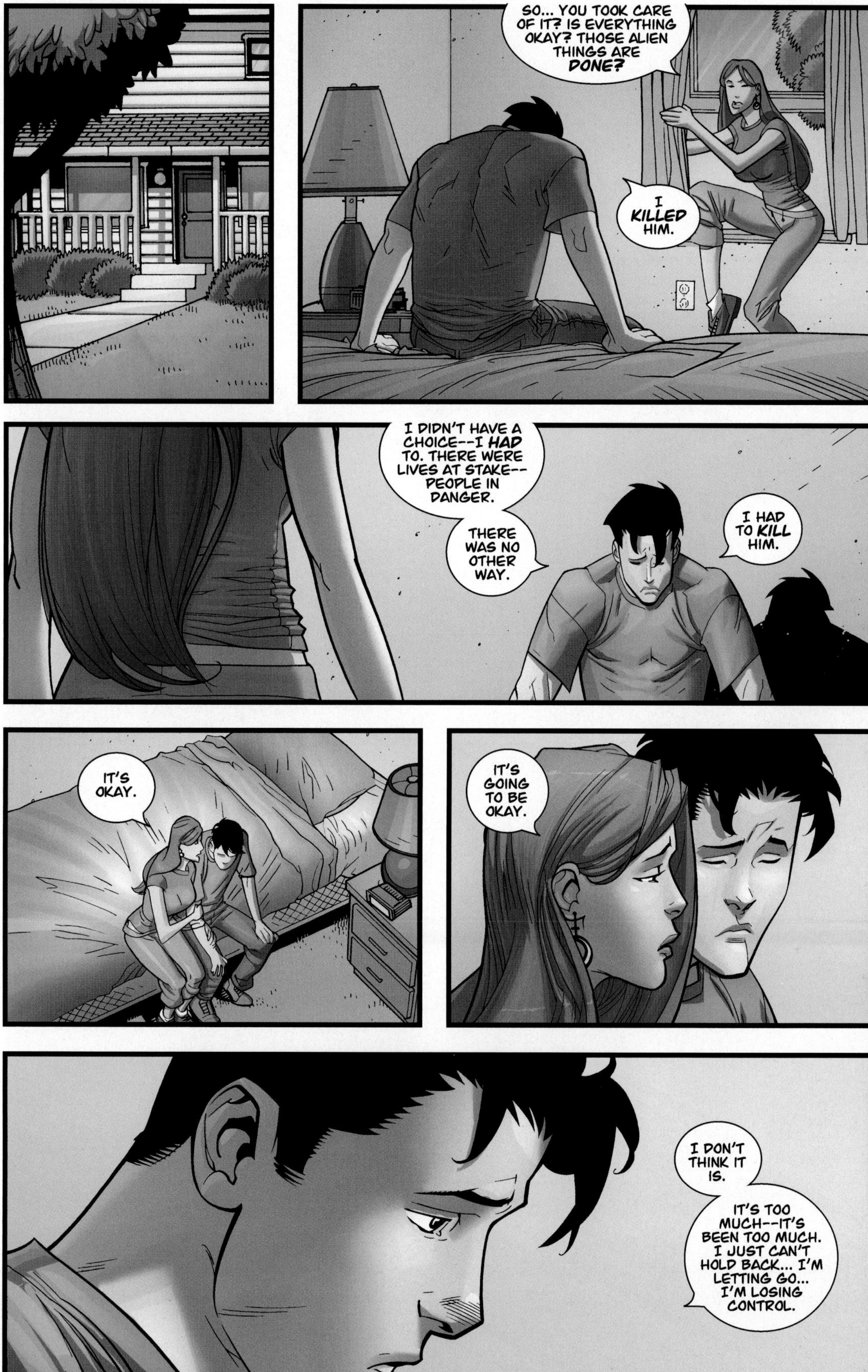

SO... YOU TOOK CARE OF IT? IS EVERYTHING OKAY? THOSE ALIEN THINGS ARE DONE?
I KILLED HIM.
I DIDN'T HAVE A CHOICE--I HAD TO. THERE WERE LIVES AT STAKE--PEOPLE IN DANGER.
THERE WAS NO OTHER WAY.
I HAD TO KILL HIM.
IT'S OKAY.
IT'S GOING TO BE OKAY.
I DON'T THINK IT IS.
IT'S TOO MUCH--IT'S BEEN TOO MUCH. I JUST CAN'T HOLD BACK... I'M LETTING GO... I'M LOSING CONTROL.

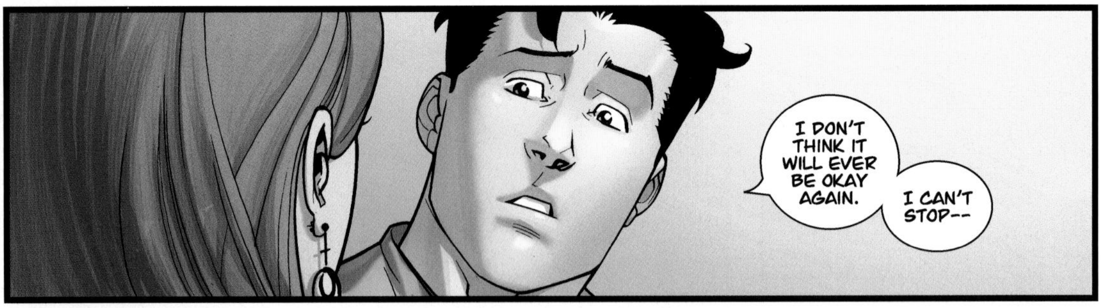
I DON'T THINK IT WILL EVER BE OKAY AGAIN.
I CAN'T STOP--

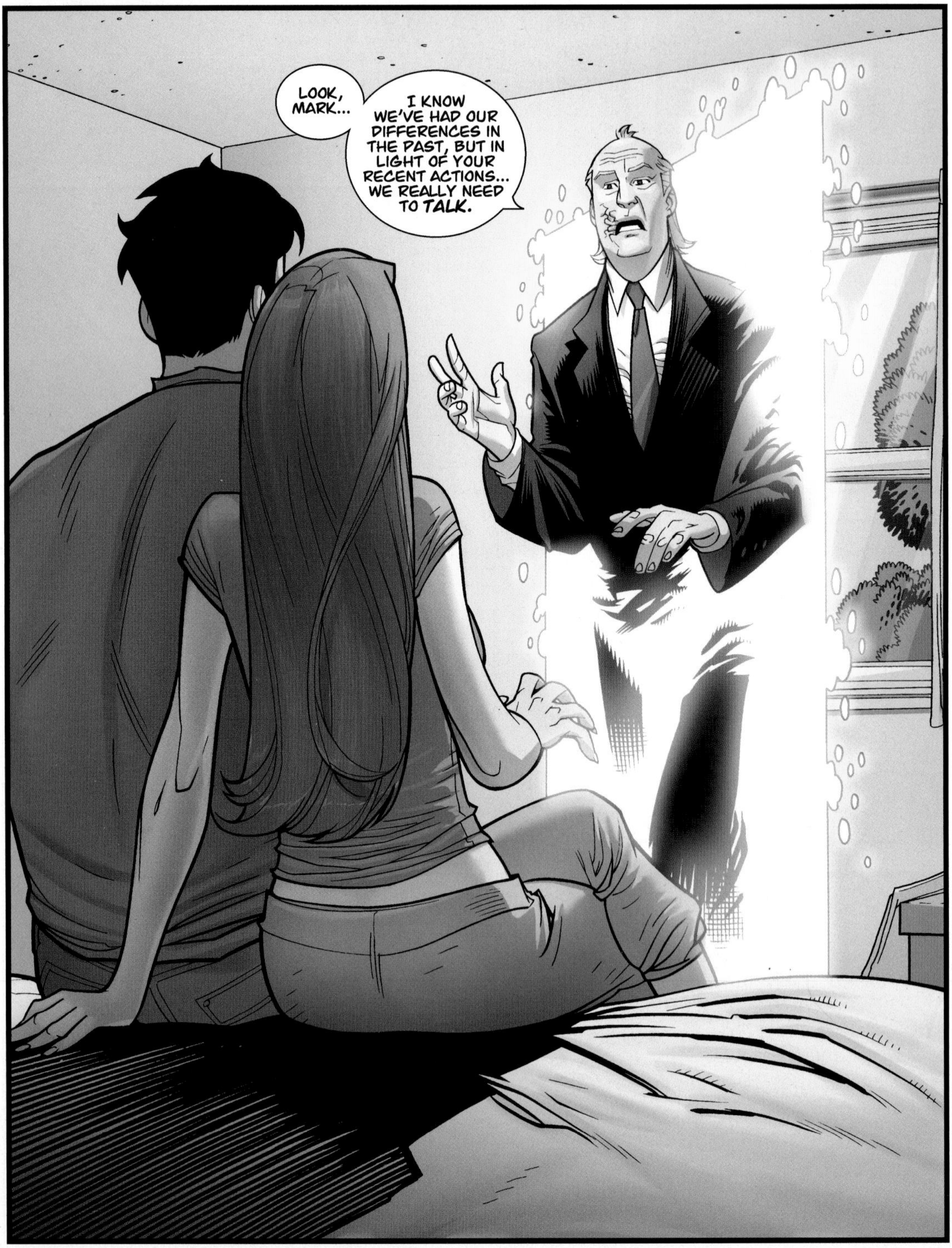
LOOK, MARK...
I KNOW WE'VE HAD OUR DIFFERENCES IN THE PAST, BUT IN LIGHT OF YOUR RECENT ACTIONS... WE REALLY NEED TO **TALK**.

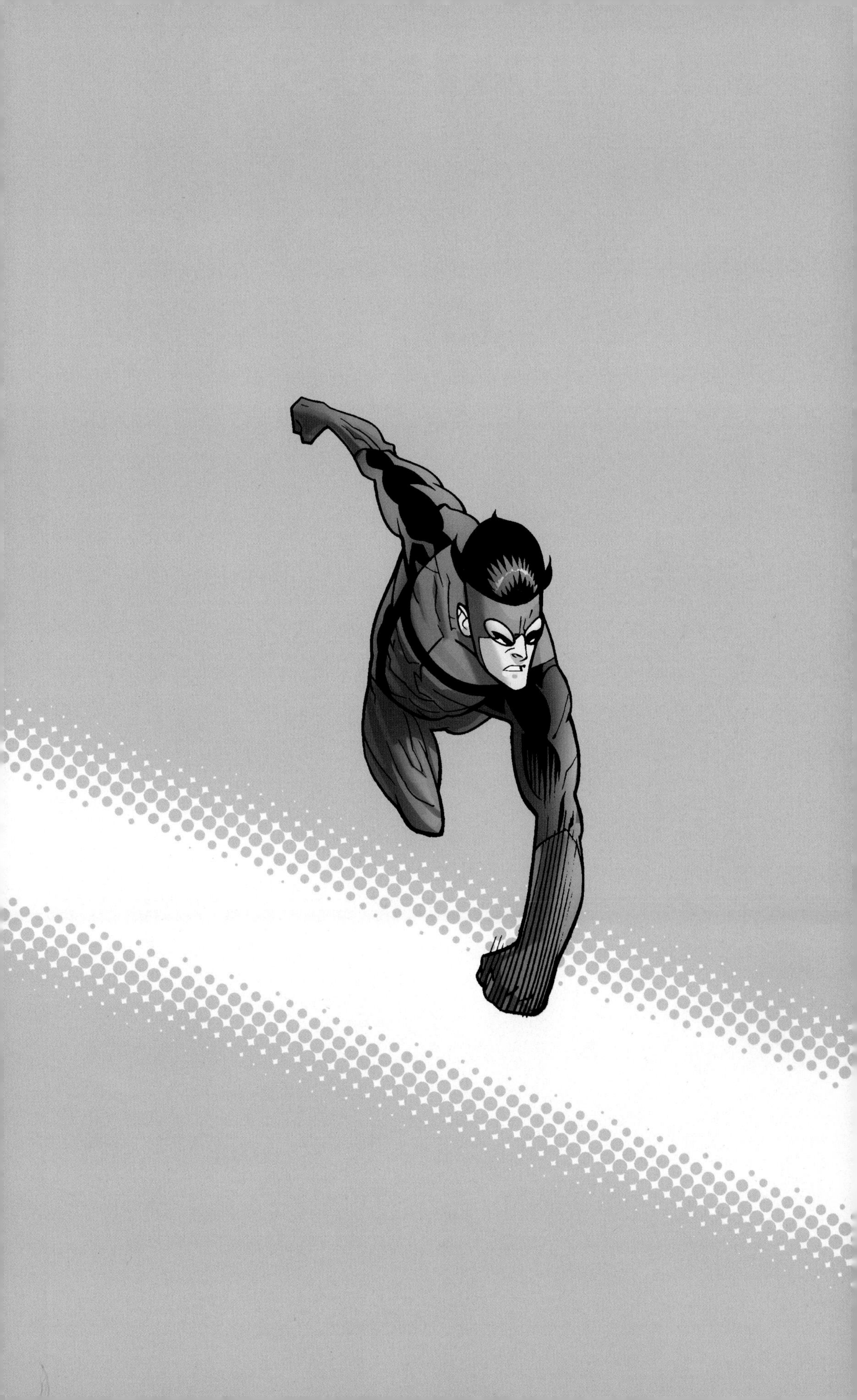

# CHAPTER SIX

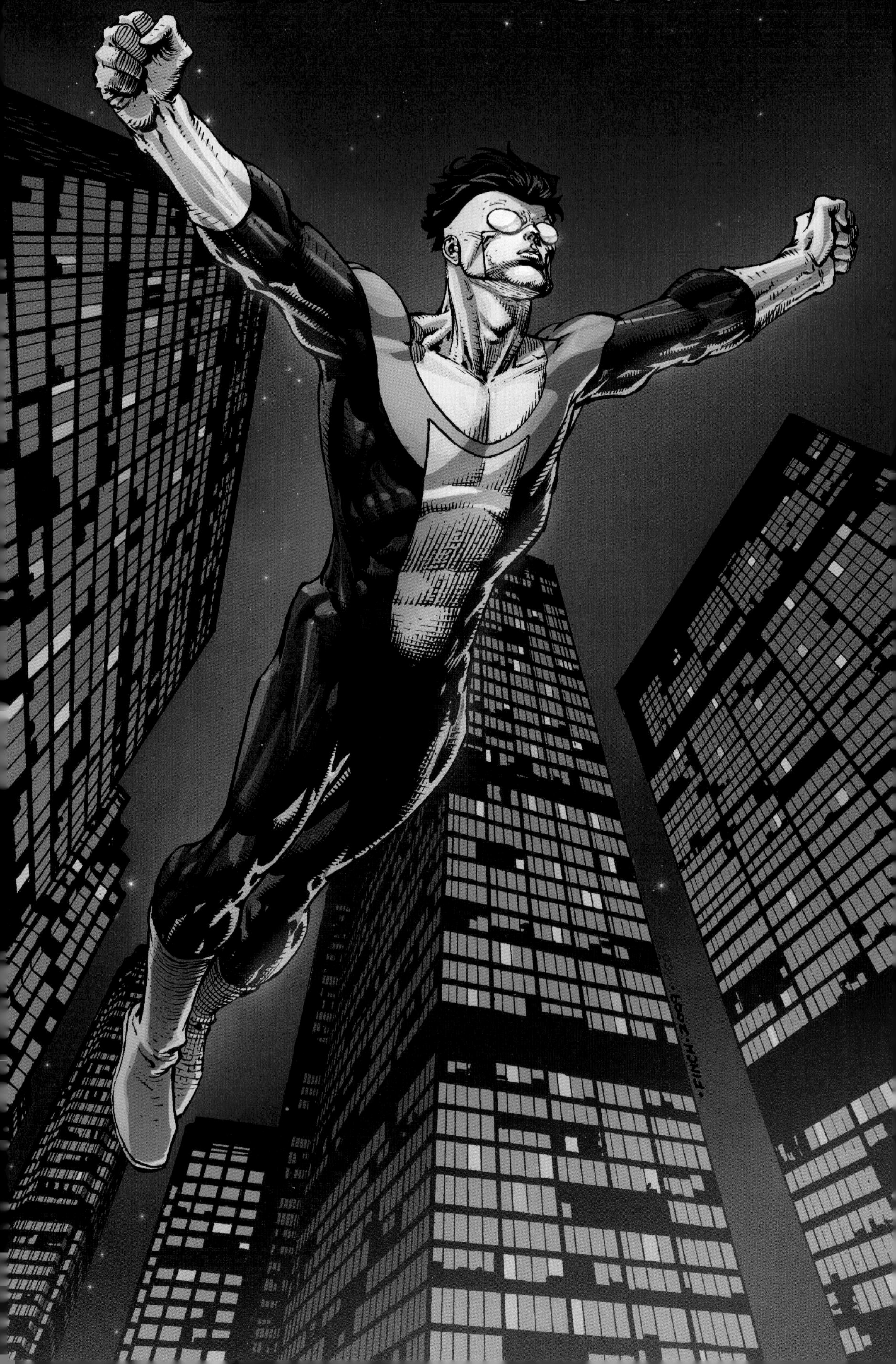

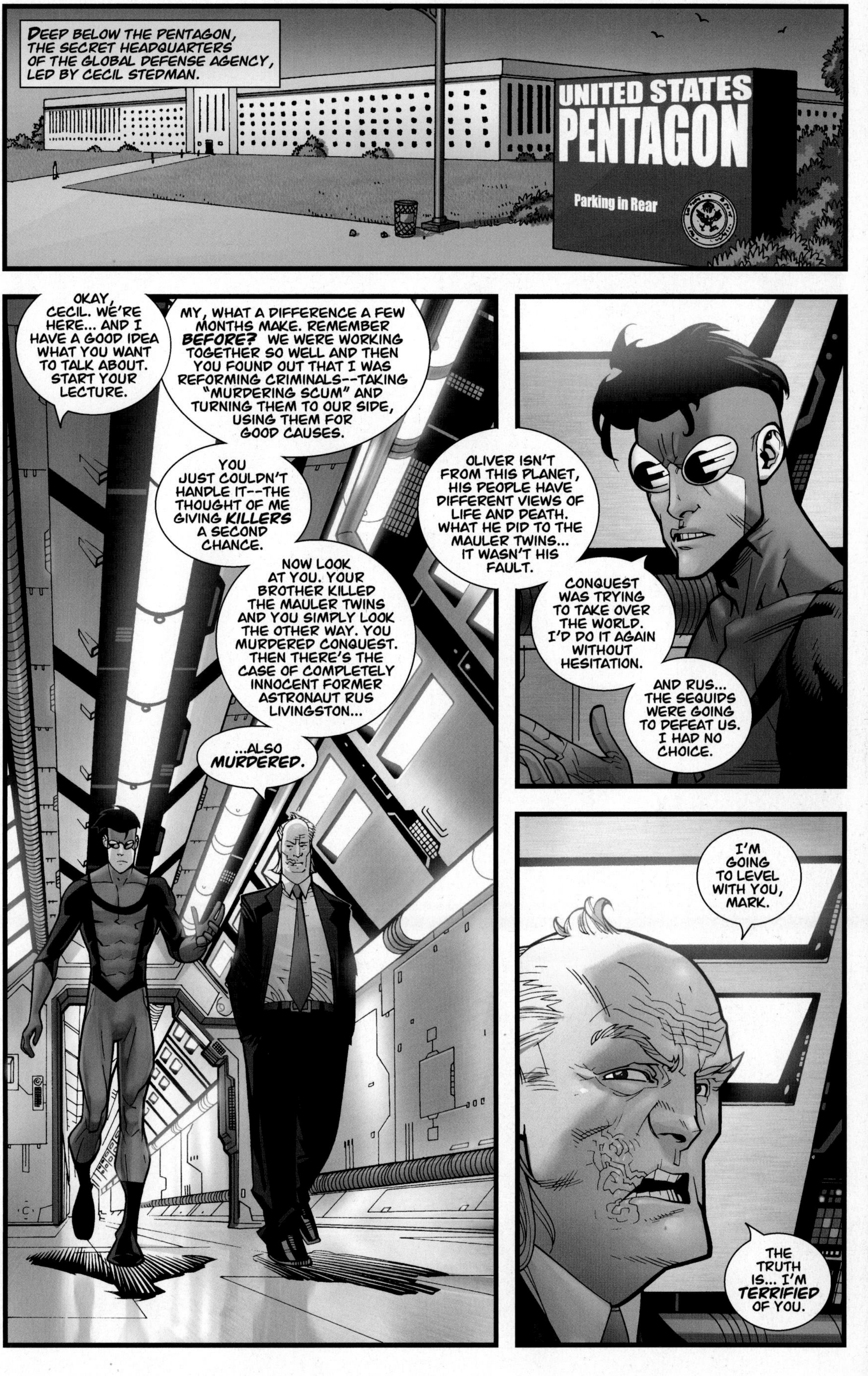
DEEP BELOW THE PENTAGON, THE SECRET HEADQUARTERS OF THE GLOBAL DEFENSE AGENCY, LED BY CECIL STEDMAN.
UNITED STATES PENTAGON
Parking in Rear
OKAY, CECIL. WE'RE HERE... AND I HAVE A GOOD IDEA WHAT YOU WANT TO TALK ABOUT. START YOUR LECTURE.
MY, WHAT A DIFFERENCE A FEW MONTHS MAKE. REMEMBER BEFORE? WE WERE WORKING TOGETHER SO WELL AND THEN YOU FOUND OUT THAT I WAS REFORMING CRIMINALS--TAKING "MURDERING SCUM" AND TURNING THEM TO OUR SIDE, USING THEM FOR GOOD CAUSES.
YOU JUST COULDN'T HANDLE IT--THE THOUGHT OF ME GIVING KILLERS A SECOND CHANCE.
NOW LOOK AT YOU. YOUR BROTHER KILLED THE MAULER TWINS AND YOU SIMPLY LOOK THE OTHER WAY. YOU MURDERED CONQUEST. THEN THERE'S THE CASE OF COMPLETELY INNOCENT FORMER ASTRONAUT RUS LIVINGSTON...
...ALSO MURDERED.
OLIVER ISN'T FROM THIS PLANET, HIS PEOPLE HAVE DIFFERENT VIEWS OF LIFE AND DEATH. WHAT HE DID TO THE MAULER TWINS... IT WASN'T HIS FAULT.
CONQUEST WAS TRYING TO TAKE OVER THE WORLD. I'D DO IT AGAIN WITHOUT HESITATION.
AND RUS... THE SEQUIDS WERE GOING TO DEFEAT US. I HAD NO CHOICE.
I'M GOING TO LEVEL WITH YOU, MARK.
THE TRUTH IS... I'M TERRIFIED OF YOU.

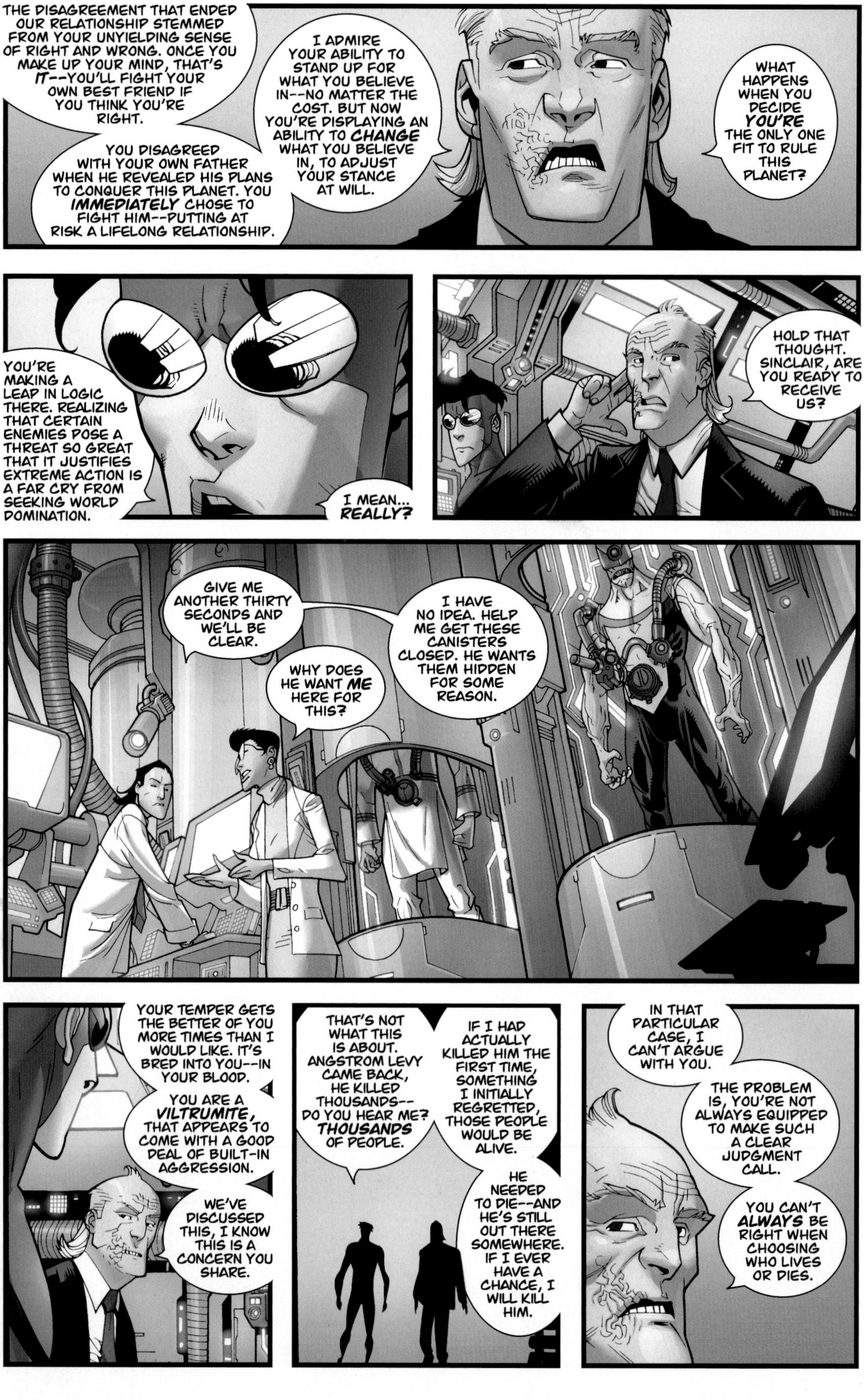
THE DISAGREEMENT THAT ENDED OUR RELATIONSHIP STEMMED FROM YOUR UNYIELDING SENSE OF RIGHT AND WRONG. ONCE YOU MAKE UP YOUR MIND, THAT'S IT--YOU'LL FIGHT YOUR OWN BEST FRIEND IF YOU THINK YOU'RE RIGHT.
YOU DISAGREED WITH YOUR OWN FATHER WHEN HE REVEALED HIS PLANS TO CONQUER THIS PLANET. YOU IMMEDIATELY CHOSE TO FIGHT HIM--PUTTING AT RISK A LIFELONG RELATIONSHIP.
I ADMIRE YOUR ABILITY TO STAND UP FOR WHAT YOU BELIEVE IN--NO MATTER THE COST. BUT NOW YOU'RE DISPLAYING AN ABILITY TO CHANGE WHAT YOU BELIEVE IN, TO ADJUST YOUR STANCE AT WILL.
WHAT HAPPENS WHEN YOU DECIDE YOU'RE THE ONLY ONE FIT TO RULE THIS PLANET?
YOU'RE MAKING A LEAP IN LOGIC THERE. REALIZING THAT CERTAIN ENEMIES POSE A THREAT SO GREAT THAT IT JUSTIFIES EXTREME ACTION IS A FAR CRY FROM SEEKING WORLD DOMINATION.
I MEAN... REALLY?
HOLD THAT THOUGHT. SINCLAIR, ARE YOU READY TO RECEIVE US?
GIVE ME ANOTHER THIRTY SECONDS AND WE'LL BE CLEAR.
WHY DOES HE WANT ME HERE FOR THIS?
I HAVE NO IDEA. HELP ME GET THESE CANISTERS CLOSED. HE WANTS THEM HIDDEN FOR SOME REASON.
YOUR TEMPER GETS THE BETTER OF YOU MORE TIMES THAN I WOULD LIKE. IT'S BRED INTO YOU--IN YOUR BLOOD.
YOU ARE A VILTRUMITE, THAT APPEARS TO COME WITH A GOOD DEAL OF BUILT-IN AGGRESSION.
WE'VE DISCUSSED THIS, I KNOW THIS IS A CONCERN YOU SHARE.
THAT'S NOT WHAT THIS IS ABOUT. ANGSTROM LEVY CAME BACK, HE KILLED THOUSANDS-- DO YOU HEAR ME? THOUSANDS OF PEOPLE.
IF I HAD ACTUALLY KILLED HIM THE FIRST TIME, SOMETHING I INITIALLY REGRETTED, THOSE PEOPLE WOULD BE ALIVE.
HE NEEDED TO DIE--AND HE'S STILL OUT THERE SOMEWHERE. IF I EVER HAVE A CHANCE, I WILL KILL HIM.
IN THAT PARTICULAR CASE, I CAN'T ARGUE WITH YOU.
THE PROBLEM IS, YOU'RE NOT ALWAYS EQUIPPED TO MAKE SUCH A CLEAR JUDGMENT CALL.
YOU CAN'T ALWAYS BE RIGHT WHEN CHOOSING WHO LIVES OR DIES.

HERE'S ONE OF THE TIMES YOU WOULD HAVE BEEN **WRONG.**

HELLO, INVINCIBLE.

WHAT? WHY ARE YOU BRINGING ME **HERE?** WHAT PURPOSE WILL THIS SERVE, CECIL?

THIS IS A **LEARNING** EXPERIENCE. D.A. SINCLAIR, HE WAS DEVELOPING HIS REANIMEN TECHNOLOGY WHILE ATTENDING UPSTATE UNIVERSITY. HE EXPERIMENTED ON THE HOMELESS PEOPLE IN THE AREA—EVEN A FEW STUDENTS.

NOW THAT THE TECHNOLOGY IS IN USE, THE REANIMEN TROOPS ARE SAVING **COUNTLESS** LIVES. BUILT ON CADAVERS NOW, THEY EACH TAKE THE PLACE OF **TWENTY** FOOT SOLDIERS.

**HORRIFIC** THINGS WERE DONE TO THOSE MEN, WE ALL AGREE ON THAT, BUT NO ONE LISTENED TO SINCLAIR, NO ONE BELIEVED HIS THEORIES AT FIRST. HE HAD TO PUT THEM INTO PRACTICE TO PROVE HIMSELF.

THEY'RE MAKING THIS WORLD A BETTER PLACE.

I'M HAPPY TO REPORT, SINCLAIR HIMSELF IS NOW **COMPLETELY** REFORMED. HE'S DEVELOPING NEW TECHNOLOGY WITH THE FULL SUPPORT OF THE GLOBAL DEFENSE AGENCY. HE'S MAKING MY— AND **YOUR** JOB EASIER.

AND HE'S ENGAGED TO BE MARRIED TO JUSTINE, ONE OF OUR OTHER SCIENTISTS. ALSO, I'VE JUST LEARNED THAT THEY'RE EXPECTING THEIR FIRST CHILD.

HI.

I'M NOT A BAD PERSON. **DRIVEN**—ALMOST DRIVEN **MAD** BY MY WORK, BUT ONLY BECAUSE I KNEW WHAT I WAS DOING WAS RIGHT—THAT THE ENDS JUSTIFIED THE MEANS.

I REGRET WHAT I HAD TO DO, BUT I FIND COMFORT IN THE KNOWLEDGE THAT IT HAD TO BE DONE—IN THE END, I WAS RIGHT.

THANK YOU FOR YOUR TIME, D.A.

YEAH... THANKS—AND CONGRATULATIONS.

SOUND FAMILIAR? THE ENDS JUSTIFY THE MEANS? DID YOU KNOW DARKWING SACRIFICED HIMSELF TO SAVE THE REST OF HIS TEAM? ARE YOU STARTING TO SEE THAT--

YEAH, I KNOW... I *GET* IT, OKAY? I WAS STARTING TO GET IT BEFORE YOU BROUGHT ME HERE. KILLING RUS, IT FELT *WRONG.* I HAD TO FORCE MYSELF TO DO IT, BECAUSE I THOUGHT IT WAS THE RIGHT THING TO DO.

BUT IT FEELS *HORRIBLE.* LIKE MAYBE I WAS JUST TAKING THE EASY WAY OUT--KILLING HIM SO I DIDN'T HAVE TO FIGURE SOMETHING ELSE OUT.

I GET WHAT YOU'RE SAYING, KILLING IS ALMOST *NEVER* JUSTIFIED. OTHERWISE, I'M JUST LIKE ALL THE OTHER VILTRUMITES. YOU KNOW I DON'T WANT *THAT.*

THESE LAST FEW MONTHS HAVE BEEN HARD ON ME-- IT'S GOT ME ALL TURNED AROUND. I'LL BE THE FIRST TO ADMIT I LOST MY WAY.

THANK YOU FOR ADMITTING THAT. LOOK, I KNOW THIS ISN'T GOING TO REPAIR OUR RELATIONSHIP OVERNIGHT, BUT IF--

WE'VE GOT A SITUATION IN NEW YORK. LOOKS LIKE WE'RE GOING TO NEED TO SEND SOMEONE IN.

INVINCIBLE-- COULD YOU-- FOR OLD TIMES' SAKE?

...

*VDDSH!*

EXCELLENT TIMING, DONALD. AND NEW YORK? WE LUCKED OUT HAVING SOMETHING HAPPEN SO CLOSE, MAKES MORE SENSE TO ASK HIM.

I'M NOT COMFORTABLE MANIPULATING HIM LIKE THIS--AND I TAKE IT YOU DIDN'T TELL HIM ABOUT CONQUEST?

MANIPULATING? THIS IS *NOTHING.* I'M JUST USING HIM OBVIOUSLY SECOND GUESSING HIMSELF TO PULL HIM BACK TO OUR SIDE. HE'S TOO *POWERFUL* TO HAVE HIM OUT THERE ON HIS OWN.

AND TELLING HIM NOW THAT WE KEPT THAT MONSTER ALIVE WOULD ONLY TURN INVINCIBLE AGAINST US... AND HE'D BE RIGHT TO BE ANGRY. WE MADE A HUGE MISTAKE THERE.

ONCE CONQUEST BROKE AWAY FROM OUR FACILITY, HE LEFT THE PLANET AND HASN'T COME BACK--MAYBE HE *WON'T* COME BACK. WE'LL WAIT UNTIL IT'S A PROBLEM BEFORE WE TAKE ANY ACTION.

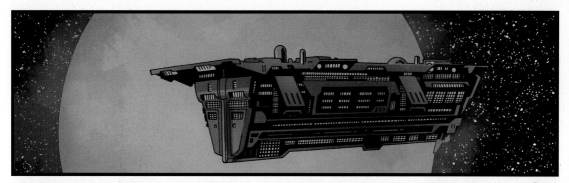

ON YOUR KNEES!

SIRE, IF YOU'LL JUST ALLOW ME A MOMENT TO EXPLAIN--

NONE MAY ADDRESS GRAND REGENT THRAGG WITHOUT SUBMISSION!

BOW YOUR HEAD!

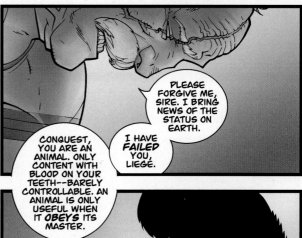

PLEASE FORGIVE ME, SIRE. I BRING NEWS OF THE STATUS ON EARTH.

I HAVE FAILED YOU, LIEGE.

CONQUEST, YOU ARE AN ANIMAL. ONLY CONTENT WITH BLOOD ON YOUR TEETH--BARELY CONTROLLABLE. AN ANIMAL IS ONLY USEFUL WHEN IT OBEYS ITS MASTER.

I ORDERED YOU TO BRING DOWN THE SON OF NOLAN AND SECURE HIS PLANET FOR MY ARRIVAL. NONE OF THESE TASKS WERE ACCOMPLISHED.

AND SO I MUST ASK...

...OF WHAT FURTHER USE COULD YOU BE TO ME?

I UNDERESTIMATED THE BOY. I TOYED WITH HIM FAR TOO LONG, I GAVE HIM TIME TO GAIN AN ADVANTAGE.

I HAVE SERVED YOU WELL FOR MANY YEARS. PLEASE FORGIVE MY CARELESSNESS AND SPARE ME.

WE HAVE LEARNED OF A TEAM SENT TO EARTH TO RETRIEVE NOLAN'S SON AND BRING HIM INTO DIRECT CONFLICT WITH US.

I DOUBT YOU HAVE TIME TO PREVENT THIS, BUT GO, CATCH THEM ON THEIR RETURN AND ENSURE NONE OF THEM ARE ABLE TO JOIN THE FIGHT.

LEAVE *NONE* ALIVE.

I BEG YOU...

DO NOT FAIL ME AGAIN.

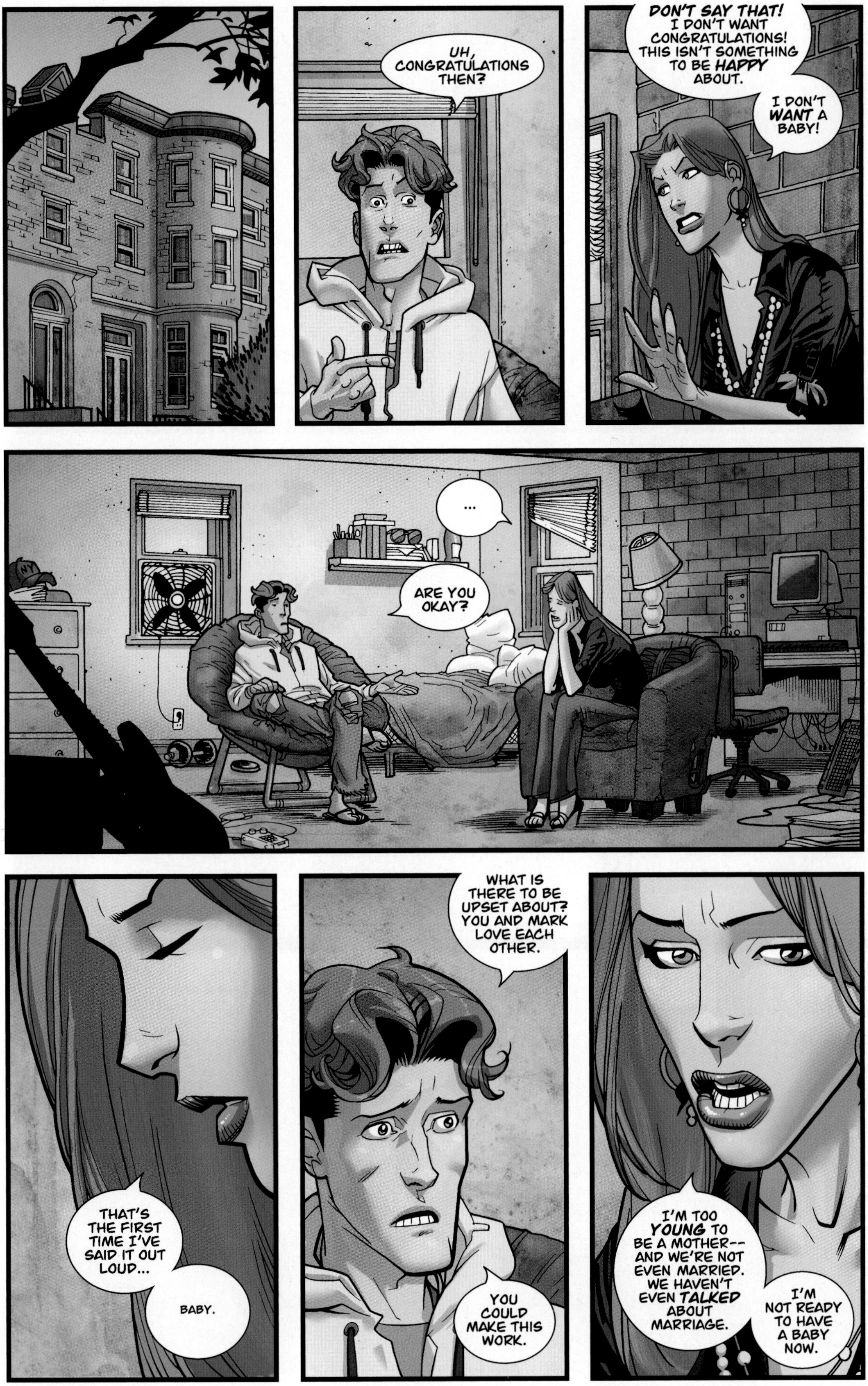
UH, CONGRATULATIONS THEN?
DON'T SAY THAT! I DON'T WANT CONGRATULATIONS! THIS ISN'T SOMETHING TO BE HAPPY ABOUT.
I DON'T WANT A BABY!
...
ARE YOU OKAY?
THAT'S THE FIRST TIME I'VE SAID IT OUT LOUD...
BABY.
WHAT IS THERE TO BE UPSET ABOUT? YOU AND MARK LOVE EACH OTHER.
YOU COULD MAKE THIS WORK.
I'M TOO YOUNG TO BE A MOTHER--AND WE'RE NOT EVEN MARRIED. WE HAVEN'T EVEN TALKED ABOUT MARRIAGE.
I'M NOT READY TO HAVE A BABY NOW.

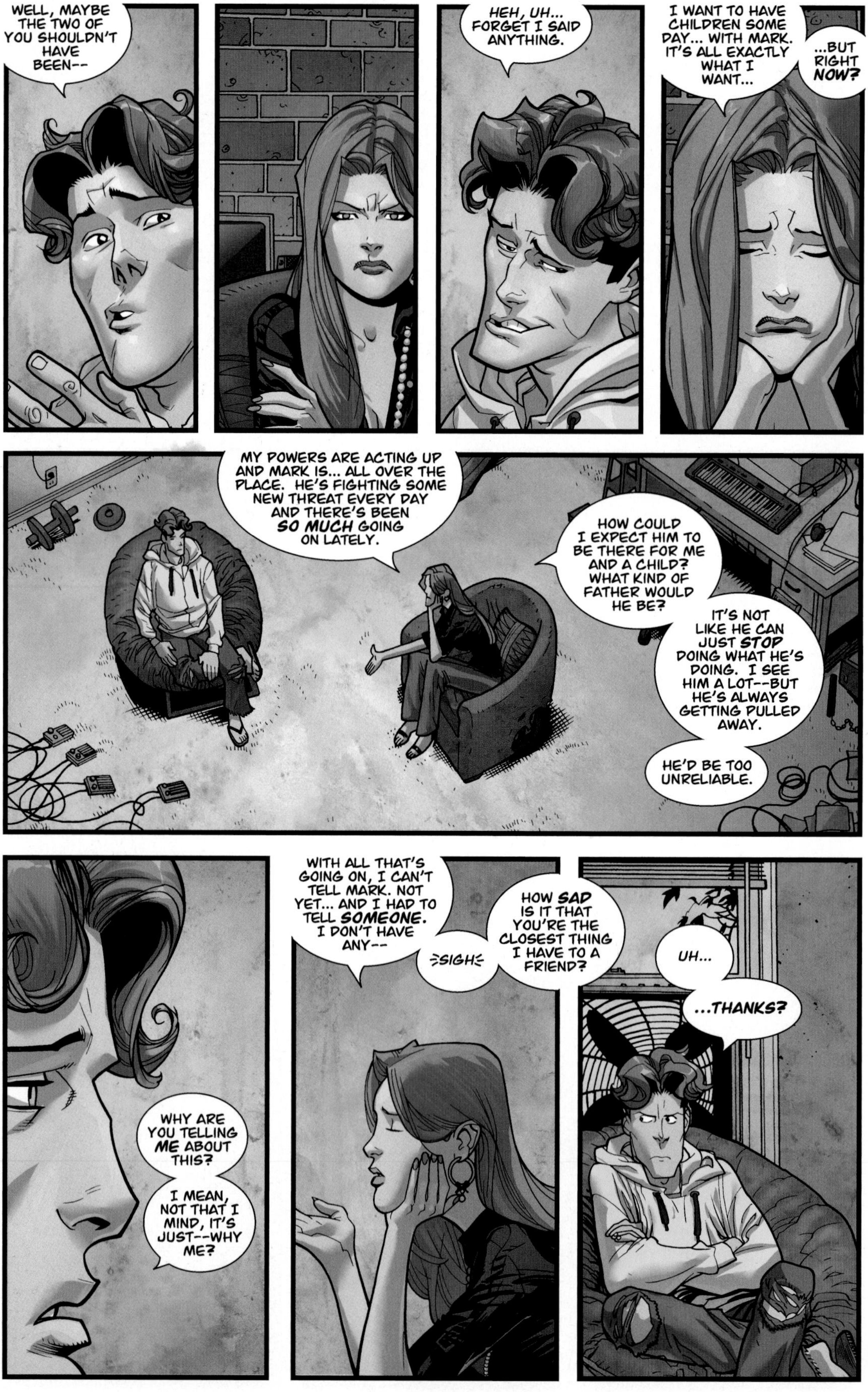
WELL, MAYBE THE TWO OF YOU SHOULDN'T HAVE BEEN--
HEH, UH... FORGET I SAID ANYTHING.
I WANT TO HAVE CHILDREN SOME DAY... WITH MARK. IT'S ALL EXACTLY WHAT I WANT...
...BUT RIGHT NOW?
MY POWERS ARE ACTING UP AND MARK IS... ALL OVER THE PLACE. HE'S FIGHTING SOME NEW THREAT EVERY DAY AND THERE'S BEEN SO MUCH GOING ON LATELY.
HOW COULD I EXPECT HIM TO BE THERE FOR ME AND A CHILD? WHAT KIND OF FATHER WOULD HE BE?
IT'S NOT LIKE HE CAN JUST STOP DOING WHAT HE'S DOING. I SEE HIM A LOT--BUT HE'S ALWAYS GETTING PULLED AWAY.
HE'D BE TOO UNRELIABLE.
WHY ARE YOU TELLING ME ABOUT THIS?
I MEAN, NOT THAT I MIND, IT'S JUST--WHY ME?
WITH ALL THAT'S GOING ON, I CAN'T TELL MARK. NOT YET... AND I HAD TO TELL SOMEONE. I DON'T HAVE ANY--
SIGH
HOW SAD IS IT THAT YOU'RE THE CLOSEST THING I HAVE TO A FRIEND?
UH...
...THANKS?

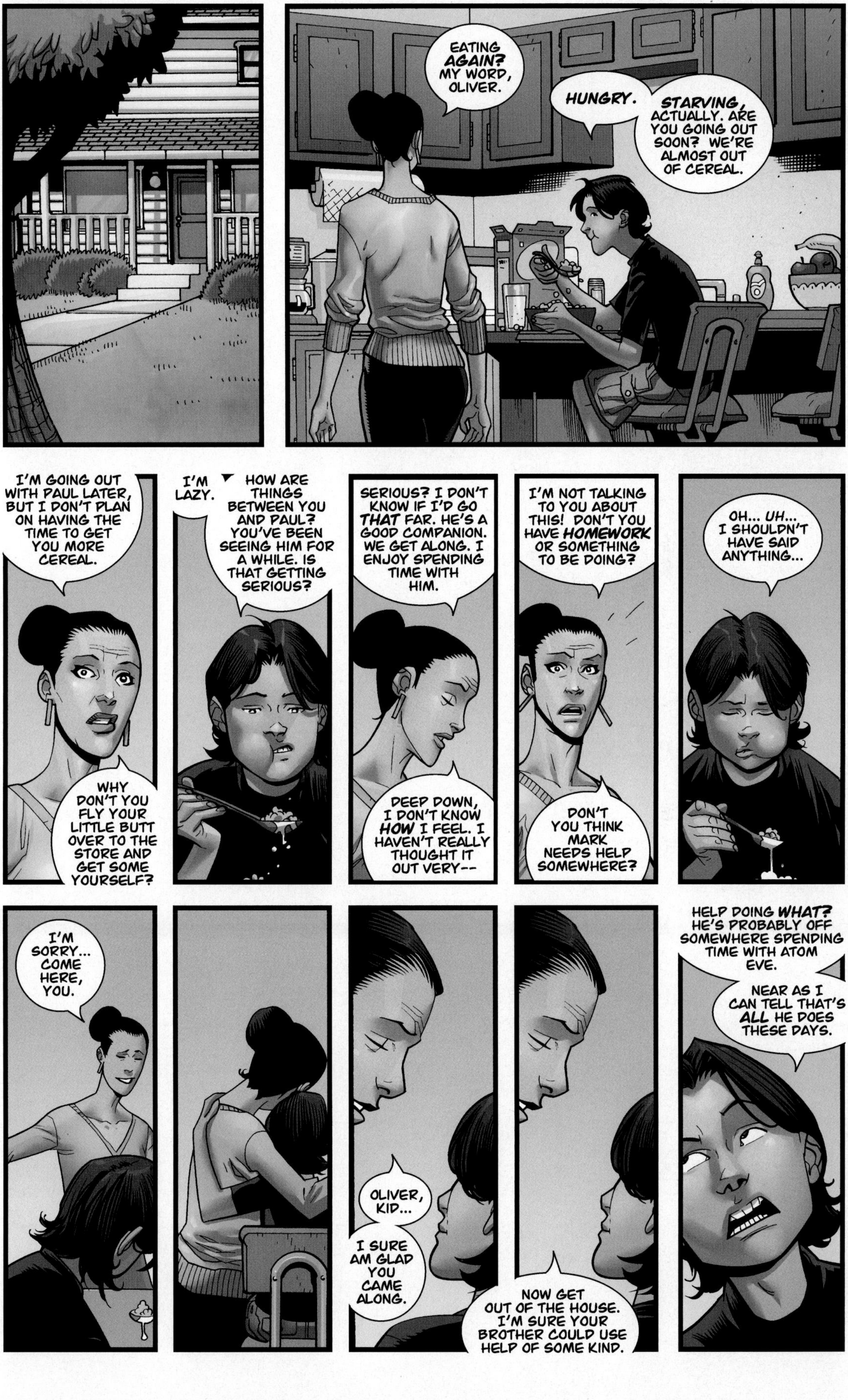
EATING AGAIN? MY WORD, OLIVER.
HUNGRY.
STARVING, ACTUALLY. ARE YOU GOING OUT SOON? WE'RE ALMOST OUT OF CEREAL.
I'M GOING OUT WITH PAUL LATER, BUT I DON'T PLAN ON HAVING THE TIME TO GET YOU MORE CEREAL.
WHY DON'T YOU FLY YOUR LITTLE BUTT OVER TO THE STORE AND GET SOME YOURSELF?
I'M LAZY.
HOW ARE THINGS BETWEEN YOU AND PAUL? YOU'VE BEEN SEEING HIM FOR A WHILE. IS THAT GETTING SERIOUS?
SERIOUS? I DON'T KNOW IF I'D GO THAT FAR. HE'S A GOOD COMPANION. WE GET ALONG. I ENJOY SPENDING TIME WITH HIM.
DEEP DOWN, I DON'T KNOW HOW I FEEL. I HAVEN'T REALLY THOUGHT IT OUT VERY--
I'M NOT TALKING TO YOU ABOUT THIS! DON'T YOU HAVE HOMEWORK OR SOMETHING TO BE DOING?
DON'T YOU THINK MARK NEEDS HELP SOMEWHERE?
OH... UH... I SHOULDN'T HAVE SAID ANYTHING...
I'M SORRY... COME HERE, YOU.
OLIVER, KID...
I SURE AM GLAD YOU CAME ALONG.
NOW GET OUT OF THE HOUSE. I'M SURE YOUR BROTHER COULD USE HELP OF SOME KIND.
HELP DOING WHAT? HE'S PROBABLY OFF SOMEWHERE SPENDING TIME WITH ATOM EVE.
NEAR AS I CAN TELL THAT'S ALL HE DOES THESE DAYS.

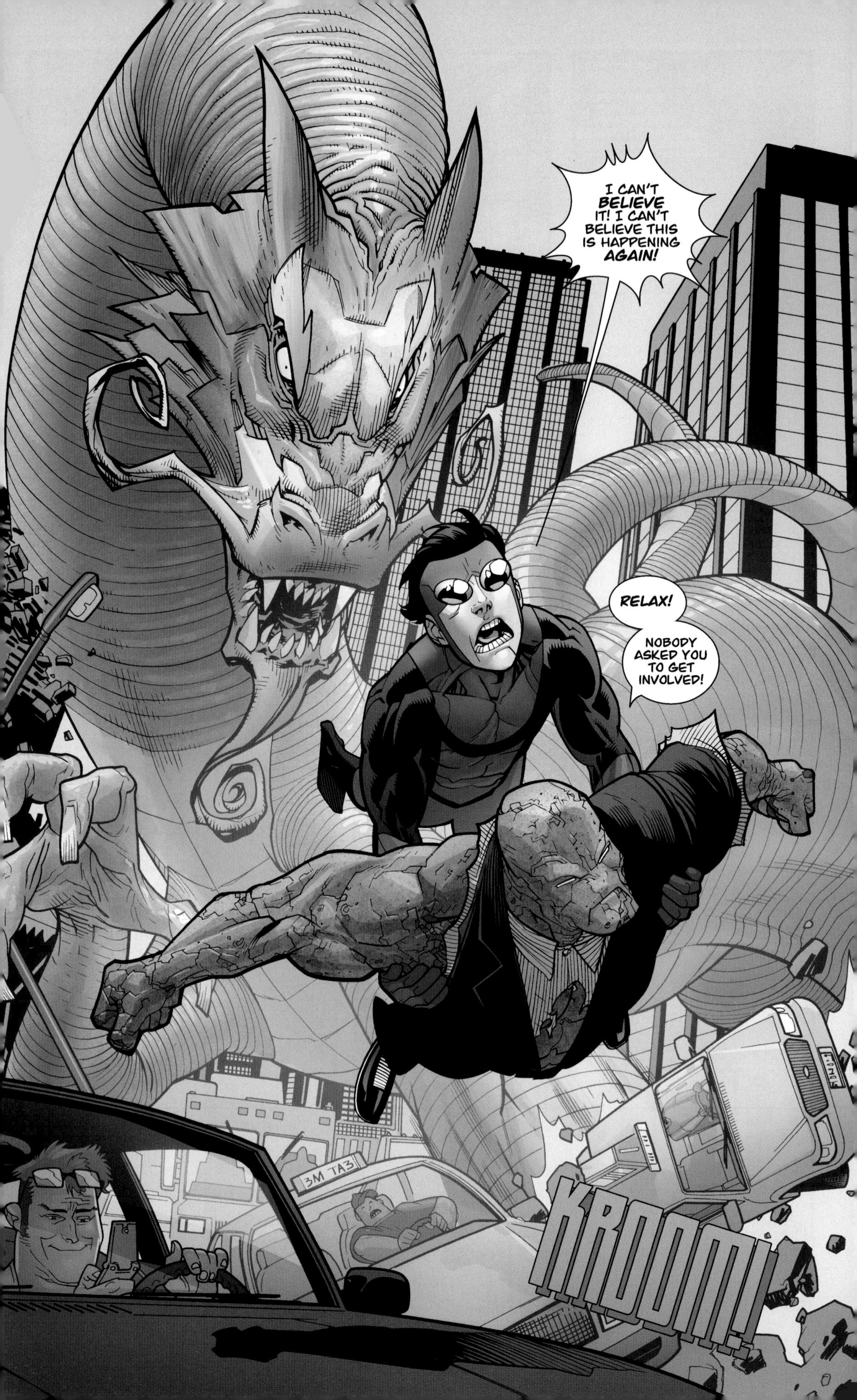
I CAN'T BELIEVE IT! I CAN'T BELIEVE THIS IS HAPPENING AGAIN!
RELAX!
NOBODY ASKED YOU TO GET INVOLVED!
KROOM!!
3M TA3

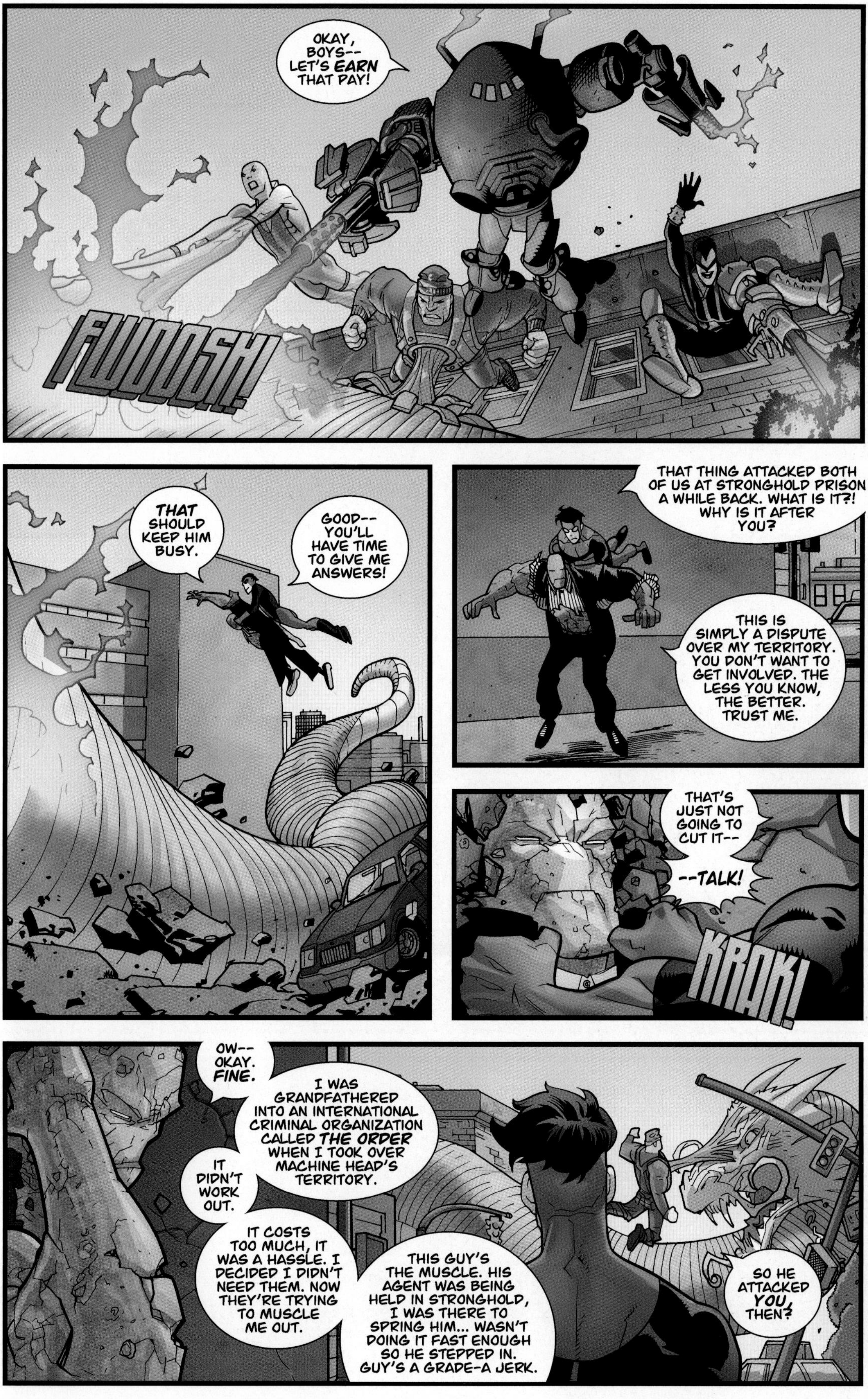
OKAY, BOYS-- LET'S EARN THAT PAY!
FWOOSH!
THAT SHOULD KEEP HIM BUSY.
GOOD-- YOU'LL HAVE TIME TO GIVE ME ANSWERS!
THAT THING ATTACKED BOTH OF US AT STRONGHOLD PRISON A WHILE BACK. WHAT IS IT?! WHY IS IT AFTER YOU?
THIS IS SIMPLY A DISPUTE OVER MY TERRITORY. YOU DON'T WANT TO GET INVOLVED. THE LESS YOU KNOW, THE BETTER. TRUST ME.
THAT'S JUST NOT GOING TO CUT IT--
--TALK!
KRAK!
OW-- OKAY. FINE.
I WAS GRANDFATHERED INTO AN INTERNATIONAL CRIMINAL ORGANIZATION CALLED THE ORDER WHEN I TOOK OVER MACHINE HEAD'S TERRITORY.
IT DIDN'T WORK OUT.
IT COSTS TOO MUCH, IT WAS A HASSLE. I DECIDED I DIDN'T NEED THEM. NOW THEY'RE TRYING TO MUSCLE ME OUT.
THIS GUY'S THE MUSCLE. HIS AGENT WAS BEING HELD IN STRONGHOLD, I WAS THERE TO SPRING HIM... WASN'T DOING IT FAST ENOUGH SO HE STEPPED IN. GUY'S A GRADE-A JERK.
SO HE ATTACKED YOU, THEN?

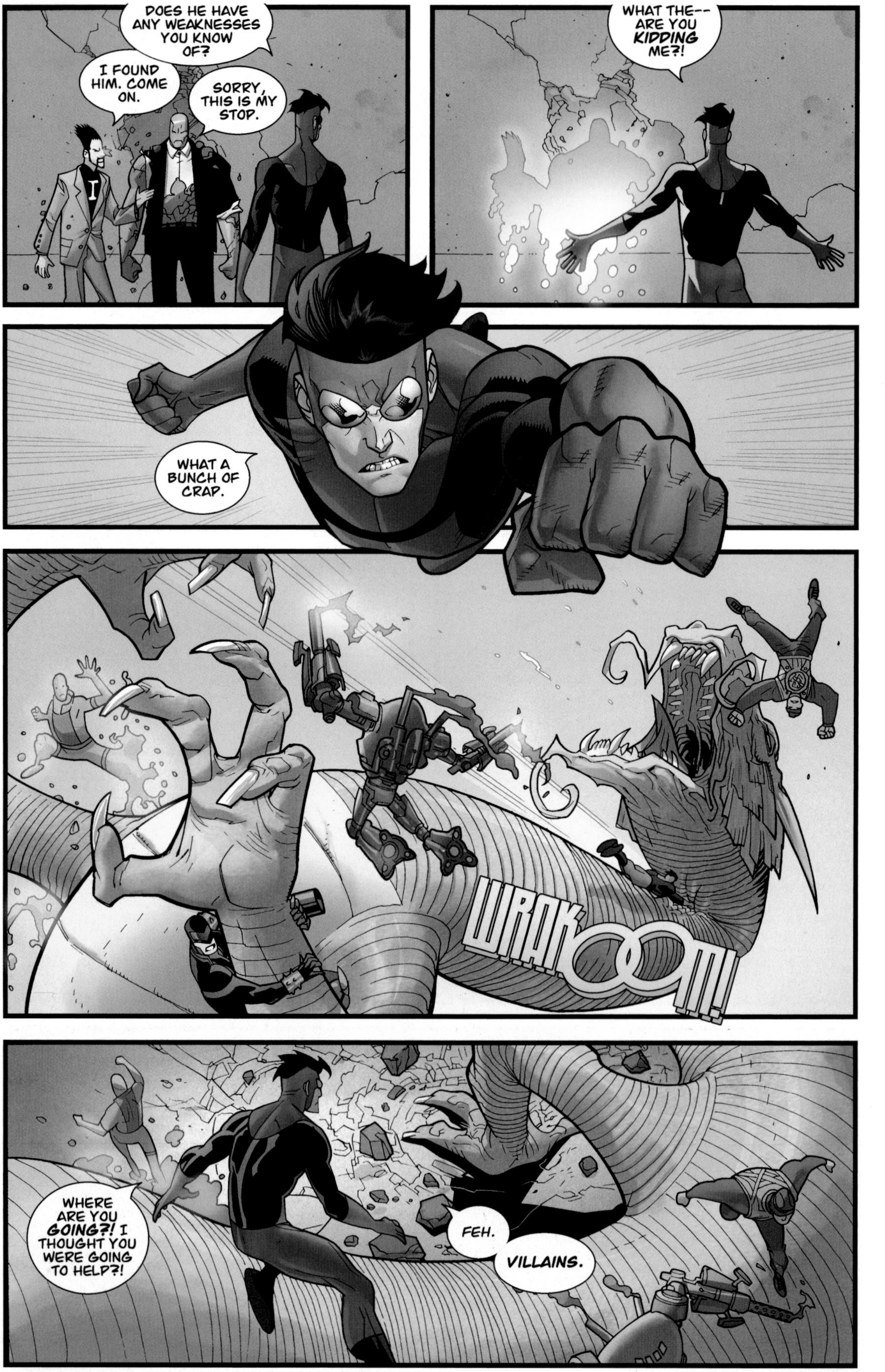

DOES HE HAVE ANY WEAKNESSES YOU KNOW OF?
I FOUND HIM. COME ON.
SORRY, THIS IS MY STOP.
WHAT THE-- ARE YOU KIDDING ME?!
WHAT A BUNCH OF CRAP.
WRAKOOM!
WHERE ARE YOU GOING?! I THOUGHT YOU WERE GOING TO HELP?!
FEH.
VILLAINS.

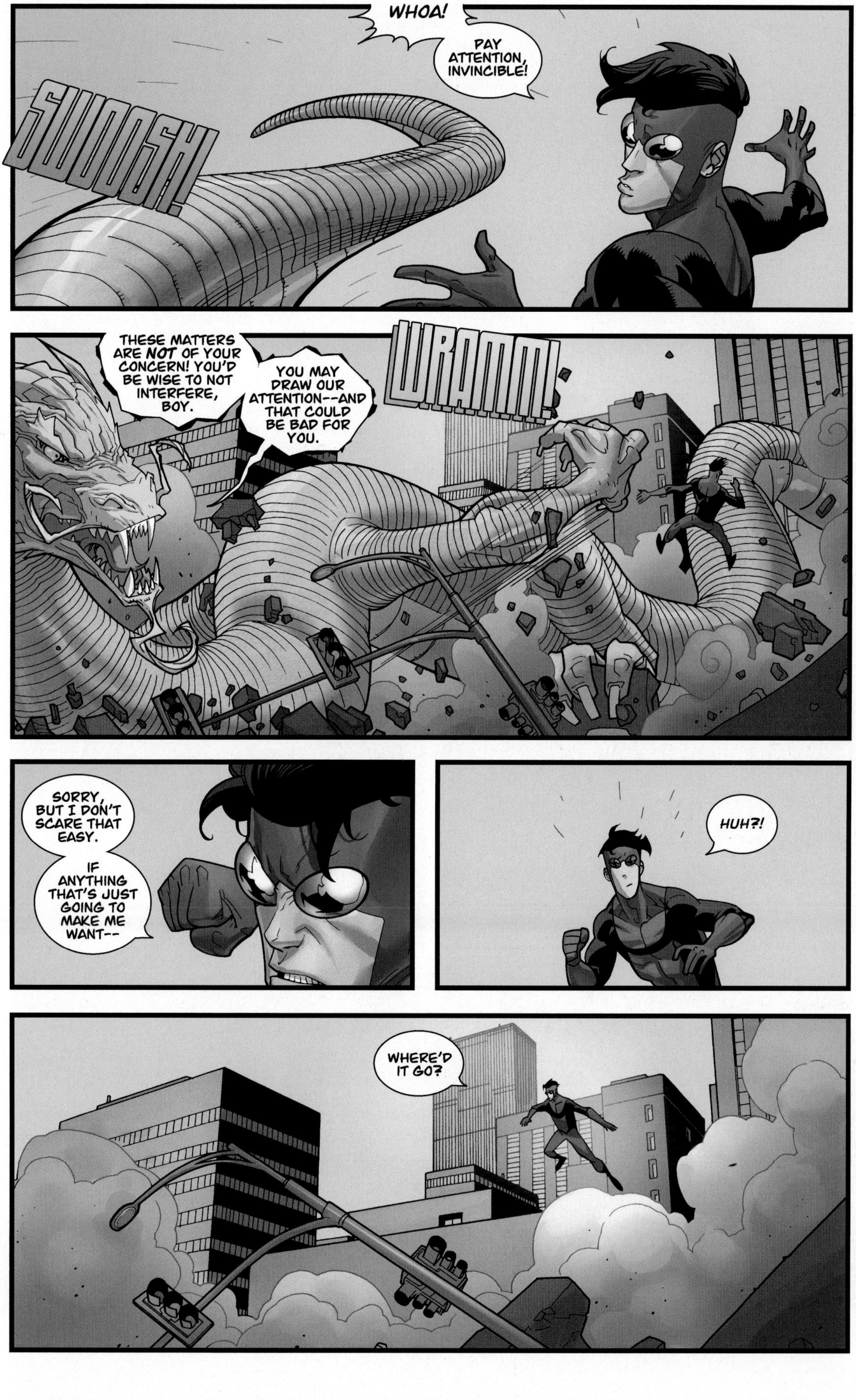
WHOA!
PAY ATTENTION, INVINCIBLE!
SWOOSH!
THESE MATTERS ARE NOT OF YOUR CONCERN! YOU'D BE WISE TO NOT INTERFERE, BOY.
YOU MAY DRAW OUR ATTENTION--AND THAT COULD BE BAD FOR YOU.
WRAMM!
SORRY, BUT I DON'T SCARE THAT EASY.
IF ANYTHING THAT'S JUST GOING TO MAKE ME WANT--
HUH?!
WHERE'D IT GO?

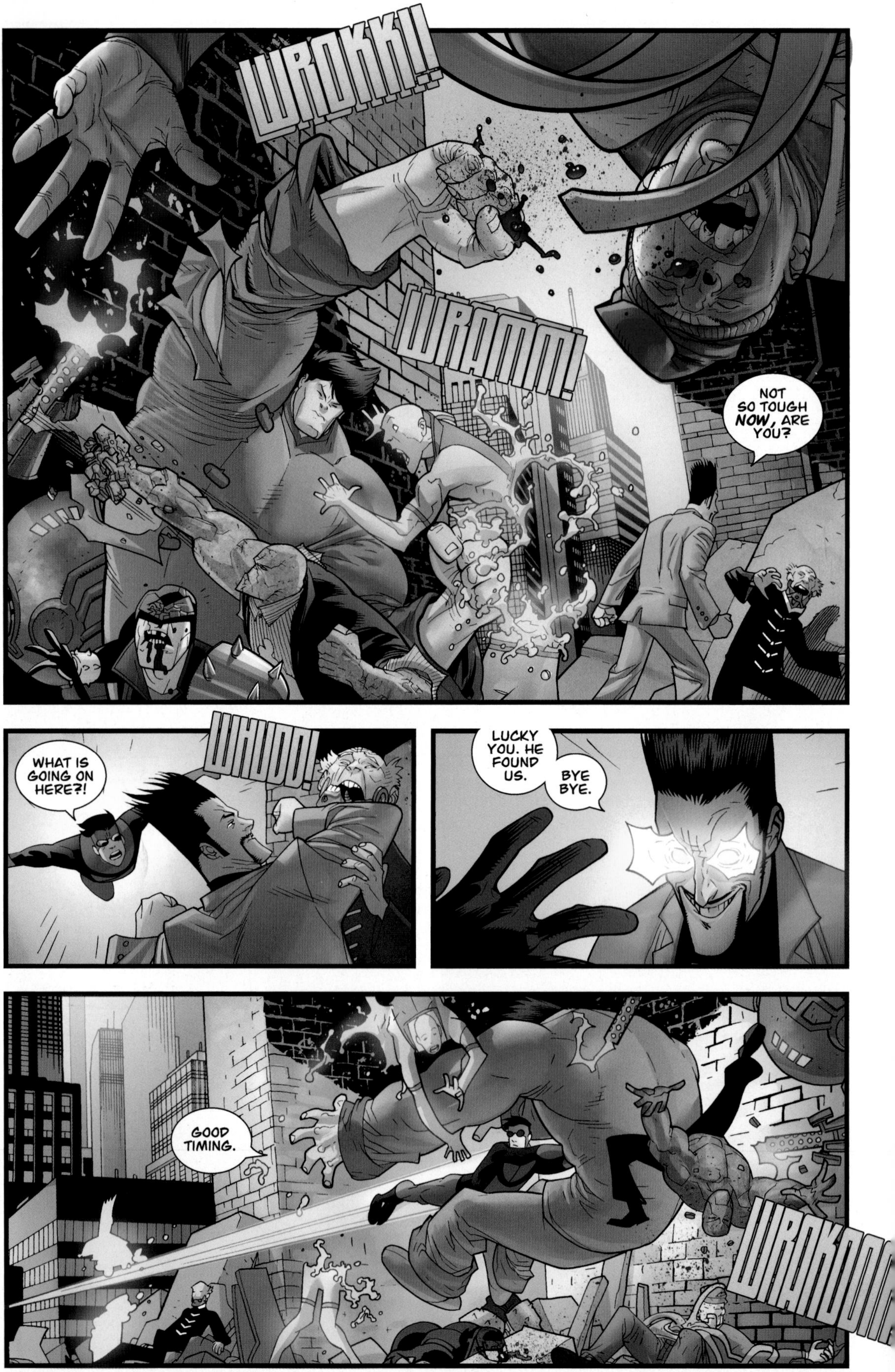
WROKK!!
WRAMM!
NOT SO TOUGH NOW, ARE YOU?
WHUD!
WHAT IS GOING ON HERE?!
LUCKY YOU. HE FOUND US.
BYE BYE.
GOOD TIMING.

ART ROSENBAUM'S TAILOR SHOP.

TAILOR
shoppe

OKAY, THEN... JUST LET YOURSELF IN.

I DON'T MIND.

MARK?

EVERYTHING OKAY?

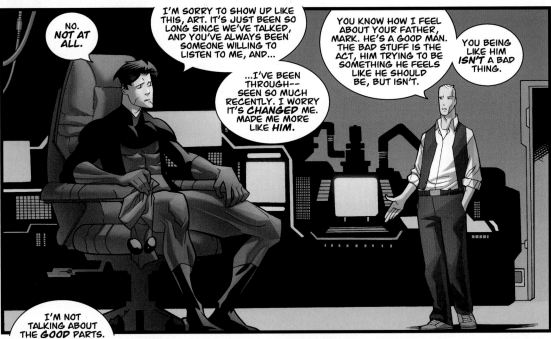

NO. NOT AT ALL.

I'M SORRY TO SHOW UP LIKE THIS, ART. IT'S JUST BEEN SO LONG SINCE WE'VE TALKED, AND YOU'VE ALWAYS BEEN SOMEONE WILLING TO LISTEN TO ME, AND...

...I'VE BEEN THROUGH-- SEEN SO MUCH RECENTLY. I WORRY IT'S CHANGED ME. MADE ME MORE LIKE HIM.

YOU KNOW HOW I FEEL ABOUT YOUR FATHER, MARK. HE'S A GOOD MAN. THE BAD STUFF IS THE ACT, HIM TRYING TO BE SOMETHING HE FEELS LIKE HE SHOULD BE, BUT ISN'T.

YOU BEING LIKE HIM ISN'T A BAD THING.

I'M NOT TALKING ABOUT THE GOOD PARTS. SOMETIMES I THINK, AND I KNOW THIS SOUNDS CRAZY...

IT'S ALMOST LIKE THIS COSTUME IS A CURSE.

I'VE SEEN THE MAJOR CITIES OF THE WORLD LEVELED, I SPENT MONTHS DIGGING OUT BODIES... PARTS OF BODIES.

I'VE SEEN MORE DEATH THAN I CAN BEAR.

CONQUEST CAME, MADE THINGS EVEN WORSE. I SAW THE DEATH OF MY GIRLFRIEND... EVEN THOUGH SHE DIDN'T ACTUALLY DIE...

I STILL HAD TO SEE THAT... FEEL WHAT IT WOULD HAVE BEEN LIKE.

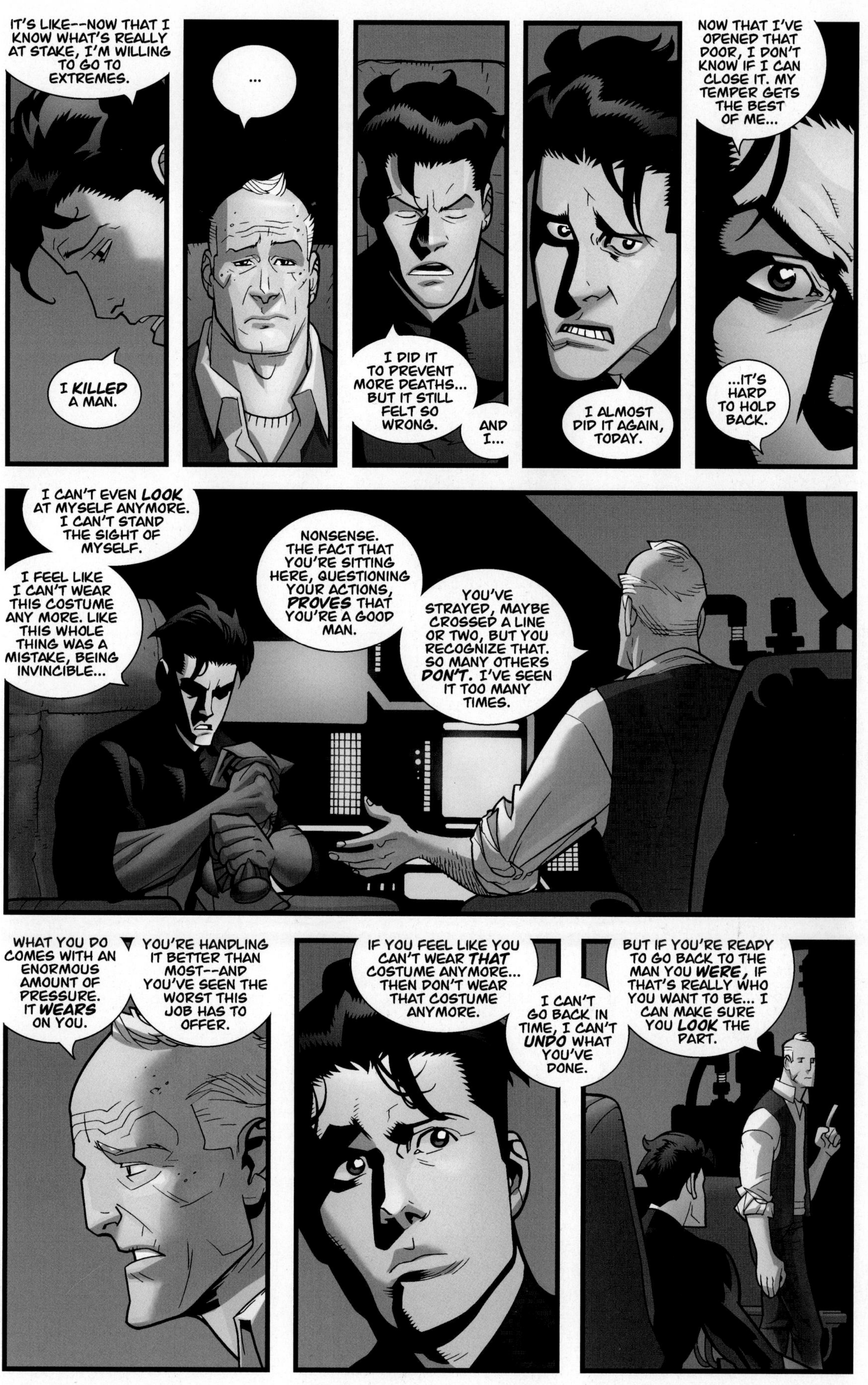

IT'S LIKE--NOW THAT I KNOW WHAT'S REALLY AT STAKE, I'M WILLING TO GO TO EXTREMES.
I KILLED A MAN.
...
I DID IT TO PREVENT MORE DEATHS... BUT IT STILL FELT SO WRONG.
AND I...
I ALMOST DID IT AGAIN, TODAY.
NOW THAT I'VE OPENED THAT DOOR, I DON'T KNOW IF I CAN CLOSE IT. MY TEMPER GETS THE BEST OF ME...
...IT'S HARD TO HOLD BACK.
I CAN'T EVEN LOOK AT MYSELF ANYMORE. I CAN'T STAND THE SIGHT OF MYSELF.
I FEEL LIKE I CAN'T WEAR THIS COSTUME ANY MORE. LIKE THIS WHOLE THING WAS A MISTAKE, BEING INVINCIBLE...
NONSENSE. THE FACT THAT YOU'RE SITTING HERE, QUESTIONING YOUR ACTIONS, PROVES THAT YOU'RE A GOOD MAN.
YOU'VE STRAYED, MAYBE CROSSED A LINE OR TWO, BUT YOU RECOGNIZE THAT. SO MANY OTHERS DON'T. I'VE SEEN IT TOO MANY TIMES.
WHAT YOU DO COMES WITH AN ENORMOUS AMOUNT OF PRESSURE. IT WEARS ON YOU.
YOU'RE HANDLING IT BETTER THAN MOST--AND YOU'VE SEEN THE WORST THIS JOB HAS TO OFFER.
IF YOU FEEL LIKE YOU CAN'T WEAR THAT COSTUME ANYMORE... THEN DON'T WEAR THAT COSTUME ANYMORE.
I CAN'T GO BACK IN TIME, I CAN'T UNDO WHAT YOU'VE DONE.
BUT IF YOU'RE READY TO GO BACK TO THE MAN YOU WERE, IF THAT'S REALLY WHO YOU WANT TO BE... I CAN MAKE SURE YOU LOOK THE PART.

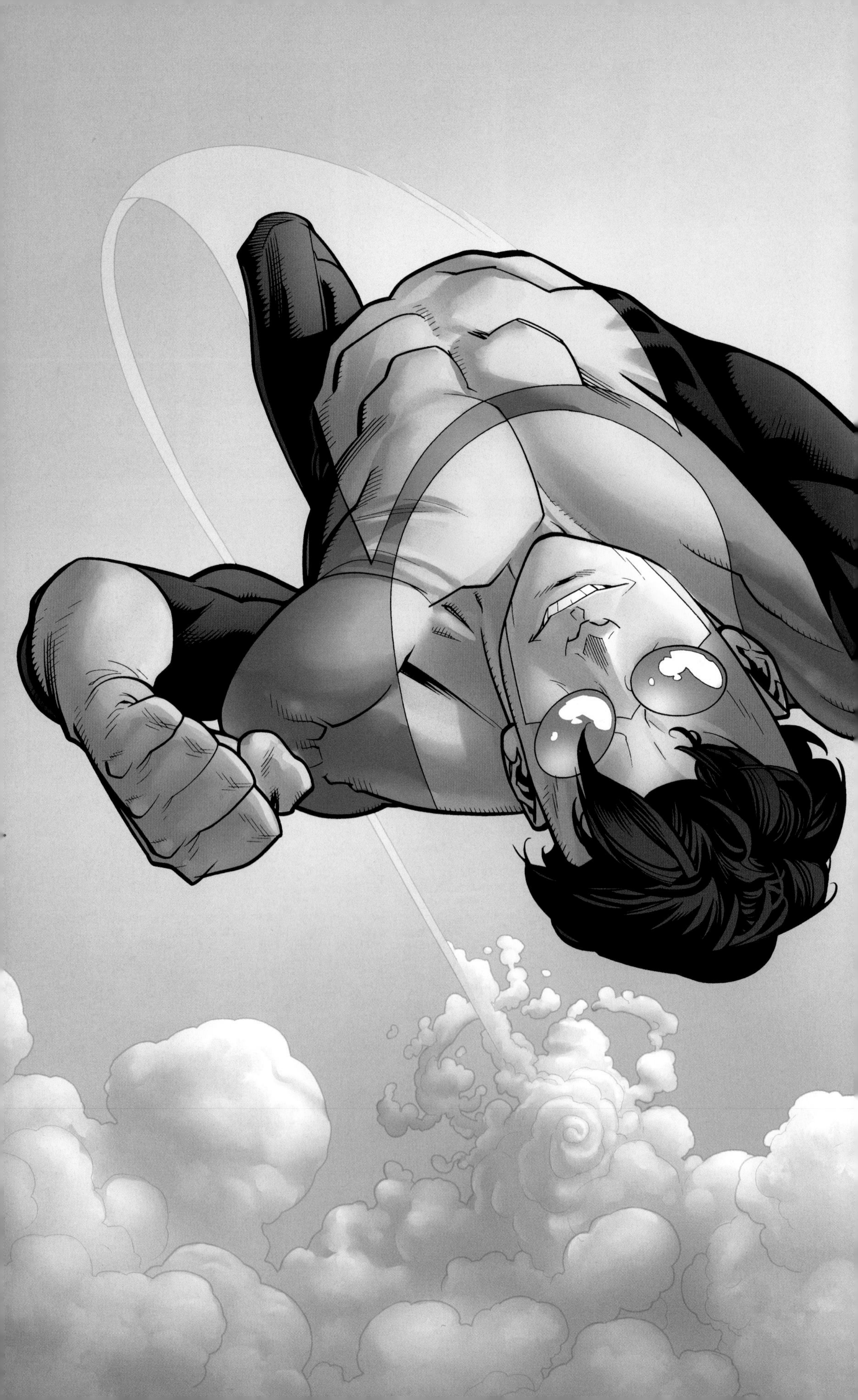

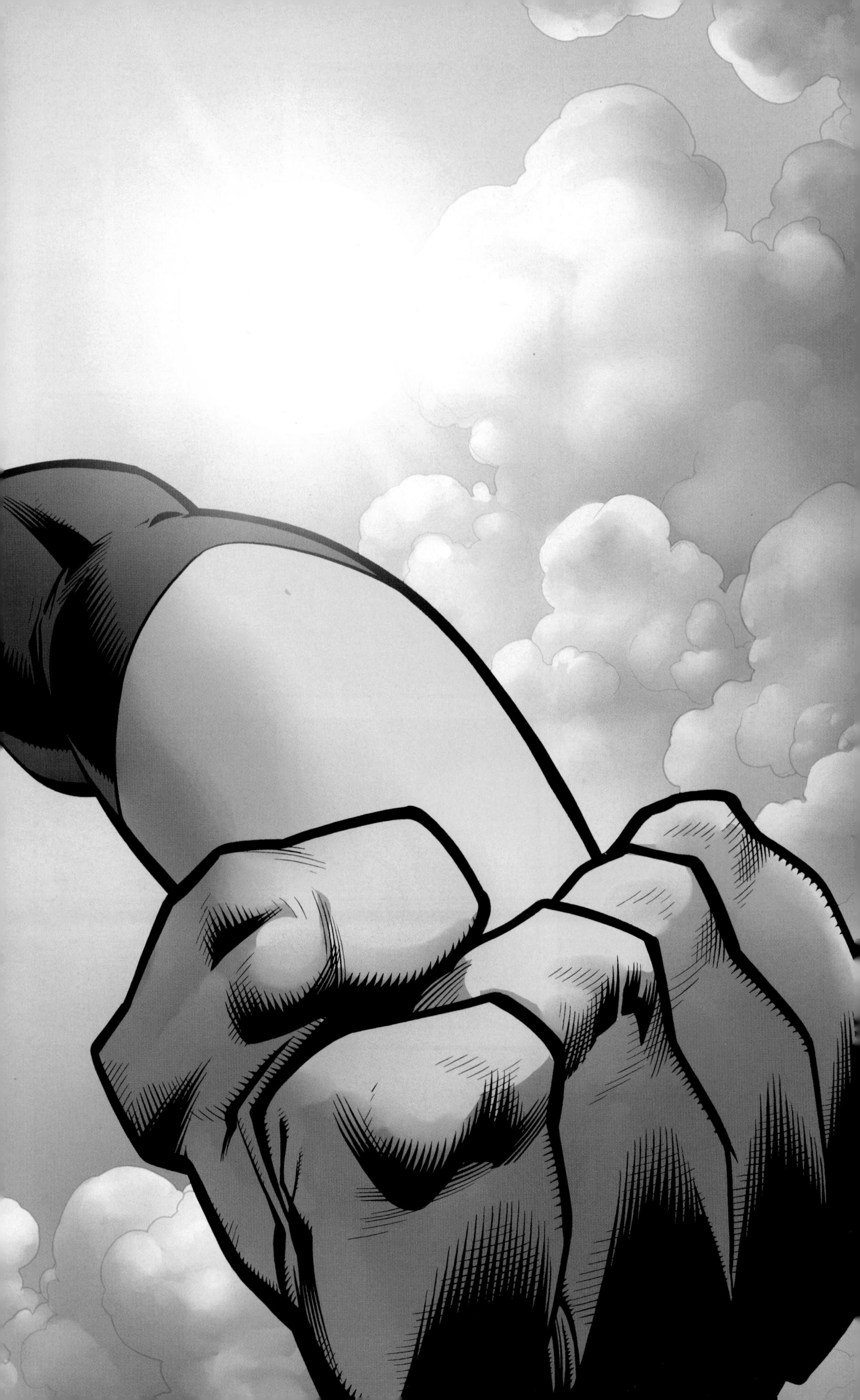

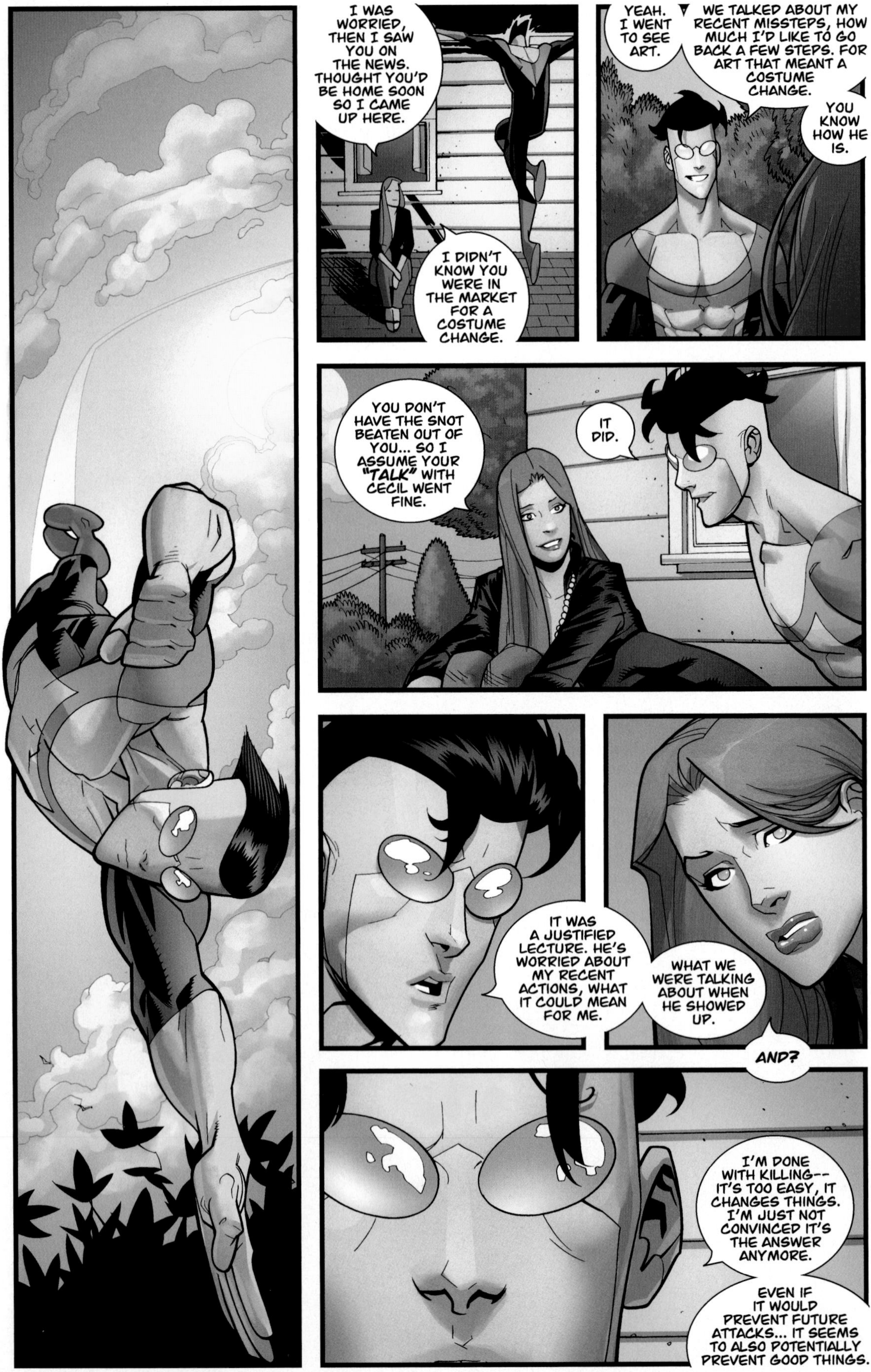
I WAS WORRIED, THEN I SAW YOU ON THE NEWS. THOUGHT YOU'D BE HOME SOON SO I CAME UP HERE.
I DIDN'T KNOW YOU WERE IN THE MARKET FOR A COSTUME CHANGE.
YEAH. I WENT TO SEE ART.
WE TALKED ABOUT MY RECENT MISSTEPS, HOW MUCH I'D LIKE TO GO BACK A FEW STEPS. FOR ART THAT MEANT A COSTUME CHANGE.
YOU KNOW HOW HE IS.
YOU DON'T HAVE THE SNOT BEATEN OUT OF YOU... SO I ASSUME YOUR "TALK" WITH CECIL WENT FINE.
IT DID.
IT WAS A JUSTIFIED LECTURE. HE'S WORRIED ABOUT MY RECENT ACTIONS, WHAT IT COULD MEAN FOR ME.
WHAT WE WERE TALKING ABOUT WHEN HE SHOWED UP.
AND?
I'M DONE WITH KILLING-- IT'S TOO EASY, IT CHANGES THINGS. I'M JUST NOT CONVINCED IT'S THE ANSWER ANYMORE.
EVEN IF IT WOULD PREVENT FUTURE ATTACKS... IT SEEMS TO ALSO POTENTIALLY PREVENT GOOD THINGS.

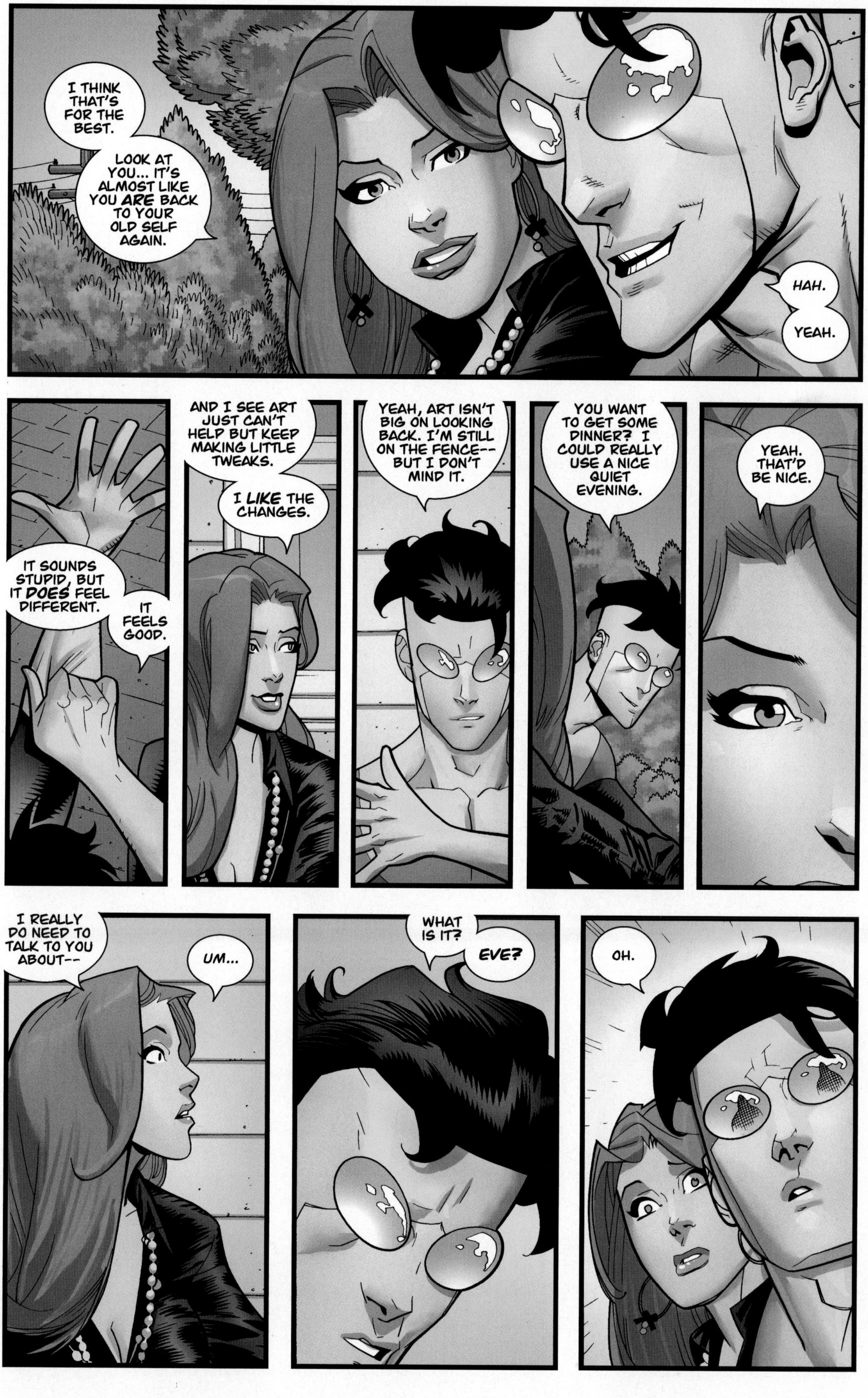
I THINK THAT'S FOR THE BEST.
LOOK AT YOU... IT'S ALMOST LIKE YOU ARE BACK TO YOUR OLD SELF AGAIN.
HAH.
YEAH.
IT SOUNDS STUPID, BUT IT DOES FEEL DIFFERENT.
IT FEELS GOOD.
AND I SEE ART JUST CAN'T HELP BUT KEEP MAKING LITTLE TWEAKS.
I LIKE THE CHANGES.
YEAH, ART ISN'T BIG ON LOOKING BACK. I'M STILL ON THE FENCE-- BUT I DON'T MIND IT.
YOU WANT TO GET SOME DINNER? I COULD REALLY USE A NICE QUIET EVENING.
YEAH. THAT'D BE NICE.
I REALLY DO NEED TO TALK TO YOU ABOUT--
UM...
WHAT IS IT?
EVE?
OH.

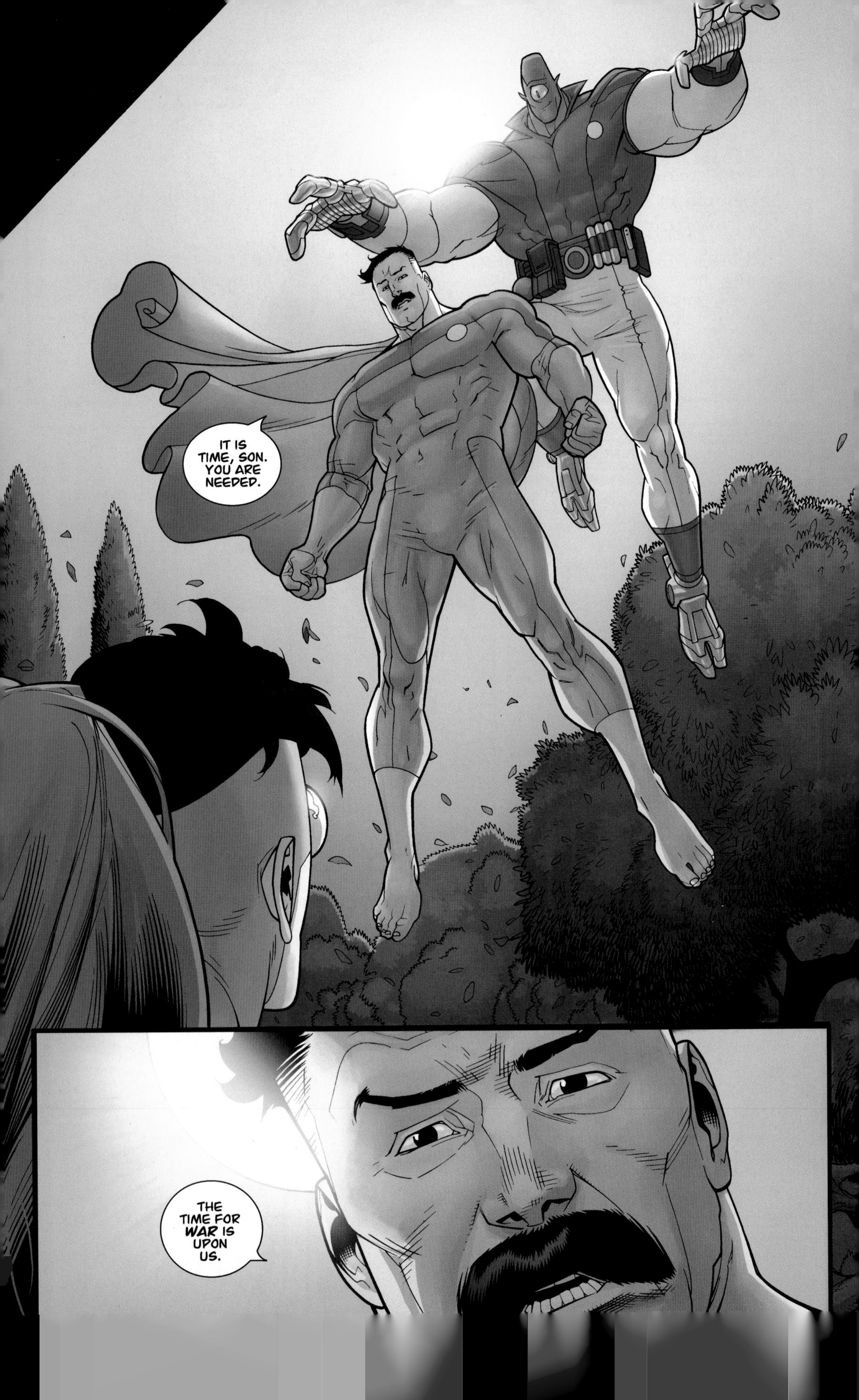
IT IS TIME, SON. YOU ARE NEEDED.
THE TIME FOR WAR IS UPON US.

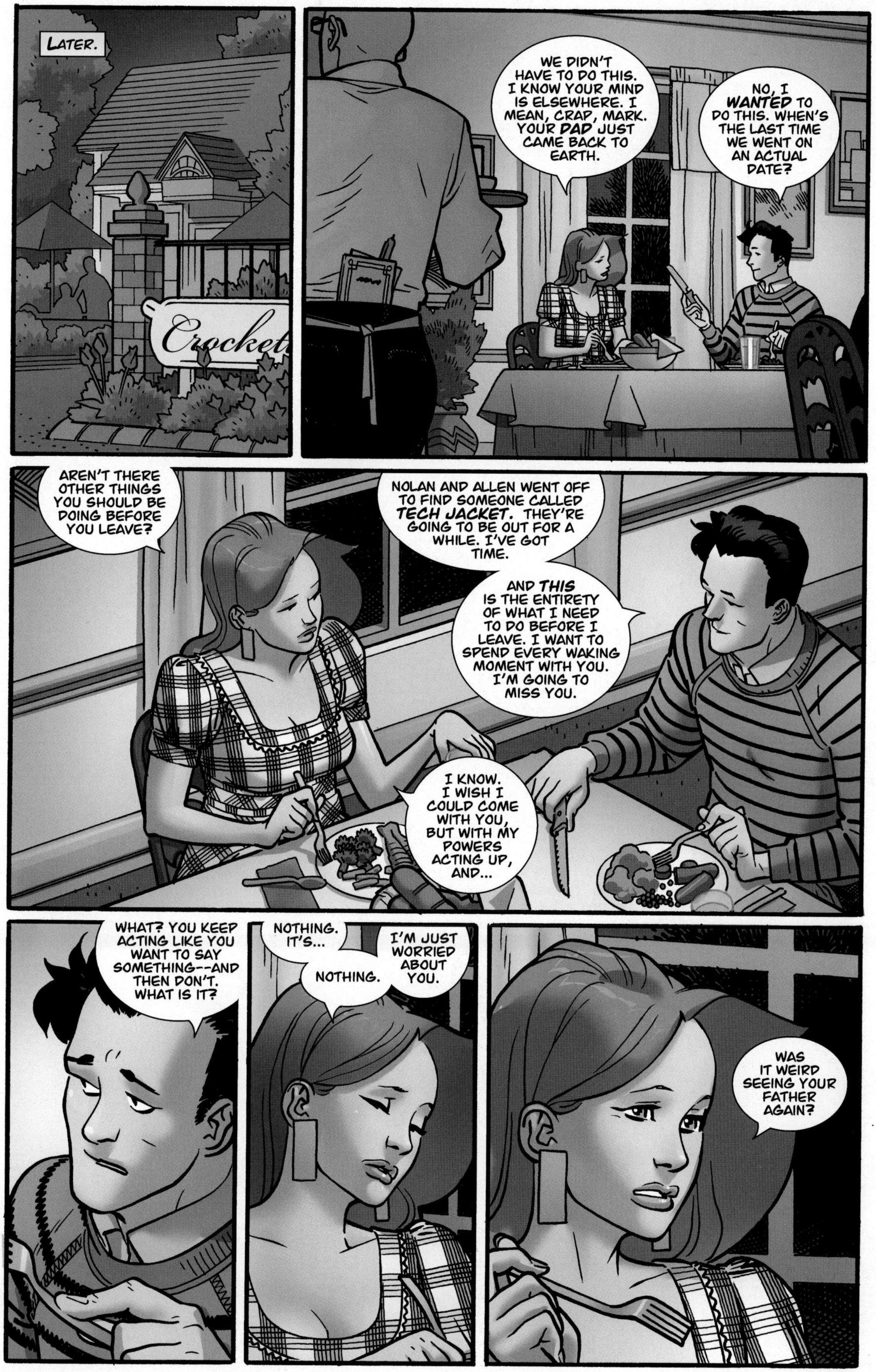
LATER.
Crockett
WE DIDN'T HAVE TO DO THIS. I KNOW YOUR MIND IS ELSEWHERE. I MEAN, CRAP, MARK. YOUR DAD JUST CAME BACK TO EARTH.
NO, I WANTED TO DO THIS. WHEN'S THE LAST TIME WE WENT ON AN ACTUAL DATE?
AREN'T THERE OTHER THINGS YOU SHOULD BE DOING BEFORE YOU LEAVE?
NOLAN AND ALLEN WENT OFF TO FIND SOMEONE CALLED TECH JACKET. THEY'RE GOING TO BE OUT FOR A WHILE. I'VE GOT TIME.
AND THIS IS THE ENTIRETY OF WHAT I NEED TO DO BEFORE I LEAVE. I WANT TO SPEND EVERY WAKING MOMENT WITH YOU. I'M GOING TO MISS YOU.
I KNOW. I WISH I COULD COME WITH YOU, BUT WITH MY POWERS ACTING UP, AND...
WHAT? YOU KEEP ACTING LIKE YOU WANT TO SAY SOMETHING--AND THEN DON'T. WHAT IS IT?
NOTHING. IT'S...
NOTHING.
I'M JUST WORRIED ABOUT YOU.
WAS IT WEIRD SEEING YOUR FATHER AGAIN?

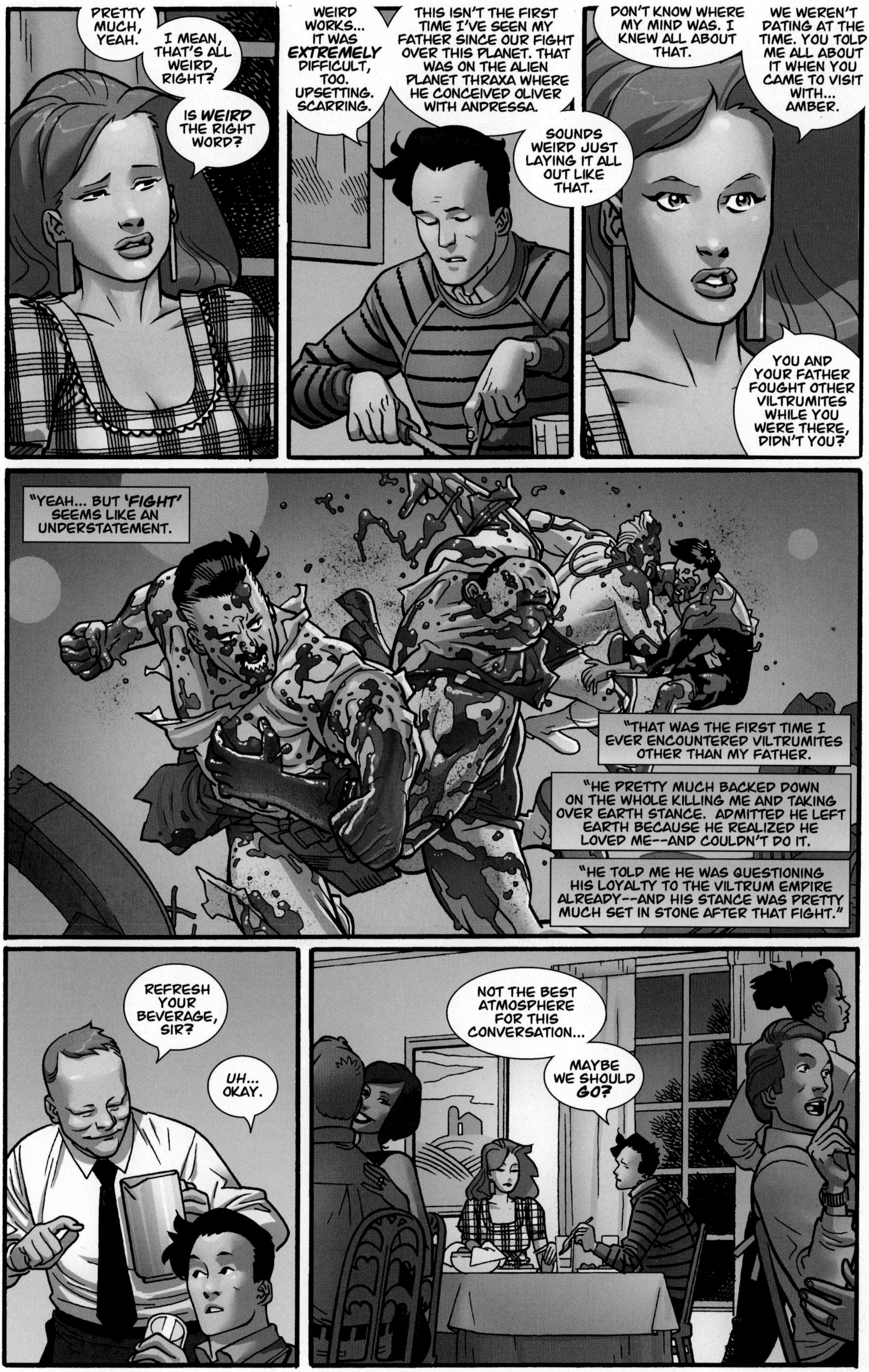
PRETTY MUCH, YEAH.
I MEAN, THAT'S ALL WEIRD, RIGHT?
IS WEIRD THE RIGHT WORD?
WEIRD WORKS... IT WAS EXTREMELY DIFFICULT, TOO. UPSETTING. SCARRING.
THIS ISN'T THE FIRST TIME I'VE SEEN MY FATHER SINCE OUR FIGHT OVER THIS PLANET. THAT WAS ON THE ALIEN PLANET THRAXA WHERE HE CONCEIVED OLIVER WITH ANDRESSA.
SOUNDS WEIRD JUST LAYING IT ALL OUT LIKE THAT.
DON'T KNOW WHERE MY MIND WAS. I KNEW ALL ABOUT THAT.
WE WEREN'T DATING AT THE TIME. YOU TOLD ME ALL ABOUT IT WHEN YOU CAME TO VISIT WITH... AMBER.
YOU AND YOUR FATHER FOUGHT OTHER VILTRUMITES WHILE YOU WERE THERE, DIDN'T YOU?
"YEAH... BUT 'FIGHT' SEEMS LIKE AN UNDERSTATEMENT.
"THAT WAS THE FIRST TIME I EVER ENCOUNTERED VILTRUMITES OTHER THAN MY FATHER.
"HE PRETTY MUCH BACKED DOWN ON THE WHOLE KILLING ME AND TAKING OVER EARTH STANCE. ADMITTED HE LEFT EARTH BECAUSE HE REALIZED HE LOVED ME--AND COULDN'T DO IT.
"HE TOLD ME HE WAS QUESTIONING HIS LOYALTY TO THE VILTRUM EMPIRE ALREADY--AND HIS STANCE WAS PRETTY MUCH SET IN STONE AFTER THAT FIGHT."
REFRESH YOUR BEVERAGE, SIR?
UH... OKAY.
NOT THE BEST ATMOSPHERE FOR THIS CONVERSATION...
MAYBE WE SHOULD GO?

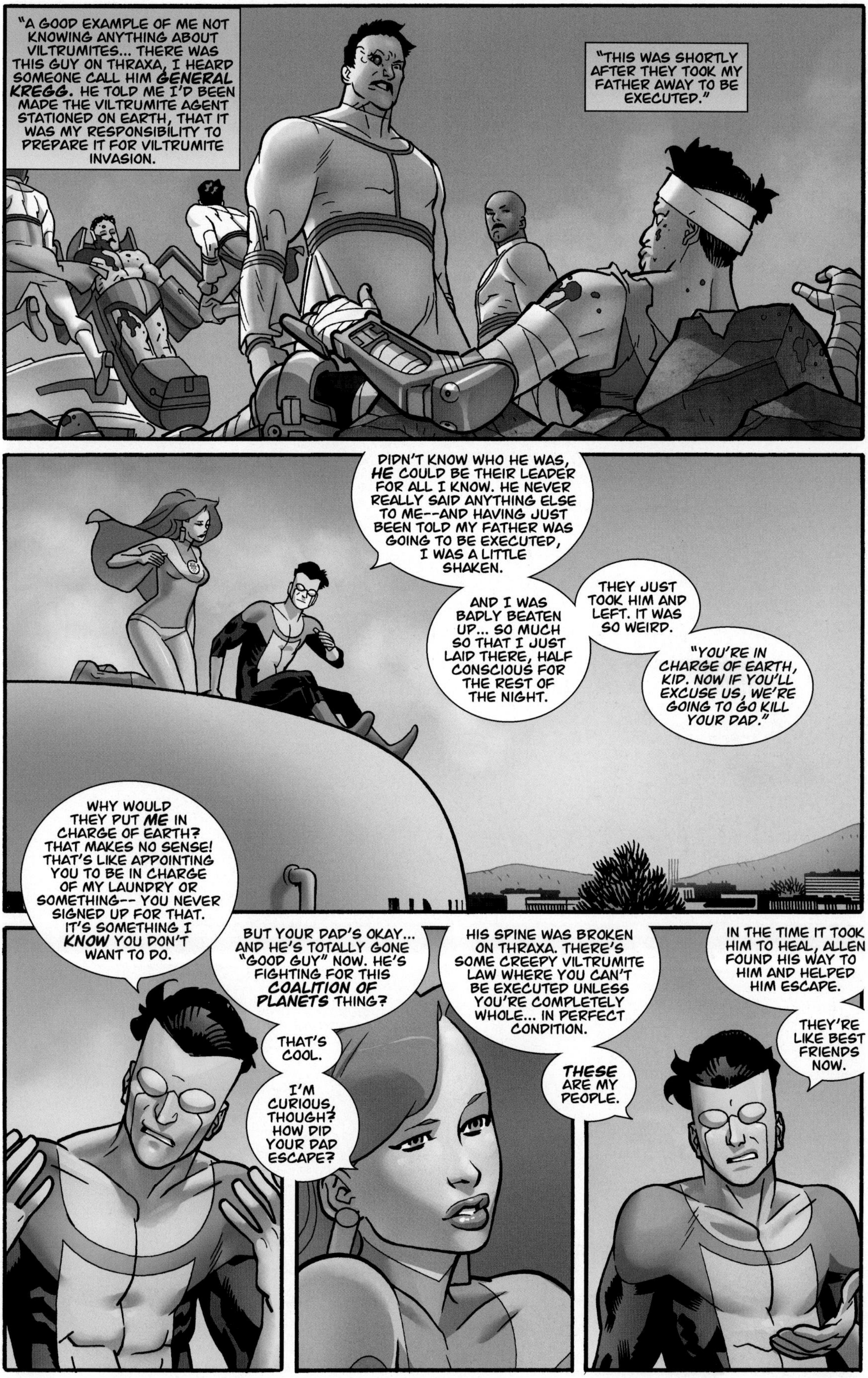
"A GOOD EXAMPLE OF ME NOT KNOWING ANYTHING ABOUT VILTRUMITES... THERE WAS THIS GUY ON THRAXA, I HEARD SOMEONE CALL HIM GENERAL KREGG. HE TOLD ME I'D BEEN MADE THE VILTRUMITE AGENT STATIONED ON EARTH, THAT IT WAS MY RESPONSIBILITY TO PREPARE IT FOR VILTRUMITE INVASION.
"THIS WAS SHORTLY AFTER THEY TOOK MY FATHER AWAY TO BE EXECUTED."
DIDN'T KNOW WHO HE WAS, HE COULD BE THEIR LEADER FOR ALL I KNOW. HE NEVER REALLY SAID ANYTHING ELSE TO ME--AND HAVING JUST BEEN TOLD MY FATHER WAS GOING TO BE EXECUTED, I WAS A LITTLE SHAKEN.
AND I WAS BADLY BEATEN UP... SO MUCH SO THAT I JUST LAID THERE, HALF CONSCIOUS FOR THE REST OF THE NIGHT.
THEY JUST TOOK HIM AND LEFT. IT WAS SO WEIRD.
"YOU'RE IN CHARGE OF EARTH, KID. NOW IF YOU'LL EXCUSE US, WE'RE GOING TO GO KILL YOUR DAD."
WHY WOULD THEY PUT ME IN CHARGE OF EARTH? THAT MAKES NO SENSE! THAT'S LIKE APPOINTING YOU TO BE IN CHARGE OF MY LAUNDRY OR SOMETHING-- YOU NEVER SIGNED UP FOR THAT. IT'S SOMETHING I KNOW YOU DON'T WANT TO DO.
BUT YOUR DAD'S OKAY... AND HE'S TOTALLY GONE "GOOD GUY" NOW. HE'S FIGHTING FOR THIS COALITION OF PLANETS THING?
THAT'S COOL.
I'M CURIOUS, THOUGH? HOW DID YOUR DAD ESCAPE?
HIS SPINE WAS BROKEN ON THRAXA. THERE'S SOME CREEPY VILTRUMITE LAW WHERE YOU CAN'T BE EXECUTED UNLESS YOU'RE COMPLETELY WHOLE... IN PERFECT CONDITION.
THESE ARE MY PEOPLE.
IN THE TIME IT TOOK HIM TO HEAL, ALLEN FOUND HIS WAY TO HIM AND HELPED HIM ESCAPE.
THEY'RE LIKE BEST FRIENDS NOW.

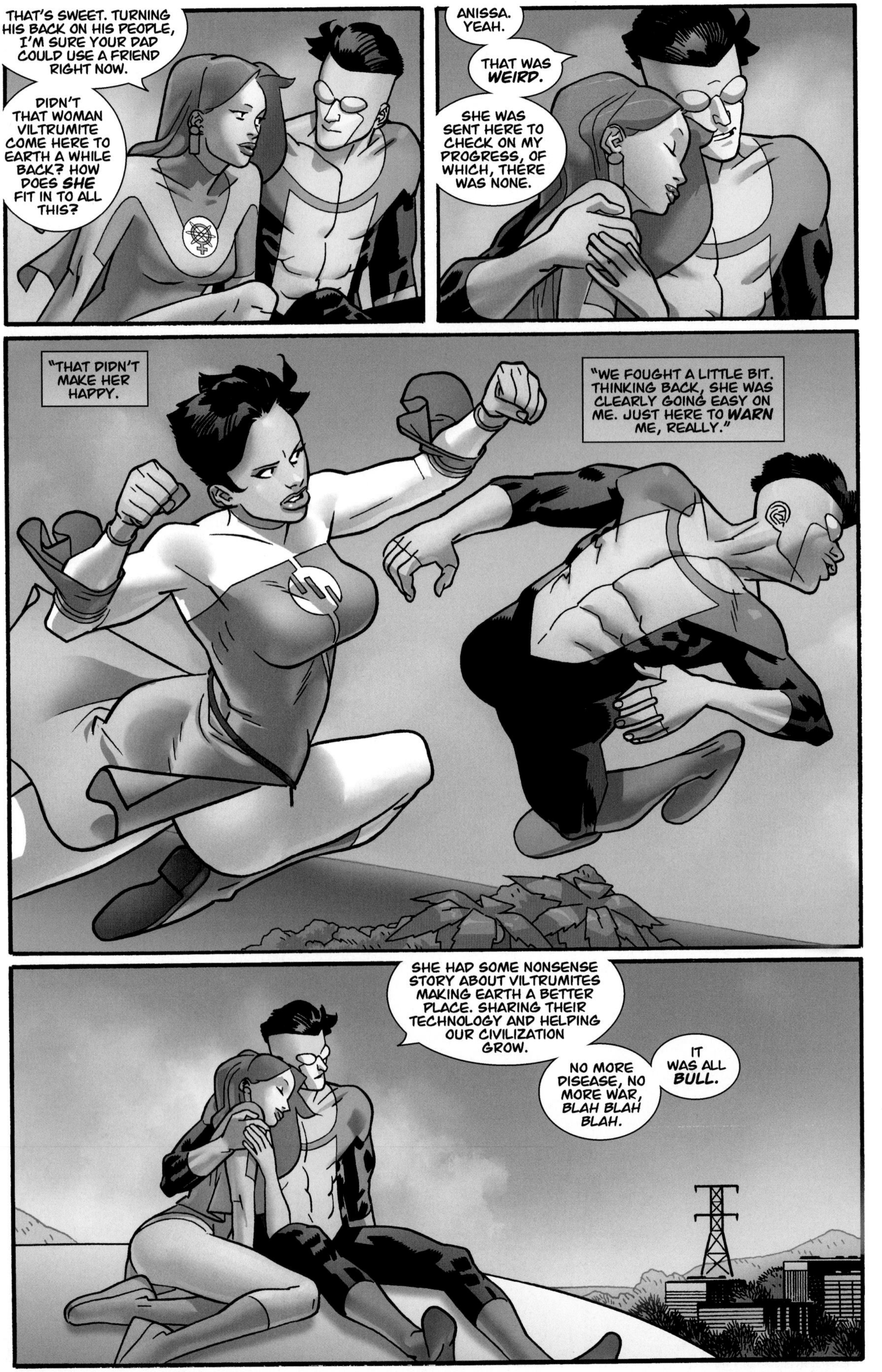
THAT'S SWEET. TURNING HIS BACK ON HIS PEOPLE, I'M SURE YOUR DAD COULD USE A FRIEND RIGHT NOW.
DIDN'T THAT WOMAN VILTRUMITE COME HERE TO EARTH A WHILE BACK? HOW DOES SHE FIT IN TO ALL THIS?
ANISSA. YEAH.
THAT WAS WEIRD.
SHE WAS SENT HERE TO CHECK ON MY PROGRESS, OF WHICH, THERE WAS NONE.
"THAT DIDN'T MAKE HER HAPPY.
"WE FOUGHT A LITTLE BIT. THINKING BACK, SHE WAS CLEARLY GOING EASY ON ME. JUST HERE TO WARN ME, REALLY."
SHE HAD SOME NONSENSE STORY ABOUT VILTRUMITES MAKING EARTH A BETTER PLACE. SHARING THEIR TECHNOLOGY AND HELPING OUR CIVILIZATION GROW.
NO MORE DISEASE, NO MORE WAR, BLAH BLAH BLAH.
IT WAS ALL BULL.

"SHE EVEN HELPED ME SAVE A BUNCH OF PEOPLE AS SOME KIND OF FORCED DISPLAY OF THE GOOD THE VILTRUMITES COULD DO.

"I DIDN'T BUY IT."

SHE WAS CLEARLY SOME KIND OF LAST DITCH EFFORT TO WIN ME OVER. IT ALL SEEMED LIKE A TRICK.

IN HINDSIGHT, SHE WAS CLEARLY THE HONEY, SOON TO BE FOLLOWED BY THE VINEGAR.

I KNEW A BIT ABOUT THE VILTRUMITES ALREADY. WORLD CONQUERORS, ALIEN ENSLAVERS, GENERALLY BAD PEOPLE... I WASN'T BUYING HER KINDER, GENTLER VILTRUMITES ACT.

SHE WARNED ME. TOLD ME I BETTER START MY WORK, PREPARING EARTH FOR TAKEOVER--THAT IT WOULD BE BETTER FOR EVERYONE IF I DID IT PEACEFULLY.

BECAUSE THEY WOULD NOT.

CONQUEST.

AND SHE SAID THE NEXT AGENT THEY'D SEND WOULDN'T BE AS REASONABLE AS SHE WAS.

YEAH.. CONQUEST.

NO NEED TO GO THERE, MARK. REALLY.

THE LESS SAID ABOUT HIM THE BETTER.

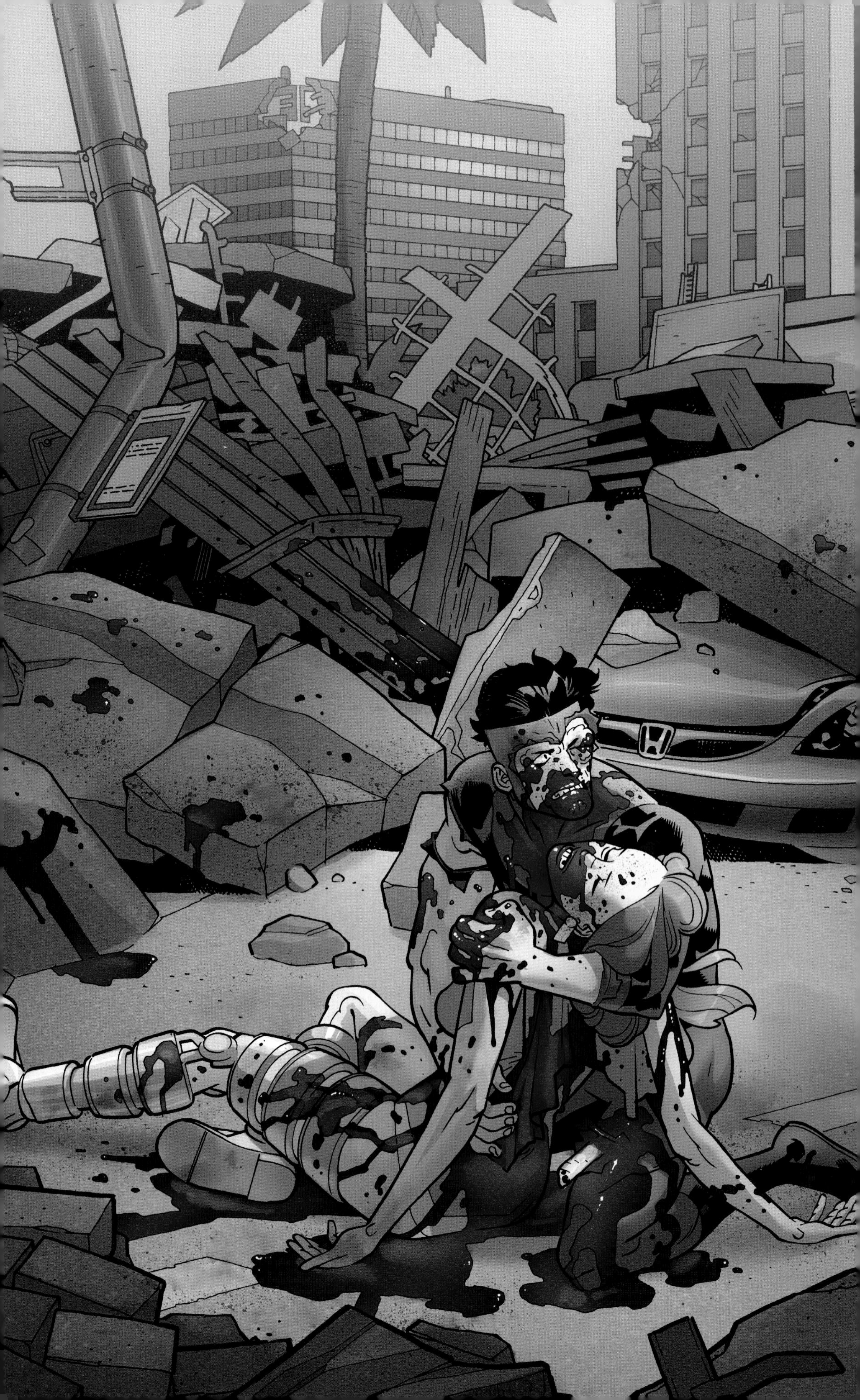

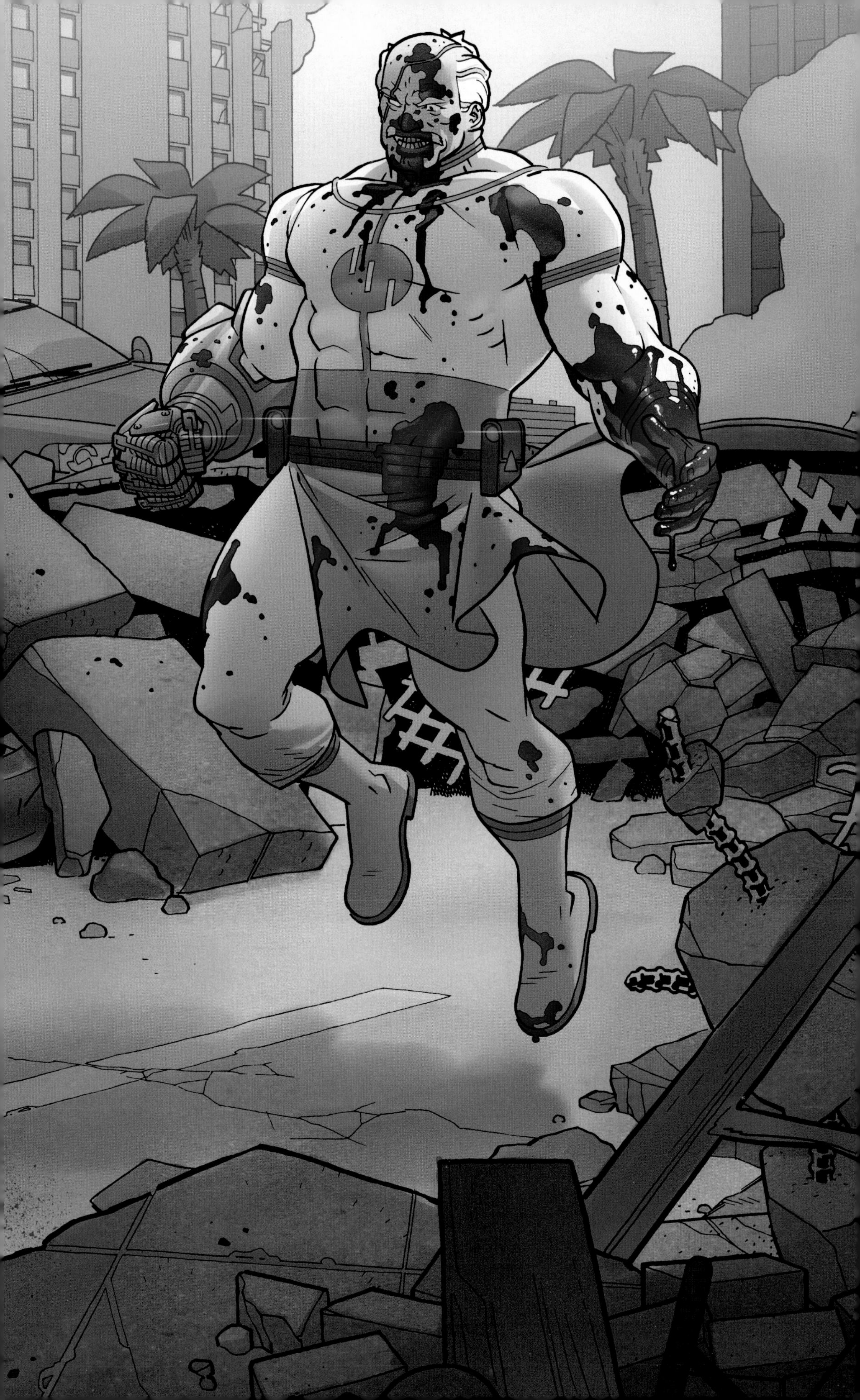

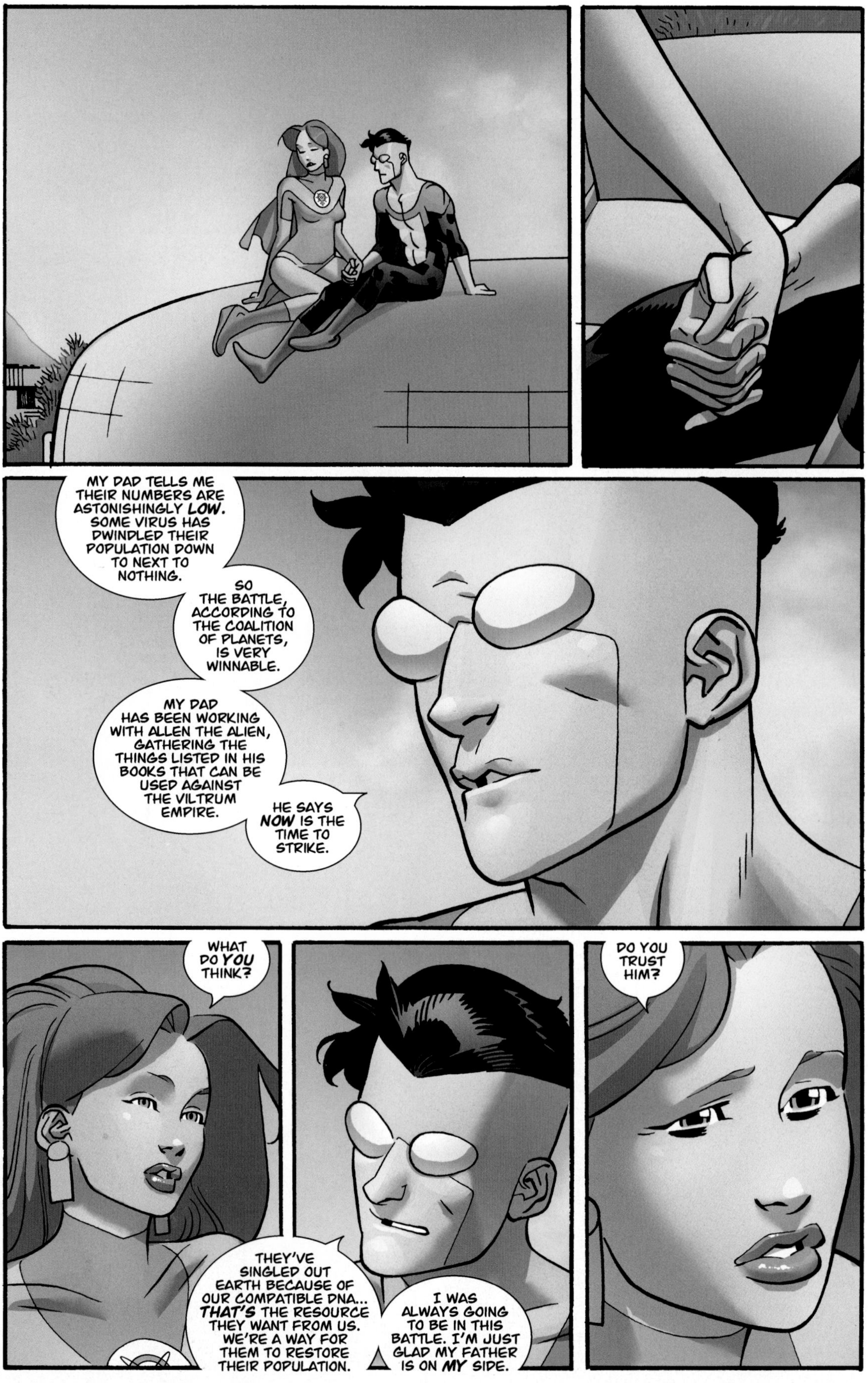
MY DAD TELLS ME THEIR NUMBERS ARE ASTONISHINGLY **LOW.** SOME VIRUS HAS DWINDLED THEIR POPULATION DOWN TO NEXT TO NOTHING.
SO THE BATTLE, ACCORDING TO THE COALITION OF PLANETS, IS VERY WINNABLE.
MY DAD HAS BEEN WORKING WITH ALLEN THE ALIEN, GATHERING THE THINGS LISTED IN HIS BOOKS THAT CAN BE USED AGAINST THE VILTRUM EMPIRE.
HE SAYS ***NOW*** IS THE TIME TO STRIKE.
WHAT DO ***YOU*** THINK?
THEY'VE SINGLED OUT EARTH BECAUSE OF OUR COMPATIBLE DNA... ***THAT'S*** THE RESOURCE THEY WANT FROM US. WE'RE A WAY FOR THEM TO RESTORE THEIR POPULATION.
I WAS ALWAYS GOING TO BE IN THIS BATTLE. I'M JUST GLAD MY FATHER IS ON ***MY*** SIDE.
DO YOU TRUST HIM?

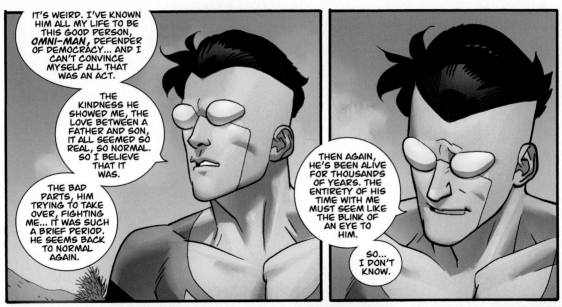

IT'S WEIRD. I'VE KNOWN HIM ALL MY LIFE TO BE THIS GOOD PERSON, *OMNI-MAN*, DEFENDER OF DEMOCRACY... AND I CAN'T CONVINCE MYSELF ALL THAT WAS AN ACT.

THE KINDNESS HE SHOWED ME, THE LOVE BETWEEN A FATHER AND SON, IT ALL SEEMED SO REAL, SO NORMAL. SO I BELIEVE THAT IT WAS.

THE BAD PARTS, HIM TRYING TO TAKE OVER, FIGHTING ME... IT WAS SUCH A BRIEF PERIOD. HE SEEMS BACK TO NORMAL AGAIN.

THEN AGAIN, HE'S BEEN ALIVE FOR THOUSANDS OF YEARS. THE ENTIRETY OF HIS TIME WITH ME MUST SEEM LIKE THE BLINK OF AN EYE TO HIM.

SO... I DON'T KNOW.

WHAT CHOICE DO I HAVE? *ALLEN* TRUSTS HIM. THE COALITION TRUSTS HIM.

HE'S DONE NOTHING BUT REVEAL THE WEAKNESSES OF HIS PEOPLE SINCE HE BEGAN WORKING WITH THEM. I DON'T SEE HOW THAT COULD BE PART OF A LARGER PLAN...

BUT WHAT DO I KNOW?

WE'RE SUPPOSED TO LEAVE TOMORROW. I DON'T KNOW HOW LONG I'LL BE GONE AND I WON'T HAVE ANY CONTACT WITH EARTH.

BUT THIS IS SOMETHING I *HAVE* TO DO-- FOR THE SAKE OF THE WHOLE PLANET.

I KNOW. I UNDERSTAND.

I--

I'LL HOLD DOWN THE FORT WHILE YOU'RE GONE.

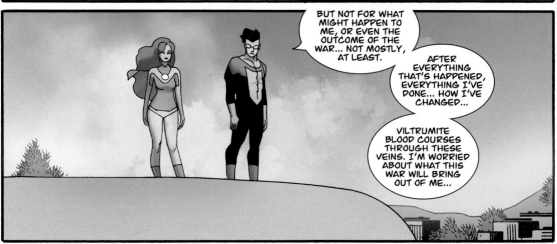

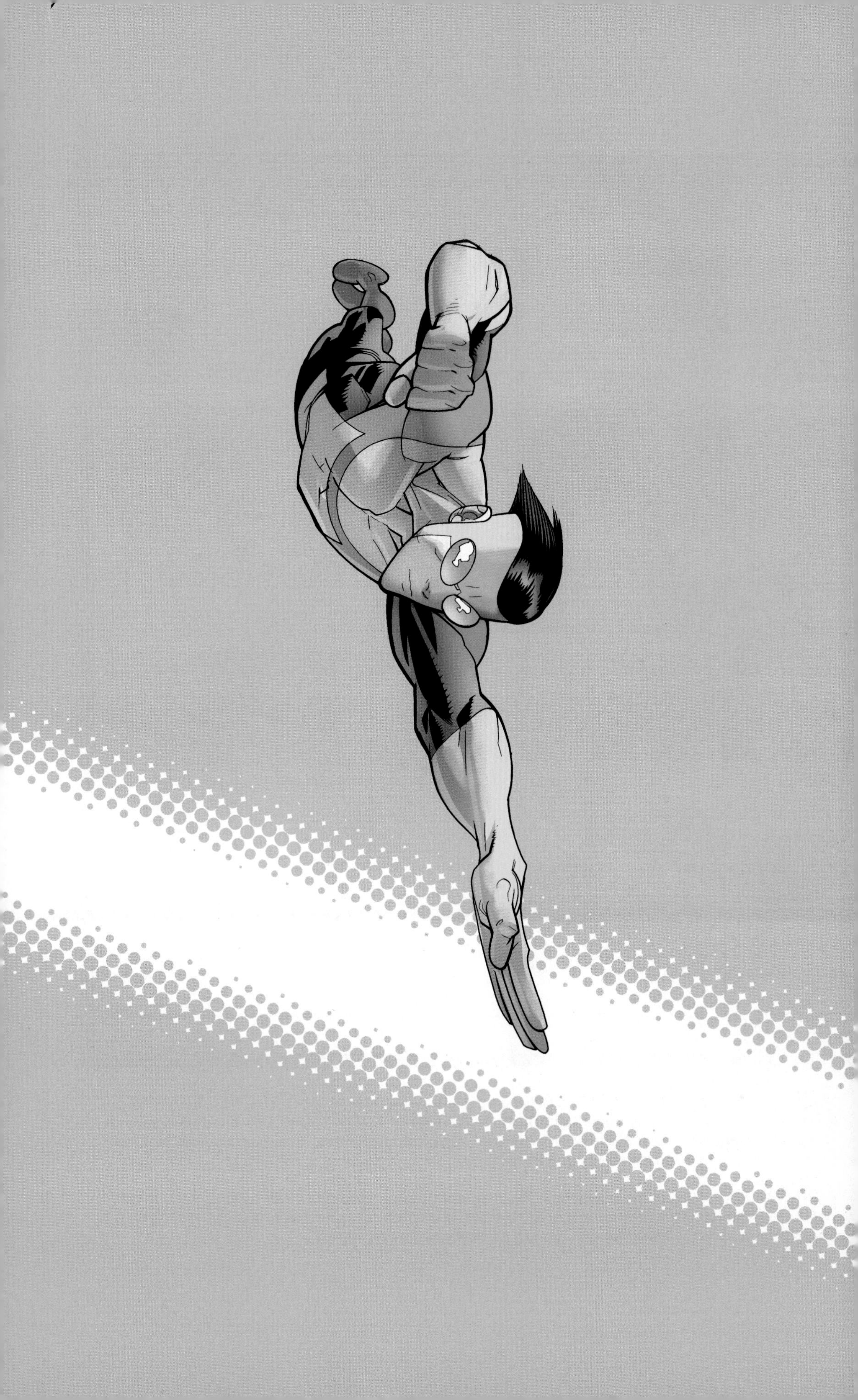

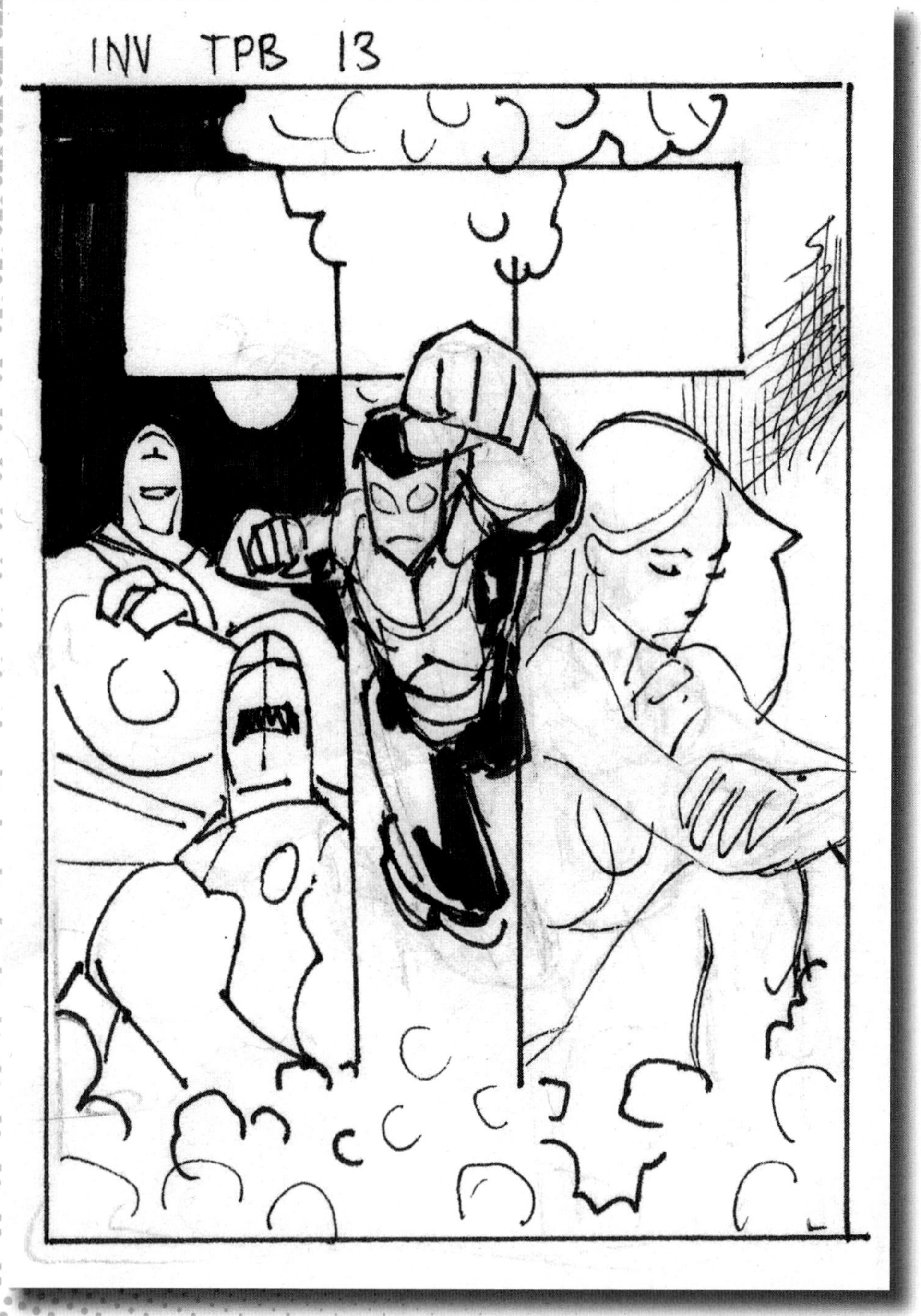
INV TPB 13

**ROBERT KIRKMAN:** Look at that, there's another awesome trade paper back cover by ye olde Ryan Ottley. I think this might possibly be the last time that Ryan will ever draw the Sequids, I mean, I've got no plans to bring them back at this point, but who knows. What do you think, Ryan? Should we bring them back--do you miss drawing those little pink things?

***RYAN OTTLEY:** I hate to admit this in front of everyone, but yes I do miss them. The reason is that I can use them to cover up a lot of background. Mindless noodling is much easier than drawing cars and buildings and stuff. So yeah, if you ever want to bring them back, I won't complain.*

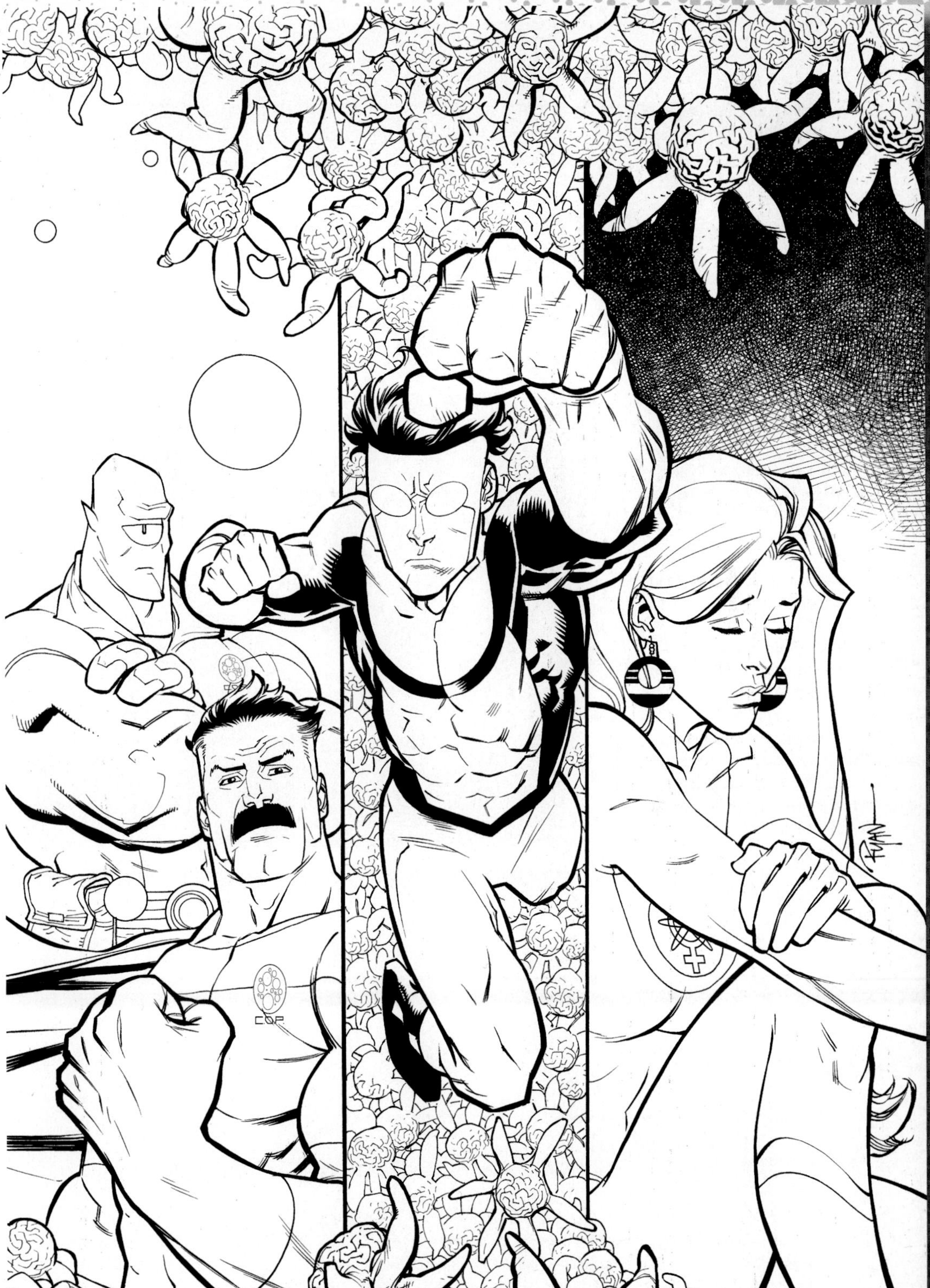

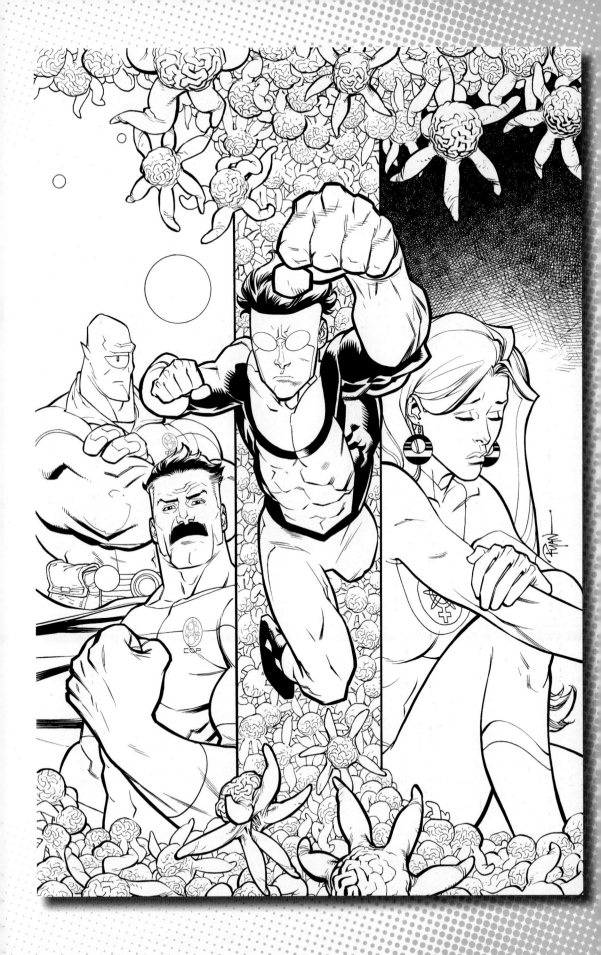

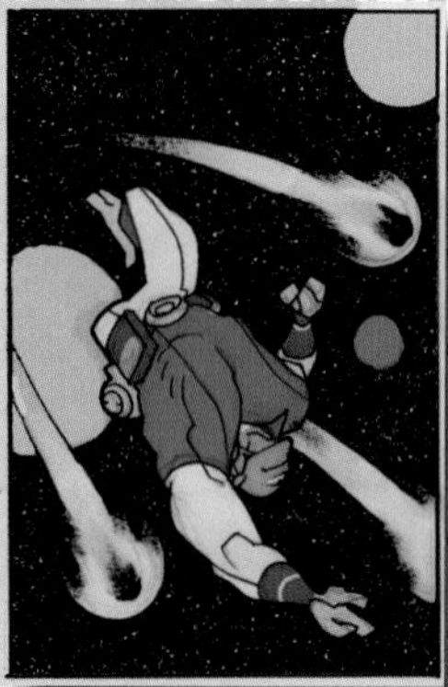

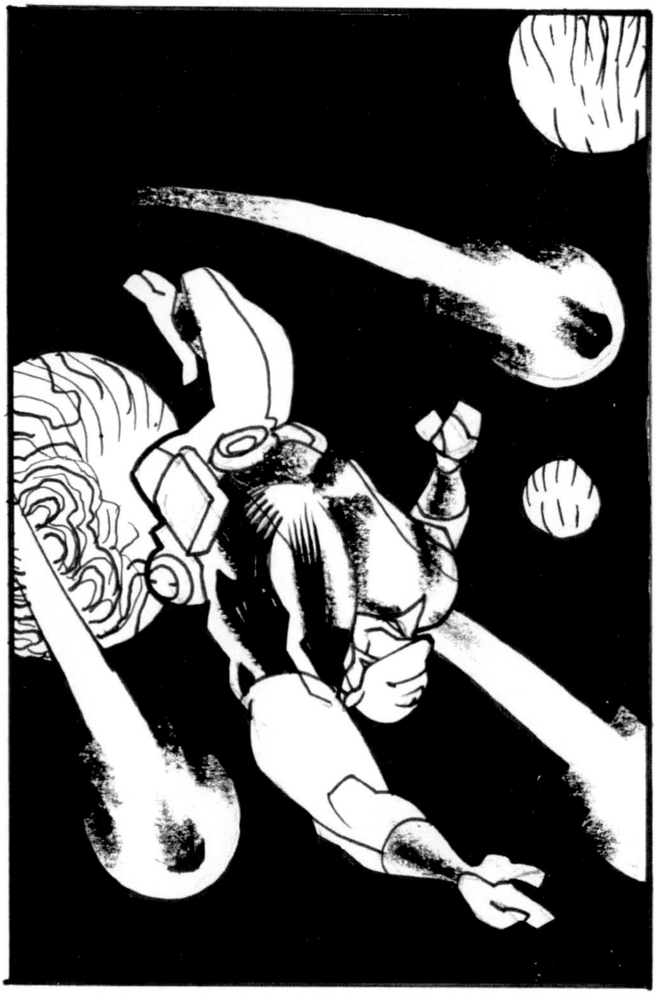

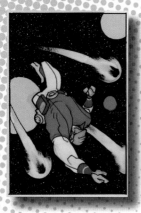

**KIRKMAN: So the plan to have Invincible co-creator Cory Walker come back to do a couple issues, focusing on Allen the Alien, had been in the works for a good long time. If I recall, we began talking about this before issue 50, when the Viltrumite War was originally planned to begin (before I ran out of room). These cover sketches were done back then when we first decided to do these issues.**

***CORY WALKER:** The two versions of that cover that feature only Allen were done in 2006, I think.*

***OTTLEY:** Well I want Cory to come back and do MORE issues, I loved having him do these two. So please, Cory, come back and do an issue every once in a while. It looks awesome AND it gives me a break. Win-win I say.*

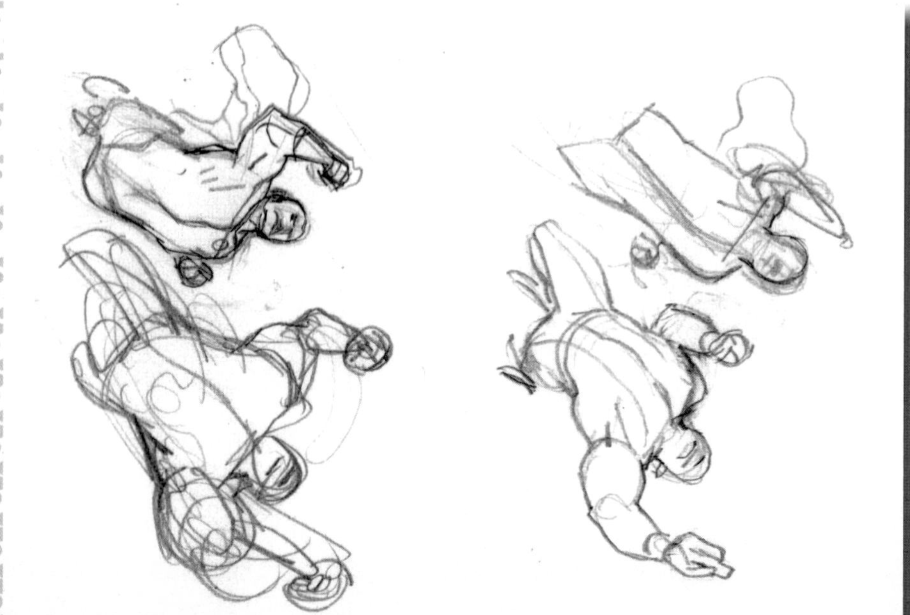

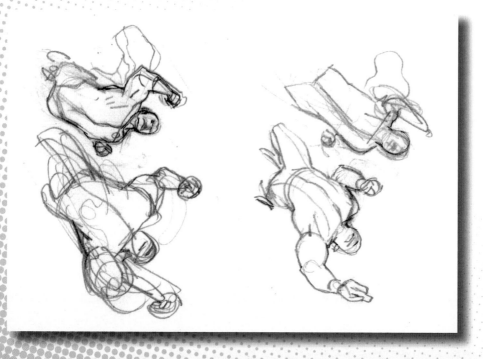

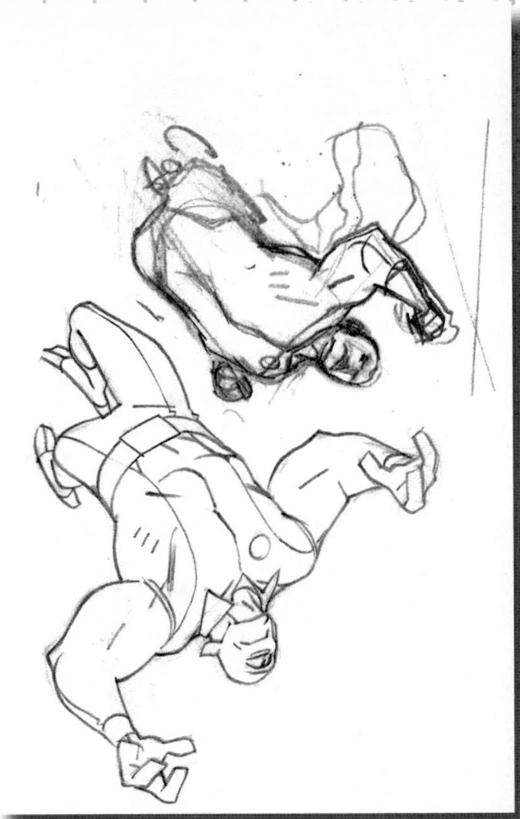

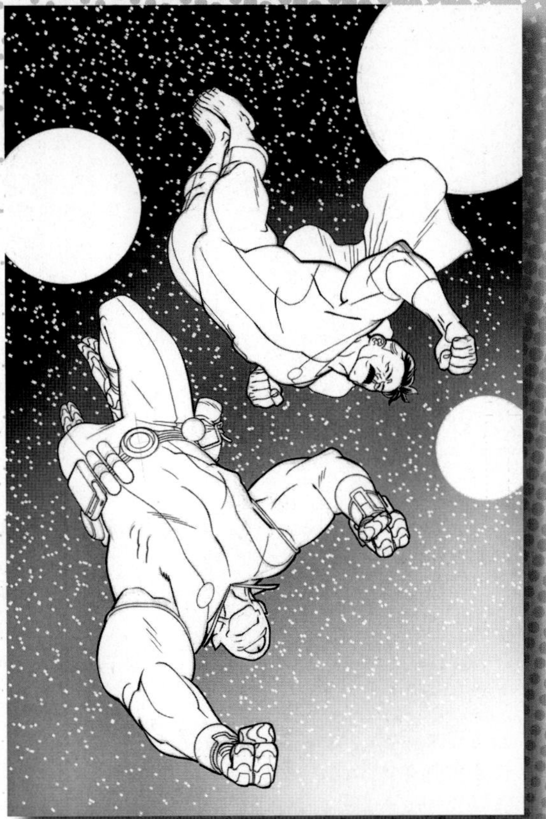

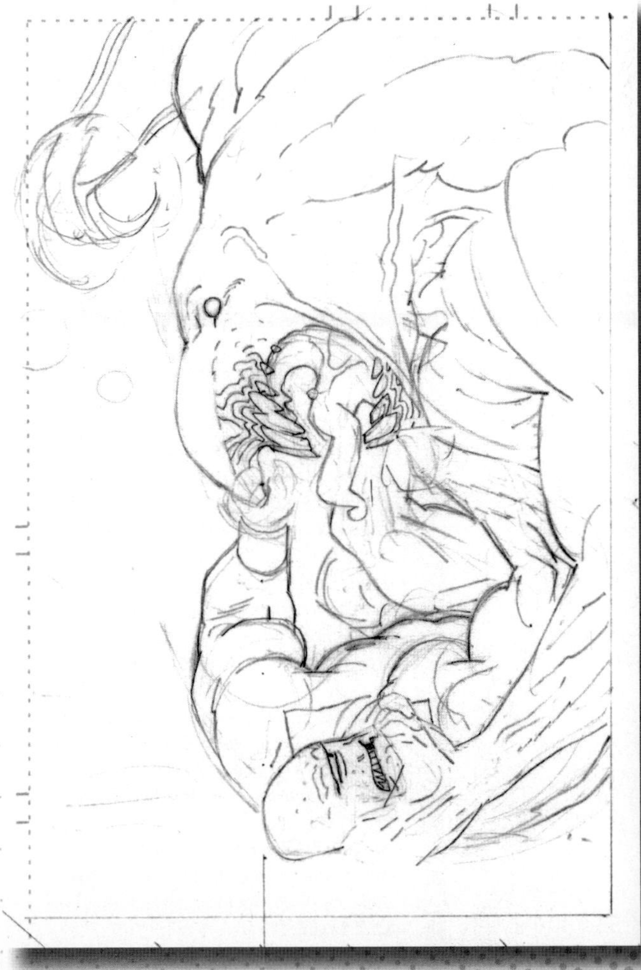

**KIRKMAN: Later, when it finally came time to do these issues, I decided to change the story up a little and have it feature Nolan as well as Allen. So the cover had to be adjusted somewhat before it became what we know and love as the cover to issue 66.**

***WALKER: I'm pretty pleased with how this cover turned out. Upside-down is the new black.***

***OTTLEY: Yeah I remember drawing the cover to 46, the one with Immortal and Allen fighting on the moon, that was Robert's idea to do the upside-down cover, he hesitated because he wasn't sure if he wanted to interfere with Cory's upside down cover. As if Cory had a copyright on upside downness. It all worked out though, and I love the hell out of Cory's covers.***

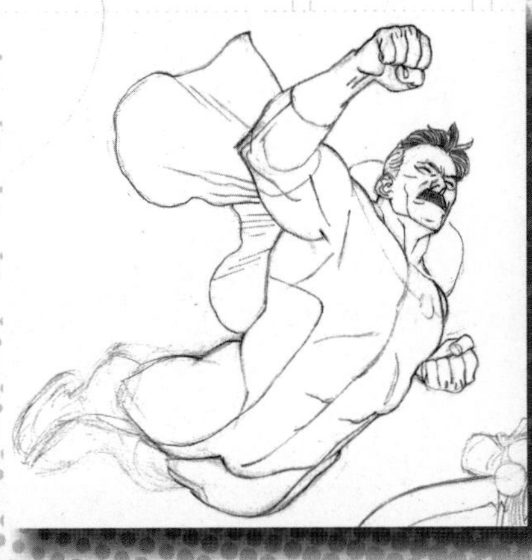

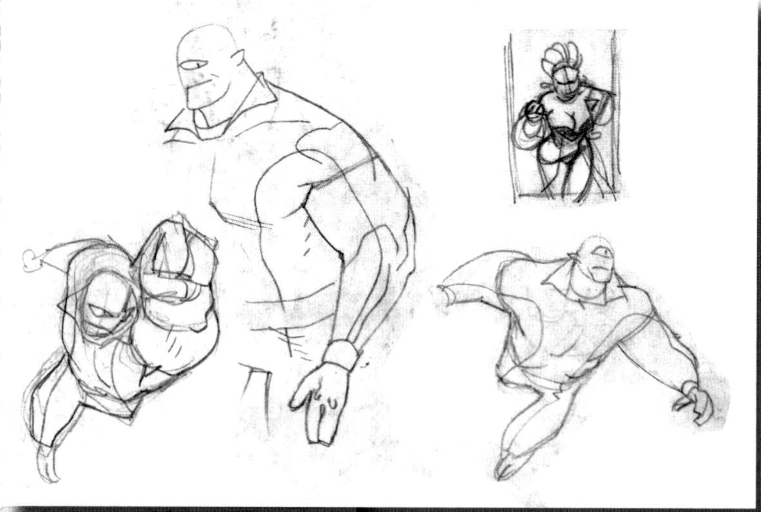

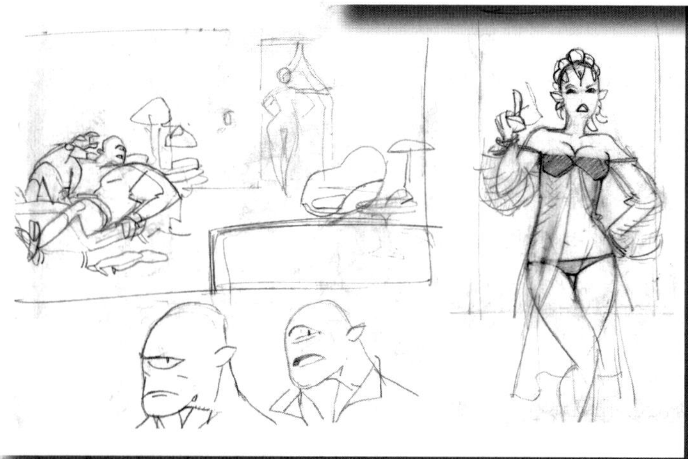

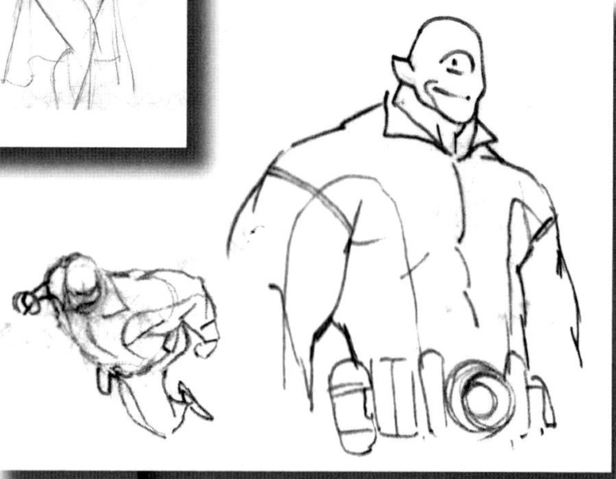

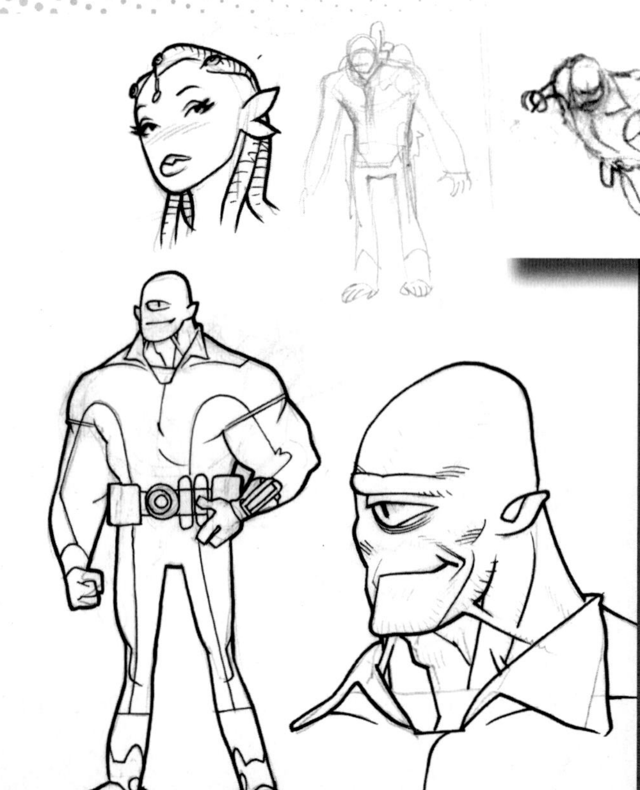

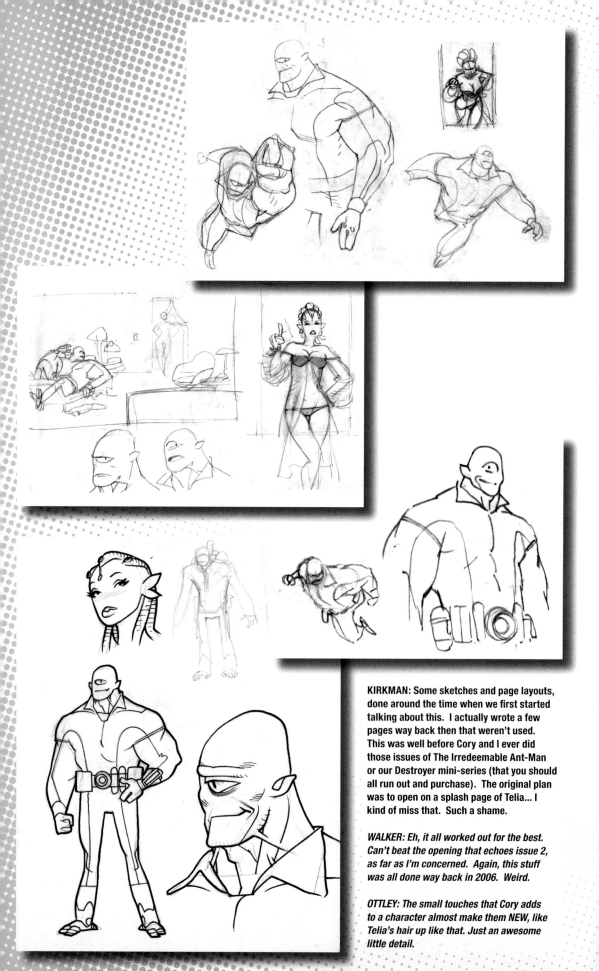

**KIRKMAN: Some sketches and page layouts, done around the time when we first started talking about this. I actually wrote a few pages way back then that weren't used. This was well before Cory and I ever did those issues of The Irredeemable Ant-Man or our Destroyer mini-series (that you should all run out and purchase). The original plan was to open on a splash page of Telia... I kind of miss that. Such a shame.**

***WALKER: Eh, it all worked out for the best. Can't beat the opening that echoes issue 2, as far as I'm concerned. Again, this stuff was all done way back in 2006. Weird.***

***OTTLEY: The small touches that Cory adds to a character almost make them NEW, like Telia's hair up like that. Just an awesome little detail.***

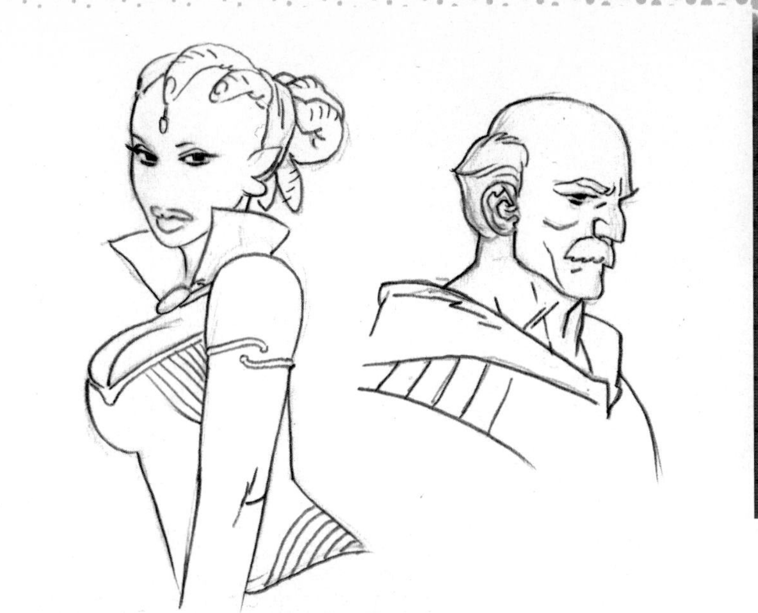

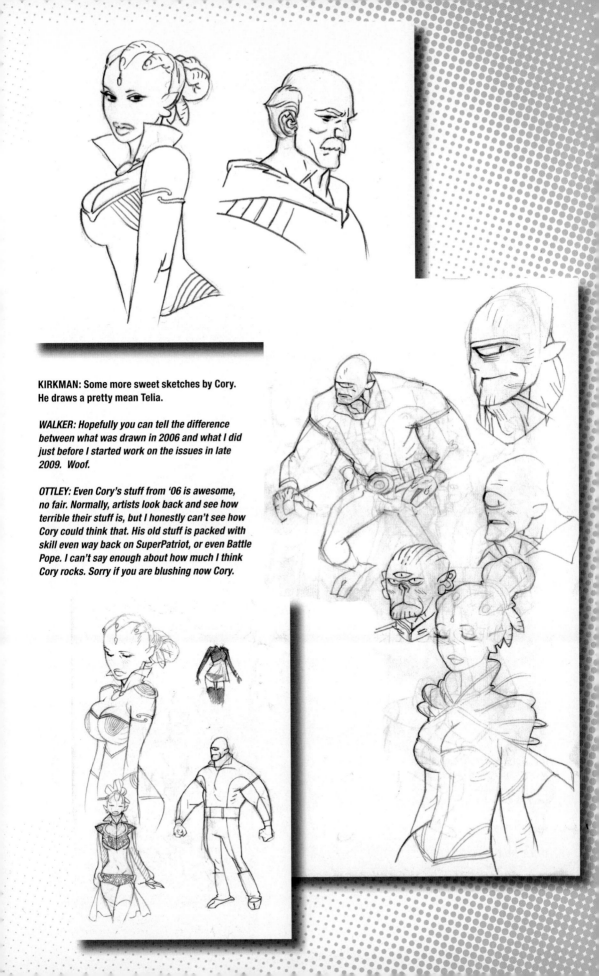

**KIRKMAN: Some more sweet sketches by Cory. He draws a pretty mean Telia.**

***WALKER: Hopefully you can tell the difference between what was drawn in 2006 and what I did just before I started work on the issues in late 2009. Woof.***

***OTTLEY: Even Cory's stuff from '06 is awesome, no fair. Normally, artists look back and see how terrible their stuff is, but I honestly can't see how Cory could think that. His old stuff is packed with skill even way back on SuperPatriot, or even Battle Pope. I can't say enough about how much I think Cory rocks. Sorry if you are blushing now Cory.***

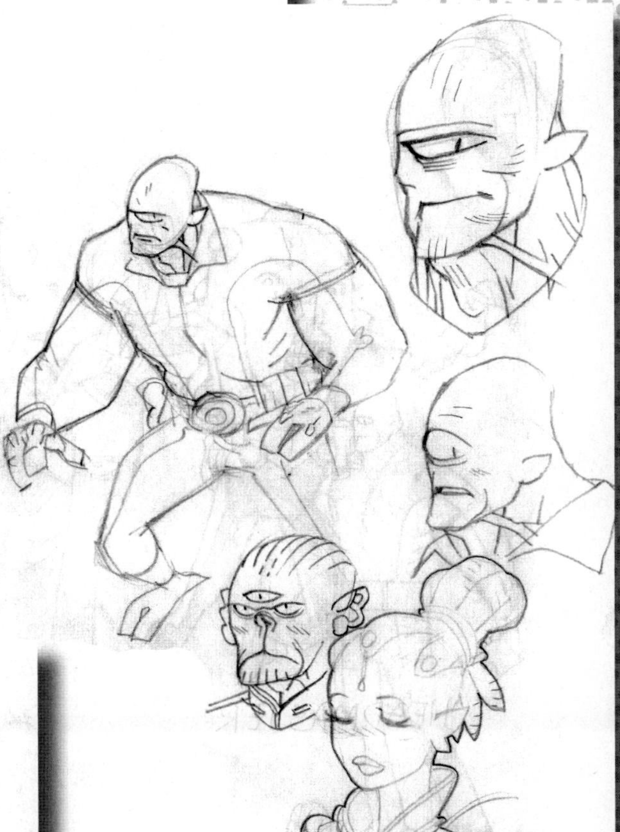

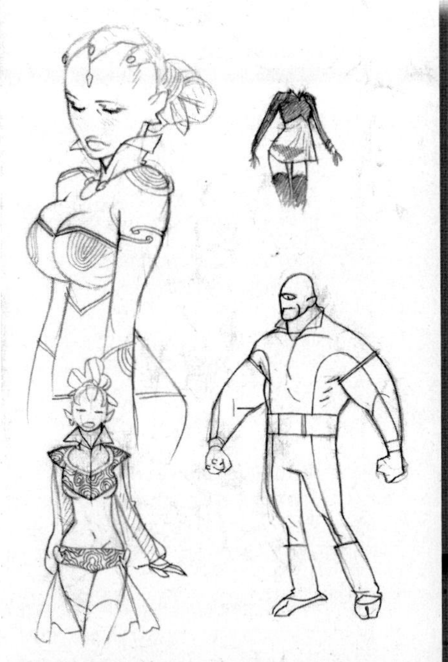

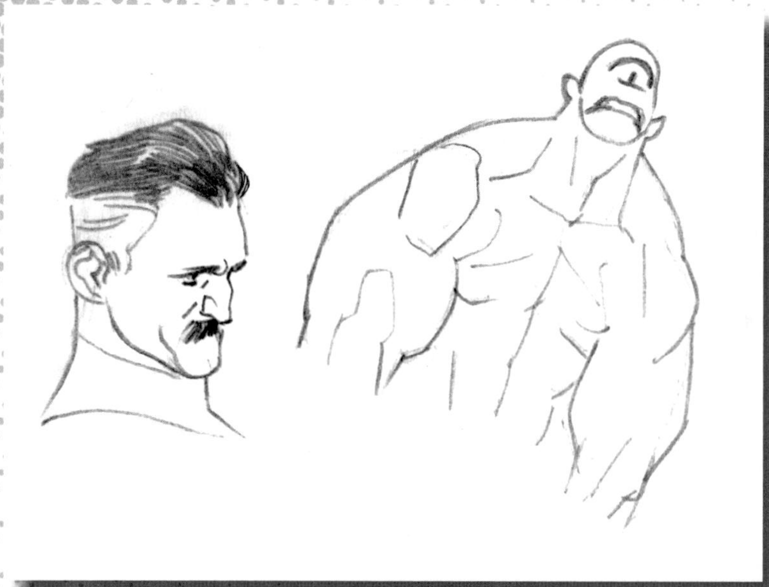

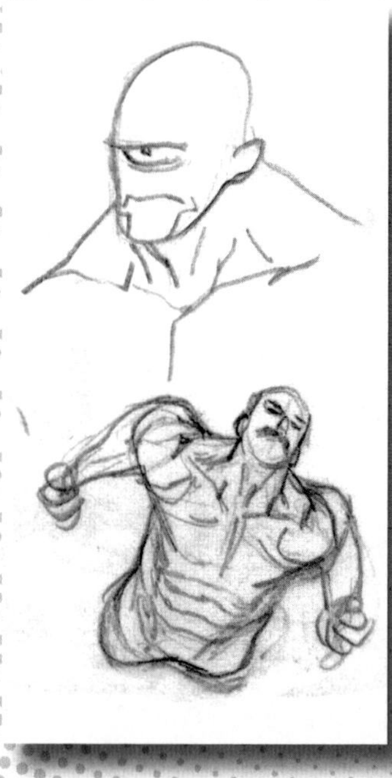

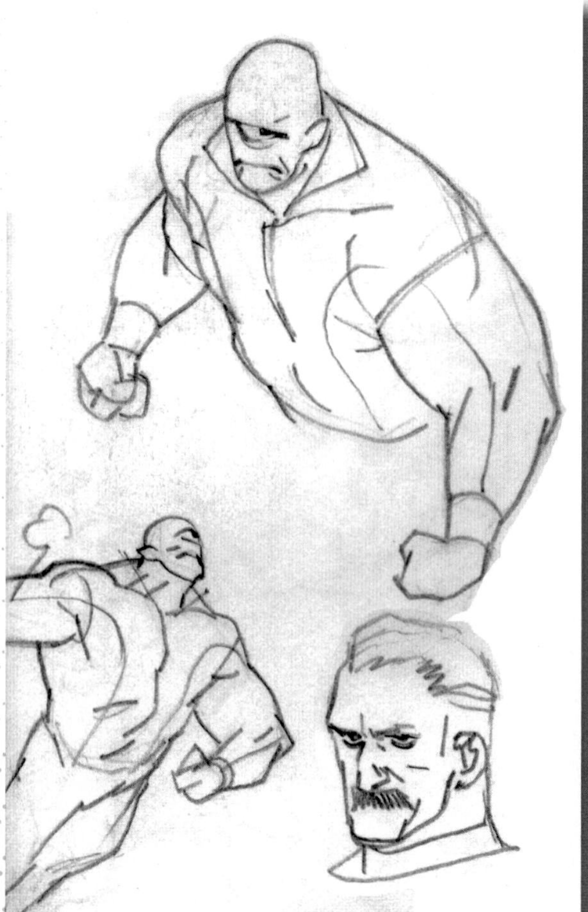

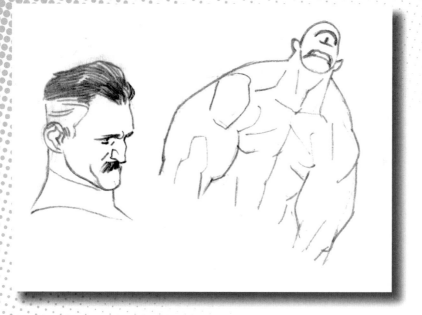

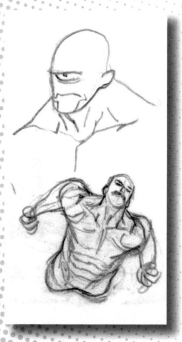

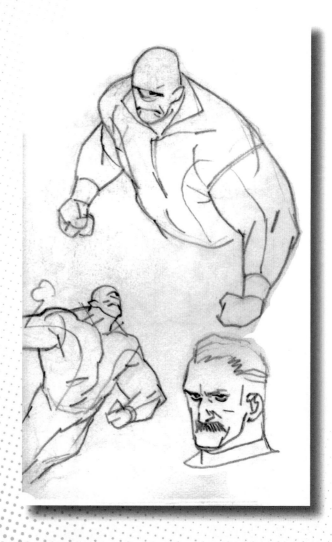

**KIRKMAN: More awesome sketches from Cory. Not really anything to add other than that Cory is great. He's such a master of the human form. Great looking stuff.**

***WALKER: I work out.***

***OTTLEY: He does, I watch him.***

**KIRKMAN: Here are Cory's designs for SPACE RACER which were done way back when the character first appeared in issue 35 of this series, when he was called Space Rider, but we'll pay no attention to that... that was just because Nolan changed the name for his book, you see. Wakka wakka. Move along.**

***WALKER: Space Racer is pretty cool. I wish I had made him a little less humanoid, but whatever. I'm no Nate Bellegarde.***

***OTTLEY: FUN FACT: Robert wanted me to change Cory's design a little bit, instead of feet, he wanted hands. Ok so maybe that fact wasn't fun at all. I should've just called it a semi-interesting fact? I don't know.***

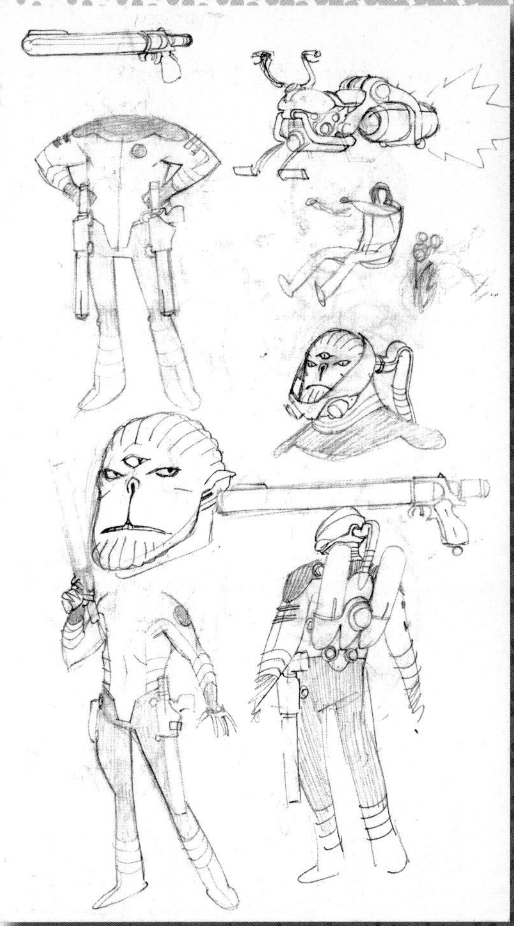

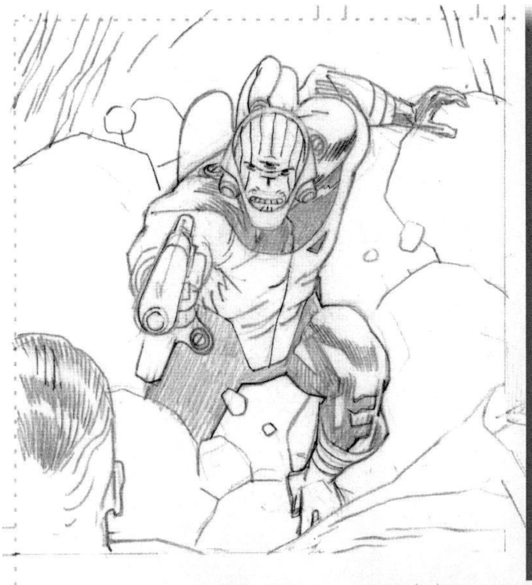

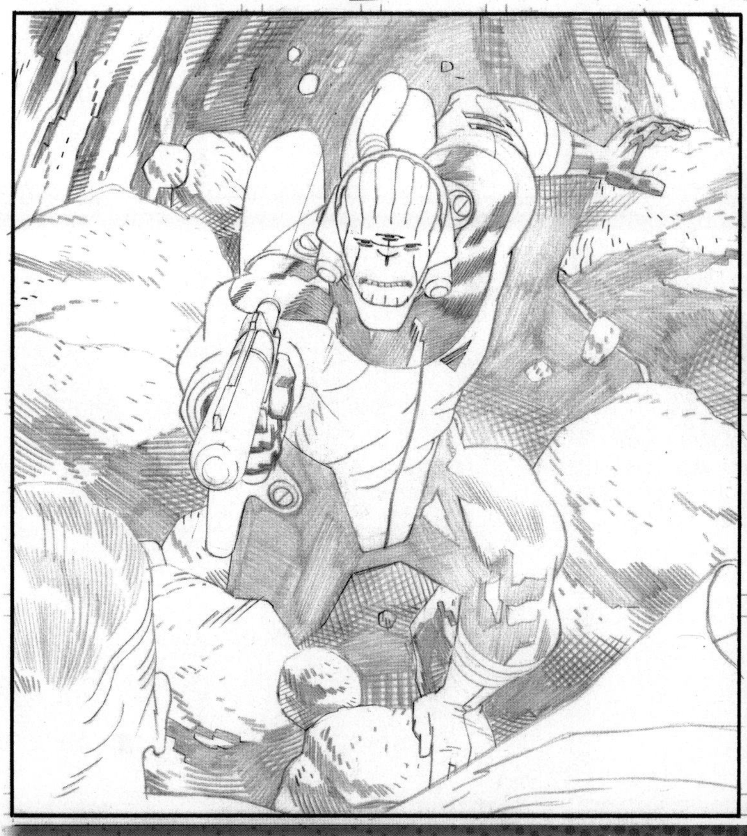

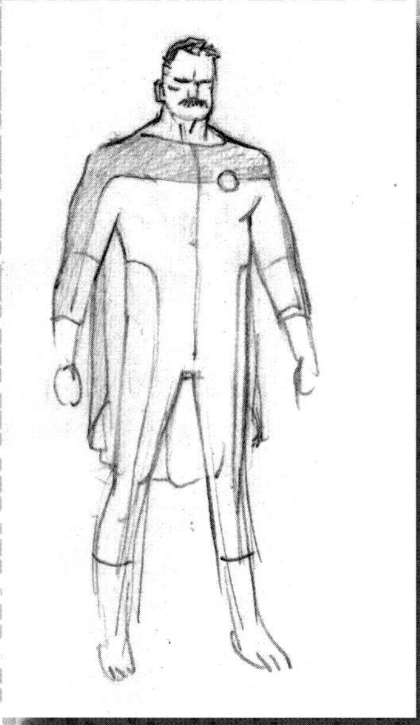

**KIRKMAN: Some variations of Nolan's costume that Cory did. I don't remember which one we picked... and have no idea how I'd go about trying to figure that out in a definitive way.**

***WALKER: The colors, Duke, the colors! To be honest, I really quite liked the blue one, but I'm glad we went with the color scheme that we did.***

***OTTLEY: He could use shoes.***

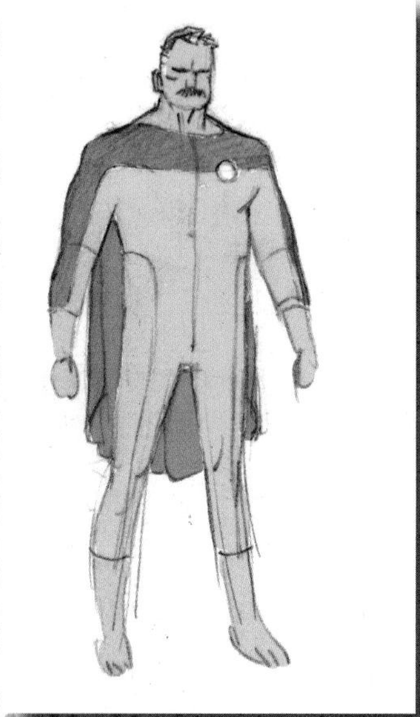

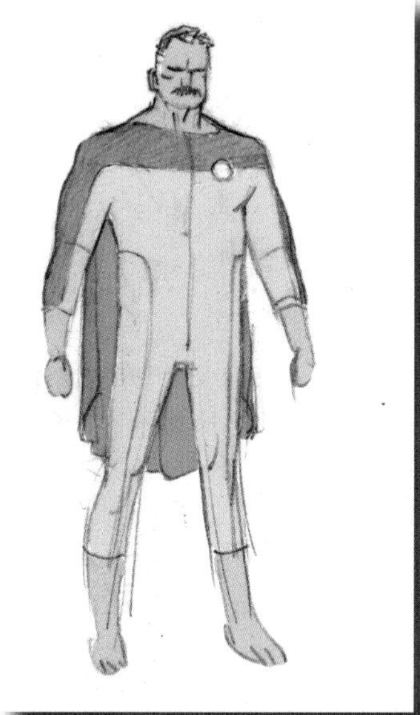

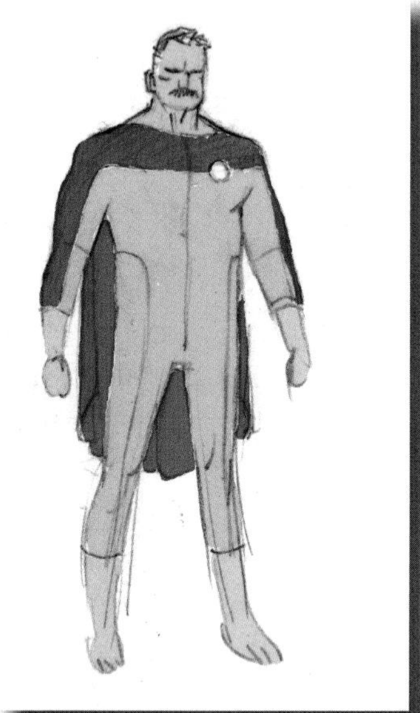

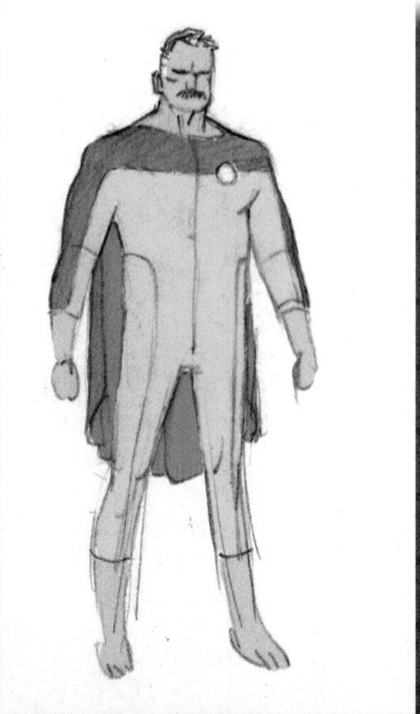

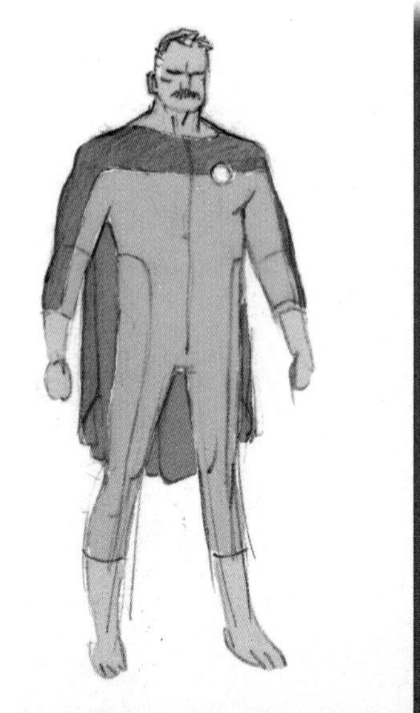

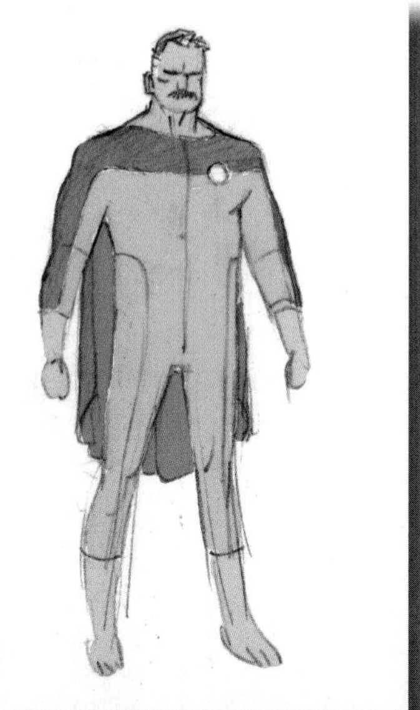

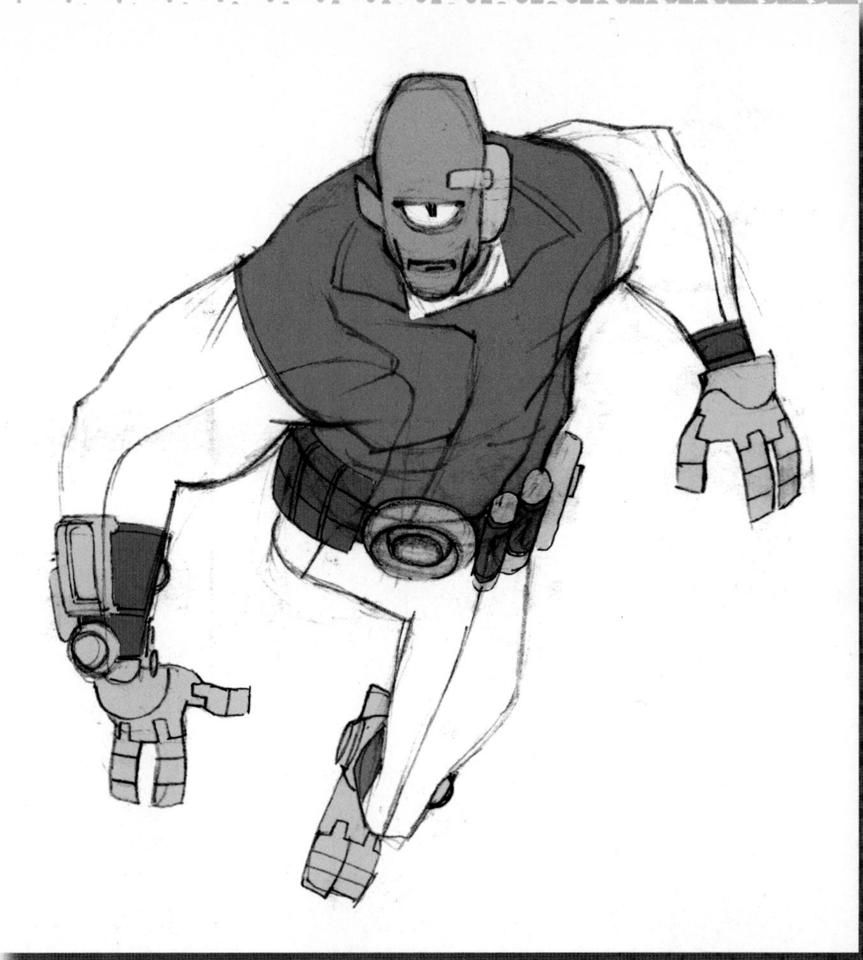

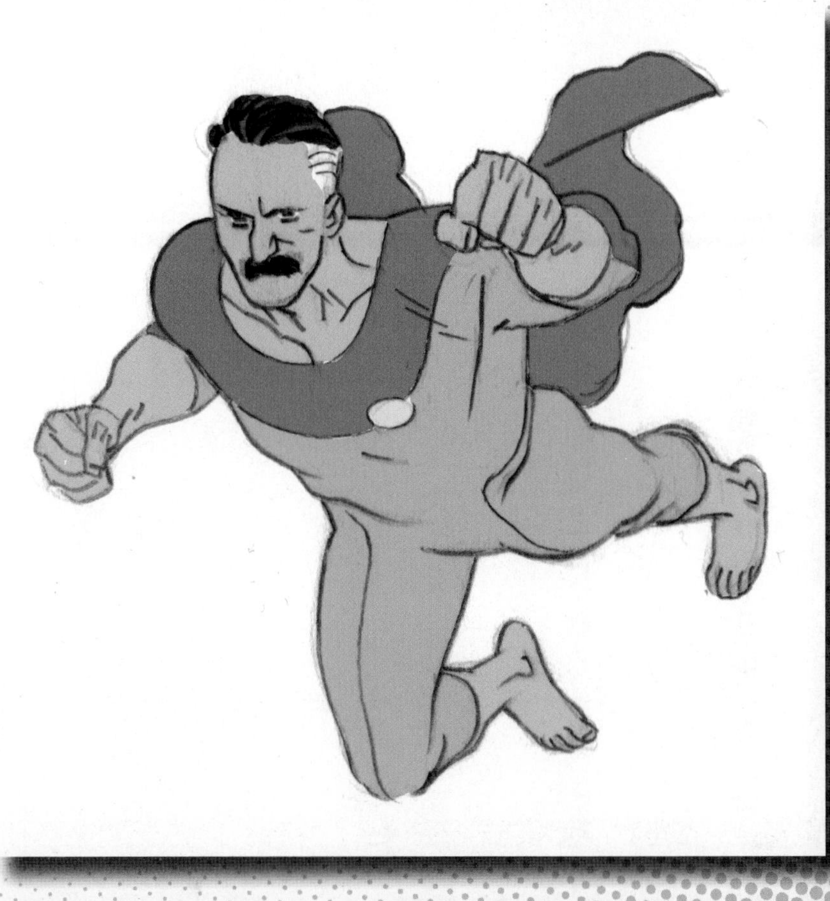

**KIRKMAN: Some cool colored sketches by Cory.**

***WALKER: Pretty cool, right? Pretty cool bare feet, right?***

***OTTLEY: Bare feet are all right. We could get into WHY he would want bare feet but we could probably fill up pages talking about what benefits bare feet would have: is it a comfort thing, is he sick of wearing boots like the Viltrumites, is it simply because he's so strong that boots would not act as protection? Like goggles on Invincible? Like metal gloves on Allen's hands and feet? so on.***

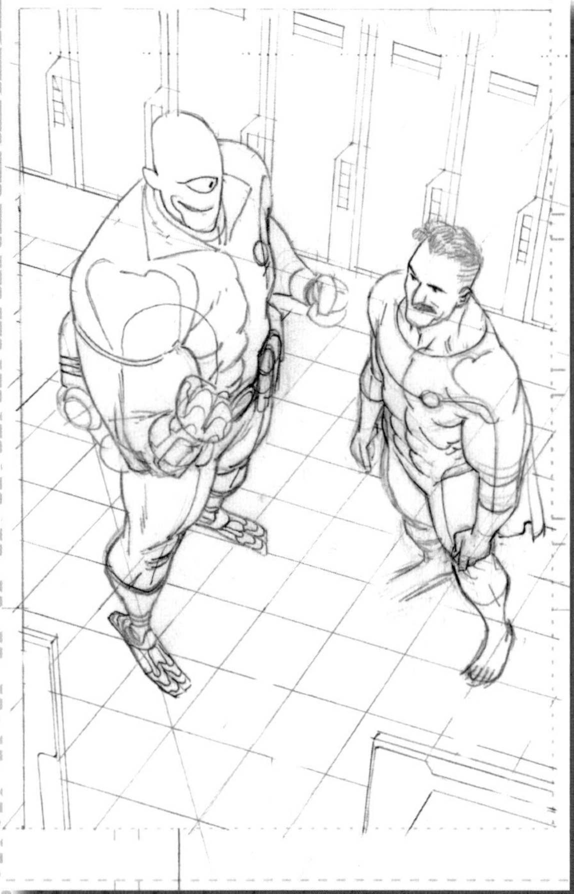

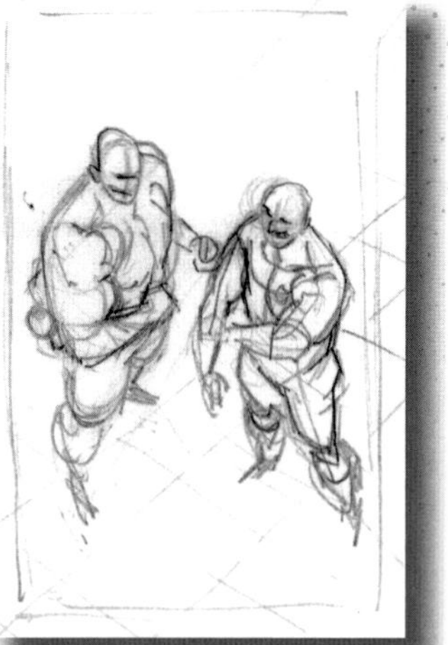

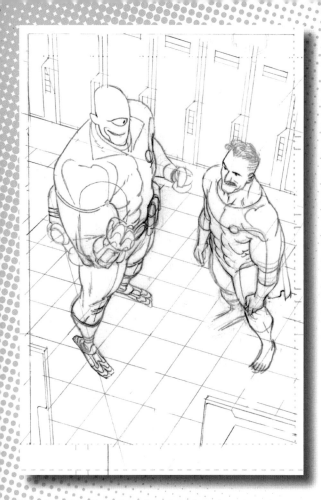

**KIRKMAN: Page layouts for issue 66. I'm going to keep writing that page of Nolan talking over and over because it's great. This is what... the fourth time? Enjoy!**

***WALKER: Look, ladies, you can see a bit of the process used to do the first page of issue 66. Any time there's a large figure on a page, or in this instance, an enormous head, I thumbnail the drawing, then resize it for the page and lightbox it. That's what happened here.***

***OTTLEY: Yeah I do that too, but Cory has this uncanny ability to draw amazing detail SO small. It's pretty mind-blowing to see the actual size of Cory's thumbnail layouts and how CLEAN they are.***

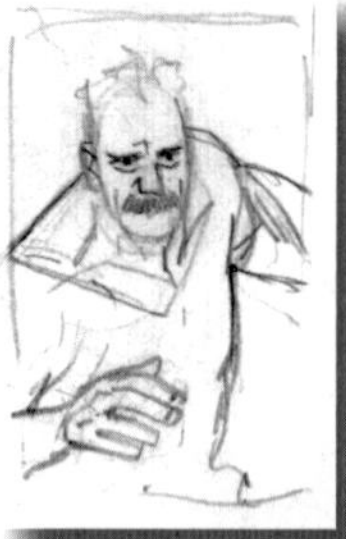

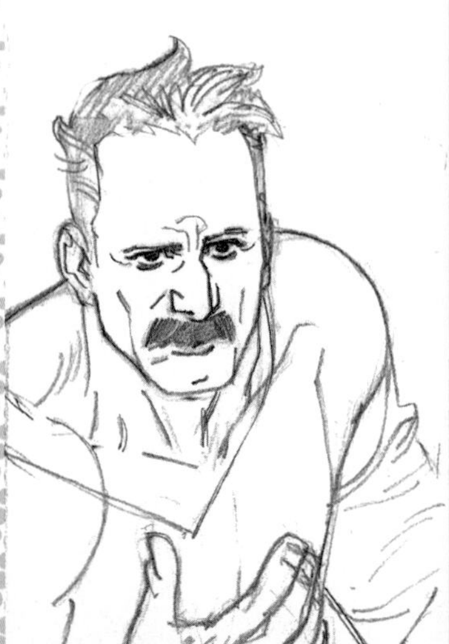

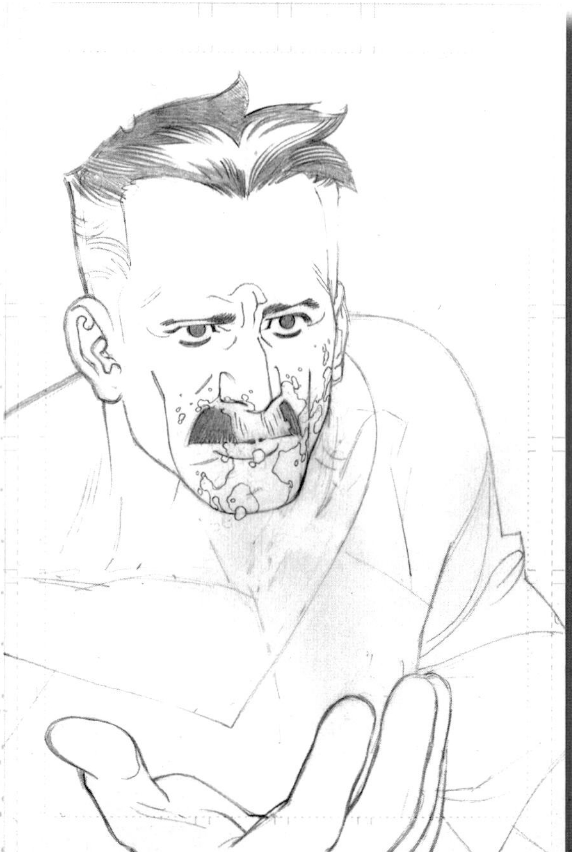

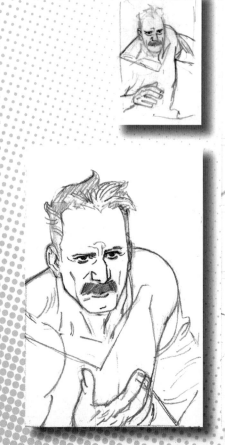

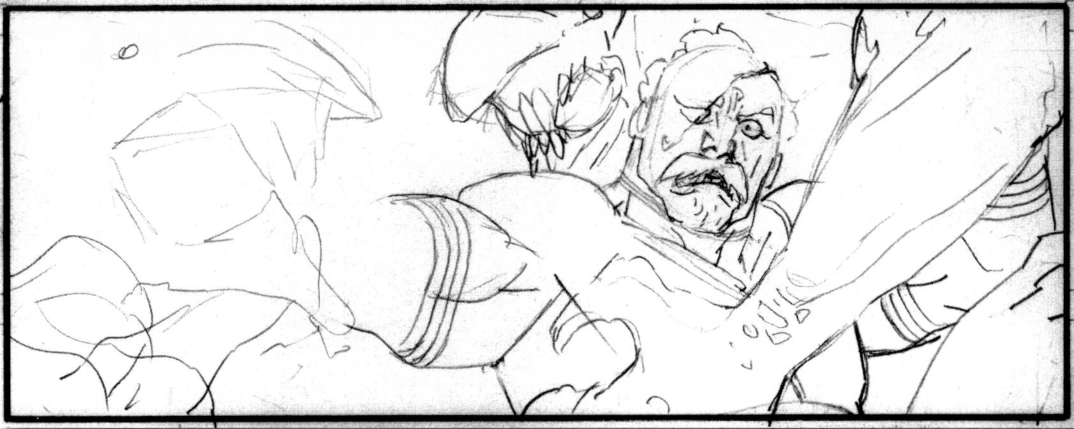

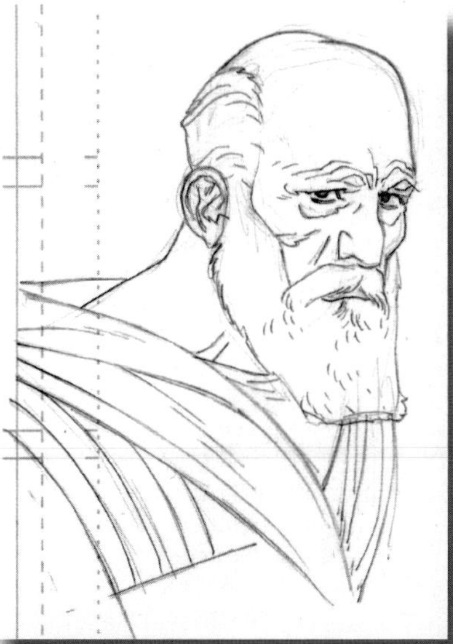

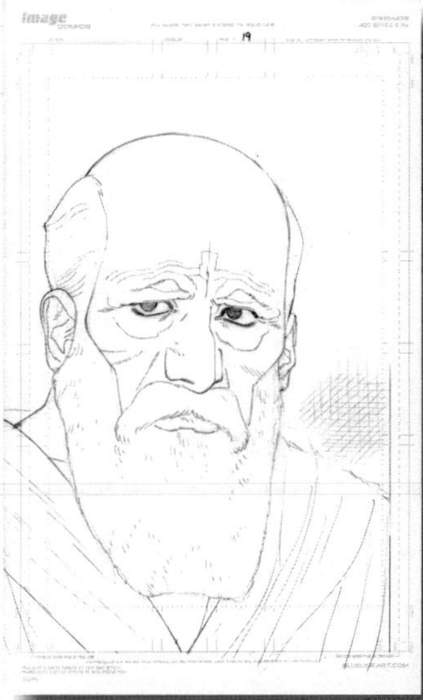

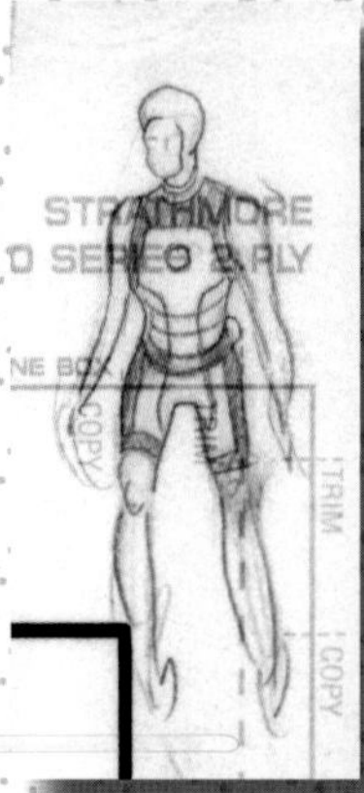
STRATHMORE

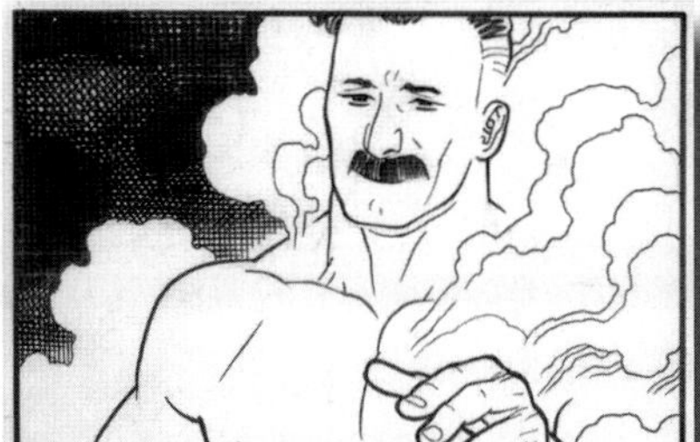

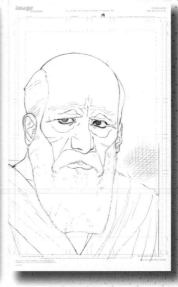

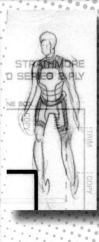

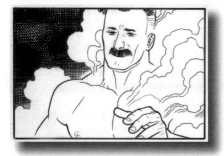

**KIRKMAN: Random stuff from Cory's issues. I feel like I'm talking too damn much! Cory... explain what this stuff is.**

***WALKER:** Well, most of it is pretty self-explanatory, but here you see the design work I did for those alien brain nerds in the gutter space of the very page they first appear on. You can also see my first pass at Thaedus from the giant head two page spread from issue 67, where I worked it to death and made it look like garbage, and then, there's little drawing I did to replace it. Also, that panel of Nolan holding the pillow over his ears is probably the best drawing I have ever seen.*

***OTTLEY:** I Love it!*

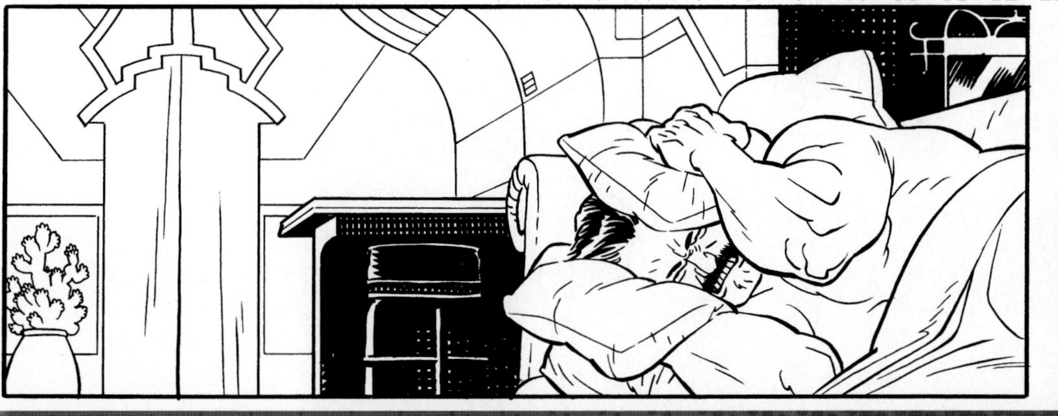

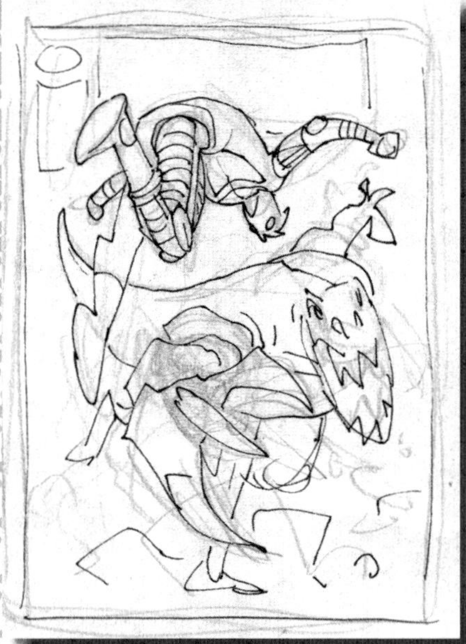

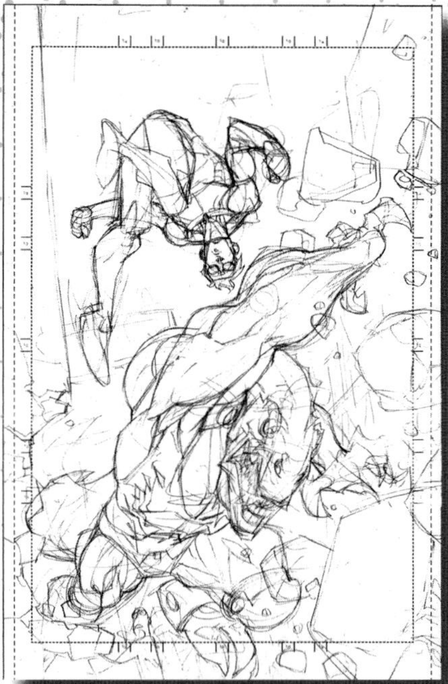

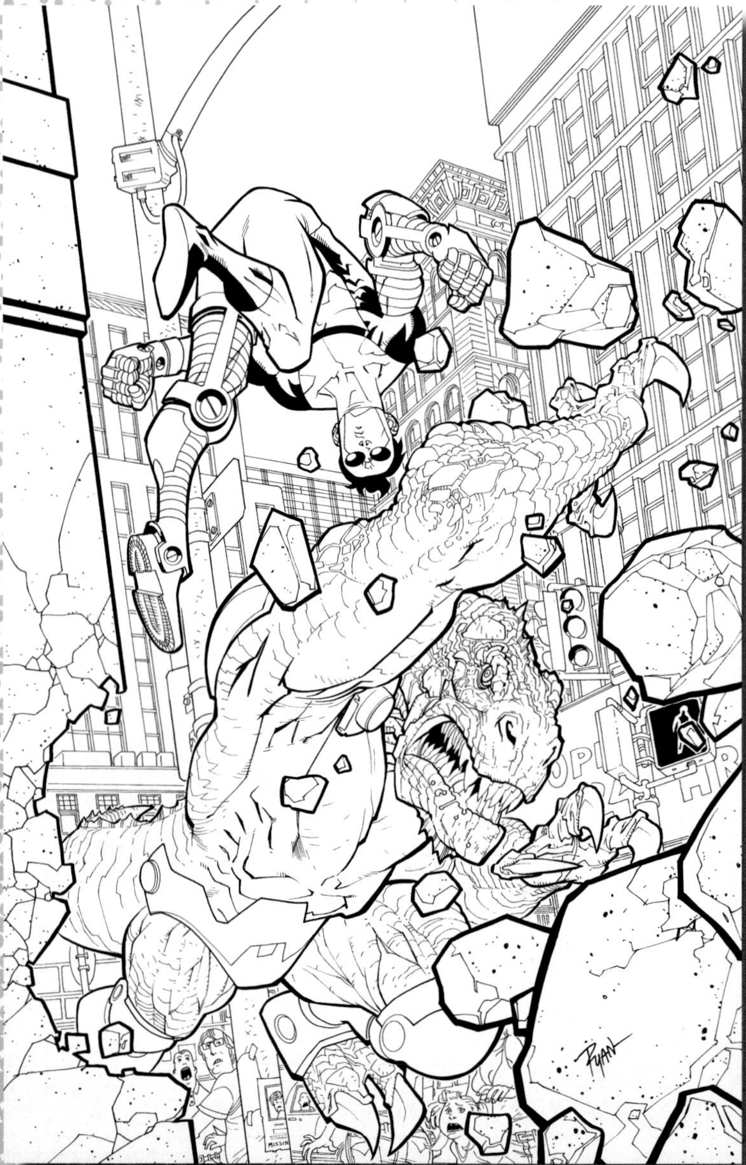

**KIRKMAN: Here's the cover to 68. DINOSAURUS! Oh, Dinosaurus. You're the first comic book character my son kind of created... or well, named at the very least. We were playing with dinosaurs one day and I asked him to name his and he replied "Dinosaurus!" He was three at the time. I think I called Ryan about three seconds later to get him started on designs. Such a cool name. And I've got big plans for this guy, we'll be seeing much more of him very soon.**

***WALKER: Dinosaurus? Pfft. The Elephant is where it's at. Totally awesome cover, though. Ryan Ottley is the king of it.***

***OTTLEY: It is a fun name, even moreso after Robert told me the story. Oh and thanks Cory. *blushes****

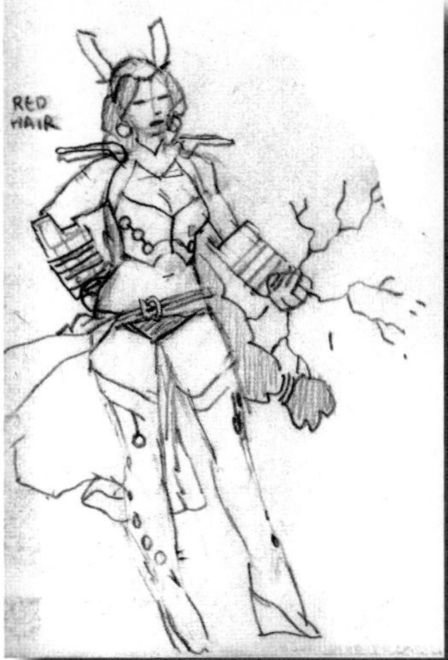
RED HAIR

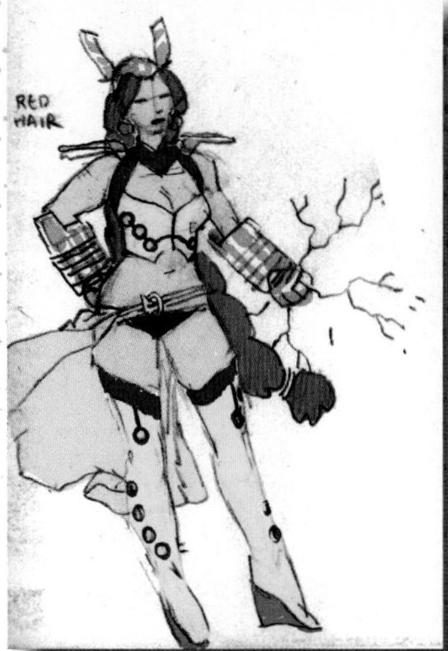
RED HAIR

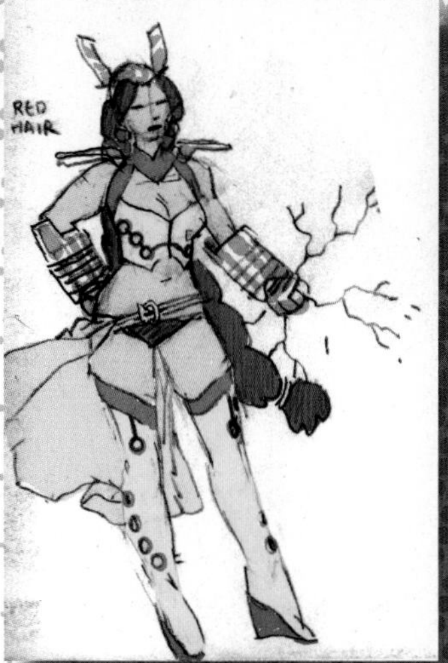
RED HAIR

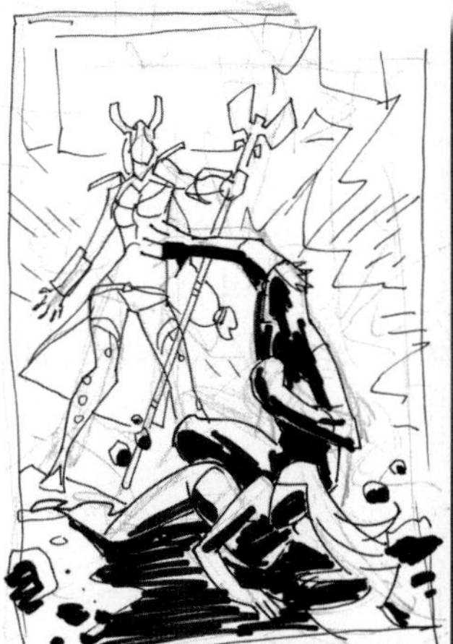

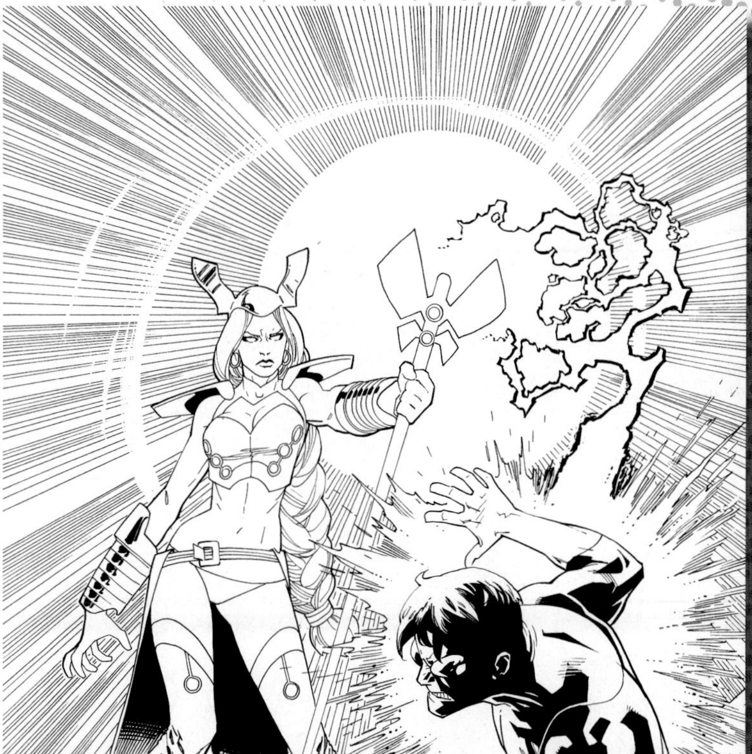

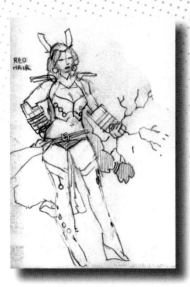

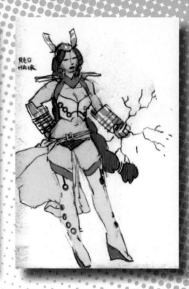

**KIRKMAN: More female villains! I've been wanting to do that for a while and that's what brought about Universa here. Excellent design by Cory Walker, which was drawn on the set of the movie PAUL.**

***WALKER: I remember sitting there, on the set of the movie PAUL, thinking, "I am going to design a Universa. Panty cape." So I did. As you see, though, my original color choices were not so well thought-out. Peach skin? Barf. Seriously, though, smooth making her green was smooth a smooth move, Kirkman. I think she turned out pretty good for a character that was designed on the set of the movie PAUL.***

***OTTLEY: Way rad, I love her design!***

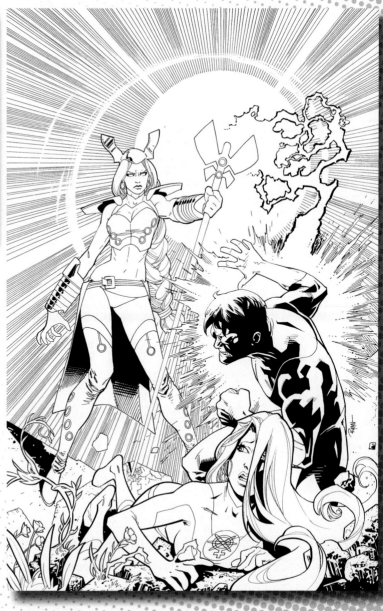

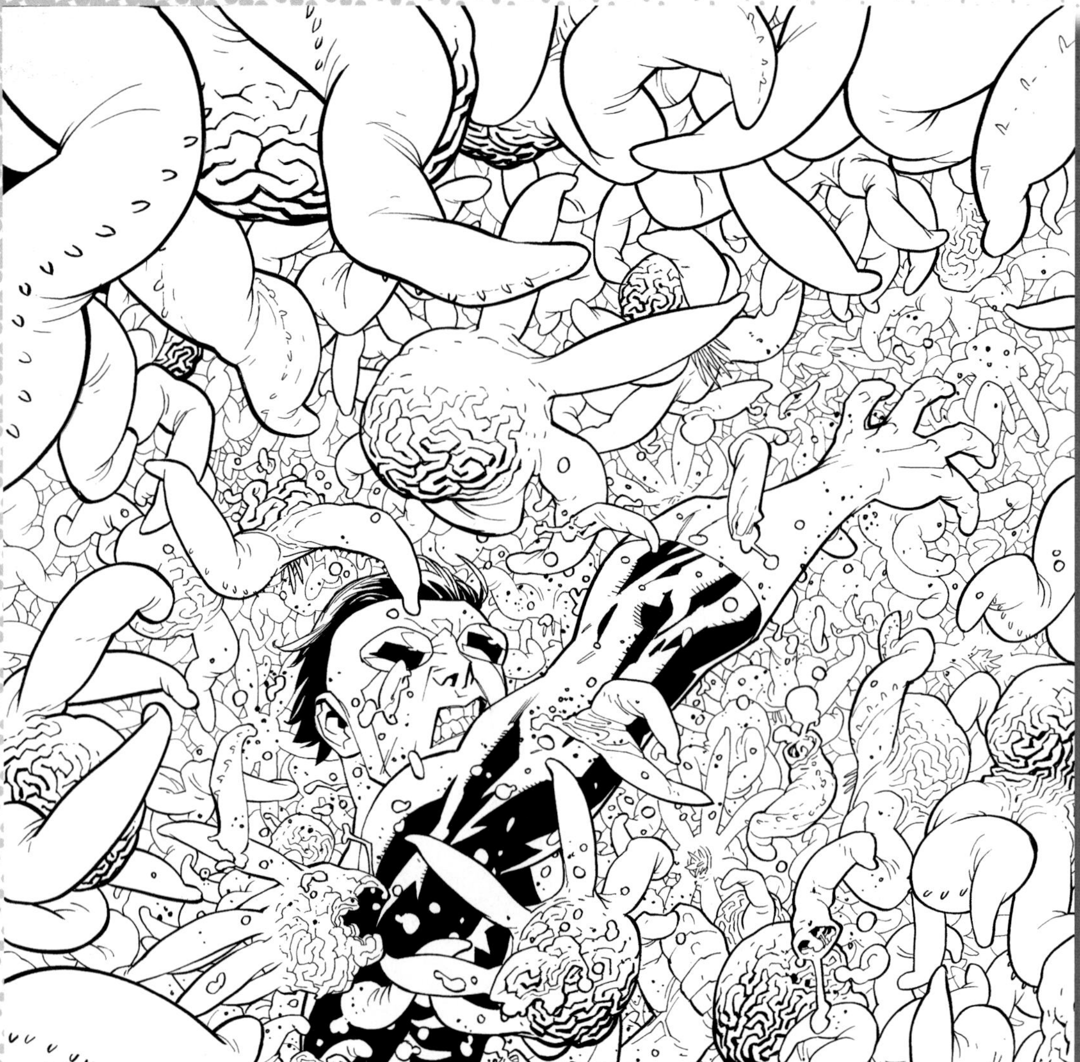
RYAN

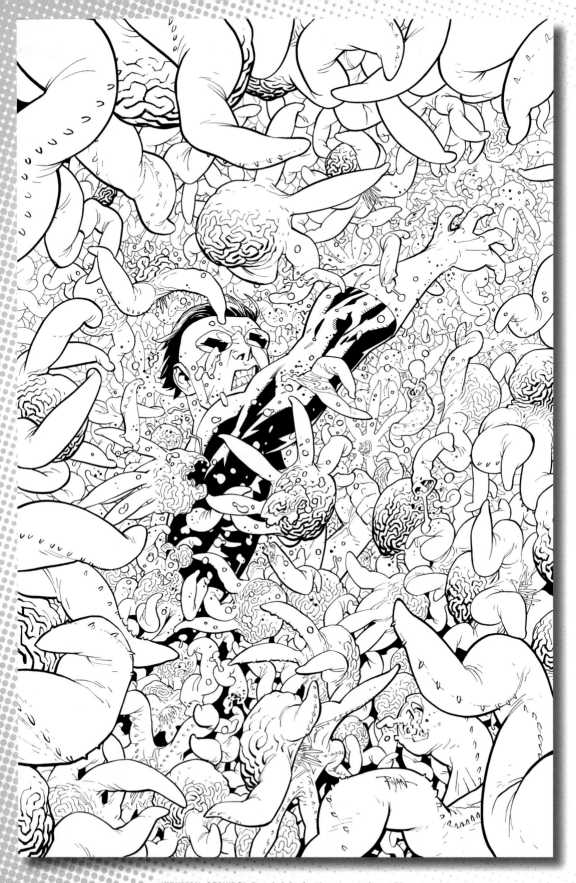

**KIRKMAN: SEQUIDS! Ryan's inks for the cover to issue 70.**

***WALKER: SO good. I love any time Ryan draws a sequid.***

***OTTLEY: I love YOU guys!***

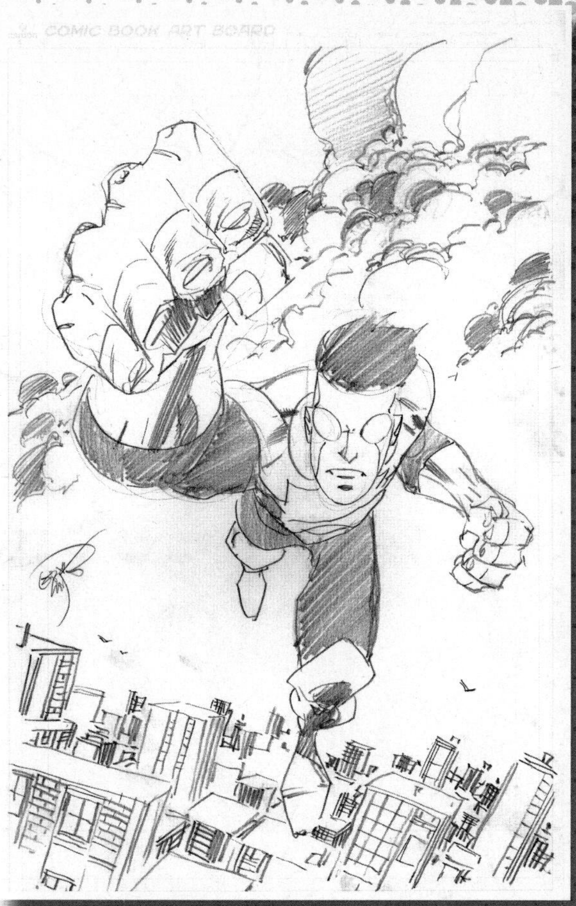
COMIC BOOK ART BOARD

**KIRKMAN: Last year at Comic-Con, Erik Larsen was drawing a bunch of commissions for people, so I threw my money in the hat and asked him to draw me an Invincible. I dug it so much that I asked if he'd be okay with me having Ryan ink the thing up so that we could use it as a cover. Erik, great guy that he is, agreed and it became a variant cover for INVINCIBLE: RETURNS #1.**

***WALKER: SO good. I love any time Ryan teams up with Erik Larsen.***

***OTTLEY: I made a few changes, I deflated that hand a bit, Erik and his huge fists. It's always great working over Larsen's pencils, he has such a fun energy in his lines.***

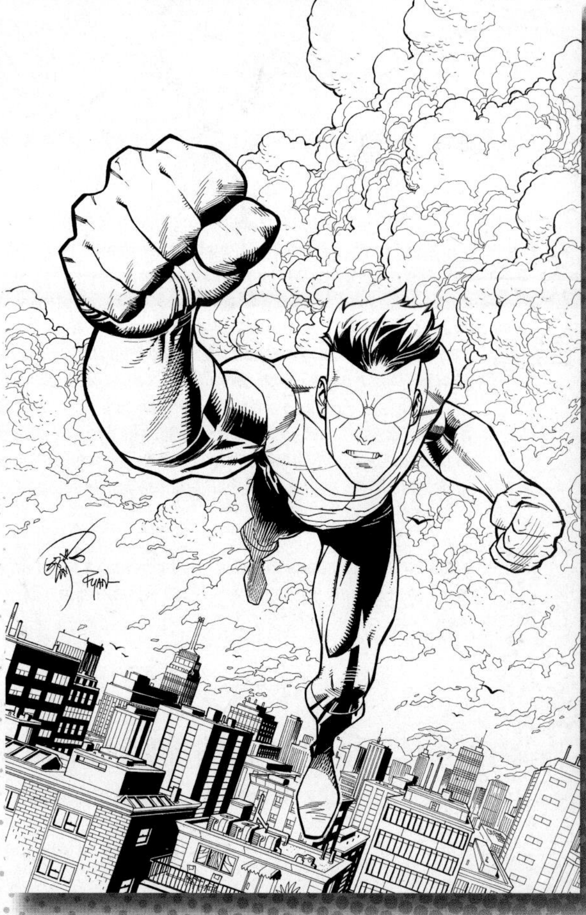

KIRKMAN: This is a pretty awesome two-page spread by Ryan Ottley... the first time Invincible appeared in his yellow and blue costume since issue 51. Man, I did not expect him to wear that blue and black costume for 20 issues... wow.

*OTTLEY: FUN FACT: Jason Howard (Astounding Wolf-Man) and I hung out with Erik Larsen at this year's San Diego Comic-Con. Jason reminded Erik that I made a big fist challenge when I drew this spread. That is HALF a page of fist there folks. I then told Erik if he wants to be the "king of fists," he needed to one-up me. Erik immediately grabbed two 11x17 pages and filled the WHOLE thing with an amazing fist, and on one side you could see Savage Dragon's face. It was absolutely glorious. I hope he uses it in a future issue of Savage Dragon, because I doubt I could ever draw a bigger fist than I did here on Invincible. Until Larsen's spread hits the printed page I am still the fisting champion. Er..you know what I mean.*

*WALKER: Nobody does it better. Ryan can do a lot of things that other guys only dream of. Drawing wicked-awesome spreads like this is one of them. Curious about the other things? Ask your sister.*

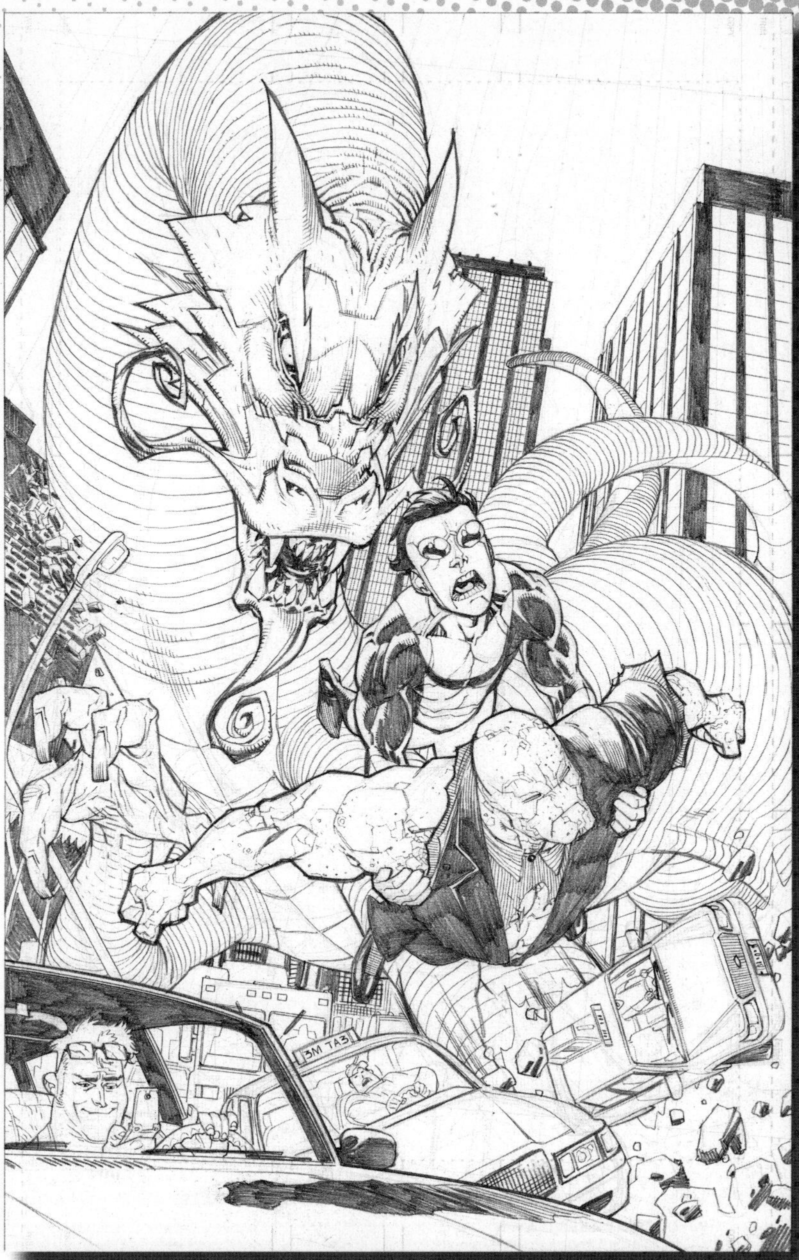

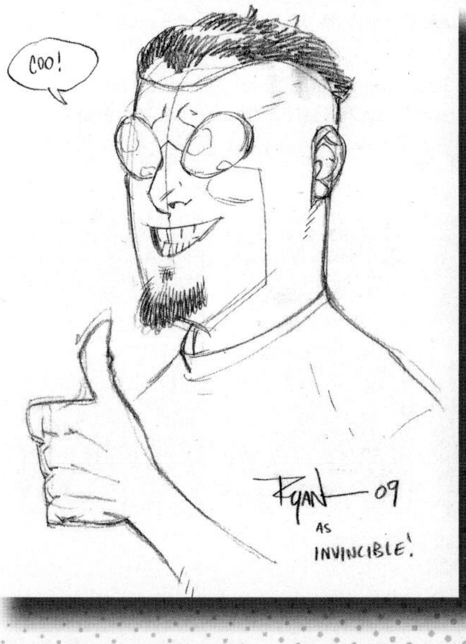
COO!
Ryan 09
AS INVINCIBLE!

**KIRKMAN: We leave you with an awesome splash page and a goofy drawing of Invincible wearing a Ryan Ottley body. Funny stuff, Ryan.**

***OTTLEY: Thanks! Peace out y'all.***

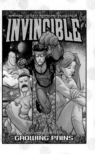

# MORE GREAT BOOKS FROM
# ROBERT KIRKMAN & IMAGE COMICS!

## THE ASTOUNDING WOLF-MAN
**VOL. 1 TP**
ISBN: 978-1-58240-862-0
$14.99
**VOL. 2 TP**
ISBN: 978-1-60706-007-9
$14.99
**VOL. 3 TP**
ISBN: 978-1-60706-111-3
$16.99

## BATTLE POPE
**VOL. 1: GENESIS TP**
ISBN: 978-1-58240-572-8
$14.99
**VOL. 2: MAYHEM TP**
ISBN: 978-1-58240-529-2
$12.99
**VOL. 3: PILLOW TALK TP**
ISBN: 978-1-58240-677-0
$12.99
**VOL. 4: WRATH OF GOD TP**
ISBN: 978-1-58240-751-7
$9.99

## BRIT
**VOL. 1: OLD SOLDIER TP**
ISBN: 978-1-58240-678-7
$14.99
**VOL. 2: AWOL**
ISBN: 978-1-58240-864-4
$14.99
**VOL. 3: FUBAR**
ISBN: 978-1-60706-061-1
$16.99

## CAPES
**VOL. 1: PUNCHING THE CLOCK TP**
ISBN: 978-1-58240-756-2
$17.99

## HAUNT
**VOL. 1 TP**
ISBN: 978-1-60706-154-0
$9.99

## INVINCIBLE
**VOL. 1: FAMILY MATTERS TP**
ISBN: 978-1-58240-711-1
$12.99
**VOL. 2: EIGHT IS ENOUGH TP**
ISBN: 978-1-58240-347-2
$12.99
**VOL. 3: PERFECT STRANGERS TP**
ISBN: 978-1-58240-793-7
$12.99
**VOL. 4: HEAD OF THE CLASS TP**
ISBN: 978-1-58240-440-2
$14.95
**VOL. 5: THE FACTS OF LIFE TP**
ISBN: 978-1-58240-554-4
$14.99
**VOL. 6: A DIFFERENT WORLD TP**
ISBN: 978-1-58240-579-7
$14.99
**VOL. 7: THREE'S COMPANY TP**
ISBN: 978-1-58240-656-5
$14.99
**VOL. 8: MY FAVORITE MARTIAN TP**
ISBN: 978-1-58240-683-1
$14.99
**VOL. 9: OUT OF THIS WORLD TP**
ISBN: 978-1-58240-827-9
$14.99
**VOL. 10: WHO'S THE BOSS TP**
ISBN: 978-1-60706-013-0
$16.99
**VOL. 11: HAPPY DAYS TP**
ISBN: 978-1-60706-062-8
$16.99
**VOL. 12: STILL STANDING TP**
ISBN: 978-1-60706-166-3
$16.99
**VOL. 13: GROWING PAINS TP**
ISBN: 978-1-60706-251-6
$16.99
**ULTIMATE COLLECTION, VOL. 1 HC**
ISBN 978-1-58240-500-1
$34.95
**ULTIMATE COLLECTION, VOL. 2 HC**
ISBN: 978-1-58240-594-0
$34.99
**ULTIMATE COLLECTION, VOL. 3 HC**
ISBN: 978-1-58240-763-0
$34.99

**ULTIMATE COLLECTION, VOL. 4 HC**
ISBN: 978-1-58240-989-4
$34.99
**ULTIMATE COLLECTION, VOL. 5 HC**
ISBN: 978-1-60706-116-8
$34.99
**THE OFFICIAL HANDBOOK OF THE INVINCIBLE UNIVERSE TP**
ISBN: 978-1-58240-831-6
$12.99
**INVINCIBLE PRESENTS, VOL. 1: ATOM EVE & REX SPLODE TP**
ISBN: 978-1-60706-255-4
$14.99
**THE COMPLETE INVINCIBLE LIBRARY, VOL. 1 HC**
ISBN: 978-1-58240-718-0
$125.00
**THE COMPLETE INVINCIBLE LIBRARY, VOL. 2 HC**
ISBN: 978-1-60706-112-0
$125.00

## THE WALKING DEAD
**VOL. 1: DAYS GONE BYE TP**
ISBN: 978-1-58240-672-5
$9.99
**VOL. 2: MILES BEHIND US TP**
ISBN: 978-1-58240-775-3
$14.99
**VOL. 3: SAFETY BEHIND BARS TP**
ISBN: 978-1-58240-805-7
$14.99
**VOL. 4: THE HEART'S DESIRE TP**
ISBN: 978-1-58240-530-8
$14.99
**VOL. 5: THE BEST DEFENSE TP**
ISBN: 978-1-58240-612-1
$14.99
**VOL. 6: THIS SORROWFUL LIFE TP**
ISBN: 978-1-58240-684-8
$14.99
**VOL. 7: THE CALM BEFORE TP**
ISBN: 978-1-58240-828-6
$14.99
**VOL. 8: MADE TO SUFFER TP**
ISBN: 978-1-58240-883-5
$14.99

**VOL. 9: HERE WE REMAIN TP**
ISBN: 978-1-60706-022-2
$14.99
**VOL. 10: WHAT WE BECOME TP**
ISBN: 978-1-60706-075-8
$14.99
**VOL. 11: FEAR THE HUNTERS TP**
ISBN: 978-1-60706-181-6
$14.99
**VOL. 12: LIFE AMONG THEM TP**
ISBN: 978-1-60706-254-7
$14.99
**BOOK ONE HC**
ISBN: 978-1-58240-619-0
$34.99
**BOOK TWO HC**
ISBN: 978-1-58240-698-5
$34.99
**BOOK THREE HC**
ISBN: 978-1-58240-825-5
$34.99
**BOOK FOUR HC**
ISBN: 978-1-60706-000-0
$34.99
**BOOK FIVE HC**
ISBN: 978-1-60706-171-7
$34.99
**THE WALKING DEAD DELUXE HARDCOVER, VOL. 2**
ISBN: 978-1-60706-029-7
$100.00

## REAPER
**GRAPHIC NOVEL**
ISBN: 978-1-58240-354-2
$6.95

## TECH JACKET
**VOL. 1: THE BOY FROM EARTH TP**
ISBN: 978-1-58240-771-5
$14.99

## TALES OF THE REALM
**HARDCOVER**
ISBN: 978-1-58240-426-0
$34.95
**TRADE PAPERBACK**
ISBN: 978-1-58240-394-6
$14.99

**TO FIND YOUR NEAREST COMIC BOOK STORE, CALL:**
# 1-888-COMIC-BOOK

THE WALKING DEAD™, BRIT™ & CAPES™ © 2010 Robert Kirkman. INVINCIBLE ™ © 2010 Robert Kirkman and Cory Walker. BATTLE POPE™ © 2010 Robert Kirkman and Tony Moore. THE ASTOUNDING WOLF-MAN ™ © 2010 Robert Kirkman and Jason Howard. TECH JACKET™ & CLOUDFALL™ © 2010 Robert Kirkman and E. J. Su. REAPER™ © 2010 Cliff Rathburn. TALES OF THE REALM™ MVCreations, LLC. © 2010 Matt Tyree & Val Staples. HAUNT™ © and 2010 Todd McFarlane.
Image Comics® and its logos are registered trademarks of Image Comics, Inc. All rights reserved.